Three Summers

www.penguin.co.uk

Also by Karen Swan

The Wild Isles series
The Last Summer
The Stolen Hours
The Lost Lover
The Midnight Secret

All I Want for Christmas
Christmas by Candlelight
The Christmas Postcards
The Paris Secret
Midnight in the Snow
The Secret Path
Together by Christmas
The Hidden Beach
The Christmas Party
The Spanish Promise
The Christmas Lights
The Greek Escape
The Christmas Secret
The Rome Affair
Christmas Under the Stars
The Paris Secret
Christmas on Primrose Hill
Summer at Tiffany's
Christmas in the Snow
The Summer Without You
Christmas at Claridge's
Christmas at Tiffany's
The Perfect Present
Prima Donna
Players

Three Summers

Karen Swan

bantam

TRANSWORLD PUBLISHERS

UK | USA | Canada | Ireland | Australia
India | New Zealand | South Africa

Transworld is part of the Penguin Random House group of companies whose addresses can be found at global.penguinrandomhouse.com.

Penguin Random House UK, One Embassy Gardens,
8 Viaduct Gardens, London SW11 7BW

penguin.co.uk

First published in Great Britain in 2026 by Bantam
an imprint of Transworld Publishers

001

Copyright © Karen Swan 2026

The moral right of the author has been asserted.

This book is a work of fiction and, except in the case of historical fact, any resemblance to actual persons, living or dead, is purely coincidental.

Every effort has been made to obtain the necessary permissions with reference to copyright material, both illustrative and quoted. We apologize for any omissions in this respect and will be pleased to make the appropriate acknowledgements in any future edition.

No part of this book may be used or reproduced in any manner for the purpose of training artificial intelligence technologies or systems. In accordance with Article 4(3) of the DSM Directive 2019/790, Penguin Random House expressly reserves this work from the text and data mining exception.

Typeset in 12/15.65 pt Sabon LT Pro by Six Red Marbles UK, Thetford, Norfolk
Printed and bound in Great Britain by Clays Ltd, Elcograf S.p.A.

The authorized representative in the EEA is Penguin Random House Ireland, Morrison Chambers, 32 Nassau Street, Dublin D02 YH68.

A CIP catalogue record for this book is available from the British Library.

ISBNs:
9780857507525 (cased)
9780857507532 (tpb)

Penguin Random House is committed to a sustainable future for our business, our readers and our planet. This book is made from Forest Stewardship Council® certified paper.

For my beloved parents, Mally and Malcolm

Prologue

Agricola Parisi, Tricase Porto,
15 September 1957

The stone rolled, lumpen, over the terracotta tiles, coming to an abrupt stop by the door jamb. Instantly, the dawn settled herself upon it, throwing down warming sunrays in thick shafts, nudging at it fruitlessly with a fluttering, whimsical breeze.

Rafaella, motionless beneath a patched sheet, stirred as the echo of the quiet knock winged its way over to her bed. She rolled onto her back and stared blankly at the ceiling, watching the fan rotate as the beautiful day danced around the room, ready for her to play. And for half a moment she felt the sap rise within her, that instinctive reach for the brightness – before she remembered she was stuck in the shadows now. Death crowded every sense and blotted out the light; she was a creature mired in darkness.

Memories of those terrible days a few weeks ago clamoured in her drowsy mind and she closed her eyes against them, but they only glowed more vividly behind her eyelids, mournful scenes flashing in rapid succession. A crimson tide in the moonlight; a shoeless foot; moist earth freshly heaped in banks beside an open grave; the porcelain whiteness of a mother's frozen visage; a coffin lowered on ropes; the nonnas' black lace mantillas hanging forward as their tears dropped to the grass . . . She could still hear the cries, too, the wails and screams and then the crushing silence that seemed to follow after horror, when words were simply not enough.

That hadn't been the end of it. There had been more to endure: questions and investigations, rumours and accusations . . . The plan was getting them through, but at what cost? Their desperate grasp for freedom had, ironically, cost them exactly that, and with every day that passed the outlook was becoming bleaker.

The sudden sun-up crescendo of the cicadas ushered in daybreak like a symphonic orchestra and she rolled onto her side, looking dully towards the vista that spread far and wide beyond her open French doors. It was the view she had known her entire life, both a comfort and a blessing: every morning she awoke to the sight of red earth and starlings, the neat lines of ancient olive groves stretching over the hills and tucking into the horizon.

But today there was something more.

Her gaze fell to the rogue stone on the balcony floor. It was crudely wrapped with a sheet of paper and tied with string. For several seconds she stared at it, knowing it could only have been thrown by one of two people; knowing it either contained very good news or very bad . . .

She rose from her bed, crossed the room and sank onto her haunches, picking up the stone and holding it in her palm like a baby bird. Already she could see the noble crest through the paper, and her heart began to pound as her fingers fumbled with the loose knot.

Very good news or very bad.

She pulled on the string and the stone rolled, unfurling from its parchment coat. She turned the paper over and her eyes fell upon two words.

Forgive me.

Summer 1957

Chapter 1

Rafaella

Tricase Porto, Puglia, 3 July 1957

The bolt of satin rolled out along the length of the cutting table, ripples catching the light like the sparkling sea that lay beyond the window. The women gasped at its beauty, a cluster of hands instinctively reaching forward to touch the liquid fabric. The lace veil they had been working on moments before, their chairs still gathered in a circle, was instantly forgotten.

'*Basta!*' Silvana Parisi cried, swatting them away and reaching for her white cotton gloves. She pulled them on with a proud smile, holding up the cut end and pressing it against herself. 'Huh? Huh?' she prompted as the women broke into excited chatter, seeing how the fabric draped and fell like a waterfall against her impressive curves.

'But how did you afford it?' Nonna Giacosa asked with her usual suspicious tone. She was not in the habit of believing in luck – or favours – and in her long memory, no one in this tiny, impoverished fishing port had ever worn something as opulent as a satin wedding dress before.

'Dante brought it back from Rome for me. He became friends with the costume designer on set.'

'I bet he did,' Gina Crespi murmured, rolling her eyes towards Rafaella and winking at her. 'Was she blonde?'

'*He* was not,' Silvana continued. 'But the fabric was left over from a costume for . . .'

She left the reveal hanging tantalizingly and several of the women gasped again. They all knew Dante Giannelli had been cast as an extra in the new Robert Leonard film, starring Gina Lollobrigida, Italy's sweetheart.

'You are telling me my future daughter-in-law will be wearing La Lollo's dress to marry my son?' Giulieta Carosa exclaimed delightedly.

'The *fabric*,' Nonna Giacosa corrected.

'And mine will be even better than hers by the time I'm finished with it!' Silvana boasted, pressing the fabric to her body again and swaying happily from side to side.

Rafaella watched her big sister, knowing it was true. Silvana could take a potato sack and make it into something beautiful, or even better – desirable. She knew exactly where to tuck, dart or pleat, and she would spend hours poring over magazines that showed the fashions worn by all the movie stars carousing in Rome. It hadn't escaped the notice of the nonnas that she was pinning the younger women's dresses ever tighter at the waist and bosom, bringing the style of the famous Fontana Sisters to little Tricase Porto. Gina's new Sunday best dress had had to be let down and out by an inch after her mother had crossed herself at the first sighting of her daughter in it; Silvana had promised to comply, but Rafaella knew she had only pinched in a half-inch instead, and Gina blamed the rest on pasta.

Silvana had promised to make a new dress for Rafaella too this summer, for she had grown fast this last year. Finally, at seventeen, she was sprouting curves that had been sorely lacking before. Rafaella had chosen a light blue cotton, which Silvana had suggested they trim with white cotton lace and pearly buttons at the bust. She couldn't wait for her sister to start on it. The peaches were already hanging heavy in the trees, which meant the summer people would be arriving any day now, and then their sleepy fishing village would burst into life for six glorious weeks.

Already there were more cars and scooters coming through on the coast road, visitors invariably dazzled as they came round the sharp bend to be greeted by a deeply coloured vision that could have come from a Cinecittà film set: dazzling turquoise waters lapping onto a small golden sand beach, flanked on one side by a long promenade where the *ragazzi* lay on towels in their swimwear, and on the other by the marina, where dozens of cerulean-blue fishing boats were moored. Along the frontage sat a handful of grand villas in Neapolitan colours: the salmon-pink hotel Villa Maria on the waterfront itself, the now-yellow Villa Blanca, blancmange-pink Villa Agosto and the pistachio-painted Villa Aymone. Set back in verdant gardens, behind high walls and trellised gates, they sat empty for ten months of the year; the villagers lived further up the hill, in the small white houses lining the far end of Borgo Pescatori and Via Santa Marcellina.

'And what are you thinking for the style?' Giulieta asked Silvana. Her eyes fell to the open page of a nearby magazine that showed a model exiting a car, displaying a wanton amount of cleavage, and her fingers formed an accusing point. 'Because Father Tommaso would have something to say if you walked down his aisle showing *that*.'

'As if her own father would stand for it!' Irma Parisi protested, seeming to find a slight in the suggestion.

The nonnas immediately joined in the consternation and Rafaella and Gina exchanged looks as the moral rectitude of the port was suddenly, seemingly, thrown into question. Was this bolt of satin not merely a touch of luxury but a Trojan horse through which Hollywood's scandalous sexual laxity would infect their seaside community?

'Neither my father nor Father Tommaso will have anything to worry about,' Silvana reassured them, haughtily tossing back her long, almost-black hair. 'The neckline will be modest—'

'High?' Nonna Masina asked, bringing a shaking, veined hand up to her own neck.

'Modest, *si*,' Silvana reiterated noncommittally.

'With long sleeves?' The shaking hand went to her wrist.

'To the elbows at the very least.'

A frown began to furrow the lined skin. 'And long . . .' Nonna Masina was far too old to get her hand down to the floor; neither knees nor hips would permit it.

'Certainly past the knees.'

The nonnas' eyebrows began to hitch upwards as they looked over at her mother, but they were interrupted by a sudden shout from outside. 'Maria!' The clamour at the table died down.

'Tch,' Gina's mother tutted as she crossed over to the green-shuttered window. '*What?*' she called out.

Rafaella could hear her grocer husband telling her their delivery of tomatoes and courgettes had arrived.

'Pah,' she muttered, swatting his words away with a hand as she turned back to the other women, her gaze falling longingly over the bolt of white satin once more.

Silvana's wedding to Luchino Carosa was to be the high point of the villagers' summer. It was all the women wanted to talk about as they did their laundry at the wash-house or leaned on pillows over their stabled front doors in the evenings. But their time was up in the dressmaker's studio. No more lace-making today. *Riposo* was over. The shutters would soon be pulled back up at the caffè and the shrimp boats would shortly be coming in with the last of the day's catch. Dinners needed to be prepared.

The nonnas got up from their stools beside the cutting table and began making their way down the narrow stairs. Silvana shared the rent on the property with the local cobbler, a new arrangement that seemed to be working well.

'Can we have a fitting of my dress later?' Rafaella asked as they carefully wound the satin back onto its roll. 'I come off my shift at six.'

'Not tonight,' Silvana said with a flick of her thick lashes. 'Luchino is taking me to see the new Mastroianni picture.' Luchino had recently bought one of the new Piaggios and missed no opportunity to impress his fiancée by whizzing her off to places beyond the train line.

Rafaella bit back her disappointment – and desperation. 'Tomorrow, then?'

Silvana raised an eyebrow. 'It's not like you to be so impatient, little sister.'

'I'm not impatient,' Rafaella shrugged. 'But my clothes no longer fit.'

'It's true, your skirts are too short. I'll have to drop the hem on that one,' Silvana said, casting a glance at Rafaella's pink-and-yellow-striped dress that now stopped several inches up her thighs.

'You already have.'

'. . . Oh.' Her sister glanced at her, a gleam coming into her eye. 'And is this sudden desperation for your blonde Romeo's benefit? Or because a certain boy is coming back to the port next week?'

'What?' Rafaella felt her cheeks flame. 'No! Why should I care what Cosi thinks about my clothes?'

Silvana's eyes widened with delight at her evident fluster. 'Who mentioned Cosi? Not me. I didn't name names.'

'Well, clearly you didn't mean Fede!'

'Why not? He's as gorgeous as his little brother.'

'He's five years older than me!'

Silvana shrugged. 'Papa is four years older than Mamma.'

'Oh, forget it!' Rafaella turned to leave.

Silvana smiled as she pinned the fabric's end to the roll to keep it from creasing, then carefully lifted it onto a shelf alongside the other bolts of cloth. It glowed like a pearl among the heavy linens and cottons. 'Fine!' she called after Rafaella. 'Come tomorrow.'

Rafaella spun back on her heel. 'Really? When?'

'During *riposo*. I've got fittings all morning.'

'OK, great! Thanks!' she cried, hearing her sister's low chuckle behind her.

Outside, Gina was waiting for her on the pavement, and together they made their way back down to the harbour promenade. Silvana's atelier (as she had started to call it) and the cobbler's were situated in a small building on the corner of Via Santa Marcellina, right at the junction where the coast road began to wind up the hill, north past the Giannellis' *trappito* towards Marina di Andrano. Most of the other village amenities were in the opposite direction, back down the hill and round the bend of the beach. Gina's family's grocery sat on the corner plot of Borgo Pescatori – they could see the tomatoes being offloaded from the blue three-wheel Piaggio truck outside – but the barber, the chandlery and Tito's Bar were further along, on a man-made island positioned between the coast road and the small lane that ran in front of Villa Agosto. It was a constant gripe among the villagers that so much land was 'lost' to those grand, empty villas while the locals had to scratch for space in the heart of where they lived and worked.

They walked along the promenade, nodding and smiling at the familiar faces they passed. There was scarcely a handkerchief's worth of space along the entire stretch, but they could name everyone they saw – the *anziani* swimming sedately in the calm waters or standing half-immersed and motionless at the concrete steps; the toddlers splashing in the shallows and watched by their mothers, talking. They passed their old schoolmates Donatella, Antonia and Clara lying out on towels and deepening their suntans.

'*Ciao*, Gina. *Ciao*, Rafa.'

'*Ciao*.'

They walked on a few steps before Gina knocked Rafaella's hand. 'You know Antonia did it with Enzo?' she whispered.

'No, she did not!' Rafaella gasped.

'Don't look back!' Gina hissed, catching her just as she was about to. 'She did. Enzo told Fon, who told Luigi, who told me.'

Gina's sources were always impeccable, and Rafaella felt a cold bullet of fear at the risk Antonia had taken. The flirtations of their early girlhood were being replaced by more serious courtships; there was a sense of competition now among the girls speeding past on the back of a boy's bike or sharing an ice cream on the harbour wall, as if finding a husband was a race and the good ones would soon be snapped up. Gina herself attracted plenty of attention from the boys they knew; she had always been petite but now she was curvy too, her body as soft as her tongue was sharp, and it was apparently an intoxicating mix. Rafaella didn't have the same-size pool to fish in and was constantly being teased by her two brothers about all the ways she was 'wrong': she was too tall, they said, and her fledgling curves were like berries on a twig. But Fon Giannelli didn't seem to care. He looked at her as if she was Venus or Aphrodite, and she was grateful for that.

They walked under the shallow archway that tunnelled through low-lying cliffs to the other side of the headland. The beachside caffè was set on the village's 'second' beach – barely more than a rug of sand on the rocks – and only open during the summer holidays. It was merely a wooden shack with some tables and chairs, but they sold coffee, affogato, gelato and granita to tourists coming back from the lido, the natural high-sided sea pools carved out of the basalt rocks further along.

Together the girls set about lifting the shutters and setting out the few small tables, casting squares of shade onto the sand with brightly striped umbrellas. A family stopped within moments and Gina served them as Rafaella went round the back and pulled a block of ice from the freezer. She began hacking at it with a pick, feeling sweat bead at her brow even in the shade.

'Here,' she said fifteen minutes later, emerging with a tub of crushed ice and setting it along the back counter – it was mirrored so they could see the goings-on behind them without having to turn around as they prepared the refreshments during busy periods. Three of the five tables were already taken, the patrons burying their toes in the sand as they sipped coffee and watched the boats at sea.

The sailing yachts were still far out, but the shrimpers were on their way back in. Even from here, Rafaella could tell the different boats by the distinctive patching of their sails, their small outboards puttering in a low gurgle as they slowly returned to port.

She turned to clean out the refrigerator but the high whine of a motor caught her attention. Looking back, she saw a sporty motorboat shoot past the headland in a sharp line before pulling hard left and beginning to turn figures of eight in the deeper waters beyond the harbour wall. Its wake instantly set the shrimpers rocking on their approach into harbour, and shouts rose up like ravens' cries.

'Who is that?' she squinted, stepping out onto the sand and shading her eyes to see better, but the figures on board were too distant to make out.

Gina gave a small tut. 'Well, I heard Gina Lollobrigida's dress fabric wasn't all Dante brought back from Rome.'

'He bought a *speedboat*?' Rafaella asked in disbelief. '. . . But how? With what?'

In the winter, during harvest season, the Giannellis ran the port's communal olive press – the *trappito* – on a plot of land at the tip of the headland just above the little caffè, atop the cliffs. But in the summer months, like many of the other men, they were fishermen. To have the money to spare for a speedboat, of all things . . .

'Dante's a film star now.'

'He was an extra on a film set!'

'Hollywood money,' Gina shrugged. 'Even the extras get rich.' She sighed. 'Who knows? Maybe he signed a contract while he was there.'

'Oh, I think we'd have heard if that was the case,' Rafaella groaned.

'Well, it's perfectly possible. I mean, with his looks . . .'

It was true Dante Giannelli had the kind of brooding Roman profile that the camera loved. Perhaps if he were playing a character other than himself, Rafaella thought, he might be convincing as a romantic hero; but whereas his brother had tentatively wooed her for months, Dante was notorious for his hot passions and cool heart.

She could make out two silhouettes on board, bracing against the wind, their cheers whooping into the sky as the boat carved loops into the sea's skin, and she knew Fon was out there with his brother. Dante was his idol, and he trotted after him like an eager puppy.

'I hope he's not going to do that all summer,' she muttered.

'Maybe if we play our cards right, he'll take us out on it,' Gina said with a coy wink. Gina, so astute in every other way, had always had a blind spot for the handsome eldest Giannelli boy, but at twenty-three, he was five years their senior and well known for his love of fast women. Hand-holding with teenagers didn't cross his mind.

'No thanks,' Rafaella grinned, turning away at last and heading for the welcome shade of the caffè. Summer was only just heating up, but already her skin was nut-brown and her long, light brown hair was turning blonde around her face.

'Hey, signorinas! Signorinas!' a voice called imperiously, and Rafaella looked up to see a couple stalking over the sand towards them. The sunlight bounced off their gleaming hair, the beach reflected in the lenses of their fashionable sunglasses. The young woman was wearing a shockingly short, brightly swirled sundress, a far cry from the muted and demure cottons of the locals.

'*Romy?*' Gina gasped. 'Cosi?' She broke into a sprint as Romola did the same, and the two friends embraced so hard they almost fell over.

Rafaella, gathering herself, was only a few steps behind. 'You're here already?' she asked, clutching Romola in disbelief. 'We didn't think you would come for another week! Your letter—'

'I know,' Romola laughed, throwing out her hands excitedly. 'But for one thing, the city was too hot! It was impossible! I told Mamma I would surely *die* if we stayed another day. Didn't I say that, Cosi?'

Cosimo drew level with his sister and grinned at them. 'She did.'

'Always the drama!' Gina groaned. She looked Cosi up and down for a moment. 'You got ugly,' she said.

'You got short.'

'I've always been short, idiot,' she laughed, punching him in the arm before allowing him to fold her into a hug. Cosimo was only older than Romola by eleven months, so the four of them had always played together as children; they had grown up like siblings, or cousins perhaps, squabbling one minute and racing into the sea the next.

Only, as Rafaella reached up with a welcoming hug too, she detected restraint in his manner as his arms closed around her, a new tension in his usually languid body. She felt the swell of muscles beneath his T-shirt, stubble against her cheek; there was little left of the boy she had grown up with in this man's body. She pulled away, suddenly self-conscious. 'You look so different! . . . Both of you!'

'Says you!' Romola laughed. 'I wasn't sure if my eyes were playing tricks from a distance! When did you grow so tall?'

'Oh, stop! Papa says I am like a weed,' Rafaella grimaced. At five foot nine, she stood almost a full head and shoulders above the other girls.

'A sunflower, perhaps! You have become such a beauty. Isn't she beautiful, Cosi?' Cosimo gave a noncommittal nod as Romola cupped Rafaella's cheek and tutted. 'All the boys must be chasing you now.'

'Oh, no.' She shook her head quickly. 'They like Gina.'

'They like Antonia!' Gina corrected with a knowing wink. 'And don't listen to her – Fon circles her like a leopard! None of the other boys can get near her.'

'. . . *Fon Giannelli?*' Cosimo blurted. 'Dante's brother? The fisherman's son?'

Rafaella felt herself taken aback by his tone. She had never known him to be a snob.

'Are you dating him?' Romola asked, looking delighted. 'You never said in your letters!'

'I – well . . .' Rafaella blustered, feeling under immediate scrutiny.

'Five months. Second base,' Gina said, winking again and making Romola scream and clap excitedly.

'Gina!' Rafaella scolded, her cheeks burning.

'Oh – as if I wasn't going to get it out of you!' Romola

laughed. 'But I can't believe you've got a boyfriend and never said! What's the big secret?'

'No secret,' Rafaella fibbed. Everyone in the village knew, of course, but it was true she had held back from sharing the news in her letters. She hadn't wanted it to get back to Cosimo, as she'd known it would. She had wanted to control the message, to see how things were between them first.

But this had hardly been controlled. And his reaction wasn't what she had anticipated.

'You can do better than him, surely, Rafa?' Cosi asked, his gaze tangling with hers like a cat's cradle.

'What's so wrong with him?' she bridled.

'You're kidding, aren't you?' He looked across at his sister. 'Don't you remember that time we caught him peering over the garden wall while we were in the pool and he tried to pretend he was bird-watching?'

'No.'

Cosi looked back at Rafaella. 'He's a loner. I always thought he was a bit odd.'

'*You're* a bit odd,' Romola said, rolling her eyes and pushing him so that he stumbled back a step.

'Just because Fon's quiet doesn't make him odd. Loads of the girls around here have a thing for him,' Gina said protectively. 'He's good-looking. And he's taller than you now, too, I reckon.'

'Not stronger, though, I bet,' Cosimo said, casually flexing a bicep. 'He always had legs like pipe-cleaners.'

'Oh, leave him alone!' Gina scolded. 'He and Raf are very sweet together.'

'Sweet?' Scorn dripped from the word. 'Well, I guess if that's what floats your boat.'

'It will be if he has even a *fraction* of his brother's charm,' Romola grinned, biting her lip as Gina gave a small squeal too. Dante's appeal to women ran across all age groups and up and down the social ladder.

Rafaella waved a hand dismissively, although she was stung by Cosimo's scorn of her love life. 'Tell us your news,' she implored Romola. 'What happened with Rocco? You said you were going to meet after Easter?'

Although they only saw each other once a year, the girls' letters were regular and always filled with gossip. Of course, Romola's were thicker, stuffed with detailed accounts of her adventures at glamorous parties and society balls. There was so much more to do in the big city, not to mention that life was exponentially bigger when you had the money and status that came with the ducal Franchetti name.

'Pah! It never happened. He threw me over for some girl he met skiing in Courmayeur.'

'No!' Gina dramatically pressed a hand to her heart. The story of Rocco's determined pursuit of their friend had kept them all on tenterhooks for most of the year. '*He* threw *you* over?'

'*Si!* But I don't care,' Romola said dismissively.

'You don't?' In her last letter, Romola had vowed she was going to marry him.

'Of course not,' she shrugged. 'By then I had met Otello, and he has a castle near Turin with three ghosts.'

'Three?' Rafaella asked incredulously.

Her comment prompted a wail of laughter from Gina. 'You're supposed to care about the castle, Rafa! Not the ghosts.'

Even Cosimo cracked a smile at that.

'But she said he has *three*!' Rafaella protested, catching sight of a couple walking round from the lido, towels thrown over their shoulders and heading towards the last remaining table. 'Oh, come – we are working. You'll have to pretend to work with us while you tell us all the news.'

'You want me to work? In this?' Romola asked in mock horror, pulling at the fabric of her turquoise-and-blue dress as the four of them walked over the sand. 'It's a Pucci.'

'A who-cci?' Gina cooed, stroking her like a pet.

Romola laughed again. 'Only the new It designer of the moment. He opened a boutique in Portofino. All the glitterati are wearing him. You really haven't heard of him?'

Rafaella smiled as this year's education began. Romola was their authority for everything stylish. 'I'm sure Silvana has.'

'Oh, she has. It was she who told us to find you here, and we could scarcely get away! She almost had the dress off me trying to examine the seams!'

'Did you hear she and Luchino are getting married in a few weeks?' Rafaella asked, her eyes shining.

'Of course! She—'

'Wait, don't say another word,' Gina said, holding up a finger. 'I'll be right back!' She ran over to the couple sitting down at the last free table to take their order.

'Do you want some Cokes?' Rafaella asked as they waited, reaching down into the fridge and holding up a couple of bottles.

'Love one,' Romola gasped, taking it. 'I'm parched.'

'Cosi?' She looked up at him, feeling a small shock as their eyes met again.

He shook his head. 'Too sugary. They make me feel sick.'

'Since when?'

'Ignore him,' Romola said, shoving his arm irritably. 'He thinks he's the big man now because he drinks Merlot and cognac.'

'I can't help it if I have a discerning palate and you don't.'

'Well, we definitely don't have Merlot or cognac here,' Rafaella shrugged, opening a cola for herself too and gulping it down thirstily. She needed the sugar. She felt shaky, as if there had been a step change in the rhythmic beat of her heart. Every year, the Franchettis' summer return to the port seemed to quicken her life force, as if pulling her from a state of dormancy; but this was different. She felt like there was quicksilver in her veins. 'Will you still be here for the wedding?'

'Of course. I love a wedding! Besides, I don't want to leave a single second before I must,' Romola said. Standing behind the counter, she looked like a flamingo in a henhouse. Usually Rafaella felt a heady mixture of fascination and awe as she readjusted to being in her glamorous friend's orbit, but she couldn't concentrate on her today. Cosimo lurked in her peripheral vision, her familiar old friend but also . . . aloof, as if he was holding himself apart.

'OK, I'm back,' Gina panted as she reached for the coffee pot, not wanting to miss a thing. 'So – when did you get here, anyway?'

'Not even an hour ago. Mamma will be furious we sneaked out,' Romola said, completely unperturbed by the deception. 'We promised we would unpack before we came to find you, but we couldn't wait. We're having our party tomorrow night and just knew you would want to know the scoop right away.'

Scoop? Rafaella and Gina both looked at her expectantly. As if the annual party itself wasn't exciting enough.

'Guess who is our guest of honour?' Romola said, clapping her hands with excitement as Cosimo looked at her sharply.

'Romy—'

'We can't guess!' Gina said, far too impatient for games at the best of times, but especially while holding a coffee pot. 'Who is it?'

'Valentina Fabiani!'

Heads turned in their direction as the name carried on the breeze.

'Valen—?' Gina breathed.

Rafaella felt her whole body tense with shock. If La Lollo was Italy's sweetheart, Valentina Fabiani was her precocious little sister. 'The bombshell from Bomba', the newspapers called her. Her latest picture had been a huge hit, and her recent visit to the Colosseum for a private tour had created traffic jams in Rome for hours.

'But how do you know her?' Gina stage-whispered. This put Dante Giannelli's brief brush with fame firmly in the shade. He had been one of three hundred extras on set with La Lollo, merely breathing the same air. But for the Franchettis to actually host a bona fide film star in their home . . .

'*I* don't. I haven't met her yet. You-know-who here met her at a jazz club on Via Veneto a few weeks ago.' Romola jerked her head towards her brother. Cosimo had the decency to look abashed as the girls stared at him incredulously.

'You're dating *Valentina Fabiani*?' Gina asked him in open disbelief.

'I wouldn't say dating, exactly . . .'

Rafaella felt suddenly sick. The sugar had hit her bloodstream, and it was so hot . . . She grabbed a cloth and began wiping the counter as Romola carried on dishing gossip.

'Supposedly she's travelling to Gallipoli for some reshoots of her next picture, so Brother Dearest invited her to stop over here for a few days. Mamma disapproves terribly, of course, but Valentina's arriving here tomorrow evening, so there is no time for indignation.'

Now it was clear why the Franchettis had arrived early – nothing to do with the heat in Rome. But then, Romola, like the rest of the Roman nobility, always spoke at an angle, everything slightly oblique.

'. . . Poor Mamma is in a terrible fluster.'

The girls knew Romola's mother would not be doing anything more arduous than choosing the flowers and deciding which dress to wear. It would be the village women, swinging into action, who would bring the party to pass – and they would do it happily, because everyone would talk about it for months if not years afterwards. Such events enhanced the legend of the noble Franchettis in their beloved summertime port.

'Right. Well, that's all perfectly normal. Tomorrow night we're partying with a film star,' Gina said wryly, nodding as she digested the news. She looked across at her co-worker and best friend. 'I guess this means our summer has officially begun. Wouldn't you agree, Rafa?'

Rafaella was staring out to sea, watching the Giannellis' boat still cutting swooping loops beyond the harbour wall as they revelled in their moment of glory.

'. . . Rafa?'

She turned back to them, dishcloth in hand, and managed a smile, aware of Cosimo's quiet gaze upon her profile. 'I guess I would, yes.'

Chapter 2

Fon

Plumes of red dust billowed into the evening sky as they sped along the dirt track, bones rattling over the hard ruts as they headed for the water tower. Several goats were standing atop the crumbling drystone wall along the far edge of the Parisis' olive grove. Fon's eyes travelled over the ancient trees, their branches already growing heavy with fruit. It was going to be another good harvest this year. Their father would be pleased – bumper crops were good news for the *trappito*.

Dante pulled hard on the wheel as they approached the corner, the old Fiat skidding on the dry earth and sending up more red clouds in their wake. Fon could see two figures ahead, silhouetted against the sunset; they were leaning against the wall but they stood up as the car hurtled towards them. The shorter one flicked away his cigarette as Dante finally hit the brakes, the lighted butt curving an arc into the dust.

'Wait here,' Dante said, cutting the engine and jumping out before Fon could say a word.

He watched his brother stride over to where the men were waiting. They wore rough working clothes and their faces were in shadow, but he recognized them – Francesco

Romano, tall and thin with his lop-shouldered stance from an old fighting injury, and Pablo Carrieri, older and bow-legged. Fon watched as Pablo handed over a small package, which Dante examined for a moment before tucking it into his jacket pocket.

His brother had returned from Rome with a new swagger. It was the second year running that their father had sent him to stay with cousins for a few days to explore job opportunities beyond the Mezzogiorno; ever since the end of the war, the poor had been draining in vast numbers from the 'land of grain and pasture' and heading for the industrial north or emigrating to Australia and Argentina. Last year Dante had only been gone a week, but this time he'd landed the job as a film extra and three days had turned into three months.

It wasn't fame or fortune that had turned his head, though. For the first time, he'd told Fon as they lay in their beds in their shared room, he had seen the power – 'real power' – that came with money. It bought luxury and women, but more than that, it bought respect, something that had been in short supply for the Giannellis for far too long. They lived in the *casino vecchio* – the 'old place', on a plot behind the grand Villa Blanca. At two hectares it was one of the port's largest plots, but the soil was especially poor and barely allowed them to grow more than their family's requirements of fava beans, artichokes and tomatoes. They grazed a few animals for milk and cheese. Their house, a low, blocky building crazed with cracks and now more black than white, had been falling into steady dilapidation for the past fifty years despite their father tirelessly fishing the seas during the summers and working through the nights in winter at the *trappito*. Nothing he did was ever quite enough to pull his family from the gaping maw of poverty.

Rome had opened Dante's eyes to new possibilities, and ever since his return he had been throwing around words like 'venture' and 'opportunity'. The world was changing, and *la dolce vita* had taken hold of the popular imagination far beyond Italy's borders. Films like *Roman Holiday* had brought the lushness and heat of the Mediterranean to the grey horizons of Britain and America; now tourists were coming over in record numbers, and Dante intended to cater to them. The motorboat, he had said, was only the start of his enterprises.

His business concluded, Dante turned away from the two men and came back to the car with a satisfied look.

'Let's eat,' was all he said as he turned on the motor.

'What were you talking about?' Fon asked, watching Pablo and Francesco slip between the trees and disappear into the shadows of the grove.

'They're just running some errands for me.'

'Parisi's men?' This land belonged to Rafaella's family, and Fon's sense of unease deepened.

'Why not? They're earning a little extra on the side,' Dante shrugged, casting him an unapologetic look. 'It's not my fault if old Emilio doesn't pay his labourers a living wage.'

Fon's gaze fell to the package in his brother's jacket, but Dante didn't seem to care about it being a secret any more than he cared to explain.

There was a gap of three and a half years between them, but to Fon it felt more like thirteen. They both had strong, distinctive Roman noses but Dante's was topped and tailed by a heavy brow and fleshy lips that sent women into a spin. Fon, although tall, was lanky and fairer than he wanted to be. He felt like a pale imitation, lacking intensity – a watercolour to his brother's oil painting. He had a feeling he would never catch him up.

'Look, it's your girlfriend,' Dante muttered, jogging Fon hard with his elbow as they whisked through the tall stone pillars marking the entrance to the Parisi *agricola*. Rafaella, coming up the road, stood on the pedals of her bike. She looked startled by their speed coming down the hill. For a moment their eyes locked, and Fon felt that sickly, tingling feeling that always fired up in his stomach when she looked his way.

In the next instant she was far behind them. He knew she had just come off her shift at the beach caffè; he had asked her to go out for gelato later, but she'd declined. Something about helping her sister with her trousseau.

'Hmm, those legs,' Dante murmured appreciatively, looking back at her in his rear-view mirror. 'She's becoming a swan at last... No wonder you're so keen.'

'I'm not *keen*,' Fon muttered sullenly. If a lifetime as Dante's brother had taught him anything, it was never to reveal his true heart's desire. It gave others too much leverage.

'No?' Dante shrugged. 'OK, fine. I'll have her myself, then.'

'No!' His sudden vehemence made Dante laugh, and Fon realized he'd been baited. But Rafaella wasn't like the other local girls. She was thoughtful, reserved, kind – that rare thing, a good listener in a world of talkers – and she deserved better than to be one of his brother's many conquests. She wasn't chasing after a husband or going with the first guy to get a scooter. She had ambitions of her own beyond marriage and motherhood, although she'd told him she wanted three children 'at the very least'. She wanted to be a writer or a teacher too, she'd confided in him once, laughing shyly as she said it, aware that it was an impossible dream. They both knew women around here didn't have careers. But as Fon had listened, he'd found he wanted to make it happen for her – even if, as a fisherman's son, that was his own impossible dream.

Dante looked over at him with a wolfish grin. 'Think you'll be her first?'

'Oh my God, stop!'

Dante laughed. 'I mean, I'm happy to put in a good word for you if you think it'll help.'

Fon stared out the window. He knew his brother could steal almost any girl with a single look. He also knew that when Dante was his age, he'd been getting far past chaste kisses; he had already proved himself a man.

'Hey, I'm only looking out for you, little brother,' Dante said, shoving his arm hard. 'It's the ones like her you have to watch out for.'

'What does that mean?'

'She's a tease.'

'She's not a tease.'

'No? So she's putting out?'

Fon looked away, refusing to dignify the question with a response. Still, he could feel the shame burning in his cheeks at his apparent 'failure' to make Rafaella his.

Dante smirked, leaning towards him slightly. 'I hate to break it to you, Fon, but she's going to keep holding out. Shall I tell you why?'

Despite himself, Fon heard himself ask the question. 'Why?'

'Because she thinks she's better than you. Thinks she can do better.'

Do better? The spectre of Cosimo Franchetti flashed through his mind. Rafaella had never brought up her friendship with the dashing duke's son, but Fon had seen them together countless times over the years, observing from a distance. He had noticed the way her eyes sparkled when the Franchettis came back to the port each summer.

'Rafaella doesn't think like that,' he murmured.

'Her father owns the biggest olive grove for ten miles. We have six goats. She does.' Dante caught him with a knowing look and held it. Fon was about to ask why the same bad luck didn't apply to him, then; but it didn't seem to matter to women if a man was poor when he had the face of a prince.

'But don't worry, things are going to change.' Dante winked, reading his mind, just as he had Fon's whole life. 'They're *already* changing. Soon she's going to be begging you to stick it to her.'

Fon ignored his brother's crassness as he looked back at him. 'Because of *Allegra*, you mean?' He had seen Rafaella watching them from the beach earlier, standing on the sand with Gina as Dante put the boat through its paces. Had she liked it? 'Will you let me take her out on it?'

Dante shrugged. 'Perhaps – one day. Let's not run before we can walk, eh? It's an expensive toy. We can't afford any accidents.' His finger tapped the steering wheel lightly, one arm leaning on the open window, his hair catching the breeze as they cruised through the woodland and back down the hill towards the port. He had a way of driving a Fiat like it was a Ferrari.

Swagger.

'Where have you been?' Monica Giannelli demanded as her elder sons walked into the kitchen.

'Sorry, Mamma,' Fon said, kissing her cheek on his way past to the tap.

'We had so much to do with the boat today. We had to get the mooring changed and fill her up, not to mention washing off the salt,' Dante said, placing a hand on their mother's shoulder. 'Wait until you see her. What a beauty!'

'You still haven't told me how you managed to afford it,' she fretted, trying to catch his eye.

'Don't worry so much, Mamma. I told you, I met a man who knew a man . . . It was a good deal,' he shrugged, taking his bowl to the table and sitting down just as their father came in. He had been mending the nets all afternoon. 'Papa, you should have come out with us. Did you see us?'

'Everyone saw you,' Carlo Giannelli replied disapprovingly.

'Carosa wasn't happy with the wake you caused on his way back in. Two of his lobster pots were toppled.'

'He's never happy,' Dante said dismissively. 'Besides, today was just the trial run. When we do the trips for real, we'll be further out.'

Fon took his usual place by the window, looking out onto the chickens, while his father and brother took the head and right-hand seats.

'*Mangiate*,' their mother insisted, using a cloth to swat at a bothersome fly. 'While it's hot.'

They all waited as their father served himself first. 'Good news, Papa. I got a good price for the sea bream at Brindisi,' Dante said.

'It's crazy, you going all the way up there to sell some fish,' their mother tutted from the stove as she reached in for the bread.

Dante glanced over at her before reaching for the package in his pocket and sliding it across the table. 'Like I told you, it was better than your guy was offering. Uncle Teo was right – there's profit to be had if you cut out the middleman.'

Their father took a quick look at the contents: more cash than he had ever seen in one place before. He looked back at his eldest son with pride, removing the package to his own jacket pocket with a silent nod before his wife returned to the table. 'Well done, my boy.'

Fon looked on, unsettled by the blatant lie. They hadn't been up to Brindisi today, and Parisi's men were no fishermen.

'So, you have heard the news?' their mother asked wearily, sitting down at last as Dante took the bowl and served himself next.

'Even five miles out at sea, I heard the news,' their father muttered. 'Everyone has gone mad!'

'*Si*,' she agreed. 'Mad!'

But Fon glimpsed a dark bead of excitement in her eyes before the disapproval won out. 'What's happened?' He was always the last to know, it seemed.

'The Franchettis are back –'

His head whipped up at the words. They were here already?

'And they're throwing the party tomorrow night. They have a guest of honour.'

'Who?'

'Valentina Fabiani.'

The name didn't seem to mean much to Monica's husband but her sons looked back at her, stunned, Dante pausing with his spoon midway to his mouth. 'Why is she coming here?'

'She is a friend of Cosimo's,' their mother shrugged.

Dante's eyes narrowed. 'Friend? Or girlfriend?'

'How should I know?' she scowled. 'All I know is the duchessa is unhappy. The boy acted on a whim again, and now it is down to his poor mother to clean up his mess. She says if it cannot be prevented, then she is at least determined to keep things elegant.' Monica arched an eyebrow to show that a line was being drawn between the noble Franchettis and their sexy starlet guest – and it was clear where their loyalties should lie.

But what did red-blooded young men care for elegance and etiquette against sexual allure? Power came in different guises; Dante was learning that. Fon, too.

'Of course, their housekeeper has been *frantic* all afternoon trying to source some calla lilies!' she continued. 'Her usual supplier only has Madonna lilies.'

'Why can't she use Madonnas, then?' Fon asked, reaching for the serving spoon.

'Not all lilies are correct just because they are lilies, Fon!'

'Oh,' he sighed. It was funny how the women of the port seemed to care about these rules in the summer months and not at all during the rest of the year.

'The nearest she can find any is in Bari, so tomorrow you and your brother are going to drive up there at dawn.'

'Wait, what? Why us?' Fon gasped.

'Clearly you don't mean *me*?' Dante frowned.

'*Si*, both of you. You're to buy eight hundred stems.'

Eight hundred flowers? Fon looked at his mother in disbelief. Surely it was a joke? Who needed eight hundred flowers for a party?

'But how?' Dante argued. Their small car couldn't even fit a goat in the back. They knew because they had once tried.

'They have said they will give you the use of their car for the trip.'

Dante paused at this. The Franchetti car was, if memory served, a glossy Alfa Romeo.

Fon remained unmollified. 'We're supposed to start with the boat trips tomorrow,' he protested. 'We've been getting everything set up today.' He had spent his morning painting advertising boards with 'Water-Ski Trips Available Here' on the quay outside the harbourmaster's office.

'It can wait for one more day. There are going to be many important people coming in for this party. We must come together to make sure it's a success.'

'But—'

'Your mother's right,' their father interjected. 'Help out the Franchettis tomorrow and your reward will come when their guests want to go out on the water in the days afterwards.'

Dante nodded, seeing the business opportunity this presented, but Fon continued to smoulder. Cosimo Franchetti coming back was never good news as far as he was concerned. The last thing he wanted was to be sent out of the port – on an errand necessitated by Cosimo's actions, no less – when the Franchettis had just arrived back in it.

Every summer it was the same: the Franchettis' return cast a golden shimmer over everything but it also unsettled the whole community. A kind of headiness came over the villagers, as if they were all drunk on beauty and excitement for six weeks straight. The women cared about nonsensical things like calla lilies over Madonnas, for one. And Rafaella Parisi's eyes would shine, for another.

Fon stared at his dinner, wishing summer had never come and that the Franchettis would just stay in Rome, where they belonged.

Chapter 3

Cosimo

Cosimo stood on the balcony and looked out to sea, watching as sunlight darted and bounced off the surface like a thousand golden arrows. Distant boats pottered past on the horizon, their sails catching the same buffeting breeze that made the cloud pines shimmy all around him. It was what he loved most about this place – the contrast between the verdant garden, so thick it was almost like a jungle, and the vast, open expanse of the Adriatic a few steps beyond their trellised gate. Both landscapes were extreme, and both were as different as it was possible to be from the ancient clamour and cheek-by-jowl jostle of life in dusty Rome.

He had spent every summer of his childhood here, riding his bike down the long, lemon-tree-lined drive and swimming in turquoise waters that were so bright, whenever he left he was certain he must have exaggerated their jewel-like hue in his mind – only to return the next summer and realize it had all been true. The air was clear here, sparkling somehow, swallows double-dipping on the thermals and hidden cicadas giving the blistering heat a sound.

Yes, this, right here, was his favourite spot in the world – standing beneath the middle arch of the pink villa in his green-striped pyjama bottoms, sipping espresso, with the bougainvillea blossoming in an extravagant froth and scented jasmine perfuming the sky. A brilliant day was dawning before him, as if just for him.

The villagers had come out in force to help prepare for tonight's party. He could hear multiple voices even over the mellifluous swish of the fan in his bedroom: shouts for help carrying things, directions for where to put them . . .

He peered around the decorative stone campana urns – they had been planted with extravagant geraniums this year, one centred in each arch along the balustrade wall. In the garden below, gardeners were sweeping away stray palm fronds and twigs that had fallen overnight. One was carrying a net as he went to skim the round swimming pool hidden in the orange grove. A blue Piaggio Ape was parked askew on the gravel below – the grocers' van. Their daughter, his old friend and sparring partner Gina, was unloading crates of fruit from the back.

He straightened up. Where Gina was to be found . . .

'You finally got out of your pit, then?' an arch voice behind him asked, and he turned to find Romola walking barefoot through the vaulted drawing room towards him. She was wearing another of her fashionable new swirly dresses that made more sense on the coast than they ever had in the city.

'It's going to be a long day,' he shrugged.

'And night – you hope!' Romola grinned, brushing past him and reaching for one of the orange slices cut and arranged on plates on the breakfast table. She sank into the deep yellow cushions of a chair, arm flopping on the rest as she bit into the segment. '. . . When's she arriving?' she asked, sounding deliberately bored and watching as he sat down on the wall, half turned to keep an eye on the comings and goings. Stone steps flanked either side of the balcony here, turning back in on themselves down at garden level; as children they used to have timed races up them. Last summer they had been more useful as an alternative entrance to the front door at the west side, when they'd broken curfew to drink beers on the beach and needed to sneak in.

Cosimo shrugged. 'Six, thereabouts.'

'Mamma's going to hate her.'

'I know.'

'She looks cheap.'

He flashed her a grin. 'I know!'

'She's furious that everyone is so excited about Valentina's presence and not our return.'

'I hardly think it's an occasion for anyone that we're back. We do come every year, after all. This is our home.'

'Oh, so we're locals?' she teased.

'Of course!'

Romola giggled, swinging a long, tanned leg. 'You have some funny ideas, Cosi.'

'What's funny about it?' he asked defensively. 'We practically grew up here!'

'No, we just summer here. And the locals only like us because we spend more in six weeks on prosecco and lobster than they make the whole rest of the year.'

Cosimo frowned. They had this argument almost every year, but this time it seemed to matter more than ever that he won it. 'So you're saying Gina and Rafa are only pretending to be our friends?'

'Well, not *them*, obviously!' Romola said, rolling her eyes. 'We were all playing together long before we understood the differences between us.' She sucked the orange juice off her finger. 'It was good seeing them yesterday, didn't you think?'

'It always is,' he shrugged.

'It's a bore that they're working now, though. What are we going to do with our days if Gina's always working for her parents and Rafa's at the agricola – and when they're not there, they're doing shifts at the beach caffè?'

'It is pretty selfish,' he agreed.

Romola laughed. 'I guess we should have seen it coming. This is how their lives will be now,' she sighed. 'They'll work in the port till they marry, and then they'll be too busy having babies to go anywhere or do anything else . . .' She gave a horrified gasp. 'You do realize this could be our last summer before all of that happens?'

He frowned. 'Don't be ridiculous.'

'What's ridiculous about it? Rafa's been with Fon for five months! That's longer than you or I have ever managed.'

'Yes, but we don't *want* to settle down.'

Romola tipped her chin down demurely and pressed a hand to her chest. 'And not follow in Mamma and Papa's footsteps? But why ever not? Their lives are so perfect!' she mocked.

He grinned and lapsed into an easy silence, sipping coffee. He loved it here. For all the glamour of their life in Rome, he felt he spent all year waiting to come back to Villa Agosto.

'God, it must be fun to be able to fly,' he said, watching a butterfly flit in the geraniums. 'I'd have that as my superpower, wouldn't you? No, wait!' He held a hand up. 'Don't tell me – you'd choose invisibility, so you could go round spying on people. Or being able to read their minds.'

Romola gave a bark of laughter as she kicked a leg at him. 'Fun! But you're wrong. I'd choose the ability to fly too.'

'You would?' Cosimo was surprised.

'Yeah, but I wouldn't be a *butterfly*,' she scoffed. 'They just flutter, looking pretty, and then die within a day. I'd be . . .' Her eyes scanned the garden, alighting on a bird darting between the trees like an arrow, catching flies. 'One of them. Sharp, agile. A weapon in the sky.'

Cosimo rolled his eyes. 'That's a barn swallow. Not an eagle!'

She laughed again, not caring either way. 'It's good news about Silvana and Luchino getting married, at least,' she said, getting back to the local gossip as she inspected a nail.

'Is it?' he asked sceptically.

'Of course. He should have asked her last year, if you ask me. It was getting to be embarrassing, him making her wait like that.'

'Right.' He sighed, looking out to sea again, not caring about the courtship of the betrothed couple. His mind was still on Rafaella and Fon. The news they were dating had come as a bolt from the blue yesterday and he hadn't been able to shake his disgruntlement. He just couldn't get his head around the thought of them together. What did she see in him? Every summer Cosimo could feel Fon's yearning to be included in their group, staring at them across the water or watching them in Tito's Bar. There was a hunger in his look that unnerved Cosimo, as if he wanted something from him.

And now he had it. Because he had Rafaella.

Romola smiled. 'Did you see how excited they all are that the dress is going to be made from the same satin used for Lollobrigida's dress in her new film?'

'No. I'd tuned out of the conversation by then.'

She chuckled. 'Dante Giannelli was an extra on set, and apparently he met someone who knew someone . . .'

'Ugh, of course he did,' Cosimo muttered. 'He's such a shameless opportunist.'

'Well, it appears opportunity is well and truly knocking. Yesterday he was showing off in that new speedboat.'

Cosimo's head whipped back round. 'Wait – that was *him*?'

'Apparently they're going to offer water-skiing trips to the summer people.'

Cosimo frowned. Tricase Porto had only ever been a tiny fishing port, never raising its eyes to consider chasing or attracting the fashionable crowds from the cities. That was precisely why he loved it here so much. It was an opportunity to get away from the back-stabbing fakery and social climbing of their everyday lives.

Romola shrugged. 'I thought it looked rather fun, actually. Could be something to do tomorrow, depending on how sore our heads are.'

'But how did he afford a speedboat?' Cosimo insisted. 'That doesn't make sense . . .'

'Gina says since coming back from Rome he's been convincing his father to let him' – she gave a wry smile and made speech marks with her fingers – 'diversify their income streams.'

Cosimo raised an eyebrow. 'Dante the businessman? That's a new one. I assumed he was on the hunt for a rich widow.'

'Well, probably that too,' she conceded.

Cosimo looked back out to sea. Slick sailing yachts often dotted the horizon, but if he wanted the jet-set lifestyle on the water, he'd go Porto Ercole. 'So much for coming to Tricase for the quiet life.'

'Ha! Everyone's life is quiet compared to yours, Cosi!' Romola said. 'It's not the place, it's the person – and *you* date like women are going to be banned.'

'Like you can talk!' he snapped back. 'You get through boys like they're dresses.'

'What can I say? I like pretty things,' Romola shrugged. She smiled; bickering was their form of affection. 'Talking of which, I had to look twice at Rafa, didn't you?'

He swallowed. 'Not really.'

'But she looks so different.'

'Different how?'

'I don't know, just different! It's not one thing. God, you're such a male.' She glanced at him. '. . . I thought you were a bit mean to her, actually.'

'No I wasn't.'

'You weren't exactly nice about her boyfriend.'

'Am I supposed to lie? I don't like the guy, never have. And his brother's even worse.'

'I know, but here's a thought – be her friend? If Fon makes her happy, be happy for her! I know we're hopeless cynics, but some people do actually get to live happily ever after. Apparently.'

The sound of a car coming up the drive made her sit up and look down, past the campana urn. 'Huh. Talk of the devil.'

'What . . .?' He twisted to follow her gaze. 'What the hell . . .?' he murmured as he caught sight of their mother's Alfa Romeo drawing to a halt, dozens upon dozens of long-stemmed flowers spilling from the open windows of the back seat and yet more wrapped in newspaper and trussed to the roof like sheaves of wheat. He caught sight of the two faces in the front seats. '. . . Is that the Giannellis? What are they doing in Mamma's car?'

Romola threw her head back laughing as the two brothers tried to extricate themselves from the floral tomb. 'Ugh! This is going to be so much fun.'

Rossanna Franchetti didn't look up from the dining-room table, which was serving as the party HQ, when Cosimo walked through.

'Good afternoon, my *carino*,' she murmured, not breaking from writing a letter on their headed paper as he kissed her on the cheek. Her skin was rose-scented, as ever, and the breeze from the ceiling fan made her dark hair flutter around her temples.

'Is Papa back?'

'On his way. He was delayed getting away. Another meeting

with the prime minister.' She glanced at him. He had showered and changed into shorts and a linen shirt, the soles of his pale suede shoes slapping on the tiled floor. He always wore them with the backs pushed down when he came here; it was one of the signifiers that he had arrived in port and summer proper had begun. A faint smile creased the right corner of her mouth. It was no secret Cosimo had always been her favourite child – so like her in both looks and manner – and she knew how he loved coming back here. Though he was no longer racing out to build castles in the sand, something of the little boy still lingered in the young man's body.

'Where are the others?' he asked, perching on the edge of the table.

'Fede is studying . . . obviously,' she smiled, still writing. 'And Romy's taken the little ones to the lido.'

'Is there anything I can do to help?' he enquired.

His mother stopped writing at last. '*You?*' she asked with a bemused smile. 'Help?'

He shrugged. 'I'm not entirely useless, am I?'

Some of the village women bustled in carrying bundles of linen tablecloths, candles and crockery.

'. . . Signoras,' he smiled as they passed, nodding at him with twinkling eyes, wordlessly taking in the changes in him from another year spent growing up in Rome. For all his monied, urban sophistication, their warm fussing around him always made him feel like the prodigal son returned. He knew he would be inundated with questions as soon as they caught up with him, out of earshot of his mother.

'Well, actually, yes, you could be helpful,' his mother replied, surprising him. 'You can take the chandeliers there,' she said, indicating two cherry-red Murano glass-drop light fittings positioned on pillows beside the table legs. 'They're too heavy for Giuseppe to carry, though that won't stop him, and the very last thing I need is him pulling his back again.'

Cosimo wrapped the chain of one around his fist and lifted it easily. He grabbed the other too, liking how his biceps bulged with the faint effort. 'Where do you want them?'

'Take them to the Apollo garden. The gardeners have set up some hanging hooks in the trees there,' his mother said distractedly, back to her letter again. 'Oh, and Cosi! Tell Giuseppe the urn in the middle arch is loose. He needs to . . .' She twirled her wrist vaguely. 'Fix it, somehow.'

'Fix it. Right,' he said, stepping out of the villa's cool, shaded embrace and down the steps, feeling the blistering heat on his skin as he walked through the sunspots between the trees. Everything was always heady sensation here, colours, smells and sounds all rich and deep – the smell of *pane di Altamura* wafting from the kitchen, the grass tickling his bare ankles as he crossed the lawn, the faint salty tang of the seaside air, the babble and cry of dozens of conversations and orders being issued as the villagers and villa labourers worked together against the tight deadline.

He thought of the woman in whose honour they were all striving – though she would never know it herself. Everyone, from his mother down to the cleaning lady, would maintain to their dying breath that this was all entirely usual. But even by the Franchettis' standards, the preparations were above and beyond. His mother might look down upon Hollywood glamour, but she'd be damned if she wouldn't still outdo it.

The formal garden sat largely forward of the villa and was bisected by the long drive, each section on either side subdivided again into quarters. The giant statue of Apollo stood centrally between two ancient stone-pine trees and was flanked on the far side by a thick wall of flowering jasmine, into which a niche had been cut and a stone bench set. It was his mother's favourite place and he had fond memories of growing up eating lunches on blankets on the grass there, as if in repudiation of the gold cutlery and white-tablecloth formality of Rome.

Judging by the number of dressed tables set around the space, this was where food would be served tonight, but he wasn't sure whether it would be eaten or simply admired. The local women had organized themselves into platoons – some were dressing serving plates with thick bunches of grapes worthy of Caesar entertaining Cleopatra, while others were doing intricate work with fruit: cutting lemons and oranges in half and fashioning the edges into zigzags for reasons beyond his comprehension.

He saw Gina crouched down by one of the tables, the tip of her tongue peeking through her teeth as she tried to balance a pomegranate on top of a fruit tower. He instinctively smiled at the sight of her and felt the itch to topple it and get a rise from her. Growing up, they had scrapped over every small thing, more like brother and sister than friends, never willing to give an inch.

'Need some help with that?' he called as he sauntered over the grass.

Gina looked up at the familiar voice – and familiar teasing tone. She grinned. 'Do *you*? Looks like you're straining a little there. Need some muscle, pretty boy? We all know you can't do any heavy lifting.'

'So I'm pretty now, am I? Yesterday you said I got ugly,' Cosimo grinned as he walked over to the first pine tree and set the chandeliers down. He waited as she came over too, five feet and one inch of sassy attitude, stopping in front of him with a hand on her hip as she looked him up and down.

'Yes, I was right the first time. Definitely ugly.'

He grinned again. 'Where's Rafa?'

'She's getting some more ice with her mother. She'll be back any moment.'

'Ah.' His gaze rose to the hook strapped to the tree branch high above them. Four metres high.

'Seriously – will you be OK putting that up?' she asked as he walked over and retrieved the orchard ladder that had been left ready, propped against the tree trunk. 'You never did have a head for heights.'

'So I'm not only ugly and physically feeble, I'm fearful too? You think so highly of me,' he said, tipping the ladder open.

'Well, someone's got to keep you humble, given how highly you think of yourself,' she quipped as she steadied it for him.

He picked up the chandelier and climbed the rungs, securing it easily by looping the chain over the hook.

'Not so fast,' Gina said as he made to come back down, and he saw she was pulling out some taper candles from her apron pocket. He bit his lip. It was true he had never liked heights, but he would rather fall from one than admit it to her.

She watched as he reached over, carefully inserting the candles into the holders all the way round the chandelier. 'So, your new girlfriend. Tell me everything.'

'There's not much to tell. I've only met her once.'

'And yet you've mobilized an army for her.'

He shrugged. 'We always throw an opening-up party.'

'Not like this, you don't. It must be a big deal if even your mamma is in a flap.'

He stopped what he was doing and pinned her with a look. 'My mother has never *flapped* in her life. She's a duchessa, not a pigeon.'

Gina grinned as he descended the ladder. 'Still, Valentina's a big deal. What did you do to trick her into liking you? Wear a mask? Adopt an entirely new personality?'

Cosimo jumped to the ground and looped an arm around her, pulling her playfully into a headlock as he had done when they were children. 'What was that? . . . I can't hear you.'

She tapped out, laughing as he lifted the ladder and they walked over to the other tree. 'Is she going to stay here in the port afterwards?'

He climbed up with the second chandelier. 'I've no idea. We may find we have nothing to talk about.'

'Oh, so you've got talking on your mind, have you? Interesting.'

He chuckled. 'It also depends on her filming schedule in Gallipoli . . . It's all very loose. I was surprised she said yes to coming here at all, to be honest.'

'Do you like her?'

'She's Valentina Fabiani! Of course I *like* her! Find me a male with a pulse who doesn't!' He hung the chandelier on the hook and looked down at her, a hand outstretched for the candles. 'You? Do you have a boyfriend yet? Please don't tell me you're still in love with Dante Giannelli.'

'Always,' she gasped, pressing a hand above her heart dramatically. 'But until he comes to his senses and notices me, I'm stuck with being groped by Luigi Vitti.'

He had to think for a moment. 'The barber's son?'

She shrugged. 'It's better than nothing.'

For once, Cosimo was lost for words. He had kissed many girls himself in this past year, but the thought of these local boys pawing at his oldest friends . . . Gina was all soft curves and lips; he could well imagine the lust she inspired. And Rafa – she was the opposite, delicate and flighty with long legs and doe eyes . . . Who wouldn't want her?

'If you say so.'

'I do. It's not like we're spoilt for choice here, you know. Not like in Rome, where you have a new girl every week!'

He glanced down, hearing her pointed tone. 'I hope you don't mean me specifically?'

'Romy tells us in her letters what you're getting up to, you know. What are you so desperate to prove, Cosi, huh?'

He shook his head and tutted. 'You girls talk too much.'

'Well, we all have a lot to say,' she shrugged.

'*You* definitely do.'

'Rafa too.'

'Yeah, right.'

'Believe it or not, our lives do continue when your family leaves town!'

'Now, that I find hard to believe,' Cosimo grinned.

'Oh, the things I could tell you,' she teased.

He glanced at her, intrigued. 'Such as?'

'Infidelities. Secret seductions. Betrayals. It all happens here as well, you know – just in patched clothes. Don't think we're not getting up to what you're getting up to.'

Cosimo swallowed, sincerely hoping that wasn't true. 'Romy was saying at breakfast she thinks Rafa's going to marry Fon.' It wasn't exactly what she'd said but the suggestion had been raised, and now he couldn't get it out of his head.

Gina paused, watching him straighten the candles in their holders. 'Well, he is mad about her,' she said in a considering tone. 'He treats her like a princess; you should see how he hangs on her every word. Who knows? Maybe they will. He's devoted, and she's a pragmatist.'

'*Pragmatist?* What kind of reason is that for getting married?'

'Rafa lives in the real world, Cosi, unlike you. To be honest, I wouldn't be at all surprised if she became Mrs Alfonso Giannelli within the year.'

The garden swayed suddenly, as if the ladder had been kicked; or perhaps it was the tree, a sudden gust shaking the branches. He climbed down quickly.

He never had been good with heights.

'Hey!' Gina called suddenly across the garden, pointing at him. 'Look who finally woke up!'

He looked over to see Rafaella and her mother struggling to carry a tin bath between them, filled with ice.

'Here, let me help,' he said, running over to them. 'Signora Parisi, please, it looks heavy,' he insisted.

Rafaella's mother smiled gratefully as she allowed him to take the handle on her side of the tub. '*Grazie*, Cosimo.'

She moved off, joining the women at the food tables, leaving him alone with Rafaella.

'Hey,' he said, glancing at her as they walked awkwardly over the grass.

'Hey.'

A small silence bloomed, both of them uncharacteristically lost for words as they carried the bathtub in pigeon steps. The reunion yesterday at the beach caffè had held surprises for them both.

'. . . She's going to love this,' Rafaella said after a moment.

'Who will?'

'Valentina. The garden looks so pretty.'

'Oh. Yes.'

'Everyone's so excited to see her.'

'They are?'

'Of course!'

'Are you?' he asked her.

'Of course!' she said again. '. . . Are you?'

'Of course!' But he winced, not just at the evident strain in the conversation, but at the lie – for the truth was, he wished he'd never invited Valentina now. She was undeniably beautiful and sexy, but what had seemed like a good idea at midnight in a nightclub now seemed a terrible proposition here in this garden, in the middle of the day.

'Good,' she smiled. 'Well, I'm glad you're happy.'

He glanced across at her again – did she really mean it? She didn't care that Valentina Fabiani was coming here as his guest and all that that implied?

Rafaella's smile hadn't reached her eyes, but before he could say anything, they reached the table that would serve as the drinks station for the night, and they set the tub down carefully on the grass. Gina had gone back to balancing the pomegranate and she came over now, hands on her hips, her hairline damp.

'Ugh, I'm actually melting!' she complained, wiping her brow with the back of her hand.

'Luckily, we have a remedy for that,' he said, grateful for the distraction she provided as he swung an arm in the direction of the round pool further down the lawn. '. . . Anyone for a swim?'

The water slipped over his skin, cool and clear, as they all swam like otters below the surface, together but apart. As children they would have retrieved any items they could get to sink to the bottom, or had races, or seen who could hold their breath the longest . . . Once upon a time he would have grabbed the girls and thrown them in or dunked them, but the innocence of childhood had faded and he found he didn't dare put his hands on either one of his old friends now. What could be hidden beneath clothing was wholly revealed poolside and it was impossible not to notice their new curves in their swimwear. Gina's bikini was in an existential crisis, desperately trying to cling on to her; Rafaella was mermaid-like as she gently fluttered her long limbs, her hair streaming out behind her, so serene and beautiful that he knew he would gladly follow her to be dashed upon the rocks.

The new tension between them all cut both ways. He had seen the way their eyes flickered too over his hard-won muscles and smattering of chest hair as he had pulled off his shirt and carelessly – but expertly – dived in. Gina was swimming around with a small, enigmatic smile on her face, as if she knew something he didn't. She probably did, but he knew better than to ask her what it was; she'd always had a way of throwing him off balance with her waspish wit, and he already felt wrong-footed as they adjusted to this new adult dynamic between them all.

'Better?' he asked, as Gina surfaced with a gasp.

'So much,' she sighed, smoothing her hair back from her face. 'I felt like a lobster being boiled alive. Honestly, Cosi – only your family could get everyone to work during *riposo*!'

'It's called enlightened self-interest,' he grinned, treading water. 'They know they'll be rewarded with the fruits of their own labour tonight, when they eat and drink us out of house and home. Isn't that right, Rafa?'

Rafaella appeared not to hear. She was lying on her back, a floating starfish, and he and Gina swapped looks, each already knowing what the other was thinking. It had always been one of their favourite games when they were kids . . . Without hesitation, he duck-dived, swimming under Rafaella and blowing out bubbles that rose up and tickled her back. She startled, wriggling at the unexpected movement below her just as he grabbed her right ankle, pulling her under water.

She folded and sank, everything going into slow motion down there as she twisted and faced him through the blue, his hands upon her waist in immediate reassurance as she got her bearings. Time seemed to stand still. Above their heads, it was the world – perfectly still and silent – that looked like the mirror reflection, and down here was what was real. They couldn't speak, clearly; there was no more hiding behind polite conversation or mannered smiles. They could only communicate with their eyes, but for a few short seconds it was as if a veil had been dropped and he was transported back to that night, last summer . . .

She kicked up to the surface, emerging with a small half-cry, half-laugh. 'Bastards!'

'Got you!' Gina laughed, splashing her for good measure.

Cosimo threw his head back, an arc of water flying through the air as his hair settled in perfect position off his face. He rubbed his face in his hands. 'Sorry, Rafa. It was too good to resist,' he said unapologetically, swimming around her like a shark.

'I'll get you back for that!'

'Yeah, yeah,' he replied, holding her eye contact and hoping she would. He wanted to see that moment of truth again, to feel it. Had he imagined it?

She splashed at him, getting him straight in the face, and it was all the ammunition he needed to dive under again and grab her by the leg. They were below water once more, his hands on her skin as he pulled her towards him – but she was slippery in his grip, a good swimmer too, and she got away, surfacing with another laugh as she raced for the steps.

She was fast – always had been – but he was taller and right behind her, the water parting as his arms ploughed through, gaining on her. She got to the steps just as his hands closed round her waist and he threw her back into the middle of the pool. He followed straight after her, diving messily now. Where she went, he went . . . Limbs and slipstreams. Bubbles and darting glances. Somewhere in the chaos, it had become a chase, and they felt themselves caught on the tail-feathers of another game, the echoes lingering from the night last summer when pursuit had led to capture . . .

'*Rafa?*'

Cosimo peered into the narrow fissure in the trunk of the mighty monumentale *tree. It had always been one of the best hiding spots in this part of the plantation, and they had often fought for it when playing hide-and-seek. She'd won tonight.*

'Let me in,' he whispered. Somewhere in the shadows, Romola was hiding too.

'No!' she laughed, giddy on the beers he'd smuggled out. 'It's mine! I got here first! Go find your own spot.'

'Shh!' He pressed a finger to her lips, shushing her as he waited for another sound to come to his ear.

'Coming to find you! Ready or not!' Gina's voice carried through the night, calling for them. It was so late even the cicadas were sleeping, the moon sweeping its monocular gaze across the silver-banded sea.

He looked back at her. 'Too bad! There's no time now,' he hissed, beginning to squeeze himself into the crevice too.

'No! There's no room!' she giggled, trying to push him back. Once upon a time, when they'd been smaller, they could have squeezed in there together, but he'd grown so much recently they'd be like two nuts in a shell now. 'Go somewhere else!' she hissed.

But he was too strong, and too determined not to lose the game, to be deterred. The fissure wasn't a sheer vertical but a diagonal slash through the trunk and he filled the space as he slid in first one leg, then the other, holding himself not so much beside her as around her. She was pressed back against the plane of smooth wood, and he braced his hand against the inside of the nook to support himself as he stood angled above her.

Rafaella looked up at him and he was suddenly aware of the intense heat of his body against hers, her breath like a hot wind upon his skin.

'Come out, come out, wherever you are!' Gina cried, her voice ricocheting through the grove. She was close now.

Cosimo didn't stir; he could hardly even breathe as Rafaella blinked at him in the darkness. Only the breeze moved, rustling through the olive leaves as they waited, suspended.

'I know you're here somewhere!' Gina slurred. They could hear her footsteps on the ground, treading over twigs and stones as she stumbled along, as drunk as the rest of them.

From the sound of it, she was only a few metres away, peering up into the canopy as she went.

Rafaella shifted but Cosimo pressed a finger to his lips as they heard Gina's footsteps pass right by on the other side of the tree. He pretended to be listening but he couldn't think of anything but the heat of her thighs between his in the tiny space, her body pressed close as they waited to be found. He knew she was drunk and that she was unused to the fuzzy, swirling feeling – unlike him; he should know better than to recast his old friend in a new mould.

He tried to cool his thoughts, but they couldn't have slipped so much as a blade of grass between them and he knew he wouldn't be able to hide her effect on him if they stayed here much longer. He closed his eyes, listening to Gina stumbling in the moonlight. Perhaps it would be better if she did find them. Release them from this dangerous confinement.

But as he looked back down, he saw the shift in Rafaella too. He could see it in the way her gaze fell to his lips, the drowsy blackness of her eyes, and he realized that what was coming next was inevitable, a gravitational pull neither of them could resist.

He scarcely had to move to kiss her but he hesitated before their lips touched, as if he knew this would change everything. He did it anyway and, almost immediately, the pressure between them grew. The tree cradled her against him and their arms and legs became as tangled as the branches. She pushed her body upwards, an instinct that made him groan, and when she looked up at him it was as if something inside her had switched on – a vital, hidden part of herself she had never even known was there.

'Rafa,' he whispered, his voice breaking on the word as desire won out . . .

*

They surfaced for the third time, gulping down lungfuls of air, his head turning frantically as he looked around to see where she had gone. He was surprised to find his sister standing on the side, looking on with amusement. '*Allora! Allora!*' she was yelling, clicking her fingers to get his attention. '*Si, ciao!* Earth to Cosi!'

'Oh, hey!' he said distractedly. Rafaella was treading water nearby, looking up at Romola too, her eyes shining and her breath coming heavily as she recovered from the repeated dunkings. She looked happy. Had she felt it too, then?

'I was calling you!'

He turned back to his sister. 'Sorry, I didn't hear.'

'Clearly!'

He squinted. The sun was right behind Romola, throwing her into silhouette. He swam over to the edge and pulled himself out easily, sitting on the side. 'What's up?' he asked, raking his hair back and hoping no one could see how hard his heart was pounding. All he wanted was to get back under the water again, to make her laugh and scream . . .

Romola straightened. 'I just took a call from your girlfriend's assistant. Valentina's on the train. You need to pick her up in an hour.'

He felt his euphoria dissipate like a bubble on a spike. 'An hour?' The station was fifty minutes from here, even when he wasn't soaking wet and in the middle of the pool.

'Yeah, so you'd better hop to it. You can't keep La Bomba waiting!'

He turned towards Gina and Rafaella with a sinking feeling in his chest, but they were looking back at him with inscrutable stares.

Playtime was over.

Chapter 4

Rafaella

Rafaella could tell the party was in full swing long before she began pulling on the squeaky brakes of her bike as she freewheeled down the hill. Music echoed across the bay, shrieks of laughter carrying into the night sky like silver arrows aiming for the stars. Her stomach was in knots as she pulled up, and she took a few deep breaths while she propped the bike against a wall.

Across the road, a few young men in suits – not from around here – were leaning on their scooters by the harbour wall; they were dragging on cigarettes and looking down onto the marina below. Were they some of Romy and Cosimo's friends, invited to the party too?

She stepped around the stone gate piers and stopped short at the sight before her. This party was invariably the highlight of the villagers' calendar, but this year it somehow seemed *more*. The garden, always beautiful, was lit like a wedding cake, the long drive strung with globe lights, and the number of guests had doubled from last year.

Automatically, she tugged on her cotton dress, trying to find another centimetre of length. It was too plain, too short and too tight. It wasn't a party dress in the slightest, but she had nothing else to wear that fit, and she couldn't fill out the curves in either Silvana's or Gina's dresses. There had been no time, of course, for her sister to see her for a fitting today, all the village women having been commandeered for the party preparations.

Not that it mattered how she looked when Valentina Fabiani was here. Rafaella could be standing here nude and no one would notice.

She walked past the lemon trees, finding reassurance in the number of familiar smiling faces she passed, for there were many, many others she didn't recognize. Where had they all come from? Rome? That was almost a day's drive away, but there were of course dozens of sumptuous villas nestled in grand estates on the hills around here, hidden by oak forests and olive groves.

'*Ciao*, Rafa!'

She turned and saw Federico Franchetti waving to her. He was dressed in an ivory silk evening jacket and chatting easily with a couple of the village men, who wore their best suits. She recognized the rare look of abandon on her neighbours' faces – for one night only, their troubles were eased. They could eat and drink with an extravagance otherwise unknown to them – there would be no portioning the cheese or counting the tomatoes on each plate tonight.

'*Ciao*, Fede,' she smiled, waving back. He was Cosi's older brother, twenty-two or thereabouts, but unlike Cosi, Fede was a rare bird to spot in the port. Always studious, he wanted to be a lawyer and seemed to spend most of his time here preparing for exams. As such, she didn't know him well, and her closeness with his brother and sister lay at odds with the polite formality of their relationship. She knew manners dictated she go over and make conversation; she was an adult now, after all, not a little girl stealing chocolates from their kitchen. But she felt overwhelmed by the extravagance on display, not to mention trepidatious about how this evening might unfold. She didn't know how to prepare herself for seeing Cosimo with Valentina Fabiani, and small talk was the last thing she wanted . . .

'Hey, Rafa!' Her name carried again, and this time she saw Gina standing by the round pool with some of the local crowd: Luigi, Gino, Antonia, Donatella. 'Get over here!' Gina yelled, beckoning her.

'Yeah! Where've you been?' Antonia called.

'Oh . . .' She hesitated as she looked back at Fede, caught between obligation and ease.

'Go, I'll catch up with you later,' he smiled, seeing her quandary and not offended in the least as he turned back to his companions. He was a master of the art of mingling, able to talk with anyone.

She walked over to the others, grateful for the reprieve. Countless beer bottles were lined along the rim of the pool wall, others toppled at their feet, and Rafaella could tell at once they were well on their way to being drunk. The blue light from the water reflected up and rippled over their faces, making the whites of their eyes shine.

Rafaella looked into the water, remembering the afternoon's escapades – only a few hours ago and yet a lifetime too, it felt – as Cosimo had dunked and thrown her into the depths, frolicking as if it was the old days. But it had been only a glancing time-slip into the past for her. She couldn't pretend it was the same. They weren't children anymore, and something fundamental had shifted between them. Even last summer she wouldn't have thought twice about their games, but now . . . She could still feel the firmness of his hands on her body, the spread of his fingers on her waist, and the fear she had kindled all year had been confirmed: the innocence between them had gone. She couldn't go back to how it had been before, even if he could.

Gina handed her a beer. 'Drink,' she commanded. Luigi had his arm draped over her shoulder and kept brazenly staring down at her cleavage, which was set off to full effect tonight in her too-tight green dress.

'Where's Romola?' Rafaella asked.

Gina irritably shrugged Luigi's arm away. She seemed perpetually in flight from her boyfriend's attentions, as if seduction by him was a terrible but inevitable fate. 'Not down yet. No doubt stuck on hostessing duties with the starlet.'

'But Fede's over there—'

'How come you're so late, anyway?' Antonia asked, looking at Rafaella's dress with a pitying expression.

'I lost track of time.' She couldn't tell them that she'd spent an hour sitting on the end of her bed, willing herself to move. To face what had to be faced tonight.

'*Lost track of time?* Had better things to do, did you?' Antonia laughed, swinging an arm around at the bedecked garden.

Rafaella looked at Gina. 'Have I missed much?'

'Not once you've got that down you.' Gina playfully tipped the bottle up to Rafaella's lips and she duly obliged, swallowing as much as she could until she began coughing.

'Edo Carosa has already been sent home in disgrace for pissing on Apollo,' Luigi laughed. 'The duchessa looked like she was going to have a stroke.'

'And they've run out of Cointreau,' Gino added. 'Which apparently is a *nightmare* . . .?'

The others groaned. Even nightmares were class-based. Theirs came as unexpected pregnancies they couldn't afford, failed harvests, injuries that left them unable to work . . .

'So, have you seen her?' Rafaella asked them all, keeping her voice neutral.

'Not yet. I think she's waiting to make an entrance,' Luigi said, taking a step back and craning his neck to look up the garden to where everyone else was standing. The open, arched balconies that ran along the front of the pink villa were hidden from sight here by the deep cover of the lemon trees.

'Or else she's getting busy with Cosimo,' Gino said with a smirk.

Rafaella looked away sharply. She couldn't see the villa, but she could see through to the lawn where the food tables had been set up; the (now despoiled) statue of Apollo was moodily spotlit and, either side, twinkling chandeliers hung from the lowest branches of the two old stone-pine trees. The nonnas, in their black dresses, were seated around a table with several bottles of red wine between them and they were all talking and gesticulating intently. Nonna Giacosa was hitting bystanders on the legs with her stick whenever they strayed too close.

There were no hard boundaries between the Tricase residents and the Franchettis' personal guests, but although they stood together Rafaella saw there was almost no mingling between the groups either, despite Fede's lone efforts. They were divided by a host of unspoken distinctions – manners in conversation, the etiquette of holding a glass. Even the pitch of the visitors' laughter was moderated to something appealing and unobtrusive. Unlike the villagers in their muted cottons, the summer people were draped in extravagant colours, their dresses cut in liquid silks and gauzy, voluminous taffetas. Jewels clung to their earlobes, throats, wrists and fingers; they wore their hair in chic chignons and updos like the ones Silvana pored over in her magazines. Rafaella knew her sister would be in her element here among so many illustrious people, her magpie eye taking in the discreet haute-couture details of outfits made in Roman or Florentine ateliers. This night alone would keep the villagers gossiping for at least a month, but all Rafaella saw was the vast breach between residents and incomers. Us and them, she thought, knowing she was on the wrong side. Knowing what it meant for her vain hopes.

'Fon was here earlier,' Gino said, catching her looking around the crowd. 'But he had to help Dante with something.'

'Oh,' she said, but it wasn't Fon she was looking for; in fact, he hadn't even crossed her mind. She was too preoccupied with what was – and wasn't – happening right here. This time last year, Cosimo would have been standing out here in the shadows with them, sneaking drinks and cigarettes; now he was inside, seducing a starlet and drinking Merlot or cognac. He had always sworn, as the four of them lay on the rocks, out of sight at the lido and past their curfew, that he would never become like his parents – by which he meant one of the 'social-climbing pseudos' or 'fakes' that populated their smart circle. He had passionately, avowedly aligned himself with his port-bound best friends – but that had been naive; she could see that now, as she looked around the decorative garden and glimpsed the lavish lifestyle that was the reality of his world away from here. They weren't the same, and the differences between them were only going to grow more apparent with every passing day.

Suddenly there was a shift in the party's mood, bodies stiffening and necks craning as one.

'Oh God,' Donatella exclaimed, clapping her hands together as a clamour rose up through the crowd. 'I think she's here! She's actually here!'

'Stick with me,' Gina said, pulling Rafaella along as they joined the throng beginning to gather below the balcony. Cosimo's parents, Filippo and Rossanna, were already standing graciously in the central arch above the dual staircase, crystal flutes in their hands. A stone campana urn had been over-ambitiously planted with a froth of geraniums so that they had to stand either side of it to be seen, but from everything Romola had ever said about her parents, distance between them was only ever a good thing anyway. Not that the villagers would know it – to them, the Franchettis epitomized grace and good fortune.

Rossanna was a noted beauty and society figure in the capital; Filippo was a senior politician for the Christian Democrat government – currently he was the minister of infrastructure – and he usually only made a few fleeting appearances in the port during the summer season, more often being detained by official business in the city. As well as being an important political figure, he was the Duke of Paliano, and nobility seemed to have been bred into his bones, drawing him with an aquiline lightness of touch so that he seemed somehow almost transparent. Never fully there.

His presence was felt now, however, and the crowd fell quiet.

'Friends,' Filippo began warmly, drawing immediate cheers again. 'Rossanna and I are honoured to welcome you to our home, to celebrate the onset of summer and our family's return to our most treasured place, Tricase Porto . . .'

There were more cheers. Rafaella couldn't see Romola or Cosimo on the balcony with their parents. Where were they?

Filippo addressed the crowd, complimenting their efforts to pull the party together so quickly and thanking them for the warm welcome as his wife stood serenely beside him. Rafaella watched the mother, but it was the son she saw: dark mahogany hair, generous smile, soulful eyes framed with lustrous lashes. Rossanna was wearing a floaty white one-shouldered dress, pearls like globes at her ears, her hair loosely pulled back at the nape of her neck and punctuated with a single white lily. She was the embodiment of Roman elegance.

But as a raucous cheer went up, Rafaella saw the embodiment of Roman glamour step up behind her, and even the duchessa was eclipsed. For a moment, Valentina Fabiani was hidden behind the urn; then the duke stepped back with his usual good manners, giving her his spot and the stage.

Rafaella gasped and felt her spirit plunge. The magazine photographs hadn't done Valentina Fabiani justice. She was exquisitely beautiful: nubile, with skin like a peach. She was wearing a red pleated silk chiffon dress, corseted through the bodice and flowing into a draped skirt. Her lipstick matched the dress and her platinum-blonde hair shone even in the darkness, her cat-like eyes darting and sharply watchful as she basked in the villagers' hysterical acclaim. She was the most famous person any of them had ever seen in real life – Dante Giannelli excepted, who was now assumed to be on first-name terms with La Lollo – and it was true that even the Franchettis' star power waned in comparison. Rafaella watched Rossanna's smile freeze, her chin lifting a quarter-inch.

'I know whose face I'll be beating off to tonight,' Gino said behind her to Luigi.

'Ugh!' Gina groaned with a shudder as they sniggered. 'Animals!'

'*Grazie mille!*' Valentina smiled, waving to her adoring audience. 'Thank you for your kind welcome. I am so happy to join you here tonight. I look forward to meeting you all through the course of this evening –'

They cheered louder still as she blew them kisses, and it was as if the lid blew off the sky. Rossanna Franchetti looked as if she might splinter into shards of glass.

'Where's Cosi?' Rafaella hissed impatiently to Gina, seeing no sign of him still on the balcony. 'Or Romy?'

Valentina stepped back, and Filippo told his guests to eat all they could and drink the cellar dry. No one needed telling twice.

'I know, it's odd,' Gina shrugged, casting around the crowd

too. 'I mean, he has to look after his girlfriend, at least . . . but what's Romy got to do that's so important?'

A sudden loud bang made everyone cry out, their bodies collectively contracting into a lowered hunch, and the sky flashed white as if split open by the gods – but no rain fell, no forks of lightning speared the heavens . . . Rafaella felt Gina grab her arm as they looked around in alarm and confusion. What was happening? From the bewildered looks passing between the Franchettis, they seemed as shocked as everyone else, although not necessarily afraid.

It came again, the ear-splitting bang – but this time, the sky glowed blue.

'It is only fireworks!' Filippo called out as the villagers quailed once more. 'No need to be afraid!'

'Fireworks?' Rafaella murmured. She had heard of them, of course, just never seen them for herself. No one here had, and their gasps began to fall into synchronicity as the explosions started coming more quickly and rhythmically. It struck her as a remarkable feat that the rich could actually paint the sky red, blue, gold, green . . .

They were seemingly never-ending, cascading in a whimsy of shapes and colours, each more beautiful than the last. Rafaella looked back at the villa again and this time she caught sight of a silhouetted figure moving past one of the windows on the upper floor. Romola's bedroom.

'Oh, Gina!' she gasped, pointing excitedly. 'She's in there!'

They didn't hesitate, slipping through the mesmerized crowd and darting over the now deserted Apollo lawn towards the kitchen at the back of the property.

'*Ciao*, Signora Cinzia,' they smiled as they burst in, waving to the Franchettis' cook, who always came down here with them from Rome.

'*Bellas!*' she cried. She knew them well, of course, and raised no protest as they passed through while she stirred the risotto. They slipped past the pantry and washroom into the grand public rooms of the villa. The rooms ran in a cascade, one into the other, most of the time divided only by an arch; they skittered beneath vaulted ceilings, past gilded mirrors and plush silk sofas, over ancient tiled floors. There was a staircase to the two upper floors at either end of the villa; the master suite and the little ones' rooms were on the first floor, and Fede's, Cosimo's and Romola's at the top.

Rafaella glanced towards the balcony as they ran for the left-hand stairs that brought them closest to Romola's bedroom. The Franchettis were still standing there with their guest of honour, the night sky beyond them a kaleidoscope of colour. Valentina was chatting intently with Filippo as the fireworks continued to boom; on the other side of the urn stood Rossanna and Cosimo. Rossanna had a hand to the urn and was pointing to the base, where some of the stone appeared to have crumbled away.

Rafaella felt her breath catch in her throat just at the sight of Cosimo talking with his mother. He was partly out of sight, but even the edges of him were thrilling. Instinctively she slowed, but Gina, bringing up the rear, pushed her onwards.

'Hurry up!' she hissed, grabbing Rafaella's arm and dragging her along.

They ran up the stairs with a familiarity that came from childhood summers spent racing along these corridors, not bothering to knock at Romola's door as they burst in.

'Rom—!' Gina panted, pulling up short so suddenly that Rafaella walked into the back of her as they both took in the sight by the window. Romola was pressed against the wall, her slight frame all but hidden by the boy kissing her, one of her legs in his grip as he pushed into her, his trousers down by his knees.

For a moment the vision was freeze-framed, as sometimes

happened at the cinema when the film reel snagged and stalled, the image flickering, blistering, burning . . . Then it was released quite suddenly, and the lovers pulled apart at the sudden intrusion.

A stunned silence exploded, every bit as loud as the fireworks outside, as they watched Romola pull down her dress and Fon fiddling with his trousers before he eventually turned. But Rafaella hadn't needed to see his face to know who it was.

She staggered back, unable to believe this was really real. Fon's betrayal was wounding enough, but Romola's . . . She was one of her dearest and best friends in the world. Rafa's entire year revolved around her return; her days were enlivened by news of her exploits – so for this to happen, when Romola Franchetti could do anything, have *anyone* . . .

'Rafa!' Romy cried, the word slurring as she saw Rafaella's eyes immediately filling with tears, her chest beginning to heave with sorrow. 'Wait!'

But it was too late. Rafaella turned and fled with a speed that was uncatchable. She was down the two flights of stairs seemingly without touching a tread, flying through the interconnected rooms like a midnight bat—

'Whoa!' She was caught and spun, hands upon her arms, eyes upon her eyes. 'Rafa?' Cosimo's voice broke as he found himself holding her and she was propelled back to that moment in their past which, for one blinding, dazzling instant, had felt like a beginning and not an end . . .

'Rafa? What's happened?'

She saw his eyes rake over her face, taking in her tears and distress, his grip tightening as he held her again in his arms. It was everything she had wanted. But not like this.

'Tell me what's wrong. Are you hurt? Who's hurt you?'

She wanted to scream that it was Romy – that Romy had taken what she wanted, simply because she could! She wanted him to know that *he* had hurt her too, throwing cold water over her fevered hopes by bringing one of the most desired women in all of Italy here, undeniable proof that he had moved on from the moment that had been everything to her and nothing at all to him.

But she pulled back wordlessly, out of his grasp. There was nothing to be said. Her dreams were dying all around her tonight, leaving only ashes in her mouth.

Chapter 5

Fon

'You're a man now,' Dante grinned, slapping him hard on the shoulder before tugging on the mooring rope and jumping aboard *Allegra*. 'How does it feel?'

Fon didn't reply as he passed over the ice box. It was heavy, and he felt the strain in his body. He felt wretched. He hadn't slept a wink, spending the night staring at the ceiling and wondering how the hell it had all come to pass.

One minute he'd been helping Dante with the fireworks his brother had secretly smuggled earlier onto the roof; the next he'd run into Romola in the hall, drunk out of her mind and immediately all over him as she'd dragged him into her room. How could he have been so dumb? He hadn't even wanted her – at least, not before she'd done what she'd done. How did she know how to do all that stuff? She was his age, and before last night, he'd not got past second base! Was *everyone* more experienced than him?

He couldn't erase Rafaella's expression from his mind, seeing how her eyes had filled with tears, her mouth falling into a silent O before she'd turned and fled. He had ruined everything with her – and for what? To prove something to Dante and show his brother he could be a stud too?

He felt hollow inside, that was the truth of it; as if his entire life had been undone in an instant. All those months of groundwork with Rafaella, trying to get her to see him as honourable, to show her he was worthy of her, meant nothing now. She would never trust him again, and he didn't blame her.

'I don't want to talk about it,' he said, pulling bottles of Coca-Cola from the plastic crate and handing them to his brother one by one.

But Dante, sticking them into the ice, didn't listen. He never did. 'I've got to hand it to you, little brother. I didn't think you had it in you, bagging a Franchetti like that. And your first time, too!' He laughed, the sound morphing into a whistle. 'I'd do the mother, for sure. She plays it cool, but I bet once she gets warmed up—'

'Keep your voice down,' Fon snapped, looking around to check no one on the other boats had heard. If word was to get around . . . Besides, he had an uneasy feeling Cosimo was looking for a reason to go off on him. They'd never been friends, but yesterday, as they'd brought the flowers in, Cosimo had looked at him with something close to contempt. 'I just want to forget about it, OK?' he hissed, even as the memories played on a loop in his mind. He kept hearing Gina's gasp as she burst in, immediately followed by Rafaella's resounding silence . . . If she had only screamed at him or thrown something at his head – as any of the other girls would have done – he might have been able to engage her somehow, but she had detached so completely it was like expecting a marble statue to bleed. Her quiet dignity was one of the things he had always admired most about her, but now it shuttered her away from him and he had no idea how to reach her.

All around them, the port residents were in varying states of recovery. The party had continued long into the night, music echoing around the small port until the sun came up.

The nonnas were now treading water at their preferred spot by the steps just past the marina, kept afloat by their strong arms and capacious bosoms. The fishermen had collectively decided to spend the day mending nets in the shade of the high harbour wall. The women were in the wash-house, but Fon had passed by on his way down here and glimpsed them sitting on the step, laundry baskets by their feet as they talked.

From the snippets he had gleaned, much had happened after his early departure – Donatella and Antonia had gone skinny-dipping in the round pool; Silvana and her fiancé had been caught in an advanced stage of 'heavy petting' by Father Tommaso behind the jasmine wall; Gino and Luigi, abandoned by Gina, had got into trouble for letting off some leftover fireworks they'd found on the roof and narrowly missing one of the paparazzi gathered outside the gates in the hope of sighting Valentina Fabiani. Giulieta Carosa had fallen into a bush, and the youngest Franchettis had stolen a bottle of Aperol and been found passed out in wheelbarrows in the garden store.

So far, Fon hadn't caught a mention of his own name, nor Romola's – much less the two connected together – and he was counting on his brother showing a little restraint for once. Dante might want to shout from the rooftops about his brother's trophy seduction, but more reputations than their own were at stake in this. If word was to get out, Romola would be disgraced, Rafaella humiliated.

'Hey!' Dante cried jovially, straightening up as he looked past Fon. 'So you decided to take me up on my offer, then?'

Fon turned to find Valentina Fabiani sashaying towards them as if she was on the red carpet at Cannes, rather than this tiny Puglian harbour. The fishermen stopped their mending, mouths agape as she passed. She wore tiny white shorts over a pink bikini, black sunglasses and a wide-brimmed straw hat. Fon thought she looked like a trifle – colourful and everything jiggling. Two paparazzi were running ahead of her and taking photographs, but she ignored them so completely it was as if they weren't even there.

'Ah . . .!'

Fon registered the change in his brother's tone. He saw how he straightened up, too.

'Your son couldn't join you, signore?' Dante asked as Fon saw Filippo Franchetti bringing up the rear, carrying the towels and trying to stay out of shot.

'I'm afraid Cosimo is feeling the worse for wear this morning,' Filippo said drily. He was wearing navy swimming shorts and a short-sleeved white shirt. Fon, realizing he had only ever seen the duke in a suit, was surprised by how much younger he appeared. There was little of the politician about him as he handed over the striped towels.

Dante rushed forward chivalrously to offer Valentina a supporting hand as she jumped aboard. 'Well, we're more than happy to assist you with hosting duties, signore,' he said, but his attention was on the starlet as he gripped her fingers, holding her gaze longer than necessary. 'I trust you enjoyed our little firework display last night, Signorina Fabiani?'

'Oh! Those were yours, were they?' Filippo asked, surprised. 'We did wonder.'

'I hope you didn't mind, signore,' Dante said. 'We simply wanted to make the signorina's trip here extra special. A way for us humble villagers to say welcome.' He smiled obsequiously.

'Indeed,' the older man murmured, looking displeased by the impertinence of hijacking the party with their own celebrations.

But Dante was oblivious, watching as Valentina positioned herself prettily on the leather bench seat, crossing her legs delicately, a coy smile on her lips. She seemed well accustomed to favours, privileges and princess treatment.

Still the paparazzi were snapping away, and Fon, like the duke, tried to stay out of shot. Dante had no such reservations and casually pulled his black shirt over his head to reveal a bronzed torso rippling with muscles.

'Have you water-skied before, signorina?' he asked, balling up the shirt and throwing it into a compartment beneath the helm. Fon saw Valentina's gaze drag over him interestedly. His brother knew exactly what he was doing – with Cosimo out of the picture, at least for the next few hours, the stage was set for him to make an impression without any competition.

'. . . A few times, yes,' she purred. 'Remind me, what is your name again?'

Dante chuckled at the pushback; Fon knew his brother would be enjoying the challenge. She was no submissive local girl, grateful for his brief attention. 'Dante Giannelli at your service, Signorina Fabiani,' he said with a small bow. 'And my brother, Alfonso.'

Fon nodded stiffly, feeling like he was caught in crosshairs as her gaze swept over him briefly, like the swinging, dispassionate beam of a lighthouse, before falling upon Dante again and staying there. Fon looked down. His invisibility was like a cloak he wore at all times, but right now he was grateful for it. Beautiful women brought nothing but trouble.

Dante clapped his hands together as Filippo settled himself on the bench seat too. 'Well then, let's get to it. The conditions are good today. The surface is like glass,' he said. 'Fon, cast off, will you?'

Fon unwound the thick rope and tossed it onto the quay, where it slapped across the leather shoes of one of the photographers as they fell back at last. Dante began expertly, one-handedly manoeuvring the boat from its mooring, a man in his element, as Fon looked around the beach in the vain hope of spotting Rafaella.

But even if he saw her, what would he say? Not the truth. He could never tell her why he'd done it. She deserved better than him, he knew that. She was the perfect woman in his eyes, but no matter what he did, he was always going to be an imperfect man.

Chapter 6

Cosimo

'They've gone.' Cosimo pulled back from the window and stared at his sister, ashen-faced against the sheets. Even by her standards, last night had been wild. 'Romy, come on, you need to get up—'

'I can't,' she blurted, pulling the covers over her head again.

Cosimo walked over and sat on the side of her bed with a weary sigh. He had barely been able to get a coherent word out of her since finding her in a heap on the floor last night, alone in her room after Rafaella, followed by Gina, had fled the villa. The shock of running into Rafaella like that – to find himself holding her, as if he were dreaming, before she had fled again – had stunned him. He'd had no time to brace, to keep her there, and Romola had been in no fit state to explain what had happened. She had thrown up twice and passed out shortly afterwards.

'You have to tell me what you did. I can't help if I don't know.'

A muffled groan came from under the sheet and he pulled it back to find tears sliding down her cheeks. 'She'll never forgive me.'

'You know she will,' he said, seeing how her dark hair was

soaked on the pillow. 'It can't have been that bad.' In all their years as friends, Romola, Gina and Rafaella had never once exchanged a cross word. Jealousy didn't exist between them.

Romola's eyes met his. 'It was the very worst thing.'

He stared at her, feeling his stomach drop as he understood her all-too-familiar look of shame. 'You mean . . . with *Fon*?' He felt immediately sick – and enraged.

Romola's face crumpled at the mention of Fon's name, fresh tears falling in confirmation. 'I didn't mean to!' she cried.

His body tensed, ready to fight. 'Are you saying he forced himsel—?'

'No, no!' She shook her head vehemently. 'Not that. I just didn't – I didn't plan it, that's all! I was upset, and he was there, and . . .'

'Why were you upset?'

She blinked at him, her mouth opening a little as if she was remembering something else too. The moment stretched out.

'Well?' he demanded, impatient. 'Tell me, Romy!'

'I . . . I can't.'

'Why not? What could have happened that was so bad it could drive you into doing something like that? You know Fon's with Rafa!'

'I know! But I didn't mean to do it! I never would have done it if I'd been in my right mind!'

'Oh, please!' Cosimo cried, getting up angrily. His foot caught on something beside the bed, making him stumble. Looking down, he saw an empty Campari bottle and bent to retrieve it. Romola paled again at the sight of it as he threw it on the bed angrily.

'Was it Papa? Again? . . . I know it was! It's always him. What did he do this time?'

Her eyes flashed with a mixture of anger and fear, but she didn't reply.

'Really? You're not going to say? You do this terrible thing to your oldest, truest friend, and you won't even say why?' he demanded.

'If I could, I would!' she said.

'What does that mean, Romy?' he cried.

'I'm trying to protect you!' she sobbed.

'Me?' He gave a cold laugh. 'You don't need to protect me.'

He was forever clashing antlers with his father, the young buck to the stag, challenging for alpha-male status. Nothing he ever did was good enough: he wasn't as clever as Fede, nor was he ambitious or politically minded. He didn't care about money, or position, or any of the things his father believed he should care about.

But father and daughter – they had been devoted to one another when Romola was a little girl. Filippo could do no wrong in her eyes and he revelled in her adoration. It was only as she grew up and came to understand the reasons for his frequent absence from home, and their mother's lingering sadness, that the scales had fallen from Romola's eyes, and a distance had grown between them that was even chillier than his relationship with Cosimo. Filippo was a vain man and couldn't bear that his failings were not only seen but reflected back at him as Romola aped his numerous infidelities with a rampant promiscuity of her own. Her reputation in Rome was beginning to precede her, and Cosimo was growing tired of acting as her keeper.

He sighed, rubbing his face in his hands. He got up and stalked over to the window again and stared out. What a damned mess! They'd only been here three days and everything was already fucked up. She'd been spinning out all year, and he had hoped coming here would calm her down and bring her back to her old self.

'Please don't hate me, Cosi,' she implored behind him.

He ignored her. From this vantage he could see above the

treetops to the perfect strip of cerulean-blue sea beyond. Sailing yachts peppered the horizon, the rich already at play on the water, and he wondered idly how Valentina was getting on with the water-skiing. She hadn't hesitated when Dante had walked right up to her last night, as if he was their equal, and begun talking to her about filming in Rome before inviting them out on his boat. He was so cocksure and arrogant – worse than Cosimo remembered. No doubt Dante believed he had a shot with her.

Had Cosimo been a fool to let her go out with him today? For his sister's sake he had pleaded a hangover by way of excuse this morning, and their father had been happy enough to go as host and chaperone instead – but would he see that the Giannellis didn't play by the rules? That, like Fon, Dante would forget himself and over-reach for whatever he wanted?

Not that Valentina was his, and not that he wanted her to be. He had only asked her here in the hope it would serve as a full-bodied full stop to that unexpected moment with Rafaella last summer. He should never have kissed her, he knew it, but he'd been unable to stop himself, even though she was his friend and there was no hope of anything more between them. Rafaella wasn't the only pragmatist when it came to marriage; Cosimo knew exactly what was expected of him, too ... And yet, it had haunted him all year, no matter how many other girls he kissed. He had thought that, in case he troubled Rafaella's dreams the way she stormed his, bringing Valentina here would draw a line under something they both needed to forget.

But he had clearly flattered himself in thinking she might still care a year later. Rafaella had breezed past it without a moment's thought. She was with Fon now, and had been for five months ... Cosimo caught his breath at the thought of Fon not just touching his sister, but touching *her*—

'Get up,' he said harshly, suddenly.

'Wh-where are we going?'

He crossed the room to go and get dressed. 'You know where.'

It was difficult to move through the port at any speed. Everyone they passed wanted to press the flesh and give thanks for the family's hospitality the night before. Romola, pale and all but obscured beneath a sunhat and dark glasses, could only murmur as Cosimo, ever his mother's son, hid his torrid emotions behind an implacable smile.

At Tito's Bar, every table was taken; some of the *anziani* were playing chess and cards in their usual spots as ice melted in long glasses before them. There were many bowed heads, most of whom weren't usually found on dry land at this hour. Cosimo glanced towards the marina; all the fishing boats were in. Over the road, the sign on the *drogheria* door was showing 'Open', though the shutters remained down.

Cosimo popped his head in and Gina's mother, sitting on her stool behind the counter, looked up. She started, immediately hastening to offer thanks like everyone else, but he quickly raised a hand. 'Please, don't let me disturb you, Signora Crespi – I was just looking for Gina?'

'At the beach caffè, with Rafa. But—'

'*Grazie*.' He ducked out again, taking his sister by the elbow and leading her across the road and down the steps to the beach. The water looked inviting, but this couldn't be put off; he could feel Romy trembling beneath his fingertips, and it didn't bode well for her that Gina and Rafaella were together. If it was Rafaella she had betrayed, it would still be Gina with whom she'd have to do battle.

They walked along the promenade and stopped at the passageway through the cliff, surveying the scene before they made their presence known. All the caffè tables were set out, customers sitting beneath the striped umbrellas. Cosimo could see Gina working behind the counter, making up some drinks. His eyes scanned for Rafaella, but there was no sign of her.

'I can't do this,' Romola quailed, drawing back.

'You can and you will. You have to, Ro,' he said firmly, not relinquishing his grip. 'It's the only way to make things right.'

But even to his ear, the words were hollow. How could they ever be right again? Romola had broken an inviolable code.

'No—'

'Gina!' he called out, catching the girl's attention so that she looked over and saw them. Romola froze, but Cosimo dragged her over the sand. He saw the way Gina stiffened at the sight of them, yesterday's jokes and teasing now a distant memory. There would be no friendly headlocks today.

'You've got some nerve,' Gina hissed at Romola as they stopped before the bar, her eyes darting towards the tables to make sure no customers were listening.

'Please,' Cosimo said in a low voice. 'Just hear her out.'

Gina looked across at Romola with an expression of outright disgust, folding her arms in front of her chest. 'Why should we?'

We. They came as a pair. Indivisible.

'Is Rafa here?' He looked around for her again.

'She doesn't want to see you.'

'Is she here?' he persisted.

'No.'

But he caught the tiny sideways flicker of her eyes towards the back door, and he turned towards it. 'Rafa, I know you're back there.'

No reply.

'Rafaella!' he said more loudly now, and Gina flinched, seeing some of the customers' heads turn. As had been his intention.

'Hush!' she hissed again. 'This isn't the time *or* the place—'

But a shadow fell across the doorframe, and Rafaella emerged. She was holding a crate of lemonade bottles, the sinews in her skinny arms straining. He wanted to take the load from her, but to do so would require releasing his grip on his sister, and he still couldn't be sure she wouldn't bolt.

'*Ciao*,' he said dumbly as he took in the sight of her.

As a girl, she had always been pretty, but over the course of this year her features had grown bolder and stronger upon slight bones, so that now she could be said to be beautiful: appled cheekbones, thick eyebrows, pale, full lips . . . She was taller, too, and very gently curved, just an italic shadow to Valentina's bombshell silhouette.

She looked at them both, wary as a doe in the woods – he didn't blame her – and he tightened his fingers around his sister's bicep. 'Romy has something she'd like to say to you.'

Rafaella looked away as if just his words had hurt her, but her feet didn't stir. Gina walked over, took the crate from her and set it down on the floor.

'Well, spit it out, then,' Gina snapped, planting her hands on her hips as Romola's hesitation turned into a pause.

'I know I don't deserve your m-mercy,' Romola began. 'What I did last night was . . . It was unforgivable.'

'Yes, it was,' Gina agreed.

'I'll *never* forgive myself.'

'Good.'

'But—'

'*But?*' Gina queried, a note of outrage ringing through the word. 'You mean you have a justification?'

'No! I . . .' Romola looked at Cosimo in panic but his eyes were squarely on Rafaella. She was still looking away, so tense he could see the pulse beating in her neck. He couldn't take his eyes off it. 'I didn't plan it.'

'Are we supposed to be grateful for that?'

'No!'

'No? So, you were just so overcome with passion, then?'

Romola shook her head desperately at the sarcasm. 'No . . . It just . . . happened. I was upset, and suddenly he was there, in the hall, and—'

'Spare us the lurid details.' Gina rolled her eyes.

Cosimo could feel the muscles in his sister's arm twitching, her entire body primed to get away from here. He redoubled his grip.

'Look . . . I know an apology can't take away what I've done, but I need you to know I've never regretted anything more in my life. If I had been in my right mind . . .' Romola leaned forward on the bar suddenly, trying to engage Rafaella's attention, but she was looking far out to sea. 'Rafa, you're a sister to me,' she pleaded. 'You both are,' she said, looking to Gina now too.

'Words are cheap,' Gina sneered.

'I hate myself!'

'Good. That makes three of us, then.'

'Gina,' Cosimo said. 'You can see she's trying.'

But Gina's eyes flashed. 'You've had to *drag* her here, Cosi. You're literally holding her against her will, making her do this! Do you think we believe she'd even be out of her bed if it wasn't for you?'

Cosimo sighed, unable to deny it. 'Look, it isn't an excuse, but . . .'

'*But*, again.' Gina rolled her eyes once more.

'. . . We've had a difficult year, OK? As a family, I mean.' His voice was low now.

'Oh, really? Did you run out of Petrus?'

Cosimo flinched at the cruel sarcasm. 'Difficult in other ways,' he said finally. 'And it's not an excuse, just . . . an explanation. We all have different ways of coping.'

'So for Romy it's by opening her legs?'

Romola gave a cry, turning away from the crude response, but Gina wasn't standing for any displays of delicacy now. 'Oh, you can do it but we can't say it?'

'Excuse me!' a pithy voice intruded, and they all looked over. A customer had his arm in the air to attract attention. 'Our order?'

'Dammit,' Gina muttered as she jumped into action, setting glasses on a tray and reaching for ice. '. . . See what you made me do?'

They watched as she hurried over to the table, and Cosimo felt Romola sense her chance.

'Rafa,' she pleaded, leaning on the bar again now that Gina, guard dog and de facto leader of their unit of two, had been removed. 'I know I can't take back what I've done, but won't you let me make this right? Tell me how I can make it up to you. I'll do anything. Anything you ask.'

Rafaella gave a shrug that was agonizing in its helplessness. 'What is there to do?' she asked dully. 'It can't be undone.'

'But . . . if I talk to Fon . . .' Romola said desperately.

'What good would that do? This isn't about him. It's about us . . . I thought you were my friend.'

'I am! Oh, Rafa, you're my best friend in the entire world!'

'Then I wouldn't want to be your enemy.'

For all Gina's rage, it was the simplicity of Rafaella's words that stung like vinegar on a knife wound. Romola fell back, seeing it was hopeless.

Cosimo stared at Rafaella, seeing the breach open up between them all – because something had shifted between the two of them as well, he could feel it. If he was honest, he knew things hadn't been the same since they'd arrived; not even yesterday, during the brief reprieve in the pool, playing like electric eels and shocking each other with every touch in

the water. That one secret kiss had changed everything. He saw that now, as they stood here opposite one another –
　Not as lovers.
　Not as friends.
　But as freshly minted strangers.

Chapter 7

Rafaella

'Hold still.' The words were muffled; Silvana's mouth was full of pins as she moved slowly around Rafaella's inert body. She was pinning the baby-blue fabric Rafaella had chosen weeks earlier, back when she had cared about how she looked for Cosimo's return.

Now none of it mattered. The villa gates had remained closed for the past few days as the Franchettis sequestered themselves behind the high walls of their garden. Their high-profile return had been followed up by a conspicuously private retreat once Valentina Fabiani had left for Gallipoli, pursued by the paparazzi on their scooters.

Something must have happened, everyone conjectured, and the port was buzzing with rumours: Signora Franchetti was on the verge of a breakdown according to the cobbler's wife, who had long served as their summer housekeeper and had counted more than two hundred cigarette butts in the bins. Fon's mother had heard that Federico was secretly a communist and had dropped out of law school to lead the trade union uprisings in Turin. Rafaella's own mother had overheard at the wash-house that a distant relative of the Franchettis had emerged and was laying claim to half their fortune.

All Rafaella knew was what she knew: she had lost her dearest, most precious childhood friends, and it couldn't be undone.

Even Gina wasn't her usual sunny self, though she tried hard to pretend otherwise. They worked their shifts at the caffè by day and sat together on the promenade each evening, legs dangling down over the water as they ate their gelato. They talked around the void that had unexpectedly opened up in their summer, never acknowledging the bitter disappointment that came from losing at the eleventh hour what they'd been longing for all year. The Franchettis might only spend six weeks in the port, but that short season provided enough glamour and excitement to make the other forty-six weeks of the year bearable.

'Step back and let me see you,' Silvana said bossily, squinting as she admired her handiwork. 'I think we could go shorter, no?'

'If you like,' Rafaella shrugged.

Silvana frowned. 'If *I* like? A few weeks ago you were pleading with me for shorter, tighter, now-now-now, and all of a sudden you don't care?'

'It's just a dress.'

'. . . I can always cut it on the shin, if you prefer?'

'If you think that's best.'

Silvana crossed her arms in front of her. '*Basta!* Talk to me. I know something's up.'

'It's nothing.'

'. . . Is it Fon?'

'What? No!'

Rafaella looked away, feeling her big sister's fingers pressing on her other metaphorical bruise; for Fon had made no attempt to contact her or apologize for what he had done. In fact, she hadn't even laid eyes on him since the night of the party. She knew he knew her daily movements well enough to be able to either find or avoid her in the port. It stung that he apparently cared so little, he couldn't even be bothered to apologize.

Was he a coward or a cad? That was the question Gina kept asking her, but Rafaella had no answer. She didn't delude herself that their fledgling relationship had been any great love story, but they had always been friends, and there had been trust between them. She had stuck up for him, aged eleven, when the other boys in school had started calling him names, and they had only stopped because she was pretty enough to have some power over them.

She knew Fon didn't have his brother's easy charm and that he could be awkward in groups; he was quiet and a bit of a loner, it was true. But it wasn't as if she was the life and soul of every party herself. And there was much to be said for having a boyfriend who actually listened when she talked and didn't just look at her with that hungry expression, like most other boys. She was a realist; she knew full well her daydreams about Cosimo were idle fantasies that could never amount to anything, and when Fon had asked her to go out with him she'd reasoned that at least he was handsome, sweet and safe.

Or so she had thought.

'Is he trying to move too fast?'

'Not with me.' The retort was out before she could stop it.

Silvana's eyebrows shot up. Nothing ever got past her. 'With someone else? Did that low-life cheat on you?' Her sisterly indignation grew with every breath.

'Silvana, just leave it—'

'Those Giannellis! They're rotten to the core, every last one of them!'

'That's not true.'

'No?' Silvana planted her hands on her hips, always a sign she was about to come in hard with the truth. 'Luchino told me they were siphoning off ten per cent of everyone's harvest at the *trappito* last winter.'

'What?' Rafaella was shocked. 'No!'

'*Si!* Where do you think they got the money for that boat, huh?' Silvana swatted a hand disgustedly in the air. 'You're better off without him.'

Rafaella swallowed. Was that true? The Giannellis ran the port's communal oil press, the *trappito*, but to skim profits off the villagers' harvests, to deceive their friends and neighbours . . .? Then again, how else could they explain affording that boat on a fisherman's income?

No one could deny the water-skiing enterprise was doing well. The paparazzi photographs of Valentina Fabiani being towed along in her pink bikini had had an immediate effect, sending an influx of new visitors to the port. Tito's and the beach caffè were seeing a surge in business as the tourists hung around before and after their excursions on the water; Rafaella was quickly growing accustomed to the background whine of the engines as she worked, hearing the speedboat ploughing back and forth beyond the harbour wall and curving hard in figures of eight.

'You can do so much better than him,' Silvana huffed.

Rafaella shrugged. 'Perhaps.' She wondered what her sister would say if she knew she had kissed Cosimo. A Franchetti! Valentina Fabiani's boyfriend! . . . Cosi, her old friend. There had been many times in the past year when she'd wanted to tell her, to confide her secret, wild hopes for what might happen when he returned; but her sister's wisdom always came with rough edges and little sentimentality, and Rafaella wasn't quite ready to have the cold truth served back to her.

'He's handsome, though,' Silvana said, doubling back on her indignation. It wasn't as if they were spoilt for choice with suitors here. If they had been, she might not have held out for a wedding ring from Luchino for so very long.

Rafaella shrugged. Was that enough? 'I suppose.' She wanted to change the subject. 'Are we done here?'

'Sure.' Silvana watched as she wriggled out of the dress and stepped into her shorts, beginning to button up her blouse. 'And of course, if he does get rich—'

'Is that your dress?' Rafaella asked, pointing to the mannequin draped with a dust sheet by the window. She knew exactly how to divert her sister's attention when needed, and besides, Silvana had been suspiciously secretive about her design, working here alone most evenings to get it done in time.

'Yes, but – wait!'

But Rafaella had already peered under the sheet. She looked back at Silvana in shock, her gold-flecked eyes wide. '. . . Has Mamma seen this?'

'Now don't panic,' Silvana said quickly, seeing her sister doing exactly that as the dust sheet slithered to the floor. 'It's not finished yet.'

It seemed to Rafaella it was scarcely begun! It was going to show a *lot* of skin, and whatever the fashions might be in Rome, in Tricase Porto a corset was very definitely worn underneath other clothes. What would Father Tommaso say? Nonna Giacosa? 'Silvana . . .'

'There will be lace sleeves!' Silvana anxiously traced over her own arms, reinforcing the point. 'And I'm going to overlay the skirt with the satin – it will not just be sheer tulle like that, of course not!'

'Of course not,' Rafaella murmured, staring at the mannequin's bare crotch through the fabric and sending up a silent prayer anyway.

'And there will be little covered buttons going all the way down the front . . .'

'If you say so.'

'I do! But you mustn't say anything to Mamma,' Silvana

said, hurriedly throwing the sheet back over the dress lest anyone should see it from the street. 'She has no vision, but I know it will be perfect when it's completed! And it is my wedding, after all . . .'

'But—'

'Rafa, promise you won't say anything?' This time, Silvana's fingers found an actual bruise on her arm as she held her insistently.

Rafaella looked back at her sister, who was bossy and always had to be right, but was also rarely wrong. '. . . I promise I won't say anything.'

'Not even to Gina?'

She shook her head.

Silvana exhaled, looking relieved. 'OK, good.' The crisis was over. 'Now scram,' she said, walking Rafaella over to the stairs to make sure she caused no more trouble on her way out. 'If you want your dress for the wedding too, then I don't have time to sleep, much less stand here gossiping. I'll see you later.'

Rafaella stepped outside with relief. The atelier was a hothouse in every way and she closed her eyes for a moment, allowing the sea breeze to ruffle her long hair.

'Rafaella!'

She looked up to find Fede Franchetti coming along the road on his Vespa, past a long line of stationary cars facing in the opposite direction. There seemed to be some sort of traffic jam further on.

'I thought it was you!' he said, stopping alongside her and giving her one of his easy smiles. 'Where have you been hiding? I came looking for you at the party but couldn't find you again.'

'Oh, I know . . .' she stammered, taking in his open expression and realizing that, unlike Cosimo, he had no idea of the drama caused by his little sister and the ongoing fallout.

Rafaella didn't doubt the sincerity of Romola's apology at the beach caffè the day after the party – she had looked terrible – but how exactly were they supposed to move past what she had done? Her actions – and Cosimo's words – had betrayed an unpalatable truth: that this was who Romola had become in the past year. And neither Rafaella nor Gina liked what they saw.

'... There were so many people there. What a party! It was crazy... Good crazy!'

He laughed. 'I'm not sure my mother would agree. The gardeners are still finding cocktail glasses in the bushes. And a forgotten firework went off unexpectedly the other morning, almost giving Papa a heart attack. He thought the communists had come for him!' He laughed harder. 'Not to mention the drains have been playing up ever since Piero...' Fede stopped himself, not wishing to be indiscreet about others' transgressions. 'Well, anyway, that's all in the past... But let's take a proper look at you – another year older. Wiser... Definitely prettier.'

She rolled her eyes. 'Ha ha.'

'No, it's true. My mother said you had become the village beauty, and for once she wasn't exaggerating.'

Rafaella blinked, stunned by the unexpected compliment. His mother had really said that? She was the most elegant, beautiful woman Rafaella had ever met. Valentina Fabiani had a shiny, surface beauty, but the duchessa's ran into sinew and bone. The very foundations of her were carved and cultivated, not just top-dressing.

Footsteps sounded, growing closer. Someone was coming, and she turned as they came around the corner and stopped abruptly.

Fon stared at them both, a pile of firewood laid out across his arms.

'Rafa,' he croaked, his shame sitting upon him like a dead fox, vivid and abrupt.

'. . . Fon.' She saw the horror come into his eyes as he realized she was standing with Romola's eldest brother and that he was cornered.

A moment beat as she watched him squirm. He deserved to feel like this, she told herself. He had made her feel all the ways she thought he, of all people, would never make her feel: worthless, undesirable, stupid . . . She had thought he was different, but whatever – and whoever – he truly was, she also knew Fede didn't deserve to discover the tawdry truth about his sister from them. It was for his sake alone that she gave Fon an imperceptible shake of her head, telling him Fede was ignorant of what had happened at the party.

'It's good to see you, Fon. I'm not sure I'd have recognized you. You're so tall now!' Fede said warmly, oblivious to their wordless conversation. He was still sitting on his bike and looking Fon up and down. Clearly Fon was in no position to shake hands when he was carrying an armful of logs, but he seemed to swell a little in the glow of attention.

'Fede – it was a great party the other night.'

'Yeah? You had fun?'

'Mm-hmm,' Fon nodded, treading a thin line between complimenting his host and insulting her. His eyes slid back towards her, but Rafaella kept her smile on Fede. She just had to keep smiling and get through this . . .

'I was just saying Rafa managed to elude me in the crowd, but you did too, I'm realizing now! It's making me question just how many people I really did catch up with!' Fede gave a ready laugh. 'And I thought I'd done rather well getting around everyone.'

Fon blushed, his dirty secret scarcely hidden below the surface. 'Well, there were so many people.'

'Yes, it was a good turnout,' Fede agreed, still watching him with interest.

Did he know of anything? Rafaella wondered. He was so well mannered, she wouldn't put it past him to pretend otherwise for decency's sake.

'So, do you know why the traffic's so bad?' she asked, changing the subject. 'I've never seen the cars backed up all the way down here like this.'

Fede twisted on his seat and looked back along the road too. 'Actually, I do. I was just swimming at Marina Serra and I passed the roadblock about a mile back. There's a house on fire and it's spread down through the trees to the road. No cars are allowed past while they're getting it under control. They're still worried it might spread.'

'Oh, that's terrible!' Rafaella gasped. 'Do you know whose house?'

'Renato Lobascio's, I think? I'm not entirely sure,' Fede shrugged, losing interest as he looked back at her again. 'But tell me – we haven't seen you at the villa since the party. It's so strange being there and *not* having you and Gina shrieking in the halls! Not to mention no one's eating us out of house and home! There's a glut of food, you know, just waiting for you . . . Where have you been hiding yourselves?'

She forced her smile wider, aware of Fon shifting his weight in her peripheral vision. Did he feel ashamed of what he'd done, blasting apart a lifelong friendship? Or was he just proud of his conquest?

'Not hiding; but Gina and I have to work these days. Sadly we're not children anymore; we can't just play all summer.'

Fede jerked his head in the direction of the villas. 'But you could come over for a drink and a swim, right? Both of you, of course,' he said, quickly looking at Fon and politely including him too.

Rafaella saw the look of surprise come onto Fon's face as he stared back at Fede, a flare of delight illuminating his eyes. He had never hung out with them as kids, always keeping to the company of the local boys – Luigi and Gino – who preferred to mock and pour scorn from a distance on the summer residents.

Fede's open smile and warm invitation were irresistible and Rafaella saw Fon smile back, allowing himself to be seduced into the fantasy of lazing idly in the lush villa garden all afternoon: floating in the circular pool as, beyond the high walls, traffic chortled past and the fishing boats chugged back into port. They would drink pink drinks and listen to music and the only blot on the perfection would be, high in the blue sky, tendrils of black smoke drifting over from a burning house somewhere in the wooded hills . . .

Rafaella cleared her throat, and Fon drew himself back sharply from the daydream.

'Honestly, you'd be doing me a favour, actually,' Fede went on in a more confiding tone now. 'To be honest, everyone's moping about there like the cat died. Valentina's gone, of course, and Papa's working. Romy's sick, but Cosi is—'

'Actually, I was just about to head home,' Rafaella blurted, reaching for her bike, still propped against the cobbler's wall. 'Papa wants me to help him do some cutting in the grove.'

Fede looked taken aback by her abruptness. 'Oh . . . But you could come just for a drink, then? It's so hot out here and—'

'Oh no,' she said quickly, quite determinedly backing away. 'I couldn't possibly. Papa would be furious. He's expecting me, you see. In fact, he'll be waiting right now.'

It was a lie; she was working with her father the following day. She could see Fede's bewilderment at her strange vehemence, but he simply smiled, far too polite to press her on the refusal. 'Oh. OK . . . Fon? Are you up for it?' He looked over hopefully.

'Uhhh . . .' Fon seemed surprised that the invitation still stood now that Rafaella had withdrawn herself. They all knew he'd never been part of their inner circle.

She shot him a sharp look. Was he really so arrogant that he would seduce Fede's sister *and* accept his hospitality?

Fon read her expression correctly. 'Sorry, I have to get back with this wood,' he mumbled. 'We're rebuilding the chicken coop today. The fox got in.'

'Chicken coop,' Fede nodded, as if such a thing had never once crossed his mind in his life. 'Shame . . .'

'Yeah.'

'Well, another time, then?' Fede called after Fon, who was now hurrying away.

Rafaella watched him go, too, so eager to leave first, not bothering to hang around to talk to her alone and apologize face to face now he had the chance.

Fede turned back to her. 'Is he always so elusive?'

'Pretty much,' she shrugged. She threw her leg over the crossbar of her bike and tried to look late. 'See you around, Fede.'

'*Certo* . . . *Ciao*, Rafa.'

She watched as he kicked back the stand of his scooter and headed the short distance towards the froth of bright pink bougainvillea spilling over the garden walls of Villa Agosto. He cut a forlorn figure but she didn't feel too sorry for him. He would enjoy his tall, cool drink in the shade, lying in the grass under the orange trees. Another afternoon of indolence awaited him, his brother and sister.

But not her.

They only summered under the same sun.

Chapter 8

Fon

Fon knelt in the dirt while the chickens pecked and fussed around him, as if *he* was in *their* way. Behind him, his mother was pegging laundry onto the washing line; his father was out on the boat. He had no idea where Dante had got to and doubted he'd get a straight answer if he asked. There were no water-skiing trips booked in for the day, so Dante had headed off 'on business' to some undisclosed place.

He had been out here for an hour now, hammering posts into the rock-hard ground and trying to channel his agitation, but even if his body was tiring, his spirit was still restless. Running into Rafaella and Fede like that had been the worst possible coincidence. To his shame, Rafaella had come to his rescue and given him the opportunity to get away without a black eye, but it had almost felt worse to push through the encounter with two-faced smiles.

Fede had been warm and generous, the age gap, which had felt so huge and unbreachable when they were children, now irrelevant. All these years, Fon's attention – jealousy, he supposed – had been focused on Cosimo; being ignored by him every year had felt like being trapped in a Siberian winter while the others summered under the Puglian sun. But today Fede had approached him as a friend, and the very things he had once hated them all for – the grand villa, the lazy days, that effortless charm – had been intoxicating. He couldn't believe Fede had invited him over so casually, as if it was nothing . . .

It wasn't nothing to Fon. He had thrilled at the invitation. In that moment he had wanted to be worthy of friendship with a man like Federico Franchetti, so affable, cultured and clever, always ready to smile at everyone. For a moment, it had felt like a door into another world had opened up, a world in which he finally belonged.

Now, away from Fede's warmth, kneeling in the dirt as chickens pecked at him, Fon's doubts surged back. What could he possibly offer in return? He was poor – worse than that, he was insubstantial. He knew that at the heart of him, he had no fixed centre. He had never been able to describe the fear exactly, but it was as if he was full of swirling shadows, hiding him even from himself. He stood unnoticed in rooms and was spoken over in conversation. Only Rafaella had ever looked past the surface with him, and now he'd ruined it with her, all for the sake of impressing his brother, to whom it was just a joke anyway.

He'd seen the disgust in her eyes and there was no coming back from it with her, he knew that. Both Fede and Rafaella were too good for him. He'd dishonoured them both, and it was only a matter of time before Fede despised him too.

Chapter 9

Cosimo

'I thought I'd find you here.'

Cosimo opened one eye to find his brother standing by the pool, holding glasses and a pitcher of margarita. He allowed a half-smile to lift the corner of his mouth as he circled his hands in the water and paddled over on the inflatable.

'Thanks,' he said, as Fede poured him a drink and handed it over. 'Where've you been all afternoon?' He pushed himself off the side again, drifting back into the centre.

'Marina Serra. I fancied a swim.' Fede stretched out in the garden chair, the soles of his feet ten shades lighter than his deeply tanned legs.

'Again? The sea here isn't good enough for you?' Cosimo drawled.

'It's fine – but I fancied a drive and getting out for a bit. I've been hitting the books all day. A change of scenery is good for the soul.'

'This *is* the change of scenery.'

'Mm.'

They both lay there for several minutes, eyes closed as the garden twitched and buzzed all around them: birds alighting on branches with rapid wingbeats, a lemon falling from one of the trees and landing on the gravel drive with a soft thud, bees buzzing soporifically among the bougainvillea and jasmine. The sun blistered overhead, baking the ground so that a heat haze shimmered. Cosimo was sure he kept catching traces of smoke from somewhere.

'Where's Romy?' Fede murmured.

'In her room.'

'*Still* sick?'

Cosimo didn't bother to reply. He hated being caught up in his sister's lies as much as her drama. He lifted his head to take another sip of his drink before letting it loll back again. 'I'm so bored.'

'I know. I just saw Rafa and Fon—'

Cosimo's head jerked up again: what? 'At Marina Serra?'

'No. On the street here. I invited them back for drinks and a swim but they said they both had jobs to do . . . I sort of got the impression they were lying, though.' Fede's voice was growing heavy, slow. He was beginning to relax.

Cosimo watched his brother, feeling his heart pound, as if he was swimming laps under water. 'Oh yeah? Why would they do that?'

'Not sure . . .' Fede drifted into silence, and Cosimo stared up at the sky. A distant plane, just a white speck from here, was charting a course west and he tried to imagine all the people strapped in their seats inside, living their different lives and completely unaware of him, lazing in a circular pool, looking up at them. 'They seemed to enjoy the party, though.'

Cosimo's eyebrows went up. 'Which one of them told you that?' It was all he could do to keep the scorn from his voice.

'They both did.'

Cosimo digested the revelation. So they were together again, then? Rafaella had forgiven Fon but not Romola? . . . He felt as if he'd been kicked in the stomach when he remembered again how she'd looked at him at the caffè – as if he was a complete stranger. He was innocent of any wrongdoing against her, yet still he had been lumbered with his sister's crimes. Guilty by association. Or bloodline. Whereas Fon . . .

He watched as a dragonfly shot into his line of sight, hovering then darting in short, rapid bursts before landing on the water's surface. He flicked his fingers, sending out ripples and watching as it took off again a few moments later. '. . . They're together now, did you know?'

Fede lifted his head, roused from his torpor. 'A couple, you mean?'

'Yeah.' Cosimo blinked back at him, seeing his brother's evident surprise. 'You don't see it?'

A small silence bloomed, Fede weighing the question as if it were a grave legal matter. 'No,' he said finally, dropping his head down again. 'I really don't.'

'Mmm,' Cosimo sighed, feeling as if there was a weight on his chest. 'Me neither.'

Over the high walls came the sound of shears snipping in a neighbouring garden, a tinny sharpness cutting at the air itself.

'He seems very different to Dante,' Fede said contemplatively.

Cosimo frowned. 'That doesn't make him nice.'

Fede chuckled.

'What?'

'You always did have it in for him.'

'No I didn't!'

'Sure you did. I saw you cut him dead myself, several times, when he'd try to talk to you and the girls. I always thought you were a bit jealous of him, actually.'

'*Me?*' Cosimo recoiled so sharply he almost lost his balance and tipped into the water. 'What would I be jealous of him for?'

Fede shrugged. 'Well, he is good-looking.'

'If you like wimps!'

Fede laughed again, as if a point had been proved. 'And he's always been good friends with the girls. I don't know, I guess I thought you felt threatened by him because he's with them year round and you're not.'

'You're talking out of your ass,' Cosimo snapped. 'I don't give him a second thought. They've always liked me better than him.'

'Well, in the past, perhaps,' Fede shrugged. 'But not now, clearly.'

Cosimo, for once, didn't argue back. Was his brother right? Had he been thrown over for Fon Giannelli more completely than he'd wanted to acknowledge? Arrogantly, he had assumed that if it ever did come to some sort of contest, he would win hands down. He was Cosimo Franchetti! A duke's son and eligible catch, according to the gossip sections of the ladies' magazines. Valentina Fabiani herself had followed him down here from Rome!

How puerile it all seemed now. He had thought turning up with her on his arm would show Rafaella their kiss had been a mistake, that he didn't care; but he'd been pushing on an open door. She cared less. She liked Fon. He'd lost her long before now.

'Think what you like, but he's not the Mr Nice Guy you suppose he is,' he muttered darkly, throwing back his head to drain his glass.

'What do you mean by that?' Fede asked suspiciously.

But Cosimo was already slipping into the water, his empty glass left behind on the inflatable mattress as he sank below the surface with lungs full of air and a head full of regret.

Chapter 10

Rafaella

The red earth was baked hard as clay, and Rafaella knew falling from the ladder at this height would mean a broken bone for sure. Still, she worked deftly, knowing exactly which branches to cut and where; her father had taken her out with him since she was a little girl, so it was second nature to her to do this. Working in the groves had always been the best way she knew to spend time with him, and she had a natural aptitude for it. She loved living in a port but had always been happiest among the trees, hearing the wind brush the narrow leaves, that light, scratchy rustle as the canopy swayed with their full heads.

She glanced down the line of trees, checking her work. The seven-hectare estate held over a thousand trees in all, and many in this section were well over four hundred years old, with massive, gnarly, twisted trunks boasting a span of over a metre. The *monumentales*, as they were known, were her family's pride and joy, ancient pillars of Puglian authenticity. Seven generations of Parisis had worked this land and they took their role as guardians very seriously. The agricola employed over thirty estate workers, but only her father, her elder brother Dado, and Rafaella herself were allowed to touch the *monumentales*. The three of them had had a productive day together until her father and brother had been called to the other side of the estate to help with a tractor problem.

Satisfied with her day's endeavours, she sank onto the ground and leaned against the trunk of the last tree, her limbs weary as she dropped her head back. She wasn't entirely done yet – she still needed to collect the offcuts into the wheelbarrow – but rests were crucial. This job was physically demanding in a different way to working at the caffè, and she knew she would be stiff tomorrow.

She breathed deeply, feeling her muscles relax as she listened to the song of wood warblers hidden in the vast oak forests that bordered the groves. The land was elevated here, situated almost at the top of the hill on the outskirts of the port, the groves planted in narrow, tiered steps at the steepest parts – as here. All she could see for miles around were treetops: mainly olives, but further away some figs, oaks, almonds, some orange and lemon trees too. They each had a unique sway in the wind, as if dancing different steps, their myriad greens uncountable. The houses were flat-roofed and low-built so from here they were hidden from sight on the hillside, no signs of human life. Beyond, the sea sparkled, a pale, glittering belt around the world now that the sun was beginning to climb down from its high perch.

She always felt at peace here, the dramas of port life left firmly behind at sea level. Up here it didn't matter if the caffè had run out of pistachios or if her dresses didn't fit or if Mamma was mad at her because she'd forgotten to strip her bed sheets . . . But somehow, what Romola and Fon had done still mattered. The double betrayal trailed after her, up and down the ladder, weaving with her through the different trees, a dark shadow stitched to her heels that she couldn't outrun. Her boyfriend and her best friend . . .

Last night, she had come home to an envelope folded into a crude aeroplane on the balcony outside her room.

I would do anything to change what I did. Can we talk? F.

Finally he had reached out; emboldened, perhaps, by their accidental meeting on the street? She hadn't been able to scream at him in front of Fede, call him every name under the sun, though she would have liked to. Had he mistaken her mannered civility for forgiveness?

She had yet to respond, unsure of her next step. The humiliation was still fresh, and she felt worthless and rejected by everyone involved: Fon, Romola, Cosi too.

Perhaps even Cosi most of all. She had tried her best to shrug off the pain of learning he was dating Valentina, but the hurt had gone deeper than she'd wanted to admit, running not just into her blood but her bones. If she was honest, Romola's betrayal gave her the excuse she wanted to push them *both* away. To protect herself from either one of them.

The friendship would have had to end at some point, anyway, she told herself. The differences they had ignored as children were now glaring and unavoidable. She had been a fool to think they could remain friends, and as for the prospect of anything more—

The sound of cattle lowing carried on the breeze, the air still slightly acrid from yesterday's fire. She was so lost in her thoughts that several moments passed before her brain registered that the sound, though not jarring, was out of place. They had some goats, but her father didn't farm cattle and as far as she was aware, neither did their neighbours.

She waited for it to come again, and it did. Downhill from where she sat, but still close.

Peculiar.

She rose and began to walk towards it, ducking around the trees, her soft hands grazing over knobbled silver bark, red dust spraying her legs as she jumped down between the levels of the stepped groves.

Shadows slipped over her, marbling her skin. Twigs cracked underfoot and beetles scuttled back under pale rocks. The lowing sounds were intermittent but growing ever louder and even from a distance she could tell there must be a number of them.

It was entirely possible their neighbours had bought a herd. Everyone had noticed the Giannellis' growing fortunes as they branched out beyond fishing and olive-pressing, and jealousy was rife. Why not them too?

She was at the furthermost southern boundary of the agricola now. Ahead was a stand of oaks. Like the *monumentales*, they were hundreds of years old, and her father had no plans to ever develop this portion of the estate; the trees spoke to him as they did to her, and he preferred to leave this section wild. As such, she rarely came down here – no one did – but as she slipped into the cool, dense shade, at least a dozen pairs of eyes blinked back at her. Rafaella gasped at the number of them. How had they got all the way up here, past walls, gates and boundaries?

The cows, unperturbed by her presence, dropped back into grazing again, their dark brown muzzles burrowing the patchy grass. She heard their massive teeth easily crunching on the acorns and . . .

Acorns?

'Move!' she cried, advancing towards them with her arms aloft, trying to make herself appear bigger. '*Basta!* Go! Go!' The animals looked up at her again with slightly more interest but they didn't back away; they were completely unafraid of her, naive to the danger they were in.

Quickly, she turned and ran back out of the copse. She had to get back to the farm office and tell her father. He would know what to do. He might even know whose cattle they were. But how long had they been there for? Was it already too late?

She was running past the nursery section where the youngest trees had been planted when she saw two men working up some ladders, shaping the crowns as she had been doing, and she pivoted, heading for them instead.

'*Ciao!*' she called, waving her arms to get their attention as they turned and looked down from the treetops. She recognized them at once – Pablo Carrieri and Francesco Romano.

'Signorina Parisi,' Pablo said, seeing the alarm on her face. 'What has happened?' He spoke with a slight lisp on account of missing some front teeth.

'There are cows in the oak grove,' she panted, trying to recover her breath. She had all but sprinted up the hillside. 'At least twelve of them. And they're eating the acorns.'

There followed a confused pause as the two men looked back at her. '*Cows?*'

'Yes,' she nodded.

'You are sure they were not the goats?' Francesco asked.

She shot him an annoyed look. 'I think I know the difference between cows and goats!'

'Of course,' he said quickly. 'But how would that many cows come to be all the way over there?'

She shrugged. 'I don't know. Perhaps a neighbour bought some and they escaped?'

The men swapped sceptical looks across the tree crowns. She could tell they believed she was somehow mistaken, that such a thing could not possibly be.

'I promise you, there are a dozen cows down in the oak wood!' she insisted. 'And they're eating the acorns. Acorns are poisonous to them, aren't they?'

'Or is that just horses?' Francesco asked Pablo.

Pablo shrugged, giving a sigh and jerking his head to indicate for Francesco to follow him.

Rafaella waited impatiently as the men came down their ladders with little haste.

'Good, thank you,' she said, turning to lead them to the exact spot. 'If you follow me—'

'Signorina, do not worry yourself,' Pablo said. 'We shall deal with it.'

'But you won't know where they are,' she said, watching as he slowly put his shears into his bag of tools.

'In the oak wood, you said. I am sure twelve cows are neither invisible nor silent.'

'But the more people we have to move them—'

'*You* are too little to frighten a goose, signorina,' he chuckled, a light wind whistling between his gappy tooth pegs. Then his expression turned serious. 'Besides, they can be dangerous if they charge; you would be trampled to death. It is no place for you. If your father was to hear . . .'

'But I hardly think moving cows is dangerous. Not if there are three of us.' She looked at Francesco, but he was wearing the same reticent look as Pablo. If Emilio Parisi was known for being an honourable and fair employer, he was also known as a devoted father; his men would not dare do anything that might endanger her, no matter how small the risk.

'OK, well, hurry then, please,' she sighed, stepping back. 'I don't know how long they've been in there. It may already be too late.'

'Do not worry, we will deal with it,' Pablo said, picking up his bag. Francesco followed, the two men heading downhill in gently loping strides.

She bit her lip, watching them go and wishing they would run. 'I'll go back to the office and let Papa know,' she called. 'He can send down some more men to help you.'

Francesco turned back. 'That won't be necessary, signorina. It will be done before they can get there.'

'But—'

'Not to mention,' Pablo said contemplatively, walking a little way back up the slope again, 'if these cows do belong to a neighbour and they have strayed onto your father's estate, his response is likely to be severe, as we know.'

Unlike some of the other agricolas, which had begun to employ *campieri* – estate guards – her father preferred to protect his boundaries himself; but as such, he sometimes came down too hard. He wasn't the only man in Puglia to equate respect with fear.

'. . . Seeing as this is just a one-off, why don't you let us find out who owns them and we'll have a quiet word?' Pablo shrugged, almost murmuring now, as if afraid they might be overheard. 'There's no need for it to turn into something bigger. I am sure it's an honest mistake and times are hard, as we all know.'

He stared at her, awaiting her agreement, and Rafaella felt that breach which sometimes presented itself, a subdivision of the Us and Them that existed even within the port. Though her family had no great wealth and certainly nothing in the realms of the Franchettis, they nonetheless had more than many: landed assets and a respectable annual turnover. Her family's agricola was the largest in the area, her father a respected man and noted employer of many locals. Bullying was not a charge she wanted levelled at the Parisi name.

'Of course,' she mumbled. 'We can keep it between us.'

'*Grazie*, signorina,' he smiled, tipping his cap at her and setting off again, heading for the shadows.

Chapter 11

Fon

The fishing boats slowly circled the buoys, taking up their positions. The deep nets had been lowered several days before, funnelling tuna in from the open sea to a series of tunnels from which escape was impossible. Edo Carosa, the most experienced and strongest of the fishermen, had been appointed *raís* of the expedition, and he had been vigilant in keeping a close watch on the numbers of fish coming in. It was late in the season for tuna fishing, but not too late, and he had finally called today as the day for the *mattanza*.

It wasn't an annual event here, not like in Sicily, where the tuna shoaled with set-your-watch predictability. On the Adriatic coast they only came every few years, when the winds blew from a certain direction and the currents were favourable. In early spring of this year, Carosa had seen the first signs and begun preparing the port for this moment. Today, even the gates to Villa Agosto had opened and the Franchettis had emerged from their self-imposed confinement, Fede and Cosimo joining the other men. The duke, as a cabinet minister, couldn't be seen to take part in the spectacle but his sons had joined in at every opportunity since boyhood, always going out with the harbourmaster, El Greco, on his boat.

They had all left at dawn, sailing beneath a pale sky towards a bright horizon. The women stayed on land as ever, waving them off. Fon's mother had been emotional. The *mattanza* – Arabic for slaughter – was physically brutal and not without risk. Atlantic bluefin tuna were beasts of the ocean, the adults weighing in at up to 250 kilos, and their thrashing tails could do serious harm to a grown man. By the day's end, the blood in the water never just came from the fish.

Rafaella had been standing there too with her mother and Gina, and for a moment, as the men made their final checks, her eyes had met Fon's. His stomach had lurched at the sudden reconnection; it was like standing in a sunspot on the surface of the moon. Three days had passed since he had seen her on the street with Fede and boldly, on an impulse, sent her his note, but she had given no reply; as her silence drew out, his brief flicker of courage had failed him, all the apologies he had formulated in his mind falling away. He really had lost her for good, and the thought frightened him in ways he couldn't quite understand.

The fishing boats – sixteen in total – travelled in single file from the marina, following Carosa's lead as he headed for the deep-water nets. Father Tommaso was in the second boat, offering up prayers as they cut over the water in solemn anticipation of what was to come. Francesco and Pablo, the Parisi estate workers Fon had seen meeting with Dante, were helping out on the Giannelli boat today. All usual duties in the port were suspended; every man in the area – barber, cobbler, grocer, chandler, bar owner, farmer – was out on the water.

Once in position at the buoys, which had been arranged in a loose square, they waited as Carosa inspected the middle area known as the 'chamber of death'. It was the centre point of the underwater tunnels, a giant submerged holding pen surrounded around and below by the nets. The fish had to have moved into it for the *mattanza* to begin.

As they waited, Fon watched the Franchettis on their boat on the other side of the chamber. To his dismay, he realized Rafaella's father and elder brother were also guests of El Greco. They were all sharing drinks, Fede and Dado chatting as if it was a cocktail party.

He watched Fede intently, feeling a spark of jealousy that the courtesy and friendliness which had made him feel so special were in fact available to everyone. Fede was just like his father: a born politician, able to butter people up with that smooth smile and easy manner. For a moment, Fon hated him. He hated how easy life was for this handsome son and heir, his many personal gifts heaped upon already ludicrous privilege. But then Fede looked up, as if sensing the scrutiny, and, catching sight of Fon, he smiled and waved across the water as if they really were friends. It felt genuine, and Fon instinctively smiled and waved back. He just couldn't stop himself from basking in the radiance that shone from that gilded family.

Cosimo, standing apart from his brother, looked out of sorts and moody, shoulders hunched as he stared down into the depths as if the sea was passing secrets to him. Fon wondered if it had anything to do with how Rafaella had turned away from him, too, as he passed by on the marina earlier – although why she should be angry with Cosimo, he didn't know.

'Fon, move that chain there,' his father commanded, pulling him from his ruminations and pointing towards the anchor chain, which had slipped from its stowage under the bench.

'*Si*, Papa.' But before he could move, Francesco reached round and did it for him. As with the chickens, Fon felt out of place and in the way here. He'd never been a natural fisherman. Neither was Dante, but at least Dante had obvious skills in other areas.

Fon glanced up and down the boat as their father ran last checks, even though he had already run through them twice. Dante stood restlessly at the other end, his muscles twitching as he struggled to remain inert. He never had been any good at waiting. He was shirtless, as many of the men were; it was mid-morning now and the relentless sun was beginning to beat down hard as they waited on Carosa's word. The *raís* wouldn't act before the auspicious moment and all eyes were upon him, everyone watching his body language as he walked round and round on his boat in the centre of the floating square. He was supported in his role today by Luchino, his son, and Piero Vitti, the barber.

Suddenly there was a murmuring. Carosa, staring down into the depths, seemed to approve of what he saw at last, for he began slowly motioning with his arms for the fishermen to begin pulling their boats together. They were all loosely connected at bow and stern by slack ropes and as they heaved, the square became ever tighter, so that eventually the boats formed a solid, rigid shape on the surface.

Buoys had been attached to the nearsides of the boats and each man began to attach the nets floating in the water to their boats. It was slow going, the sodden nets heavy on their arms, but they knew they had to conserve their energy; the real work was yet to come. The minutes ticked past and some of the men began to sing a chant called the *cialoma* – it kept their nerves steady now they were in the shadow of battle.

Once the nets were secured to the fastened boats, Carosa patrolled the square chamber area looking for potential breaches. The fishermen awaited his approval like soldiers on inspection parade; every man knew his task and took the responsibility seriously.

Finally, Carosa's boat puttered back to the middle of the chamber and a silence fell. Then Carosa lifted his arms and began flicking his hands rapidly upwards. No one needed telling twice as immediately the men – as young as seven and as old as seventy – began to haul in the nets. They were immensely heavy, dragging as they did to depths of thirty metres, and it took the four or five men in every boat to begin to raise the floor.

At first, all that could be heard was the chanting of the *cialoma* and the grunts of the men as they pulled hand over hand, the nets beginning to spool at their feet. But then the water within the square began to froth and roll, the perfect blue glass surface breaking up and turning white. Sharp fins pierced the surface like arrowheads as the tuna were forced ever upwards by the tightening nets, towards an airy sky and suffocation.

Fon felt himself sweating as the tension of the net floor increased. It was growing flat, and the men groaned from the effort of hauling it up with the weight of tonnes of tuna lying upon it. There were dozens upon dozens of them and the water looked like it had come to a boil, a tuna stew in a square pot, the massive black bodies violently agitating the surface.

The *mattanza* had begun in earnest now, the *raís* moving quickly around on his boat in the middle of it all as he directed the fishermen on all four sides towards their quarry. Now that the nets had been largely raised to within a few feet of the surface, the men picked up their weapons – rods and harpoons – and readied themselves. Getting the tuna into the boats was the most perilous and exhausting part of the endeavour. Each fish could be easily double the weight of a grown man, and they would all be flailing in desperate death throes against the oxygen and spears that assailed them.

Fon went to reach for the rod he had used since he was a little boy, but Dante took it from his hands and replaced it with the harpoon Francesco had been holding instead.

'It's time for him to graduate to the real action, wouldn't

you say, Papa?' his brother said, looking at their father. 'He's a man now, not a boy.'

Francesco looked displeased – he was several years older than Fon – but hierarchies didn't just apply to El Greco's boat, and on their own craft, the Giannellis were the bosses. Carlo hesitated, then nodded. Fon took the harpoon without a word as Dante handed Francesco the rod instead.

He handled the weapon, feeling both excited and apprehensive at the task ahead of him. He had grown up working with his father on the sea, but they caught sardines, the nets bulging with thousands of tiny, slippery silver fishes. Plunging a spear into the solid flesh of a 250-kilo beast was a very different proposition, surely almost like stabbing a man. As a boy, he had longed for the moment when he would join the ranks of his father and the other men and do battle, but now that it was here . . .

He was out of time. A tuna had landed itself near their boat; Carosa was screaming at them to act and Dante, without hesitation, plunged a hook into the thrashing creature and dragged it in towards the side. Bright red blood gushed into the dark water.

'Hook it!' Dante shouted as the fish wrestled madly from side to side, trying to tear itself free. With no time to think, Fon felt his arm swing, and his spear plunged through the firm flesh too, pinning the tuna on its other side. Beside them, Pablo and Francesco reached around and got the rods underneath it, levering it up. Between the four of them, with their hooks and poles and grunts and cries, they were just able to hoist the fish out of the water and haul it behind them onto the deck.

The boat rocked from the movement and Fon looked back, seeing the massive body still thrashing until his father reached back and killed it with a well-positioned blow of his club. It was a quicker, more humane death than suffocation.

The fish was huge, 180 kilos at least, but there was no time to revel in glory. The sea was a twitching, convulsing frenzy, the water already running red; Carosa's two assistants were in the water now, standing on the nets as they struck blows upon the surface to stun the fish and make it easier for the fishermen to hook them and drag them out. It was dangerous work.

'Again!' Dante cried, hooking another. And another.

Fon lost track of time. It was impossible to gauge the minutes, or even hours, in this gladiatorial combat, his body beginning to move into autopilot – swing, hook, pin, haul . . . Every time he thought the sea square was coming off the roil, more black bodies would surface and the frantic writhing would be stirred up again.

At last Luchino and Piero hauled themselves out of the water and back onto the boat in the centre of the melee. Both were bleeding. They had sustained vicious cuts from the shoal's desperate death throes and they sank onto the benches as the *raís* threw fresh water on their wounds. Almost all the fish had been clubbed into submission, but Dante's eyes were following one that remained: a big one, clearly still with some fight in it.

'He's a monster,' Dante said, pointing as the massive tuna edged and writhed towards their boat. '. . . He's ours!' He ran to the end of the deck, warning off Gino Pampanini and the Crespis, none of whom were professional fishermen. 'Leave him to us!'

The other men backed off, even though they were closer and the angle was better. Dante leaned out, plunging his harpoon into the mighty flank and beginning to drag it in. Fon knew his brother wanted the glory of this prize kill – it was one of the biggest catches of the day, and now everyone was watching. He ran over to help alongside their father, Francesco and

Pablo, all leaning over the side with their weapons, trying to get an angle to assist.

But Dante had over-reached himself, and as the mighty fish resisted death it twisted violently, flinging him into the scarlet water. No longer pinioned, it tried to swim away, but the depth was too shallow and it found itself half beached on the net floor instead. It used its tail to try to propel itself but Dante, still recovering from his somersault into the water, couldn't right himself in time, and every swipe drew a fresh cut along his bare skin. The pain smarted and he cried out, unable to find his feet on the net. He was swallowing water; Fon saw the whites of his eyes bulge as panic took over.

The men were shouting furiously, urging Dante to move away, but as the tuna writhed, wriggled and thrashed it landed on top of him, crushing and pinning him below the surface.

Without thought, Fon leapt in, tasting the ferrous tang in the salt water as he half swam, half waded to the centre of the chamber of death. It would not be his brother dying here today, he resolved as he grabbed the injured beast by its tail and dorsal fin. With a strength he hadn't known he possessed, he hauled it off his submerged brother.

Dante exploded upwards, gasping for breath as Fon drew his arm back and plunged his spear into the fish, once, twice, twenty, thirty times. He didn't know. He didn't count. All he knew, when he finally stopped, was that the fish was lying motionless in a scarlet sea and everyone was cheering his name.

He turned around to find Luchino and Piero holding Dante under the arms as he coughed and spluttered and gagged. He was covered in blood – Fon supposed he must be, too – but it only made his brother's teeth gleam all the more brightly as he gradually got his breath back and smiled with relief.

He beckoned Fon over towards him and the two brothers embraced.

'I underestimated you,' Dante panted, leaning heavily on Fon as the men chanted his name in unison. 'I thought you were weak. But you're like me – a natural-born killer.'

The boats arrived back as they had left, in single file, but laden now with their bounty. As they passed the sea wall, the captain of each vessel hooking the sharp left turn into the marina, the crews dived jubilantly into the turquoise water to swim straight ahead to the beach. The men's victorious roars ricocheted around the port.

There was still work to be done. The tuna needed to be offloaded and hoisted by their tails onto the weighing scales before they were quartered up and sold off to the wholesalers who had come in from Gallipoli and Brindisi as word of the *mattanza* had spread. Afterwards there would be a feast on the beach for the whole village; the women had been preparing all day. But for the next few minutes, as boats were moored and ice-laden carts brought down to the harbour's edge, they could play – and they made the most of it. The surface of the sea was shattered again as they all splashed and threw one another about in a final testosterone-fuelled frenzy, showing off in front of the girls sunbathing on the promenade.

Rafaella was there with Gina and Antonia, Donatella and Clara, and Fon felt a thrill that she was witness to these celebrations of his bravery as the other men threw him skywards, catching him by the ankles in the water, dunking and dive-bombing him before throwing him up again. A crowd of mothers and *anziani* gathered on the beach, aware that something momentous had passed on the hunt. Fon felt as if he was bursting out of his own body. He had never had any of his brother's charisma, none of his swagger or confidence, but today, for the first time in his life, he felt *seen*. He was not a nobody.

The girls, relenting to the boys' constant pleas, jumped in too and shrieked and screamed as they were picked up and tossed about. Fon, sensing the moment was upon him, reached for Rafaella and spun her round to face him. Her smile died away as she saw it was him, but for once he was undeterred.

'Rafa, I'm sorry,' he said urgently. 'You have to forgive me.'

'I don't have to do anything,' she said, jerking her chin in the air, droplets of water dripping from her lashes and jaw and hair. 'You did what you did. You made your choice.'

'But it wasn't a choice,' he said boldly, his grip firm on her waist. 'It was a madness that came over me. I was trying to prove something . . . to throw the monkey off my back.'

'I don't know what that means!' she cried. 'What did you have to prove? To whom?'

He hesitated – he could apologize but not explain – and she turned away in disgust, but he caught her and held her there.

'I messed up – badly,' he admitted. 'And then I made it worse by staying away from you. I'd convinced myself I'd blown it, that I was no good for you, but I know now that's not true. I'm capable of being more, of being a better man. I'm going to show you how sorry I am for what I did. And I'm not going to stop until you believe me.'

She stared back as if surprised by this new, forthright version of him, and he stepped in closer, his body almost touching hers. He lowered his voice. 'I won't lose you, Rafa. Not for her—'

He felt hands on his legs, someone – two people, under water – knocking at his thighs as he stood there, before he was suddenly lifted up and Dante and Francesco hoisted him onto their shoulders. Still he looked down at Rafaella, his arms wheeling for balance, not sure if he was about to be thrown again. 'Meet me tonight!' he insisted, wobbling precariously. 'Let me make it up to you!'

Gina swam over and came to stand by her friend. 'What's going on here?' she demanded, butting in as ever. 'She doesn't want to talk to you!'

'You have to make her let me apologize.'

Gina looked surprised by his boldness too. '. . . And why should she do that? After what you did?'

'Because we all fuck up! And I deserve a second chance.'

'Pah! You've shown her what you are!'

'He's the man of the hour, is what he is,' Dante said, butting in too and slicking his hair back with one hand as he held Fon on his right shoulder. His body was stippled red with deep lacerations and lashes, but they were irrelevant compared to almost drowning. 'My brother saved my life today. He didn't hesitate when everyone else did. He acted on instinct, and sometimes that's the right thing to do, sometimes it's wrong. But isn't it better to have a man who acts with purpose? And passion?'

Gina's face changed on the last word. Fon didn't need to be able to see his brother to know Dante had pinned her with one of his scrutinizing looks, as if suddenly noticing her properly for the first time. Perhaps he was. Gina was wearing a tiny black-and-white-striped bikini, her luscious curves buoyant in the water. She couldn't possibly know how good she looked to the male gaze.

'We'll pick you both up tonight at ten, after the barbecue,' Dante said, a self-assured smile curling the words and needing no confirmation from the girls as he and Francesco began wading ashore, carrying Fon home to a hero's welcome.

Their mother rushed forward into the shallows, her arms outstretched.

'My boy!' Monica cried, clutching Dante close, not caring that she was getting soaked.

'It's OK, Mamma,' he reassured her. 'Fon saved me.'

'He's being dramatic, Mamma! As if he would have allowed himself to be killed by a fish!' Fon quipped, just as Dante and Francesco tipped him backwards off their shoulders into the shallows.

Fon emerged laughing, whipping his hair off his face the way Dante always did it. He glanced back. Rafaella was still staring, Gina talking by her side, and he felt himself grow in stature even more. Had his brother's words struck home? In the space of a week, Fon had been recast as a man of action. Of passion and purpose.

Unlike Cosimo Franchetti.

Fon could see him and Fede swimming across the bay, towards the steps where the nonnas bathed near the gates of the grand Villa Agosto. For once, neither of them was the main event. The Franchettis might have power, position and money, but they belonged to the past. It was the Giannellis, enterprising and dynamic, who were the future. Under his brother's stewardship they were coming into their prime at last, and nothing was out of reach, not even the Franchettis' own women. Not that it was Romola he cared for. But Fon was learning fast that fortune favoured the brave, and he could have whatever – and whomever – he wanted, if he was just bold enough to claim it.

Chapter 12

Cosimo

The flames leapt high into the sky, embers curling and twisting against the darkness as the villagers danced the *pizzica* on the sand. Everyone was in high spirits.

Everyone but Cosimo.

The haul from the *mattanza* had been the port's best ever, and the wholesalers buying for Asian markets had paid full price to take it off their hands. The fishermen might not be rich, but no one was going to starve this winter.

'You look like you'd rather be in Rome,' Fede said, sinking into the sand beside him and handing him a beer.

'I think I would.'

'. . . Funny, given you seem to spend all your time in Rome wishing you were here.'

'That's not true.'

'Isn't it?' Fede pinned him with a quizzical look but Cosimo stared instead at the burning logs. 'So why aren't you hanging out with all of them, then? Because you're usually inseparable, and no one's working now.'

Fede jerked his chin towards the figures on the other side of the flames. Rafaella and Gina were with Clara, Antonia and Donatella; Luigi, Gino, the Giannellis. They looked golden in the firelight as they laughed and messed about, making jokes with a familiarity from which he'd been shut out. Dante was leading the celebrations, of course, but Fon was by his side tonight, and Cosimo saw how Rafaella followed him with her eyes – wary but watchful.

With him, on the other hand, she was doing a great job of pretending he didn't exist, that he hadn't come back here at all.

He sighed. *Was* there any point in staying? He still didn't understand how he had become so grossly implicated in the debacle. He hadn't betrayed Rafaella, yet he saw rejection in her eyes every time they glanced at one another.

He stared down at the sand. He didn't think he could hack another five weeks of this. Everyone else greeted him with their usual friendliness, but without the tether to Rafa and Gina, he felt merely tolerated. For the first time in his life here, he felt like an outsider.

'Cosi?' Fede prompted. 'Tell me what's going on. Have you had a fight with them?'

'No.'

'Then why did Rafa look like she'd rather drink tar than come over to ours the other day? And why is she ignoring you now?'

'It's nothing to do with me.' Cosimo shook his head quickly. 'Romy . . . got into a tiff with them, so . . .'

'About what?'

He hesitated, knowing his elder brother was unaware of their sister's party-girl status in the capital. '. . . Girl stuff.'

'So now we're all the enemy? That doesn't sound like Rafa,' Fede frowned, looking over at the group beyond the fire. They were playing a game with a playing card, holding it to their mouths as they sucked in their breath. Gino was passing the card to Antonia but he exhaled, the card falling away as she leaned in for it and received a kiss instead. Everyone laughed loudly as she pretended to be annoyed.

Cosimo sighed, letting his head hang down, elbows looped over his knees. It was the sort of game they'd played as thirteen-year-olds in Rome, but things were always behind out here. That was one of the reasons he loved it. He had kissed Rafaella playing hide-and-seek, of all things, in the moonlight!

'Well, have you heard from Valentina?' Fede asked, changing the subject.

Cosimo exhaled sharply. No topic was safe, it seemed. 'No. They're doing some night shoots, so the hours make it hard to stay in touch.'

'Ah,' Fede nodded. 'She seemed nice . . . Very friendly.'

Cosimo glanced at him, checking for traces of sarcasm, but that wasn't in his brother's nature. 'Nice' and 'friendly' were not the adjectives most men would use for Valentina. Drop-dead sexy, stunning, beautiful . . . but also demanding, selfish, shallow, vain. 'Actually, I'm not sure I'll be seeing her again.'

'No?'

'We're not really a match,' he said diplomatically. The truth was, they'd barely spoken; they had little in common when they were sober, and from the moment she'd arrived at the villa she had seemed far more interested in the trappings of nobility and talking to his parents. He hadn't knocked on her bedroom door that night – too overtaken by the events between Romola and the girls – but neither had she knocked on his, and it said everything that neither of them was affronted by the other's lack of interest. Cosimo, for his part, couldn't think of anything but Rafaella and how to heal the rift his sister had caused between them all.

A hushed gasp from the group caught his attention. Dante was doing a magic trick on Gina; whether or not it was working, there was a look of enchantment on her face.

'Well, at least *they* seem to be talking again,' Fede murmured, nodding across the beach towards their parents in animated conversation with some of the port's other wealthy summer visitors. There were a few well-off families who never saw one another in the city but flocked together here like close friends, taking mutual comfort and refuge in each other's company at these larger village events.

'Thank God,' Cosimo muttered. The Franchettis came from a class in which how things looked mattered more than how things really were, and no one gathered here tonight could possibly imagine the wall of silence that had sprung up between them after the party and remained in place now for almost a week. He didn't know exactly what had caused it this time, but he could take a guess; their father was of a generation for whom fidelity was a concept, not a concrete requirement. He was required only to be discreet.

'You know, if Romy's not back on her feet by tomorrow, I really think we should call for the doctor—'

A cascade of laughter made them look up again and Cosimo watched as Gina jumped onto Dante for a piggyback, his fingertips pressing into the soft flesh of her thighs as he ran with her as if she was a child.

The rest of the *ragazzi* were getting up to go, too. Cosimo had heard them making plans to go into Tricase town for gelato. No one seemed to care that Tito's sold gelato right here; they wanted to travel five miles inland instead. The boys wanted to show off on their bikes and the girls wanted to ride pillion, arms and legs squeezed tightly around the boys as they took the bends too fast. It was exactly the kind of thing he did back home with his dates, and he knew exactly what it led to.

He watched as they all started walking up the beach, heading for the scooters parked by the harbour wall. Some of the parents called out curfews and hands were raised in acquiescent reply. Fon said something to Rafaella and she nodded; he ran ahead with the sort of machismo and swagger more associated with Dante.

'I guess we could take her back some food?' Fede went on, his thoughts still on their sister – but Cosimo was already on his feet, sprinting over the sand and around the fire.

'What are you doing?' he panted, catching Rafaella by the arm and spinning her round. She looked up at him in alarm, the gold flecks in her eyes illuminated by the firelight.

'What?'

'Are you seriously doing this? You're going to forgive him and not us?'

She pulled her arm back. 'Cosi—'

'How can you do that?' he hissed. 'Romy won't leave her room! She hates herself for what she did, but you're going to forgive *him*?'

She looked stunned by the accusation. '. . . Your betrayal was worse.'

'Mine?'

'Yes! Yours, Cosi!'

He spread his hands out as he realized this really was personal. His suspicions were right. She was angry with him, not just Romola. 'How? *I* haven't done anything!'

'No?' Her eyes burned into his, her breathing coming heavily, and he saw silent accusations run across her face. What wouldn't she say?

'What did I do? Tell me!' he implored.

'You left, Cosi! That's what you did. You left, and you said nothing all year. You didn't write. You didn't call. You didn't have the decency to say to my face that what happened last summer was a mistake! And then you just turned up here with *her* like nothing had ever happened!'

'Hey, is he bothering you, Rafa?'

Cosimo, stunned by her verbal onslaught, her tongue

loosened by beer, turned to find Dante standing in the sand beside him, Gina still clinging limpet-style to his back.

Dante's eyes narrowed, but there was a smirk on his lips. 'Want me to get rid of him for you?'

'What did you say?' Cosimo asked, immediately squaring up to him, fists already clenched.

Dante shrugged Gina off like a rucksack and she sprawled backwards onto the sand – but Dante, forgetting her already, was oblivious. He had only Cosimo in his sights, and there was a look of delight on his face that this was actually happening. Cosimo wondered just how long Dante had wanted to land one on him. Years, no doubt. The man bristled with jealousy.

'I don't like the way you're harassing my brother's girlfriend,' Dante sneered, pushing him roughly on the shoulder. 'Perhaps you should pay more attention to your own girlfriend. She certainly seems to be crying out for a real man.'

'*What* did you say?' Cosimo repeated in disbelief.

'You heard me. You need to stop being so careless with pretty things. On the boat the other day, if your old man hadn't been there, I'd have—'

Cosimo swung his right arm, but it only glanced against Dante's cheek as the other man dodged the punch.

'Hey, it's not my fault if you can't keep her satisfied!' Dante grinned. 'Just like it's not my brother's fault if your sister can't keep her legs closed—'

This time Cosimo's punch landed, but not before the words were heard – as Dante had intended – and a collective gasp whistled around the crowd as the scandal was finally unleashed. Dante staggered back with a stunned look, but he was a street fighter and rallied quickly, charging towards Cosimo and tackling him, throwing him onto his back and winding him. Unable to breathe or defend himself for several vital moments, Cosimo lay there as Dante attacked with a flurry of jabs. He could hear screams – not his – rising up as the villagers descended on them, pulling Dante off him.

In the melee, Cosimo seemed to have connected with Dante's jaw once or twice, because Dante's mouth was bloodied; but it was Cosimo who'd taken the drubbing. He could feel his left eye beginning to swell up, a rivulet of blood trickling down his brow. In the background he could hear his mother's voice frantically telling Filippo to 'do something, do something!'

'What in God's name is wrong with you both?' El Greco asked, his stocky, tattooed arms outstretched as he stood between them, keeping them apart. 'What is this about?'

'Why don't you ask him?' Dante sneered as Cosimo got unsteadily to his feet and brushed himself down. He was shaking with rage, adrenaline coursing through his bloodstream, but their showdown was over – for now. It had to be. For Romola's sake, nothing more could be done while they had an audience. His head was ringing and he was pretty sure he had broken his right thumb, but he'd be damned if he would show this *contadino* any weakness.

Fede came and stood by his shoulder. 'Let's just leave it,' he said calmly, authoritatively, shooting a warning look at Dante, who had once been his childhood friend. They had grown apart years ago, recognizing that they were very different people. Both understood, more clearly than Cosimo and the girls, that there was more dividing them than uniting them.

Dante obliged, but his smirk indicated he'd already done and said enough for one night. Cosimo could see the shock in everyone's eyes as the comment about Romola echoed through their minds. The Giannellis had disrespected the Franchettis in plain sight of the entire port. It felt as if the old order had been upended.

Cosimo looked over at Rafaella, still watching from a distance and trembling in dumbstruck silence. Fon was by her side again. He handed her the bike helmet and she took it, her feet moving even as her eyes remained upon Cosimo, and Fon began leading her away with a victorious look.

They were still going for gelato. He was still going to get what he wanted.

And what Cosimo wanted too.

Chapter 13

Rafaella

The piazza was buzzing as they parked up, scooters everywhere and huge crowds of *ragazzi* mingling. Boys sat on their Vespas drinking beer while girls clustered at the gelateria, choosing flavoured scoops, aware their bare legs were being admired in the bright lights.

'She's such a slut,' Donatella said, licking her gelato provocatively as she leaned between Gino's legs, sitting sideways on his scooter.

'She's got that look about her,' Antonia chimed in. 'You can see it in her eyes. Thinks she's better than everyone and can just take whatever – or *whoever* – she wants.'

Rafaella offered no comment, but the conversation wasn't about her anyway. Not really. She might be the wronged party in this scandal, but this wasn't about defending the victim; even Fon's role in it all seemed incidental. No, this was a takedown of the mighty Romola Franchetti, and there was not one person here prepared to defend her honour. Several times Gina had looked over at Rafaella as the other girls bitched, their old loyalty to their childhood friend still hard to shake off despite everything; but each time, she bit her tongue and let the gossip run. They owed Romola nothing anymore.

Like Donatella with Gino, Rafaella was leaning against Fon, who was also sitting on his bike sideways. Their group had parked in a loose circle and were now holding court as ever more people came to listen in. Word had quickly spread through the piazza about their exploits at the *mattanza* today; Dante was standing now with his shirt fully unbuttoned from showing off his war wounds to everyone who asked. There were at least two dozen girls making eyes at him and admiring his muscles as well as his injuries, but his attention was wholly focused on Gina, his hands moving casually, proprietorially over her body with growing familiarity as they all talked.

Rafaella had never seen her friend look so happy. Gina had never held out any realistic hope that her crush on Dante might ever become more than daydreams (or dirty dreams) but no one was in any doubt that they were on an inevitable path now. Poor Luigi looked desolate, cast off without apology, but there was nothing he could do. He was no match for the handsome older man.

Fon's hand was squeezing lightly on the back of Rafaella's neck, pressing on muscles tired from her work reaching in the olive grove. A small groan escaped her and she felt him swoop closer.

'Is that good?' he asked, his mouth right beside her ear.

She nodded, closing her eyes, feeling the effects of all the beer on the beach and still trying to shake off the day's drama. It had been a long, slow day waiting for the men to come back from the sea but as soon as they had – leaping victoriously into the water and hailing Fon as a hero – the hands of the clock had swung at triple speed: suddenly she and he were talking again; he simply wouldn't *let* her cut him out, her forgiveness becoming implied as she accepted the plates of food he brought her and the steady stream of drinks, allowed him to drive her here, to hold her hand . . .

All because she'd wanted to get back at Cosimo, to make

him suffer as she did. Her jealousy had got the better of her at last and she could no longer be the bigger person. Romola's casual betrayal had bled into his indifference as they had both shown her, in their different ways, how insignificant she was to them, how unimportant her feelings – and she hated them for it.

Her only power, she saw now, was to keep them out of her life. Romola was lying low, of course, but Rafaella had denied Cosimo the chance to talk to her this morning on the promenade; ignored his gaze as she played in the sea with the others on their triumphant return; refused to look over as he stared at her through the flames of the beach fire ... And it had worked. He'd lost his composure at last, grabbing her in front of everyone and demanding to know why he was being punished. Her heart had soared in that moment, revelling in his touch and his anger and jealousy ... But then Dante had become involved and fists had flown; it had become about the men. She'd had to pick a side. And how could she possibly pick his when he was going to leave again in a few short weeks and she would still be here, living among them?

Fon's fingers pressed harder against her neck muscles, as if more of a good thing could only be better. She knew how much he was trying to make it up to her – she saw the contrition in his eyes whenever he looked at her. Even Gina, trying to find positives, had said at the caffè this afternoon that it was no bad thing for a man to have a little 'experience'.

Another groan escaped her and she opened her eyes again to find Dante staring straight at her, scrutinizing her with his brother. It was an unnerving experience, being held so directly in his gaze. He scarcely seemed to blink, as motionless as a hawk watching a mouse scuttle through the grass far, far below ... just waiting to strike. His grip tightened on Gina's thigh, but to Rafaella he gave only a tiny, almost imperceptible nod, as if granting approval of what he saw. As if something had been decided.

'What do you say, Rafa?'

'What?' She tore her gaze away, looking at the others.

'We want to go swimming tomorrow after work,' Clara said. 'Your father will let us take your boat, won't he?'

'Come out on ours,' Fon said generously, pulling on her shoulders a little so that she looked back at him. He smiled. 'We'll take you. Our boat's bigger and faster.'

'No! It's a girls' trip!' Donatella pouted. 'We don't want to be with you boys all the time, you know. When will we get to talk about you otherwise?'

Everyone laughed, even Dante. As if he already knew every little thing they would say anyway.

Chapter 14

Fon

Fon sat on the back of his bike, his arms looped around Rafaella's shoulders, convinced this was the best day of his life. She was a little bit drunk, he could tell, because every so often her head would fall back against his chest for a moment before she corrected herself with a mumbled apology, as if she was doing something wrong. She didn't know she made him feel like a king. He could feel the stares of the other guys lingering on him enviously, wondering what he had that they hadn't, to get a girl like her.

Sex, and the promise of it, pulsed everywhere here in the midnight heat. From the moment they'd arrived in the piazza he could taste the pheromones in the air, just as he had the blood in the water this afternoon. It tinged everything, an invisible stain, infecting them all with lust and heady delight at being young and alive.

Every person here was beautiful, handsome, sexy ... but there was a hierarchy nonetheless. He had watched heads turn as Dante and Gina walked hand in hand ahead of them to get their gelato, Gina wasp-waisted and full-bosomed in tight white capris and a knotted black blouse. Dante sauntered beside her, enjoying the other men's envious looks and not in the least bit threatened by them, his cut lip and facial bruises only adding to his legend.

Fon could see that he and Rafaella, as a couple behind them, made a very different proposition to Dante and Gina's swarthy, pulsing, visceral energy. Rafaella looked virginal in her white shorts and yellow cotton lace blouse, her lissom figure like the stem to Gina's blowsy bloom; and he – fair-haired, tall but wiry – was no match for his brooding matinee-idol brother. But they complemented one another in their own way, a clean-cut style that came from good bones, not swagger. As the looks landed, he'd been emboldened to reach for her hand and clasp it in his own, a public proclamation that she was his.

The Fon of last week wouldn't have presumed to be so bold, scared that one wrong move would send her running, laughing, from him. But the adrenaline from the day, as well as the fight on the beach (he knew perfectly well he was the one Cosimo really wanted to punch), was still pumping through his veins, and he felt fearless. He was learning fast now, the rules of the game revealing themselves to him at last. He had done the very worst thing he could do to Rafaella but she had forgiven him simply because he had told her he wouldn't accept *not* being forgiven. Just as Dante had told Gina he would bring her here tonight; a statement, not a request. For all these years Fon had deferred to those he admired, but he saw now that being a real man meant being assertive. Respect wasn't simply given; it had to be commanded. Women wanted men with resolve and purpose. They wanted to be able to submit – and Rafaella was no different. He had to be the man she wanted, even if it meant forcing himself to fit into that new mould. It didn't matter if he didn't believe it of himself; it only mattered that everyone else did.

Her hand had felt small in his as he led her towards the

counter, eyes landing on them like mosquitoes, each one with a little bite. He had glanced over at her, seeing the apprehension on her face at the overt attention they were attracting, and realized she really didn't know she was beautiful. She was completely unaware of the effect she had not just on men, but women too, who looked at her whether they wanted to or not, trying to break down her beauty into elemental components they could mimic and recreate. Even Dante kept staring, and Fon knew she wasn't his type – she was too strait-laced, too elegant; he liked a coquette – but beautiful women of all types reflected well on him. On them.

Fon swept Rafaella's hair to one side and dropped his head down to kiss the curve between her shoulder and her neck. She fell still but didn't pull away and as he came back up, he locked eyes with his brother. He was growing in his estimation, he could feel it.

Dante winked lazily back at him, his own arm draped over Gina's shoulder, his hand within grasping distance of her breast but not making contact. He was a gentleman, here.

Following his lead, Fon looped his arms round Rafaella's shoulders again, pulling her in to him. She reached up and clasped his wrists as if holding him there, and he felt giddy with happiness and beer even though he knew he had to play it cool. For the first time ever, her body language chimed with his: anyone who wanted her would need to get past him.

Cosimo Franchetti included.

Chapter 15

Cosimo

Breakfast was eaten in silence, though that was nothing new; their family dealt in denial. Their father was all but hidden behind the newspaper at one end of the table, their mother sipping her espresso with glacial rage at the other.

Romola, her alibi blown, had been forced out of her room at last, but in the face of her parents' frigid anger her depression had turned to defiance. She was wearing a bikini at the table, sitting with one leg up on the chair, sucking crumbs off her fingers so that Cosimo half wondered whether she was drunk again. She was making herself into everything their parents deplored – noisy, uncouth, slatternly – but their mother busied herself with making sure the little ones finished their figs and walnuts. Their father hadn't looked at her once.

Cosimo had overheard them lecturing her on their return from the beach last night. The issue wasn't that she had had sex; the only matter of significance was with whom, and sleeping with a Giannelli sat somewhere between eating faeces and running through the streets naked.

Romola helped herself to another *pasticciotto*.

'That's your fifth,' their mother said.

'I know,' Romola shrugged, grabbing another for good measure.

Cosimo looked on. His sister always did this – starving herself for days at a time, then eating till she was almost sick. As with her drinking, there was a recklessness to it, almost as if she was trying to hurt or punish herself in some way.

She wasn't the only one feeling bruised. His black eye had come out overnight and he had almost no range of movement in his right thumb. The doctor had been sent for.

'They're still running with that story, Papa?' Fede asked, breaking the silence.

Cosimo looked over again at his father, hiding behind bureaucracy. The headlines were doom-mongering over the British and French uproar about Nasser's nationalization of the Suez Canal Company; but in smaller print, further down the page, his own name was typed in black and white: *Franchetti Landslide Shame*.

Eighty-six villas had collapsed and thirteen people had been killed in May when a heavy storm had swept floodwater through a new development in Copertino, near Lecce.

'It's been weeks now,' Fede frowned. 'Why are they still coming for you?'

There was a pause before Filippo shook out the pages, closed and folded them, and laid the paper on the table. 'Because I, to quote our American friends, am where the buck stops. I'm the minister of infrastructure. I may as well have built those villas myself.'

'Yes, you may as well have,' Romola said bullishly, eyeballing him. 'But hey, at least the men who died were only poor construction workers – so they don't really count, right?'

Filippo let the jibe slide as he reached for his coffee. He behaved as if she hadn't said anything. As if she wasn't even there.

'Right?' Romola sat forward, hunched over the table.

Cosimo glanced at their mother, knowing she couldn't bear elbows on the table. Just as Romola couldn't bear to be ignored. 'Can't you hear me, Papa?'

Filippo's head swivelled. '. . . Is there something you wish to get off your chest, Romola?'

Cosimo saw how she swallowed at his sudden directness, the chilling coldness in his voice, seeming to shrink back into herself a little. For all her badgering, she always withdrew at the vital moment, as if she wanted to spar but not wound; bite but not kill.

Cosimo cleared his throat. 'I think what Romy's trying to say is that—'

'Romy doesn't know what she's trying to say,' their father replied, swinging his attention to him now. 'That's the problem. She hears things she doesn't understand. She sees things she doesn't understand. She's no great thinker, capable of debating on this.'

Cosimo bristled at their father's arrogance. 'But her point is it *does* all go through your office.'

'Exactly,' Romola said, drawing courage again from him; they had always stuck together. 'The amount of building permits being issued isn't viable! I heard that over four thousand building permits have been issued in the past four years.'

'Oh? And where did you hear that exactly?' Filippo asked witheringly. 'An opinion piece by Italo Calvino? Some pretentious, drunk philosopher at one of your parties?'

'. . . It just seems a lot.'

'People need houses, that's a fact, and whether you like it or not, the old ways are dead. The war changed things for ever. People want to live and work in the cities now.'

'But the old city centres are being abandoned! In . . . in Palermo alone, the population has dropped by two-thirds—'

'Palermo is a law unto itself. And besides, that figure is

wildly exaggerated,' Filippo scoffed. 'But people do want the electricity and running water you can have in the modern blocks – that *we* enjoy as a matter of course. Are you saying we should insist they continue to go without?'

'No, that's not what I'm saying. Of course not—'

They were stopped by their mother's quiet chuckle at the other end of the table.

'What's so funny?' Filippo frowned.

'Oh, nothing,' Rossanna sighed. 'It just always tickles me when you present yourself as a man of the people.'

There was a silence.

'Please, carry on,' she murmured, twirling her wrist. 'It's fascinating. I do so love discussing politics at the breakfast table.'

Cosimo knew it was a clear command to drop the subject – she was a stickler for etiquette – but Romola was in no mood to appease either their father or their mother.

'All I'm saying is, everyone knows there's corruption. That these construction companies and the workers they use, and the concrete, and even the sand quarries they use to make the cement, are fronts for—'

'Oh for heaven's sake, Romola!' their father barked. 'It is for local councillors to issue permits as they see fit. I hardly see how I can be expected to police the disbursements and control the activities of regional authorities, when clearly I don't even have control over my own family!'

His outburst was met with another frigid silence. They all knew it was more a response to his wife's needling sarcasm than his teenage daughter's baiting, but it was the break in protocol Romola had been looking for and she fell back at last, as if somehow satisfied.

She took another bite of the pastry.

'Well, it'll all blow over, Papa,' Fede said, ever the diplomat. He looked as if he regretted raising the subject in the first place. 'They'll turn their attention to someone else next week, I'm sure.'

'Oh, I know so.' Filippo smiled at his eldest child. They had always been close, and Cosimo was sure Fede was only at law school as a precursor to following in their father's footsteps as a politician. Fede felt the weight of duty, as the first-born son, to make their father proud and continue the noble Franchetti name in public service, whereas Cosimo had no idea where his own future lay. 'Remember what I keep telling you. Keep your friends close and your enemies closer. Politics is all about the long game – and long memories.' He patted the small leather-bound notebook beside his coffee cup; he carried it everywhere with him. It was as much a part of his identity as his crested signet ring – or at least it was to them, always on the dinner table, bedside table or his desk. 'Do you think I rose to this position on account of my pretty face?'

Rossanna's head snapped up at the pithy remark. 'No. Just your name.'

Just then the housekeeper came in. 'Signore Russo on the telephone, signore.'

Filippo rose with a sigh of relief. 'Well, on that note . . .'

They all watched as he went to take the call with the secretary of the Council of Ministers, the PM's right-hand man. The tension in the room departed with him and Cosimo saw their mother physically soften as she pushed her knife and fork together on the plate and sank back in her chair.

'What are your plans today, boys?' she asked, looking over at them.

'Studying,' Fede replied. Sometimes Cosimo wondered if his brother worked so hard because it gave him the perfect excuse to hide away from the rest of them.

'Really?' She looked disappointed. 'I had thought we might—'

'I have exams when I get back, Mamma,' he said quickly. 'But don't worry, I'll make sure I get out for a bit. I'll go down again to Marina Serra for a swim later.'

'And you, Cosi?' their mother asked.

He hesitated. His day lay before him like a white sheet with not so much as a wrinkle to divert him. '. . . I'm not sure. I thought Romy and I could—'

'No,' their mother said, cutting him off with a dismissive shake of her head. 'I'm getting my nails done in Tricase, and she's coming with me.'

'But I don't want to get my nails done,' Romola protested.

'What you want is neither here nor there. For the rest of this holiday, you're going to remain in my eyeline at all times.'

'But you can't do that!' Romola gasped, looking horrified.

'Watch me.' Their mother pressed her napkin to her mouth and set it down as an indication that both the meal and the conversation were at a close. She looked at Cosimo. 'The little ones are going back up to the Parisis' again today.'

'Oh.' Helping out on the agricola and learning some rural skills was something they had each done when they were younger. Clearly no Franchetti would ever need to know how to prune an olive tree or press the oil, but it was a favour granted by Emilio Parisi that paid lip service to the idea of the family being integrated into the village, even though Cosimo now suspected idle, rich children were far more hindrance than help.

'Would you drop them there at ten for me, please? They'll need collecting at three.'

'Sure.' He sat a little straighter. He had humiliated himself on the beach last night. What if he ran into Rafaella there? . . . Worse, what if he didn't? Despite everything, he still wanted to see her. If he could just explain . . .

'But our nails won't take five hours,' Romy said in a worried tone.

'No, but afterwards we're going to Mass. And *you* will be going in the confession box.'

On a Thursday afternoon? Romola sank back in her chair, darting a murderous look towards Cosimo across the table, but he could only shrug in return.

It was official. This summer was a bust.

Chapter 16

Rafaella

Antonia, Donatella and Clara were already waiting for them by the time Rafaella and Gina walked round from the other side of the port. 'We brought some refreshments,' Antonia winked, revealing a bottle of Campari in her bag.

Gina looked delighted, but Rafaella still had a headache from the night before. She had drunk far too much beer by the fire and afterwards at the piazza.

'See you later,' Gina called to El Greco, who sat in his chair in the shade of his harbourmaster's house. He waved back, making a note of their departure in his log.

They jumped aboard her father's tiny red boat, *Principessa* – it was only big enough for puttering around the local coves – and Gina cast off the mooring rope as Rafaella put her hand to the tiller, guiding them carefully through the tight meander of the marina into open water. They waved to the *anziani*, standing in the water for their pre-dinner dip, as they passed; there had been much for them to discuss today, picking over the *mattanza* and last night's fight just as the *ragazzi* had done in the piazza. (It seemed to Rafaella that people didn't change with age; they just steeped into deeper versions of themselves.) There was a general sense that ancient, invisible lines had been crossed, as if tectonic plates were shifting and about to change their landscape for ever.

The breeze picked up as they headed south along the rocky coast, shallow cliffs rising above the water, jackdaws and rock pigeons nesting on the rocks. Rafaella enjoyed the sensation of her hair being blown off her neck and she stretched gently, grateful for a chance to rest at last. It had been a long day on little sleep and she had been tempted to go straight home after her shift, but the girls all wanted to regroup after last night. Donatella hadn't been lying when she'd said they needed to talk about the boys, and Rafaella had been surprised to find Gina uncharacteristically tight-lipped all day about Dante's goodnight kisses, insisting on waiting specifically to tell her now, with the others.

It was the first time Rafaella could recall Gina holding back from her. Was it an omen of things to come? A shift in the tectonic plates of *their* friendship?

They drank from the bottle Antonia shared around as they passed the numerous grottoes and caves that characterized this stretch of coastline, cutting a line past the narrow Canale del Rio, where some smart yachts were lying at anchor.

Marina Serra was only a short way further along, distinguished by two natural sea pools that sat behind a chasm in the front of the cliffs. Unlike the Tricase lido's short and stubby plunge pools, here they were long, snaking channels and meandering canals.

Rafaella threw out the anchor at their usual spot, the chain rattling as it spooled out. They were still in open water in front of the cliffs, only a narrow gap in the rock face revealing the cavity behind and the sea pools on the other side. Visitors in passing yachts could easily glide past without ever knowing what they were missing.

The girls stripped down to their bikinis, passing around the bottle for a last gulp before diving into the azure water.

They laughed and carried on talking as soon as they surfaced, treading water or floating on their backs as they let the stresses of the day finally leave their bodies; they were all on their feet for twelve hours a day at their various jobs. It felt good to be weightless for a while.

Rafaella dived down a few times to look at the fish; she had always loved swimming into the underwater caves and looking for octopus and starfish. When they were little, she and Dado had trained themselves to hold their breath for as long as they could. Her record was two minutes nine; his was two minutes forty-four. She had never managed to beat him and, once he had grown tall, knew she never would.

'Come on!' Clara called, leading the way to the rocks. Rafaella hoisted herself up on the side of the boat, reaching for the diving knife and fastening the sheath to her right thigh before following after them.

By the time she stepped sideways through the crevice the others were already in the shallow pool, kicking their feet idly. She was aware of their eyes running over her as she made her way through. Her body didn't look like theirs yet and she wasn't sure it ever would, despite what her mother and Silvana said. It seemed to her she took more after her father: lean and lanky.

'Oh, that's so nice,' she groaned as, like the others, she lay back and let her legs float forward, planting her hands on the rock bed. The water was bathtub-warm.

'That's what you said to Fon last night,' Donatella said in a teasing voice and with a wicked look. 'You know, the noises you were making were *almost inappropriate.*'

Rafaella stiffened. They were? 'I was drunk. I'd had too much to drink,' she mumbled.

'Yeah? How drunk exactly?' Antonia leered.

'. . . Not *that* drunk,' Rafaella replied, knowing exactly what she was alluding to.

'Ugh, who could have predicted that?' Antonia rolled her eyes, immediately losing interest. 'Gina? What happened with Dante after you left?'

'And don't say "nothing"!' Clara cried, butting in. 'He was *claiming* you last night! He wants you!'

Donatella kicked her feet excitedly in the water. 'He's so gorgeous!'

Gina looked back at them with shining eyes and a rare lack of guile, and it suddenly occurred to Rafaella – had her friend been deliberately holding back her joy all day because she knew Rafaella's feelings about Dante? She had never hidden her frank dislike of him, and she felt a frisson of anxiety in her stomach now as Gina leaned in conspiratorially to the other girls, ready to confide.

'Well, we kissed . . .'

Clara squealed, clapping her hands over her mouth.

'But we just kissed!' Gina added hurriedly.

There was no 'just' about it; Rafaella knew this was the apogee of her best friend's lifelong dream.

'Tell us everything!' Donatella gasped. 'I'd give my right lung to kiss him just once!'

'Well, you won't have to,' Gina crowed, pushing up her bosom provocatively. 'I intend to make sure he never looks at another girl again!'

'Is he good?' Clara whispered. 'Can you tell he's experienced?'

Gina lowered her eyes, looking up at them all from beneath long lashes. 'He knows *exactly* what to do.' She gave a shudder as she pressed a hand to her heart. 'When I think what I've been suffering with Luigi, jabbing his tongue into my mouth . . . It's been like kissing an electric eel! Whereas with Dante . . .' She closed her eyes, the rapture on her face leaving them in no doubt about how good it had been. 'Now I understand what they mean when they say you melt into them.'

Rafaella thought the girls themselves were looking like half-melted gelati as they listened, limp and breathless. 'But what about Luigi?' she asked, the voice of reason.

'What about him?' Gina shrugged. 'We're over.'

'But you've been going out with him for months.'

'So? There's no going back now. I just couldn't! Dante has *ruined* me.'

All the girls, except Rafaella, groaned in chorus. 'So you're actually serious about seeing him again?' she asked, trying to keep the alarm from her voice. Dante's reputation with women was notorious. Couldn't they see he was just going to use her?

A smile grew on Gina's small mouth. For all her voluptuousness, she had the face of a doll, her chin coming to a small point, her bow lips falling in a natural pout. 'He wants to see me again tomorrow.'

'Not today?' Antonia asked.

Gina's smile faded as she picked up on a hidden jibe. 'He couldn't do today.'

'Oh.'

'What does *oh* mean?' Gina asked tartly.

Rafaella flinched. The two girls' friendship had always teetered on a knife-edge of contempt.

'Well, it's just I would have thought if he was really keen—'

'He's in Specchia all day. He won't get back till late.'

'That's funny – what's a fisherman doing in Specchia?' Antonia puzzled. The large town was ten kilometres inland.

'His *father* may be a fisherman, but that's the very least of Dante's enterprises now,' Gina said indignantly.

'Enterprises, eh?' Donatella sounded impressed. 'So he's a businessman, is he?'

Gina kicked her legs, splashing water into their faces and moving the moment back into harmless teasing. 'You know he is! You're just jealous!'

They laughed. 'Perhaps!'

Rafaella looked on uneasily.

'So where's he going to take you tomorrow?' Clara asked, still hanging on every word.

'He hasn't said yet.' Gina glanced at Rafaella. 'But I need to be looking good for it. I was going to ask Silvana if she could take my green dress up an inch. It's short, but not short enough.'

'You want it done by tomorrow?' Rafaella laughed. 'Good luck! I've been waiting for my dress since spring and she's still not done it! Nothing fits me.'

'Don't we know it,' Antonia quipped with a roll of her eyes. 'Why *do* you always dress like you're that little girl in that book? What's it called? The scandalous one?'

Lolita? Rafaella kept quiet, but swallowed at the intended dig. '. . . Silvana's working all hours on her wedding dress, so that has to come first at the moment. She hasn't had a chance to get to it yet.'

Antonia shrugged. 'Whatever. Fon clearly likes it. He couldn't handle a real woman, though.' She struck a pose like a burlesque dancer, her breasts sticking up through the water like torpedoes.

'So things are completely good between you two now, are they, Raf?' Clara asked more diplomatically. 'You've forgiven him?'

'Yes. He made a mistake, but he's very sorry about it.'

'He's a man!' Donatella said with a 'what can you do?' tone, as if that explained it.

'More than that – he's a Giannelli!' Antonia chimed in with a wink. 'Strong urges.'

'He's growing more handsome by the day, too,' Clara said. 'Hey, Gina – soon he'll be giving Dante a run for his money!'

'Pah!' Gina snorted, waving away the bold claim with a swat of her wrist. 'Never! I've got the best Giannelli brother!'

'Who wants to hear about *my* date?' Antonia asked with a gleam in her eye. Francesco Romano had turned up at the piazza shortly after them, joining the group at Dante's insistence, and to everyone's surprise she had taken up the offer of a ride back on his bike. Like Dante, he was at least five years older. He hadn't grown up in the area, and although he worked for Rafaella's father, she had only seen him a handful of times in the few years since he'd lived here. Their conversation the other day in the olive grove had been the first time they'd actually spoken.

The others squealed in readiness for yet more scandal, but Rafaella felt the need to cool off. There was a competitive undercurrent to all this gossip that set her on edge.

'I'll be back in a bit,' she said. 'I'm going to look for some *percebes* to collect. I promised Mamma.'

The others didn't care, already engrossed as Antonia went straight into graphic details; she hadn't 'just' kissed her date, of course.

Rafaella swam away, slipping beneath the surface and feeling the water stream over her. She could see the sunbeams falling in thick shafts through the shallows, warming her skin as she made her way through the channel. The sun was hanging low now, like the ripest peach on a tree, and shadows were beginning to creep. The pools were emptying out, the day's stragglers walking up the steps cut into the cliffs and carrying their towels as they headed home for dinner. In another hour, it would be dark.

She rolled onto her back, drifting towards the end of the pool, which turned in a dog-leg, taking her out of sight of the girls. She knew that at the inside corner, just past the bend, there was a tiny inlet – no more than a notch, really, but its sheltered position made it an ideal spot for the barnacles to cling onto. She ducked under water again as she turned in, to get a better look at the amount of barnacles on the rocks.

They were thickly layered amid the kelp, and she reached for the diving knife strapped to her thigh.

There was enough here to harvest.

She went to surface, but as she looked up, she saw two pairs of feet – men's feet – on the ledge. They were entwined, the water lapping up to their ankles.

Her eyes widened as she realized what was happening and, through the water, caught a glimpse of their faces.

Rafaella pushed away in alarm, turning under water and immediately swimming back into the main channel of the pool. By the time she broke the surface, she was panting, desperate for air as she tried to make sense not just of what she had seen –

But whom.

Chapter 17

Fon

The stars were out in all their glory, speckling the midnight sky like threaded diamonds. The conversation and laughter from Tito's Bar reached down to the water's edge, but not the lights; Fon and the others moved unseen in the darkness below the harbour wall. *Allegra* was moored up, hosed down, the tank refilled and the advertising board folded on the back, ready to entice tomorrow's punters.

Dante jumped aboard, handing back the board to him, motioning for it to be left on the harbourside.

'Are you going to tell me what's—?'

Francesco whipped round and pointed a finger in his face, silencing him. 'Shh.' He glanced back at the harbourmaster's house – the light was on in the bedroom above the office, where El Greco resided – before jerking his head, indicating for Fon to hop aboard too. Dante was already at the front, releasing the bow rope.

Fon frowned at the excessive secrecy but did as he was told, knowing better than to ask any more questions until they were out on the water. They were dressed all in black, wearing gloves, and even their faces were smeared with ash so that they looked like untethered shadows. It all seemed over the top for stealing a few lobsters from Edo Carosa's pots.

Francesco cast off on Dante's command, but Dante didn't turn on the engines. Instead, Francesco handed Fon an oar.

Fon gave him an incredulous look. Was he serious? They were going to row a speedboat? But Francesco wasn't smiling as he dipped his own oar into the inky water and the boat began to slip its mooring in almost total silence.

They had to turn slightly into the channel, and Fon used the oar to push against the tiny red boat beside them – *Principessa*, belonging to Emilio Parisi. Some joker had left a half-empty bottle of Campari on the side, and it toppled loudly into the belly of the boat.

In the darkness, the sound seemed to amplify, an anomaly in the slumbering quietude. The men froze, waiting for footsteps, shouts, faces appearing over the wall. Fon flinched, knowing he had already messed up. No doubt this was why his brother never included him in his 'endeavours' . . . But no one came, and after a few moments of floating in the centre of the marina, they began rowing again. They had to almost hug the sea wall to keep out of sight – Tito's regulars would be sitting at their tables sipping on limoncello and looking out to sea – but there was a new moon working in their favour. This was probably not a coincidence, Fon realized. Slowly, silently, they slipped round the wall and into open water. Still the engines remained off. Only once they had borne left and rounded the headland by the lido did Dante ignite them.

In an instant they were flying, the boat skimming across the surface and making Fon's eyes water. Francesco stood up ahead with Dante at the helm as Fon sat on the bench seat, gripping the sides. He let his mind wander as they headed out towards the sites where Carosa liked to drop his pots. It was far too dark to make out the sea caves, the cliffs melding seamlessly with the sky now the port was behind them, and the villas and fishermen's cottages were shrouded by night's velvet veil. From this viewpoint, it felt like being in the middle of space, everything black and indistinct. Only the slight bobbing of the waves passing beneath the boat gave Fon any sense of place.

On and on they flew, over the sea, the minutes racking up. Fon peered into the darkness, realizing he was unable to pinpoint a single light anywhere. He had lost his bearings now but he could tell they weren't mirroring the coast. They were heading out into open water. Clearly they weren't out here to cheat their neighbour.

His brother and Francesco were staring into the wind, their hair streaming back as they flew along in solemn silence. They stood rigid, like black chess pieces, the mood tense. Fon swallowed uncertainly, but he knew better than to ask more questions. All would become clear soon enough.

It was another thirty minutes before Dante pulled back on the throttle and they slowed.

'How far out are we?'

'Six miles,' Dante murmured, but his attention was on Francesco.

Fon frowned. That was the international waters boundary.

Francesco appeared to be straining to hear something. Other engines were distantly rumbling through the water. 'Over there,' he said, pointing north-north-east.

Dante pushed down on the gears again, the boat quickly picking up speed once more.

'I can see them,' Francesco called over the wind, still pointing into the night. 'One o'clock.'

Dante adjusted course slightly as Fon looked out, gradually becoming aware of a growing density in the dark. They were bearing down upon a blacker-than-black mass that revealed itself as a small cargo ship as they drew closer.

Dante put the engines into neutral and reached for their father's torch. It was an old military piece, with an angled head and signalling filters; an American GI had given it to him when they'd fought in Taranto together during the war.

Fon watched as Dante double-flashed twice. Moments later, the signal was returned.

'Get ready,' Dante said, turning towards him. 'Do as they say and don't ask any questions. Don't look them in the eye and, God help you, don't drop anything. You got it?'

Fon nodded. He still didn't know what was going on but he was instinctively nervous, especially when Francesco cracked his knuckles too, a nervous tic.

They slowly idled towards the boat. There was another blue-hulled speedboat, almost identical to theirs, pulled alongside, and boxes were being tossed down to it from the mothership.

In a flash, Fon understood. *Bionde* – cigarette smuggling. Everyone knew about it; it was Italy's unofficial second economy, post-war. But it had never crossed his mind that his brother might be part of it.

Dante hung back, waiting their turn; there was no apparent rush but Francesco still kept a wide-eyed watch, casting around the horizon with a nervy look. The patrol boats of the Guardia di Finanza were fast and powerful, and no one here fancied a midnight chase.

Quickly it was their turn, the speedboat ahead of them peeling away from the ship and disappearing north up the coast, into the night. Dante brought them alongside, the engines gurgling as ropes were thrown down and Francesco hurriedly tethered them together.

'Giannelli!' Dante called up, identifying himself. A man in a cap and overalls emerged from the darkness and stared down at them, scrutinizing their disguised faces. '*Ciao*, Esposito,' Dante said, flashing his distinctive smile.

The man's face was fleshy and pockmarked. His gaze swung over them, sticking on Fon. 'Who's this?'

'My brother, Alfonso. He's working for me now,' Dante said.

'. . . Where's Pablo?'

'His wife's birthday. It would have aroused too many suspicions if he'd left.'

Fon remained motionless as Esposito studied him for a few moments more. '. . . I see the resemblance,' he grunted, before swinging back his arm and beckoning the closest man behind him, who got down on his stomach. 'You got the message? It's a large cache tonight.'

'*Si*,' Dante nodded. 'It won't be a problem. Arrangements have been made with all the relevant parties.'

'They can be trusted?'

Dante nodded again, so calm. 'They're aware of the repercussions if not . . . Eight hundred kilos, yes?' he asked, reaching forward to pass a thickly stuffed envelope to the man lying on the deck by Esposito's feet. It was passed to Esposito, who inspected the contents.

Satisfied with what he saw, he nodded and took a step back. The men behind him began to move in a synchronized pattern, passing boxes along the ship to one another, the nearest man tossing them down to Francesco. The system was simple, silent and quick.

'Pass them back to me,' Dante said brusquely, placing Fon where he had been standing and pulling back a tarpaulin.

Fon fell into line, doing as he was asked, and quickly the back of the boat was stacked with cigarettes, five hundred packets in each box. Fon glanced back and saw other speedboats hanging back in the water, just as they had done. Even in the dim light, he could make out another seven . . .

When the last box had been thrown, Dante secured the tarp over the cargo and Francesco untethered them. *Allegra* gently drifted away from the cargo ship.

'Until next time,' Dante said, getting the boat started again and curling away without further ado, heading south.

For several moments, as they adjusted to the high speeds again, no one spoke. Fon could see that his brother and Francesco were visibly more relaxed now the trade had taken place without incident. In fact, it had been an exercise in efficiency.

'Why didn't you tell me this was what we were coming to do?' Fon asked him.

'You would only have panicked,' Dante replied, casting him a sidelong glance. 'Better to just do it.'

Fon fell quiet again, trying to take it all in. 'Does Papa know?' He remembered that evening on the Parisi estate – Pablo and Francesco handing over another envelope of cash, which in turn Dante had given to their father.

'He does now. It's been working well for Uncle Teo up there. Why not down here too?'

Uncle Teo? The penny began to drop. 'So you mean, in Rome . . . you weren't really an extra on a film?'

Dante grinned. 'I mean, we *mingled* . . . But no, that wasn't my day job. The cousins were showing me the ropes.'

'And Mamma? Does she know?'

Dante scowled, looking scandalized. 'Of course not!'

Stupid question. '. . . Who sells on the *bionde*?'

'Kids, mainly. In the towns.'

Fon thought of his brother's frequent trips – to Ruffano, Taurisano, Specchia . . . He remembered seeing children at the traffic lights there, running to the cars between red and green. Not begging, as he had thought, but making lightning-quick trades . . . 'So that's why you bought the boat. It's not for the water-skiing at all.'

Dante shrugged. 'Well, it makes a small return, so there's no harm in it. And it provides a great cover story. Plus, the women love it.' His eyes glittered with that familiar wolfish look. 'I'm taking little Gina out on it tomorrow.'

Fon looked away. He wanted autonomy over his life the way Dante had over his own. He wanted to be able to have choices, to make his own decisions.

The journey back seemed quicker as he sank into his thoughts. He didn't stir until Dante cut the engines as they approached the port. The lights were off at Tito's now, the tables cleared and everyone in their beds. To Fon's surprise, Dante didn't swing the boat around the harbour wall but instead let it run forward on its own momentum, straight up to the narrow beach. Francesco jumped out in the shallows, Fon looking on as he waded onto the promenade and unlocked the door of one of the three caves that lined the curve of the cliffs here.

How did he have a key? One of the caves belonged to the mighty Gallone family, who had ruled Tricase town for almost five hundred years – no one had access to their cave; but the other two were civic property, and access to those was controlled by El Greco.

Fon glanced across to the marina. The light at the harbourmaster's still gleamed from the upstairs window.

'Don't worry about him,' Dante murmured, seeing Fon's apprehension. 'We have an agreement. He looks the other way when required.'

Fon was surprised. 'You've bribed him?' How many people were involved? How many others knew about it?

'That's a strong word. We prefer to see it as a mutually beneficial arrangement.'

Francesco was wading back now, and Dante went to the back of the boat and unfastened the tarpaulin.

'And you're going to store it all in the caves there? Right where everyone is walking past?' Fon was incredulous.

'Not for long. It'll be moved again at first light, after the fishing boats have left . . . Come, help us get this unloaded.'

Dante passed the first box down to Francesco, who waded back to shore again with it on his shoulder.

Fon looked down at the dozens of boxes. 'How much will you make on all this?'

Dante smiled. 'A lot.'

Fon wanted specifics, but he knew his brother wouldn't get into details with him. Not in front of Francesco. And not while he thought Fon was still a kid, naive about the ways of the world.

For a moment he hesitated, sensing he was at a crossroads, before he jumped down into the water. It was still warm, even at this hour. He looked back up at his brother. '. . . Will I get a cut?'

'If you show me you can be reliable and we make it a regular thing.' Dante studied him. 'Do you want it to be?'

Fon swallowed. What he wanted was for the world to see him as something he knew he wasn't: a strong man. A real man.

'Yes,' he said, taking a box and setting it on his shoulder as he'd seen Francesco do. 'I want in.'

Chapter 18

Cosimo

The umbrella shadows were stubby on the hot sand as he watched from the promenade archway, waiting for exactly the right moment before heading over. The caffè was busy today and Rafaella, doing the shift alone, was run off her feet.

As she disappeared round the back for more ice, he saw his chance, sprinting over to the only empty table and sitting down with his back to the bar, looking out to sea. The Giannellis were out in their speedboat, towing a novice water-skier who was spending more time in the water than on it.

It was several minutes before he heard the clink of glasses being set down on the counter behind him. He had got his breath back, but his heart was pounding nonetheless as he sat motionless, listening to her shoes slapping against her soles as she crossed the sand towards him.

'*Ciao!*' she said. 'What can I get y—?'

The words dropped like stones from her lips as Cosimo looked up at her. His black eye had almost swollen shut now, but he kept smiling through the humiliation. '*Ciao*, Rafa.'

She stared at him with wide eyes, incredulous at his

presence, his nerve. 'What are you doing here?' Her cold tone left him in no doubt exactly where he stood with her. He was still the enemy.

'I've come for a Coke.'

'No, you haven't. What do you want?' She glanced around anxiously, as if it was a crime for them to speak together.

He splayed out his hands and saw her clock the bandage on his splinted thumb. A spasm of concern flickered over her face and for a moment he thought she would sink into the chair beside him and reach for it, tenderly. There was always a gentleness to her movements, her nature . . . But she pulled back. Exactly as he had that night last summer. Her words on the beach had haunted him precisely because they were true; she had seen right through his ruse.

'*Just* a Coke,' he reiterated. 'Please.'

She drew in a small, sharp breath, trying to work out his game. A silence stretched between them. '. . . Fine. A Coke, coming up.'

He heard her steps retreat and forced himself not to stir, his arm laid out in languid fashion on the table belying the rapid acceleration of his pulse.

Stage One was completed: initiation of contact.

The idea had come to him in a flash when, on his way to drop the little ones at the agricola again, he had seen Gina and her father getting into their blue Piaggio truck. Cosimo had struck up conversation and Signore Crespi had mentioned they were going to the wholesaler in Brindisi – a job that would take the best part of the day. Gina had glowered at Cosimo throughout, as if reading his intentions and making it clear they were still in enemy camps. But he was resolute: divide and conquer was the only way forward. He needed to get Rafaella alone.

A double-masted yacht sailed into view and he watched it dispassionately as it tracked the horizon. They could be beautiful and certainly fun on the right day, but he'd been on enough yachts over the years not to be impressed by them. The funny thing about wealth, in his experience, was that when you could have anything, increasingly there was less to want. He certainly wouldn't rather be out there on deck than sitting at this small wooden table on the sand, under this red-striped umbrella, waiting for a Coke. From her.

'One Coke,' Rafaella said, setting down the bottle and a glass on the cork mats.

He smiled up at her but she wouldn't meet his eyes. 'Thanks.' She turned to leave, not wanting to spend a spare moment in his company. 'Could I have some ice with that?'

'There is ice,' she said, pointing to the glass.

'Yes, but . . . more ice.' He smiled again. 'Please.'

This time her eyes flashed angrily. She picked up the glass and stalked away, returning moments later with it filled almost entirely with ice. He would scarcely be able to pour any Coke into it.

'Happy now?' she asked.

'Not really,' he said.

'What else do you need? You've got Coke. Ice.'

'. . . I mean, the ice is fine, but really I just want to talk.'

She rolled her eyes as if she had known this was his intention. 'I have nothing else to say to you.'

'That's not true. There's everything to say—'

But she was already marching back to the bar.

'Why can't we just talk?' he called after her.

Cosimo sighed and stared back out to sea. Clearly they were going to have to do this the hard way.

He watched as she served the other customers with her usual sweet smile, unaware of how their gazes lingered on her as she took their orders. Unlike Valentina or Romola or even Gina, who all played up to their seductive powers, she had no idea she was beautiful, her face shyly downturned whenever a customer flirted with her.

Like them, Cosimo couldn't take his eyes off her. It was the first opportunity he'd had to look at her for any sustained period of time since coming back to the port and he was trying to absorb her beauty, as if to contain it was to control it. She was like a painting he couldn't walk past – the more he looked, the more he saw.

She had grown a lot taller in the intervening year, he already knew that, and her hair was longer and lighter than he'd remembered, falling almost to her waist – but somehow in all these years he'd never noticed before the slenderness of her hands or the delicacy of her wrists and ankles. He'd never considered that mole on her right thigh, nor the small scar on her left knee, which made him irrationally jealous because it told a story about her that he didn't know . . .

Suddenly his annual ten-month absences from here felt like a huge aberration as he was confronted not just with evidence of the life she lived away from him, but also just how much of it there was. He'd never before stopped to consider what happened in her life while he was gone, arrogantly assuming that his experiences – more glamorous, colourful, louder in every respect – dwarfed hers. And perhaps that was true, but it didn't mean her life stopped. It didn't mean nothing happened in her quiet hours here.

In the past, Fon, Luigi and Gino had merely been background characters in his seaside summers: skinny local boys, throwing rocks and revving their two-stroke engines. Now they were giving the girls love bites and pushing their luck as far as they dared. And Cosimo couldn't not see it, for what had been so painful about his return this year hadn't just been this estrangement of their friendship but the fact that for the first time ever, Rafaella and Gina hadn't dropped their lives for him and Romola. They were continuing with their daily movements as they did in April and May, October and November – and Cosimo was seeing that *he* was the bit player, on the stage for a mere six weeks from July.

He watched her clearing a table, wiping down the surface. She was wearing cream shorts and a pale pink blouse beneath her serving apron, her brown legs flashing as she loaded the tray with empty glasses, bottles and bowls. At some angles the sunlight glowed behind her, affording him glimpses of the outline of her tender curves, and it took his breath away every time.

But she never looked his way.

'. . . Your bill.'

He looked up to find her setting down a receipt on a saucer. 'Actually, I'd like another Coke, please.'

'But that'll be your fourth.'

'Yes,' he agreed.

'You do not want a fourth Coke. You said they're too sugary.'

'I'm thirsty,' he shrugged.

She sighed. 'You've got plenty of Cokes in your house.'

'How do you know?'

She sank onto one hip. 'Because you always do.'

'Perhaps, but I like the view here,' he smiled, trying to win her over with what he'd been assured was legendary charm.

She didn't look charmed. Was it the black eye?

'Why?' he pressed, as a small silence bloomed. 'Is there a limit on the number of Cokes I can buy from you?'

'No, but . . .' She sighed, refusing to be drawn into explanations, much less conversation. 'Fine. Coke number four coming up.'

She took away the receipt and he waited for her to return with the fresh bottle and the clean glass loaded with ice, all the way to the top, impossible to drink from.

'Thanks,' he grinned as she set them down in front of him.

She began to turn away but stopped herself. 'Are you planning on doing this all day?'

'For as long as it takes,' he shrugged.

'As long as what takes?'

'For you to talk to me.'

She hesitated momentarily – he could see her weighing the short-term pain of conversing with him against the long-term relief of his departure – and he lunged for the opportunity.

'What did you mean when you said I just left? You knew it was my last night.'

Her eyelids fluttered at the words, her breath catching in an uneven rhythm. 'Right. It was your last night,' she nodded. 'Every year you come and then you go. It was nothing different.' She shrugged, turning to go again, but he knew there was dissension in her agreement, a frill of sarcasm upon her words.

'No, wait!'

She stopped.

'. . . You're right. It was different and I'm sorry . . . I'm really sorry, Rafa.'

She looked down. 'What are you sorry for?'

Her words came out soft, pink and tender, too delicate for this harsh exposure. They belonged in a crepuscular half-world between memories and dreams.

'For not being stronger in the moment. I shouldn't have done it.'

She looked back at him. 'So you regret it?'

'Of course,' he lied. 'We'd had too much to drink, and . . . I crossed a line. It was all my fault. I should never have done it.'

'I see.'

He watched her, seeing her processing the apology, but sensed he still hadn't gone far enough. He swallowed. 'And . . .'

'And?'

He tried to read the look in her eyes. What were the words she wanted him to say to make everything right between them? 'I regret not speaking to you about it afterwards. You're right, I should have come to see you before we left the next day – or written, maybe? . . . I should have done that.'

'Why didn't you, then?'

He fell quiet. How could he tell her it had frightened him, the strength of feeling she aroused in him? That he'd never known how it felt to be so connected to someone, as if their souls had touched?

She gave a small scoff as his words failed to materialize. 'Forget it. I already know why.'

She turned away a third time but he caught her by the wrist. 'What do you know?'

'I know it meant nothing to you. *I* meant nothing.'

'What? No . . .'

'We were friends, Cosi. Best friends. I thought at the very least I deserved better than to be treated like all those other girls you go around kissing and discarding.'

'You did! You do! . . . You're everything to me, Raf.'

'Right – that's why you left without speaking to me. And when you did come back, you brought Valentina Fabiani with you! Because I'm everything to you!' She gave a small incredulous laugh, as if she still couldn't believe what he'd done, and he saw for the first time how deeply he'd hurt her. He felt his heart pound harder at the realization that his ruse to hide his feelings had been so very successful. Because it was all true – he had used Valentina as a human shield, to send a message that he had moved on, when nothing could have been further from the truth.

'You've got this all wrong,' he said with rising desperation as his faltering apology began to unravel.

'I don't think so,' she said flatly. 'You brought her down here and you threw a party for her! And then on top of that, your sister seduced my boyfriend there – because both of you think you can do whatever you want to me. I don't matter to either one of you.'

He knew he had to speak plainly now. To put it all on the line and tell her how he felt. 'Raf, when I kissed you, I didn't think it meant anything—' he began, half rising from his seat, needing to bridge the physical gap between them.

'It didn't! I *don't* care! I'm with Fon now anyway!' she cried, and she pushed on his shoulder so that he fell back down into the chair. 'Just leave me alone, Cosi.'

'I can't do that.' She'd cut him off before he could finish. He had intended to say, *I didn't think it meant anything to you.*

'Signorina,' a man hailed her from one of the other tables, hand in the air as he gestured for the bill.

She smiled and indicated she had heard before looking back at Cosimo with angry eyes. 'Just go,' she hissed under her breath. 'You'll burn if you keep sitting there, you know!'

He watched her go, sand flying up behind her – his heart already in flames.

'We're closing up,' she said, smacking down the bill for five Cokes. She hadn't met his eyes as he'd placed the latest order, seeming to have accepted her fate of serving him all morning, and he could see she was still not receptive to any further conversation. He had come here prepared to play the long game; so be it. He would need to change tactics.

'OK,' he said, reaching into his shorts pocket for the lira banknotes and handing over too much. 'Keep the change,' he said quickly, stopping her before she could leave for the till.

It worked. She hesitated, and he knew she didn't want his charity. She didn't want anything from him.

'When do you reopen?' he asked before she could push back.

She looked at him in surprise. 'Four. But . . .'

'I'll see you at four, then,' he said briskly, getting up from the chair. In spite of her new height, he still towered over her, and he felt the electric charge of her body so near to his as he looked down at her. Just as it had been between them that night, last summer . . .

She stepped back as he began to walk away. He could feel her eyes on him all the way across the sand as he headed home to get ready for round two.

'You're late.'

'By six minutes,' she muttered, not looking at him as she unlocked the side door of the caffè. She would have seen him waiting here as she'd come through the archway and realized how this afternoon was going to pan out.

Waiting on the other side of the counter, he could hear her throw down her bag and switch on the coffee machines, crashing and banging angrily before finally unlocking the shutters. He was leaning on his elbows, already smiling at her, when she drew them up.

'Need any help?'

'Not from you.'

Her hostility didn't faze him now; he was growing used to it. Unlike Gina, who was unpredictable and fiery, as likely to throw a punch as an insult, Rafaella only ever said what was necessary to keep him back.

'Huh. It's just, Gina said she'd be away all day, so I thought you might need a hand.' He saw her surprise at the comment, the intimation that Gina had spoken to him, perhaps even forgiven him.

'I've got it covered.' She reached for her cloth, polishing non-existent stains. '. . . I suppose you want a Coke?' she asked sullenly.

'I suppose I do,' he replied. 'I'll sit at my usual table, shall I?'

His sarcasm was not appreciated. He could feel the quiet

rage bristling from her as she went round unfolding chairs and pulling up umbrellas, pointedly getting to his last.

His instincts told him to help her, to do it himself – but she brushed against him as she leaned forward on tiptoe to fasten the rope pulleys, her blouse lifting to reveal a snatch of toned brown stomach at his eye level, and nothing on the planet could have induced him to move.

'Thank you,' he murmured as the small square of shade fell upon the sand – but not onto him. The sun had, of course, moved during *riposo*; he had spent the duration lying in their round swimming pool, trying to soothe his sore, reddened skin.

He moved his chair into the shade, this time positioning it so that he faced the bar and not out to sea. For one thing, he couldn't stomach watching Dante pull one more figure of eight on the water, acting like the local big man for the tourists.

'One Coke,' Rafaella muttered, returning a few moments later with his bottle and glass full of ice.

'Thanks,' he smiled, giving a sigh of his own as he picked up the bottle and held it, as if for a toast. Just the sight of it made him feel sick. 'Let's see if I can break my record, shall we?'

'We're closing,' she said, giving his table a perfunctory wipe as she set down his bill three hours later.

He reached for the money in his pocket and placed it on the table without even glancing at it. 'So, same again tomorrow?'

She looked at him with disbelief, the first time she had looked at him properly in hours. He had been sitting here for more than seven hours, all in. The skin on his face was red and tight and there was now more sugar than blood in his bloodstream. Sunstroke was a definite possibility tonight, to go with his black eye and broken thumb.

A glimmer of amusement climbed into her eyes at the beaten-up, bedraggled sight of him, and he felt his hopes soar. He'd happily break his leg, too, and it would all be worth it if she'd forgive him.

'What?' he grinned, feeling giddy in her gaze. She had always lost their staring contests when they were kids. He'd always known how to make her laugh and he crossed his eyes, doing exactly that.

She shook her head wearily as she grinned back, worn down by his stubbornness. 'You're an idiot.'

'I am,' he agreed. Insults were always a good sign; it was mannered reserve that set him on edge.

A moment pulsed, a moment in which he knew his entire summer hung in the balance, and he held his breath as he waited to see which way the axe would fall.

Finally she set down the cloth and pulled out the other chair, sinking into it with an exhausted groan. He watched how her eyes closed as she took the weight off her feet, the muscles in her long legs growing soft, her mouth parting as she tipped her head back and breathed deeply for several moments. His eyes raked over her with a yearning that would have frightened her if she had seen it, and he tried to remember the time – all those years – when she had been 'just Rafa': quiet and obedient compared to other girls, but also ticklish, and a fast runner, and a brilliant diver, and good at guessing riddles.

When exactly had she become more? He knew their kiss had changed her for ever in his eyes – he had spent the past year trying and failing to forget it – but what had been the trigger for it in the first place? It was the question his mind returned to, over and over, as he fell into the memories: hide-and-seek in the dark, tipsy on smuggled beer, Gina calling their names as they squeezed into the narrow gap in the trunk of one of the *monumentales*. The scent of her skin awakening something in him; that look in her eyes in the final moment before their lips met – clarity, comprehension, surrender.

He had tried to brush it off, putting it down to lust, hormones, drink and whatever else he could think of. He had returned to Rome as planned the next day, picking up his life – but he hadn't been able to forget it. And being back with her now, even in silence, even faced with hostility, he had the sense that his life was here. Rome had simply been distraction and noise.

'You're going to be in pain tomorrow,' she said, staring at the sea.

He shook his head, watching her. 'No. Everything's going to be better now.'

She squinted at his boldness and he watched her profile as she gazed at the horizon, seeing the tiny microspasms of her muscles even though her body was almost unnaturally still.

'You were right earlier, you know. What you said about Valentina.'

Her head whipped round as she pinned him with a surprised stare.

'. . . I did bring her here to make a point. I was a coward. I didn't know how you'd feel about me after what I'd done, and she was a way to . . . pretend nothing had happened.' He clicked his tongue against his teeth. 'But it was cruel. I hate that I hurt you.'

She made a small scoffing sound. 'You sound like your sister.'

'Because we've both behaved badly to you. You're such a good person, Raf, but me and Romy, we're . . . we're ruined.'

'Spoilt, certainly.' She watched him, still reluctant to forgive. A moment stretched out as she regarded him closely. 'What you said the other day, about things being difficult for you both. What did you mean? Romy's never made any suggestion in her letters that there were problems.'

He felt himself recoil at the question. Discretion was the utmost virtue in their family, but if he wanted any kind of chance of winning back Rafa's trust, he couldn't dodge the truth.

'Things are bad between our parents. Really bad,' he said quietly. 'Romy is convinced they're going to get divorced.'

She watched him. 'They're not going to get divorced,' she said, not unkindly.

'I keep trying to tell her that. If nothing else, the shame alone would deter our mother. But Romy . . . she gets so anxious and acts out.' He sighed, running a hand through his hair as he felt his own body tense. 'They behave as if nothing's wrong, that's the problem; we're all living with this pretence everything's fine, when it *clearly* isn't. I think her behaviour is a way of trying to . . . bait them? That perhaps she thinks if they have to acknowledge her situation, they'll have to deal with their own?' He shrugged, drumming his fingers nervily on the table. 'I don't know.'

She didn't respond for several moments, just looked straight at him, so clear-eyed it was like catching the wind in his hands. 'I'm sorry that's happening to your family, Cosi. It sounds awful.'

'It's not a justification, though, for how we behaved towards you,' he said quickly. 'I'm not trying to make excuses. Neither Romy nor I want to lose our friendship with you. It's the most important thing to both of us.'

Her eyes flashed in his direction. Did she hear the sincerity in his plea, even though it was only half true? He wanted more, but even friendship was a reach. As she herself had said, she was with Fon now; she'd moved on. This was the most he could hope for.

'. . . Our friendship is the most important thing,' she agreed finally.

'Yes? So you can forgive us?'

She barely hesitated. 'If you can forgive Fon.'

Fon? He was taken aback by the counter-charge. 'Well, it's not like he and I were ever close . . .'

'No, but he is my boyfriend now. And if we're going to . . . be friends, and spend time together this summer, you have to be able to get on.'

He felt her scrutiny as the words landed like hot coals on his skin.

'Can you get over what he did with your sister?' she asked.

With. Not *to*. The word choice was deliberate – mutual complicity, mutual guilt – and his eyes flashed up to hers. Clearly no one was forgiven yet.

'Well, can you?' she pressed.

Cosimo felt the answer catch in his throat. It wasn't Fon fucking his sister that provoked his rage, tormented him. '. . . Of course I can. Romy can handle herself.'

She watched him for a few moments more. Could she hear the lie quivering through his words?

'It's fine, Raf,' he insisted. 'I just want everything to go back to being how it was before.'

She looked down at the table and gave a small smile, as if she was having a silent conversation in her head and he was locked out of it. 'OK,' she shrugged. 'Then I guess it's all settled. Everything can go back to how it was before.'

She got up, but he caught her hand lightly, not wanting to let her go. 'You really mean it? We're really friends again?'

'We really are,' she nodded, looking down at him for a moment with an expression that sent electric jolts through his body. She smiled but when she slipped her hand from his, he felt like a kid glove being dropped to the pavement.

He watched as she walked away, the status quo restored. He listened to the sounds of her closing up the caffè – no more crashing and banging, no more anger. Just calm, steady routine, life continuing on as it always had. Peace had broken out and they were friends again.

He'd got what he'd come for. But it didn't feel like a victory.

Chapter 19

Rafaella

'Knock, knock.'

Rafaella looked up from her narrow bed, the book falling from her hand as she saw Romola's face peering round the doorway. '. . . Oh,' she said, unable to hide her surprise. She felt her heart switch up into a gallop, a flutter of happiness in her stomach.

Romola hesitated, looking terrified. 'Is it OK that I've come? Cosi said he saw you yesterday and that . . .' She shifted her weight, looking like she wanted to sprint away. 'But I can go if you'd rather . . .'

'No.'

Rafaella regarded her – she had lost weight and looked pale; she didn't look like she'd stepped outside all week. Romola had punished herself harder than Rafaella could ever have managed.

She scrambled from the bed and went towards her with arms outstretched, their embrace long and hard as their faces pressed into each other's shoulders and the terrible tension between them was finally crushed. Cosimo's drawn-out, ridiculous and stubborn apology on the beach yesterday had been followed up with bright smiles between them in church this morning, even though his black eye still looked sore and awkward whenever he moved his face.

'I'm sorry,' Romola said when they finally pulled apart, looking her straight in the eye this time.

'I know,' Rafaella nodded, appreciating the sincerity. 'But . . . it's done. In the past. Let's leave it behind us now.' She squeezed Romola's shoulder. 'You look like you need some sun. Shall we sit?'

Rafaella led the way to the small balcony outside, where two small wooden chairs were set. The farmhouse was large, arranged over two floors, with all its doorways and windows shadow-painted with blue trim. Her bedroom was positioned at the back of the house, looking over the crest of the hill and surveying the south-westerly aspect of the estate. Lines of olive trees, planted in diagonals, stretched away into the distance until they butted up against the oak forest that lay like a giant green lung between the port and Tricase town.

They sat down together on the chairs, currently drenched in sunlight, and automatically put their bare feet on the stone wall. They had spent many hours sitting here as young girls, talking into the night as the cicadas ticked and the stars came out. 'I always forget how beautiful your view is here,' Romola said, breaking the silence as they gazed out.

'No sea view, though.'

'Oh, overrated if you ask me. I mean, all you're really looking at is the horizon – a blue line that looks the same in Rimini as it does here . . .' Romola shrugged. 'The sea's only interesting when you're actually on it, looking back at land. This, though . . .! This could only be Puglia!'

Rafaella smiled at the overcompensation. Romola held an opinion on everything and she had nothing if not the strength of her convictions.

'Your dress is so pretty,' she said, her gaze wandering over Romola's sundress. 'I was admiring it in church earlier.'

'You were?'

The dress was lilac-and-white-striped cotton, with a square-cut neckline and mother-of-pearl buttons. 'Is it from your new designer?'

'Pucci?' Romola laughed. 'Oh, no! This is nothing. Just a –' She stopped herself. 'I mean, I do love it, though. It's so pretty, isn't it?' She gasped as an idea came to her. 'Why don't you try it on? It would look so much better on you than me!'

Rafaella smiled as she shook her head. As little girls, they had often swapped clothes, she and Gina prompting looks of amusement as they skipped through the port in silk, with Romola alongside in patched linens. More often than not, come summer's end, the local housekeeper would find clothes left behind on the bed as she closed up the house, with orders to give them to the girls now that Romola had 'outgrown' them.

But they were no longer little girls. Clearly. 'I'm not trying on your dress.'

'But I want you to have it!'

'Romy, we're not doing that. You don't need to give me something. I told you, it's behind us.'

Romola swallowed, and Rafaella could tell she felt awkward being diffident. It wasn't her usual role, but it felt difficult just reverting to their old footing again. No matter how hard they both wished it, things couldn't go back to exactly how they'd been.

'I wish you'd confided in me,' Rafaella said quietly.

Romola's head whipped round.

'Cosi told me when we spoke yesterday – about your parents' . . . difficulties.'

There was a horrified pause. 'He shouldn't have done that.'

'Don't be angry at him,' Rafaella said quickly, seeing how the alarm settled on her friend's face. 'I made him explain. I couldn't forgive until I had some sort of sense of . . . why.'

'Yes, well, it doesn't really follow logic.'

'Pain never does.'

Romola seemed to shrink in the chair. 'I guess I thought if I hurt him, like he hurts us . . .' A small noise escaped her, and she looked away. 'Oh God, I'm such a terrible person.'

'No, you're not,' Rafaella said quickly. 'You're just suffering.'

'. . . I feel . . . I feel so ashamed that this is what we are. People think we're so wonderful! A noble family with no problems! But where's the nobility in our father sleeping with our mother's friends? With the nannies? With his own –'

She stopped herself as her voice rose through the octaves. She was trembling and Rafaella put a hand over hers. 'You're not your father. You get to choose who you want to be . . . You're eighteen years old, and your whole life is ahead of you. Be better than him.'

'Be better than him.' Romola echoed the words, as if trying them for size. She gave a small snort of derision. 'Well, that shouldn't be hard. It's a low bar.'

Rafaella gave a small laugh. 'You're a good person, Romy. Don't forget that.'

'I'll try,' Romola said, squeezing her hand and looking touched.

Rafaella looked back out over the trees, wishing she didn't have to be the one doing all the forgiving. It was draining having to be bigger than she felt, saying words she scarcely meant. Telling Cosimo they could be friends had almost undone her yesterday.

'. . . Hey, so what are you wearing to the wedding?'

'Silvana's made me a dress.'

'Could I see it?'

'Of course.' Rafaella got up and returned a moment later with the blue dress her sister had just finished. It was looser and longer than she had wished now it had the extra panel and lace hem her mother had insisted on after coming to her last fitting. In fact, it was so modest, it looked like the kind of dress they might have worn at first communion.

Romola's smile froze. 'Ah,' she said diplomatically. '. . . Sweet.'

Rafaella giggled at the true Romola coming through at last. 'I *know*. It's terrible! But Mamma got involved.' She rolled her eyes.

'I've got a brilliant idea! We should go shopping and buy you a new one!'

'Where? With what?'

'My treat!'

'I've already said no to any of that.'

'But you can't go to your sister's wedding dressed as a ten-year-old!'

Rafaella shrugged as she hung the dress back on the wardrobe door. 'Who really cares how I'm dressed? It's Silvana's day.' She came to sit down again, stretching out her long, tanned legs.

'Yes – but you're not invisible, you know,' Romola protested. 'You deserve to look pretty too.'

'I know that.'

'Hmm.' Romola looked at her doubtfully. She watched Rafaella watching her father and Dado working in one of the groves; it was Sunday, but they had gone straight out after Mass, worried about a possible olive fruit fly infestation. 'You know, Cosi is *really* happy now that we're all friends again.'

Rafaella suppressed a flinch. 'Me too. I've missed you both.'

Romola gave a small laugh. 'He had to go without dinner

last night. He felt so sick he couldn't stomach anything! And he's got a temperature. Mamma can't understand what came over him, sitting out like that!'

'He was such a pain! He sat there *all* day, holding up a table that other customers could have used – but every time I went near him to get him to go, he just ordered another Coke!'

'Well, thank God you gave in! He said he was almost sick, but he was braced to go back down every day for as long as it took.'

'That would have been dangerous. Gina would have given him a much harder time than me!'

'Yes, he said he was banking on breaking you early.'

'Well, I have always been the soft touch,' she shrugged self-deprecatingly.

Romola reached over and touched her arm. 'No. You're strong, just in a quiet way.'

Rafaella gave her a small smile, but looked away.

She didn't feel strong. She felt stranded, beached. Stuck on a rock she didn't want to be on. She was glad she could put the incident with Romola behind her, but with Cosimo . . . she didn't know how to rewind her feelings for him. He wanted them to be just how they had been before, but the kiss had changed everything for her. She kept trying to forget the way she had felt in his arms that night. She was a realist – she knew her future lay here in the port, not in some fancy villa in Rome. Her daydreams of a life with Cosimo could never become a reality. But she had peered into Pandora's box, and what she'd found there had ruined her. No matter what her head told her, her heart said differently.

In the months after he'd left, she'd pined, waiting for a letter or at least some passing comment from Romola that he had asked after her. Nothing had come except careless mentions of his many conquests in the capital, and she'd finally forced herself to face facts. Cosimo might never be hers, but the way he'd made her feel ... she could find that with someone else, surely, just as he had? For five months now, she had been chasing that thrill with her boyfriend, with scant success. Only on a handful of occasions had Fon made her catch her breath, and that was usually accidental rather than by design. She knew the scarcity of Cosimo's presence brought novelty, excitement and glamour that Fon couldn't possibly compete with; but why, with Fon, did it always feel like she was kissing a friend, whereas with Cosimo it had felt like kissing the stars? What was she doing wrong?

Romola flexed her foot, and Rafaella admired her painted toenails. 'You know, it's so weird being here when you and Gina are working all the time.'

'Yeah ... sorry,' she shrugged. 'No more school holidays now. Summer is just hotter for us, not different.'

Romola looked immediately embarrassed that her seasons were marked by different locations: Cortina in the winter, Tuscany at Easter ... For Rafaella, the port was her only landscape, and living and working here all year round were her only options.

'Not that that's your fault,' Rafaella said quickly. 'It's how it is.'

'I just wish it wasn't,' Romola sighed.

'Me too. But it just means we have to make the most of the days we do get together.'

'I agree. Like on Sundays.'

Rafaella looked over at her, hearing a pointedness to the words and seeing in her friend's bright eyes that she had a plan. Romola never didn't have a plan.

She gave a mischievous grin that was just like her brother's. 'What are you doing this afternoon?' she asked, straightening in her chair.

Rafaella smiled back, a bubble of excitement in her stomach. Whatever this was leading to, she knew she would do it. '. . . Nothing special.'

'Because Cosi and Fede want to go down to El Ciolo.'

El Ciolo was a small swimming cove, far south on the road to Santa María di Leuca. The cliffs were precipitous and especially high there, but the water was beautiful.

'That's a fair way.' Rafaella pushed her feet against the wall and tipped onto the back legs of the chair, trying to push down her excitement at the prospect of a day out with the Franchettis. With Cosimo. 'How are they getting there?'

'Fede's going to take his new car with the food and towels. You and Gina could go with him, or ride on the scooters with me and Cosi. Whichever you prefer.'

'Gina knows about this?'

'She's outside with the others, waiting for us.'

Rafaella almost fell off the chair. '*What?* . . . You mean while we've been talking in here all this time . . .?'

Romola jumped up, looking delighted with her well-executed surprise. 'I had to see for myself that things were really all right between us. They understood. But we should really get going now.'

'But wait – I can't just . . . go! What do I need?' Rafaella asked, following her into the room and turning on the spot in a panic. Cosimo was outside?

'A bikini.'

'That's it?'

Romola shrugged. 'That's it.'

'Mamma, we're going to El Ciolo,' Rafaella said, putting her head into the kitchen a few minutes later. Her mother was making ravioli, rolling a bowl along on its rim to score the divisions.

'Be back by seven!' she said in her best warning voice. 'I need you to help me with Silvana's veil.'

'*Si*, Mamma,' Rafaella nodded, even though she was terrible at embroidery.

They walked outside to find Cosimo and Gina sitting on the two Lambrettas and chatting with Fede, who was leaning against a brand-new bright yellow *cinquecento*. The tiny cars were the latest sensation, found everywhere in Rome, but not yet down here. In fact, this was the first one Rafaella had seen in real life.

'Nice car, Fede,' she smiled.

'Thanks!' he said, patting the roof affectionately.

'Bikes aren't good enough for him,' Romola teased.

'That's not true! It's just, I need to study in the bigger libraries sometimes, and it's too far by bike,' he protested.

Rafaella watched him. Was that true? Or did he have other reasons for wanting to be able to travel far and wide?

'So – everything all right?' Cosimo asked, looking at his sister anxiously.

'*Si!*' Romola said, wrapping an arm around Rafaella's shoulder in proof and squeezing her gleefully.

Cosimo and Gina visibly relaxed. The cold war had ended.

'How are we doing this, then?' Cosimo asked. 'Fede's saying he has to stop on the way to collect something.'

Or see someone? They would be passing Marina Serra to get to El Ciolo, and Rafaella couldn't forget what she'd seen there.

'. . . So one of you can ride with me and the other with Romy.'

Rafaella felt herself stall. She should definitely go with Romola . . .

'I'll go with Romy,' Gina shrugged. 'Seeing as I'm already sitting on her bike.'

'Great, so then you're with me.' Cosimo gave Rafaella the most platonic smile she'd ever seen.

'. . . OK,' she said, going over to him and positioning herself on the scooter side-on.

'Actually, you'd be safer sitting astride,' he said, half turning his head towards her. 'It's ten kilometres and it'll be better balanced for me on a fast road . . .'

'Oh . . . sure,' she said, changing position and swinging her leg across so that her body was behind his. She sat as far back on the seat as she could.

Fede climbed into the little car and patted his door excitedly. 'See you down there, then?'

'See you down there!' Romola said, switching on her ignition and looking over at Rafaella and Cosimo. She paused. 'I know it's a disgusting prospect, but you will have to actually touch my brother if you don't want to die!'

'Well, obviously,' Rafaella muttered, inching forward. 'I was just being . . . considerate . . . It's hot out here.'

'Certainly is,' Gina quipped, watching them intently.

'Race you, Cosi!' Romola cried, pulling away in a flurry of revs, making Gina squeal and punch one arm in the air.

'No, Ro!' Cosimo called after her. 'I'm not . . .!' He half turned back to Rafaella with a sigh. 'I'm not racing her.'

'I'm glad to hear it.'

He nodded. 'We'll just take our time and get there safely. Enjoy the views.'

'Sounds great. Will your thumb be OK?' She looked at the bulky dressing on it.

'Oh, that. Ignore it. Looks worse than it is. I've only kept it on to appease Mamma. It's actually fine. I'll take it off when we get there.'

'OK.' Beneath her hands, she could feel the vibration of his voice through his chest. She could detect the thud of his heartbeat against his ribs. She could feel every muscle in his back as he moved, kicking off the stand.

Cosimo cleared his throat. 'Hold me tighter,' he said, pulling on her arms. 'Just to be safe.'

She shuffled in closer to his body, feeling her legs flank his, her body fully pressed against his back now.

Was it her imagination or had his pulse quickened?

He revved the engine once, twice, and as he pulled away, she rested her cheek against his shoulder.

Just to be safe.

Chapter 20

Fon

Allegra cut over the water, throwing up a seam in their wake as they sped down the coast. Dante hadn't needed telling twice when Fon had relayed what Gina Crespi's mother had told him at the beach; they both understood the risk. Territory, once gained, could never be ceded.

The sea was busy. Summer was in full swing now, and the locals were out today as well as the visitors. Sundays were always crowded with small rowing boats and fishing craft hugging the creviced coastline, but *Allegra* didn't count as a local boat. Her size, speed and glossy blue hull drew admiring glances from those idling on the sailing yachts as the two brothers flew past, bare-chested with the wind in their faces.

Dante looked over and grinned, as if Fon's thoughts were bubbles he could catch. They had grown closer this summer than Fon had ever thought possible. Against all odds, he was catching him up, and his decision to join Dante in his contraband enterprise appeared to be the right one; their father had come up to him last night, after the latest envelope had been handed over, and clapped his shoulder proudly. No words – but Fon knew that he knew. He approved.

Ahead lay the small inlet, its high, stepped cliffs leading back to a small sandy beach, some sea caves on the approach. There was talk of building a bridge to span the cove, but at the height required – forty metres high and a narrow road – it was an engineering riddle.

From the road, the approach down was via a narrow, steep, winding dirt track flanked by drystone walls, but by sea they could simply curl in as easily as Rafaella tossing her long hair. Dante pulled a wide arc into the cove, sending up spray in a rooster's tail behind them as Fon's eyes scanned for her, finding her quickly on the rocks. He recognized her by the pale blue bikini she wore, which always made her skin look so tanned – the one with little bows on the hips. Her hair was slicked back, dripping down her shoulders, and she was clambering up, her long legs at full stretch, laughing and calling out to Fede as he prepared for a dive.

A few metres higher up, Gina lay on a towel beside Romola, the two of them eating peaches, talking and watching the others. Fon tensed. In his haste, he had forgotten Romola might be here; the last time he had seen her, he'd been inside her ... She was wearing an orange, pink and yellow swirled bikini, the top pushing her breasts up provocatively, the briefs extra low-slung on her hips. She was flaunting her body, wanting attention, even though no one there was watching.

Certainly not him.

But Romola wasn't his main problem. Clearly, Rafaella had forgiven her now too, and that meant the Franchettis were no longer *personae non gratae*. If Fede and Romola were here, then . . .

He scanned the cove for Cosimo, knowing he had to be here too, and found him seconds later in the water, swimming in and calling something up to his brother. Rafaella joined in too, saying something that made Fede laugh. His arms dropped down onto his thighs, the sound echoing around the bay.

Fon felt his jealousy curdle at the sight of their close friendship, those old familiar feelings of being an outsider roused again, that prickling sense of inadequacy needling him. They all looked like great friends once more, the way they'd always been over the years: so tight, so intimate, never letting anyone else in. All his life, Fon had watched from the sidelines, seeing how everyone came alive in their company as the rich kids threw open their gates and hosted parties and carelessly told stories about a world he would never see, much less be able to offer.

He remembered a time, many years ago now, when he'd tried to find an opening into the group. They had all been playing bat and ball on the beach and someone had mishit, sending the ball far out into the sea. Fon, lying on the promenade with Luigi and Gino and watching from a distance, had taken his chance and called out that he would get it for them, diving in. But by the time he'd swum back with it, they had gone – the game abandoned, the lost ball forgotten as they went back to the plush villa in search of other distractions.

The boys had torn him up over it, laughing at his pathetic eagerness to be their friend, and he had taken a step back then, cutting off the Franchettis at any opportunity. They only ever extended cool manners to him anyway, but he saw the reserve grow in Cosimo's eyes as the slights mounted up and an unspoken enmity began to breed.

This summer, it was coming to a slow boil. His moment of madness with Romola had thrown him into the heart of their dynamic, upsetting the fragile balance of their ecosystem. Suddenly he was a central character, whether Cosimo liked it or not, and Fon wasn't going to give up his advantage now. Especially when Rafaella was *his* girlfriend.

He watched, still unnoticed by them, as the boat glided in. How long had they been here, he wondered, before he'd caught wind of their plans? An hour? More?

Dante cut the engines and threw the anchor out. It landed with a heavy splash, and finally Cosimo and the others turned. Gina sat straighter, recognizing Dante at once, her body taut with excitement even at this distance. Romola didn't stir, though she stared back at Fon like a cat on a wall. Fede hadn't noticed them yet and he executed a perfect dive into the water. But Rafaella . . . she had fallen still on the rocks and was shading her eyes, trying to see Fon better, as if trying to believe he was really here.

Fede resurfaced, blinking the water from his eyes as Fon jumped onto the front of the boat. '*Ciao!*' he called, waving his arm widely.

No one replied. Did they not recognize him, perhaps?

'Do you want to join us on board? We've brought drinks!' he called again, but no one replied to the offer, and he felt suddenly awkward. He felt himself grow small . . . He was being iced out. They didn't want him here. He'd overstepped.

'Hey!'

He looked down to find Fede treading water beside the boat and smiling up at him warmly. Saving him from public humiliation. '*Ciao*, Fede.'

'*Ciao*, Fon. Fancy seeing you here.'

'We needed to give the boat a run. We're testing the engines; the inlet manifold sounds a bit loose.'

'Ah.' Fede nodded.

'You?'

'We're just swimming, brought a picnic. Thought we'd make a day of it . . .' Fede looked over and saw Dante standing at the helm with an expectant look. 'Why don't you both join us? There's plenty of food.'

Fon hesitated, turning towards his brother, who looked

less than pleased by the lukewarm reaction to their arrival. Only Gina had seemed glad to see them.

'*Ciao*, Fede,' Dante said, before calling over to where Cosimo now stood on the rocks. '. . . *Ciao*, Cosi!'

Cosimo shifted his weight as if startled by the casual greeting, clearly remembering their last, unfriendly meeting when they'd fought in the sand. Fon saw him glance quickly towards Rafaella as if checking for something before replying. '. . . *Ciao*, Dante.'

Dante smiled, seeming satisfied that a fragile peace had been brokered. 'Sure, why not?' he said, taking Fede up on his invitation. After all, it hardly needed to be pointed out that the brothers were dating two of the three girls in their group.

He dived overboard with no preamble and popped up a moment later, flicking his hair back, no hands. 'Come on, Fon,' he said casually, holding onto the anchor chain and bobbing with the movement of the boat before letting go and heading for the rocks.

Fon dived in after him, surprised to find Fede waiting for him as he surfaced. 'The water's lovely, isn't it?' Fede asked. 'Always so clear here.'

Fon nodded dumbly. He wasn't used to social conversation. In his house, the men didn't speak unless something needed saying – the nets need mending; fetch the eggs. They didn't discuss the clarity of the water.

They swam in together and began climbing the cliffs. The rocks were sharp underfoot but easy to grab, and they were soon up with the others. Rafaella was sitting on the towel with the girls by the time they reached the ledge, beads of water still drying on her skin. She looked nervous, like a doe caught in an open meadow, as she patted her hair dry. This was their first time all together as a group, the various factions socializing as one, and Fon knew it was up to him to prove to her that only she mattered to him, and not Romola.

'*Ciao*, Rafa,' he said, going over and kissing her on the mouth. He felt the weight of everyone's gaze upon him as he claimed what was his – and by distinction, discarded what was not. '. . . *Ciao*, Romola,' he said, nodding briefly in her direction. 'Gina.'

'Well, what a coincidence this is,' Cosimo said stiffly. He was standing astride the rocks like a young god, trying his best to look nonchalant, but Fon could see he was rattled by their unexpected appearance.

'Not really. We ran into your mother,' Dante said, turning to Gina, 'and she told us your plans.' He shrugged. 'What can I say? I was missing you.'

'I find that hard to believe, given you've not called me in days,' Gina replied with her usual arch tone, but the look in her eyes was giving her away as he sat himself by her feet.

'I've been very busy . . .' he murmured as he began lightly stroking the arch of her right foot with his thumb while maintaining eye contact. 'But that doesn't mean I haven't been thinking of you every single minute . . . You've cast some kind of wicked spell on me, Signorina Crespi.' He winked, and Gina looked as if she might slide off the rock. Fon could have sworn his brother had tied a string around her heart and was slowly pulling it towards him, hand over hand.

Fon stood awkwardly, unable to find an obvious place where he should sit too – there was no space on the towel with the girls, and sitting behind Rafaella would set him outside the group. He turned and looked back down at the cove instead. He had only ever been here a couple of times – his father always used to say it was too far to justify the fuel. But that wasn't something they had to worry about anymore.

Far below, the water sparkled an emerald green so clear

that he could see the fish darting. Fede had been right; the water really was lovely here. There were a few groups of sunbathers on the beach, some others floating in the shallows, but the trek down there was so steep, most people went to the other coves with easier access. Usually only people with boats came in here.

'Do you really think they'll build a bridge?' he asked no one in particular.

'Yes,' Fede nodded authoritatively. 'The permission has already been granted.'

Dante gave a small laugh. 'Well, of course it has.'

'What do you mean by that?' Fede asked, seeming puzzled by his tone.

'Only that your father is not slow to issue building permits,' Dante said with a shrug. 'He's a great friend to "developers", I hear.'

Fede's mouth set in a grim line. 'You shouldn't believe all you read in the newspapers.'

'You assume he can read?' Romola asked tartly, quick-witted and sharp-tongued as ever.

Instantly the sky contracted around them. It was a return to form, the sort of imperious comment she would always have made in the past – and in the past, the Giannellis would have had to take it. But her position was no longer unassailable. She had compromised herself with Fon, and everyone here knew it.

Everyone but Romola, it seemed. She had missed a lot during her retreat after the party.

'But he's right, of course,' she continued, oblivious to the new order. 'Papa *is* a great friend to developers – and many other influential people besides. He's got the prime minister in his pocket. He *owns* the entire cabinet.'

'Now who's believing everything they read?' Dante smirked.

'Oh, it's no vain boast.'

'No?'

Romola shrugged. 'We've all seen it for ourselves.'

'Seen what?'

'The diary our father keeps. He's got all their secrets—'

'Romola!' Fede snapped, shooting her a sharp look. He didn't like immodesty. 'That's enough.'

'What?' she shrugged. 'I'm only giving him some friendly advice not to upset the wrong people.' She flashed a look in Dante's direction, refusing to be intimidated by the older man.

There was a pause, and Fon wondered whether the ceasefire had fallen already. But to his surprise—

'Well, then, amen to that,' Dante said with rare docility. 'I'll try to remember my place next time. What would I know about such things? I am, after all, the son of a humble fisherman.'

A tension settled over the group – there wasn't much that was humble about the speedboat on which they'd arrived – and Fon watched as Dante caught Gina's eye and winked again, as if he'd refrained from arguing just for her sake. Gina smiled, grateful and flattered by the courtesy.

'Well, when they do build the bridge, I'll jump it,' Cosimo said with a grin.

'Of course you will!' Romola rolled her eyes, bored by her brother's boast. 'Because that's absolutely worth dying for!'

'Is it deep enough?' Fon asked, peering down as he looked over the edge. The water quickly ran from emerald green through to sapphire blue. It was an innocuous enough question – or so he had thought.

'Of course. It's just a question of nerve.'

Fon immediately heard the jibe in the comment; Cosimo was trying to make him look small in front of the girls, thinking he was still dealing with the old Fon of yesteryear. 'Yeah, you're right. It wouldn't bother me.'

'No?' Cosimo chuckled, clearly disbelieving.

'Of course not.'

'Well, you could always jump from here,' Cosimo suggested. 'Why wait years for them to build the bridge? It would only be a few metres higher than this anyway.'

The girls stiffened as the boys' boasts began to escalate.

'What? No! You can't jump from all the way up here!' Gina protested. They'd been jumping from the rocks halfway down a few minutes earlier, but up here they had to be thirty-something metres high.

But it was too late. The gauntlet had been thrown down and Fon knew he had to act. He couldn't lose face in front of his brother, nor Rafaella. 'I'm game if you are.'

'. . . Sure. No problem.'

Fon saw the way Rafaella's head whipped round as Cosimo was brought into his own dare. 'But you can't!' she gasped, protesting now too.

'Rafa's right, this is madness, Cosi – even for you! It's too high,' Romola said, looking alarmed.

Fon waited for someone's – anyone's, his own girlfriend's – attention to lift off Cosimo and settle upon him instead, but he might as well have been invisible. It was several moments before Rafaella even seemed to remember him; her gaze always swung to Cosimo as if he was her magnetic north.

'Fon, you could be hurt,' Fede said.

'Oh, don't worry about me. *I'll* be fine,' Fon replied, but he was surprised to see Fede's genuine concern.

A beat pulsed between them before Fede, seeing his appeal to reason had failed, turned to his brother instead. 'Cosi,' he said warningly. 'Don't be rash.' He was looking at Cosimo with open alarm. Fon knew his own brother felt no such apprehension for him – Dante would rather see Fon die in an act of bravery than survive as a coward. He had to be bold. Grasp the nettle.

'We'll dive, yes?' he said, and began swinging his arms in alternating criss-crosses over his body, warming up and hiding his nerves. 'Jumping's far too boring.'

Fede looked at him again with a silent entreaty to stop raising the stakes, and Fon understood suddenly the connection between them: they were the sensible ones in their families, the diplomats, the ones no one would think capable of anything reckless or wild. Cosimo always outshone Fede, just as Dante always outshone Fon . . . Fon swallowed, wishing he could oblige Fede in this, but it was too late.

Cosimo showed no sign of backing down. 'Well, of course,' he said. 'It's not worth bothering with a jump.'

'No, please,' Rafaella said now, pushing up onto her knees and beseeching them both. 'I really don't like this. It's far too risky.'

'Don't worry – *Cosi* will be fine,' Romola said pointedly, and Fon found her gaze pinned on him with contempt, as if he was something she'd found stuck to her shoe. She seemed to have forgotten that she had been the one to throw herself upon him at the party, her lips on his neck and her hands scrabbling at his belt.

Wordlessly, he moved right to the edge of the rocks and looked down. The cliffs were steep and vertiginous here, but small rockfalls caused bulging in some places. If they misjudged and picked the wrong spot, or didn't leap forward far enough, they would break their necks.

Fon was regretting ever opening his mouth. He was regretting chasing over here out of fear that Cosimo would lure Rafaella away from him, as he did in his nightmares . . . But he also knew those fears weren't unfounded. There was a magnetism between the two of them that he could detect even though they were standing apart, not looking at one another. It was silent, invisible, but it was there. He knew it even if the others did not – even if they themselves did not!

It breathed and had a pulse. It was alive in spite of absence and distance and arguments. In spite of *him*, her boyfriend.

Cosimo had chosen his spot a few feet away and, as he glanced across, Fon saw the uneasiness in his face as he checked out his rival's position. Was Fon's better? Safer? The bravado had slipped at last and as Cosimo looked straight at him, bruised and strangely sunburnt, Fon glanced pointedly at Cosimo's injured hand. The thumb wasn't splinted now – taken off, no doubt, while he swam – but it was swollen and bruised black and blue. From this height, they would need to use their flexed hands as buffers to absorb the impact and protect their heads . . .

He felt his confidence grow. 'Ready?' he smiled.

Cosimo nodded. For Fon, this boiled down to honour; for Cosimo, ego. They were locked in a battle of wills and neither would fall back.

'Dante, count us down,' Fon said, swinging his arms up, feeling himself become bigger, taller, more expansive . . . The momentum was with him. It was now or never.

'Three!' Dante cried from behind them – the only person here who wanted to see this happen – and Fon braced himself for the coming moment when he would become airborne: he envisaged his feet leaving the rocks as he soared up and outwards, as if leaping over a rainbow.

'Two!'

He imagined Rafaella's eyes on him, tracking his flight, before gravity caught him in its clutches and he began the inevitable plunge down. He saw it all.

'. . . One!'

Chapter 21

Cosimo

Cosimo felt the bone break – again – as he blasted through the surface of the water. From the height they had dived from, it was like hitting concrete. Unable to hold the protective pose, his arms parted, exposing his head to some of the impact, and he felt stunned as he arrowed ever downwards, into the blue. Pain suffused his body, rippling through bone and muscle, and he had to fight the instinct to open his mouth and cry out.

This had been a mistake. Pride before the proverbial fall. He shouldn't have goaded Fon in the first place; he should have known he wouldn't back down – not in front of his brother . . . Rafaella . . . all of them. He'd thought he had the measure of his rival, the boy who had always hung back and watched from the shadows – he well remembered how Fon had trailed them as kids, peering over the garden wall while they splashed in the round pool, wanting to be included but always overlooked. Now that he was finally having his moment in the sun, there was no way he would step aside, not for anything.

What was it, this unarticulated rivalry driving them both to risk life and limb? Cosimo knew why he hated Fon – he had two very good reasons to despise him, as far as he could see – but why did Fon hate him so much? Was Fon's contempt for him the reason he'd fucked Romola, even though it risked everything with Rafaella? Had it been some kind of power play?

His body curved naturally as his descent slowed through the water, easing him upwards again, and he surfaced a few moments later with a gasp, his hand limp and throbbing as he kicked and took some breaths. He groaned loudly as the air hit his face and the pain in his thumb redoubled itself. He opened his eyes to see a row of concerned faces staring down.

'Oh my God, Cosi!' Romola cried, scolding him. 'We thought you'd knocked yourself unconscious!'

How long had he been under? 'Well, thanks for rushing to my aid, then! Don't all jump at once!'

From down here, they were almost indistinct, and yet he could make out Romola and Gina and Rafaella and Dante and Fede and . . .

Fon.

Fon was staring back down at him, too.

Cosimo blinked in confusion as realization slowly dawned . . . He hadn't done it. Fon had chickened out.

In disbelief and shock, he threw himself backwards in the water like a breaching whale. '*Woohoo!*' he yelled, a mighty war cry that seemed to gather energy from the deepest part of his soul, ricocheting off the cliffs, sounding into the caves. He felt euphoria building inside him, blocking out the pain in his hand and the ringing in his head.

He had won! Faced him down, in front of them all!

Her!

But as quickly as it had come, his joy dissipated. Oh God, what had he done? Rafaella had been protective of Fon on the beach yesterday, insisting Cosimo forgive him as she had done. Instead, Cosimo – always rash – had humiliated him at the first opportunity.

He was an idiot! Impetuous, vainglorious . . . Those were always his father's complaints about him anyway, and perhaps he was right.

Cosimo submerged himself again as he swam back to the base of the cliffs and slowly, flinchingly, began to climb the rocks. His thumb was throbbing but he used his other fingers to hook onto the handholds and pull himself up.

The others were waiting with apprehensive expressions as he finally reached the ledge. There were no cheers or congratulations. They all knew what he'd done. Dante looked mutinous, his hand proprietorial upon Gina's bare calf, his fingertips leaving white impressions in her skin when he moved.

'Did you hurt your hand again?' Romola asked, immediately noticing the strange way he was holding it and rushing over.

'It's fine,' he said quickly. 'Agh,' he gasped as his sister turned it over; the swelling was already doubling.

'Clearly not,' she said, making him wince as she gently tried to move it. 'You idiot! Mamma will kill you!'

'It's fine,' he muttered. 'Just a thumb.'

'I hope it wasn't my jaw that broke it?' Dante asked, lightly mocking and trying to regain a footing against his brother's humiliation.

Cosimo held his tongue – he'd done enough damage for one hour – as Romola returned to her place on the towel beside Rafaella. He noticed she wasn't looking at him, and neither was Fon.

He'd really messed up. Too late, he realized he should have held back. Always too late. He acted before he could think.

'Well, let's eat,' Fede said, throwing Cosimo an irritated look as he began opening up the picnic hamper Signora Cinzia had prepared. He brought out small containers of fried fishes, olives, *bombette* and *cartellate*. 'I, for one, am starving.'

As they ate, Romola began recounting a story about a disastrous shooting trip in Tuscany where the host had accidentally shot his own dog, mistaking it for a boar. Cosimo watched how Rafaella and Gina hung on her every word, eyes shining as they waited for the inevitable punchline. She'd always been the natural leader of their trio but she no longer eclipsed them in the way she once had.

Nonetheless, he saw his sister returning to herself, recognizing that she had been forgiven and things were settling back into their old order. Summers in the port had always been about life lived more deeply – music, laughter, pink drinks and pasta – but the girls' estrangement had felt like an echo of the problems in their family, in which everything was slowly fading to white and silence.

Their father – oblivious to his family's domestic dramas – was back in the city, of course, their mother drifting through empty flower-scented rooms, beautiful and bored. Even Fede, ever the diligent scholar, had taken to escaping the silence for long tours on his scooter, and the little ones preferred the red dust and chaos of their pastoral adventures on the agricola to the lush greenery of the villa garden.

But sitting here, eating and listening as the others talked, he felt their life colouring up again, the blood pumping once more through their veins. They were all together like the old days – just with two more faces in the crowd. For Rafaella's sake, he knew he had to accept it. And for Gina's, too; anyone could see by the way she looked at Dante that she was smitten. Keeping the peace meant accepting the Giannellis were part of their landscape now.

Fon was sitting on Rafaella's other side, a gap of less than a centimetre between their legs as they listened to Romola's story, and Cosimo found himself watching it with the intensity of a hawk to a mouse – as if his own entire existence inhabited that tiny space; as if he could somehow lever a distance between them and keep them apart, off the path of what Gina had suggested was increasingly an inevitable destiny.

Would Rafaella really marry him?

He watched them together, trying to get a reading of what they were to one another. Despite their proximity, Fon was sullen and distant and cold – although that was no surprise, not right now. Cosimo's glory had come at great cost to Fon's pride.

For Rafaella's sake, Cosimo knew he should have been more generous and never tried to bait her boyfriend, much less go head to head with him . . . But that was like asking a lion to clip its own claws, because he couldn't tame how he felt. Desire was like water, impossible to turn around. At best, it could be held back or redirected – but he had tried both of those tactics, and it was still there.

He'd never known this torment. Girls everywhere flocked to him but Rafaella felt unreachable. On the scooter on the way down here, he had driven slowly, pointing out the house that had burned down the other week, pretending to care about the view; anything to draw out the moments while she was holding onto him. The feel of her body pressed against him, soft and taut all at once, made his stomach drop and loins stir, and when she'd pressed her cheek to his back he'd been assailed with a violent tenderness that made him almost skid the bike. She aroused every emotion in him across the spectrum but was wholly oblivious to it.

He watched as her leg gradually leaned against Fon's, closing the tiny gap in which he'd tried to lever some hope. It was only a casual intimacy – not a kiss, nor even the touch of a hand – but Cosimo felt himself snuffed out.

Chapter 22

Rafaella

'*Mamma mia! Mamma mia!*'

Her mother's wails rang through the house and Rafaella heard the sound of curious feet slapping on the terracotta floors before there was another cry: 'Get out! *Basta!*'

Rafaella reached her door in time to see her little brother Gio being sent away with a flea in his ear, unsuccessful in passing along the message that the Carosas had arrived outside. The wedding party was due to start their procession to church, but inside the farmhouse everything was in disarray.

Gio, like their father and Dado, was wearing his Sunday suit with a pale pink rose in his jacket buttonhole. Rafaella too was ready, wearing her new, limp blue dress. It never would have passed Silvana's scrutiny if she hadn't been so taken up with her own gown, but Rafaella had meant what she'd said to Romola that Sunday afternoon before they'd gone to El Ciolo: it didn't matter how she looked. She was far more concerned that her sister – hollow-eyed from late nights at the atelier and secretive about the design – was planning some sort of sartorial coup, only revealing the dress when there was no time left in which to change it.

From the cries echoing through the house as she walked down the hall to her sister's room, she feared the worst. She could hear the two women bickering even before she had opened the door.

'. . . Mamma?'

Silvana and her mother, both wet-eyed, looked back at her as Rafaella gasped. The bride was indeed a revolutionary, a wasp-waisted corset unapologetically announcing itself, straddling the hips over a full satin skirt. The lacework – as Silvana had promised – covered the corset and décolleté all the way up to her throat, and her arms were covered with tight bracelet sleeves, but that was scant comfort for their mother, who couldn't ignore the shock value of an undergarment being worn as an overgarment.

'Do you see what she has done?' their mother cried, throwing her hands up. 'How can she wear this? *This?*'

'Mamma, please,' Silvana cried, wheeling on her heel and pacing the room. 'This is the fashion now! In all the movies—'

'*Movies?* It is your wedding dress! You will be in church!'

'Yes, and look – my arms are covered. My neck is covered. My legs—'

'I see your ankles!'

'Who cares about my ankles, Mamma?' Silvana cried. 'They are not blasphemous!'

'Ai-ai!' their mother cried, wringing her hands. 'Father Tommaso! He will not marry you! Luchino will walk out!'

Rafaella came further into the room, putting an arm around their mother and feeling her shake. 'Mamma, it's not so bad as you think. Silvana is right. These are the fashions now.'

'But not here!'

'Everything always gets here eventually.' Rafaella looked at her sister, seeing how her dark hair had been pulled back tightly, a narrow trellis of lacework pinned along her centre parting beneath the veil. 'I think she looks beautiful.'

Silvana smiled gratefully, but their mother could not be mollified. 'No! We are disgraced!'

'Mamma, no. See? She has white gloves, too. She is perfectly modest – nobody will—' A knock interrupted her.

'Gio mio, if you don't scram!' their mother yelled.

To everyone's surprise, Romola peered round the door. Like Rafaella, she gasped. 'Silvana! Your dress!'

Irma Parisi gave a cry as the denunciations began.

'– It is the most beautiful I have ever seen!'

Irma stopped mid-wail and stared at her. '*Che?*'

'Signora Parisi, you must be so proud!' Romola exclaimed, rushing into the room and clutching her by the hand. She was wearing a sensational full-skirted navy net dress with red polka dots, and it was a testament to Silvana's creativity that she still looked second-best in the room. 'Never, anywhere, have I seen a wedding dress as beautiful as this!'

'*Che?*' Irma whispered again.

'*Si!* Mamma took me to Florence for the couture and there was nothing, *nothing*, so lovely as this! *Si bellissima!* But *modesto!*'

Rafaella looked across at Silvana, the two sisters catching each other's eye. How long had Romola been standing out there? She had to know that her opinion, as the duke's daughter, carried weight. They watched as Irma blotted her eyes, standing a little taller as she looked back at her eldest daughter, trying to see her with a new gaze.

'Silvana, you must promise me – promise me, when I become a bride, you will make my dress,' Romola insisted. 'You must promise me now or I won't let you leave this room!'

Silvana laughed. '*Certo!* If that is your wish.'

'Then I shall tell Mamma it is agreed!' Romola proclaimed, walking around her as if she was a mannequin, hands clasped over her heart as she marvelled at all the little features – the pleated detailing of the corset on the hips, the lace-covered buttons . . . 'Thousands of hours must have gone into creating this.'

'*Si*,' Silvana agreed wearily.

'And it shows! I will only wear a dress by Atelier Parisi, or I shall not marry at all.'

'Atelier Parisi . . .?' Irma murmured.

'But before then, seeing as I have no groom . . .' Romola gave a wry look. 'You must let me order a dress from you before I go back to Rome! I will need a gown for a ball I am attending in October. All my friends will be begging for your number when they see me!'

Irma blinked, dazzled by this sudden reversal of fortune, and Rafaella spied her chance. 'Mamma, they are here. The Carosas are waiting.'

'Already?' Irma breathed with a fresh look of alarm, patting her lashes dry and smoothing her hair.

'*Si*. We must go.'

'*Si, si*,' Irma said, as Silvana pulled on her white gloves. She went over to her daughter to fuss over her veil. 'We must hurry.'

Rafaella saw Silvana's gaze snag upon her dress, a look of regret coming over her face now that the distraction of her own had been removed.

'Don't worry, I'll take Rafaella to help her get ready,' Romola said, reaching for Rafaella's arm.

The others – Rafaella included – looked at her in surprise. Amid all the drama, there hadn't been time to wonder why exactly she was here.

'You remember, Silvana, you admired my rosebud dress and asked whether Rafaella could wear it today?' Romola asked the bride.

Silvana, to her credit, only paused for a half-beat. '*Si!*' she cried. 'I almost forgot! That is OK, isn't it, Mamma? Rafaella needs something special too.'

'Well, hurry then!' Irma cried, too dazed and flustered to have another confrontation. And if it was a Franchetti's dress . . . 'The Carosas are waiting!'

'*What* are you doing?' Rafaella whispered as Romola pulled her from the room, giggling all the way along the hall back to her bedroom.

'As if I would let you attend your sister's wedding in that rag!' Romola exclaimed, pinching the thin fabric.

'But—'

There was a dress bag on Rafaella's bed, and she walked over to it. Inside was an ivory silk dress embroidered with pink rosebuds. It had a narrow skirt and wide straps that sat on the edge of the clavicle, swooping into a deep criss-cross V front and back.

'I cannot wear this!' Rafaella exclaimed, stepping back. 'It's too beautiful!'

'And what sort of ridiculous comment is that?' Romola cried. 'Dresses are made to be worn, Rafa! And if you won't let me buy you something, then borrowing this will have to do. Hurry now . . . Hurry!'

Rafaella didn't have time to disobey. She shrugged off the sundress and stepped into the cocktail gown, feeling the satin lining slip over her skin. Romola was as skinny as she was but its couture construction hugged her every curve, making her feel like a woman for once and not a girl. She didn't even need to see herself in the mirror to know she loved it but Romola turned her to look anyway, her head on Rafaella's shoulder as they admired her reflection. She looked elegant, sophisticated . . .

'*Si bellissima*,' Romola sighed.

'Do I look like your friends back home?' Rafaella asked, scarcely recognizing herself.

Romola kissed her cheek. 'Silly! You *are* my friends back home.'

Chapter 23

Fon

'What are we doing out here?' Fon asked as they sat in the car, watching from a safe distance as the wedding procession meandered its way down the hill. Silvana had made for a striking bride, the sharp silhouette of her dress making an impact even from afar. But he had only had eyes for Rafaella, transfixed as she walked arm in arm with Romola, looking unlike he had ever seen her before. Gone was the local girl covered in sand and red dust, with salty hair and bare legs. In her place was a stunning fashion model, her lissom limbs somehow elongated by the dress's narrow design. Her hair shone as she walked through the sunspots on the tree-lined road, laughing as she and Romola talked, looking as close as sisters. It felt impossible to believe he had come between them even for a moment. He felt the itch to jump from his seat and join them, to shadow her all the day long; for he knew exactly whose eyes would be following her too.

He still hadn't been able to shake the humiliation of his cowardice on the cliffs at El Ciolo, made all the more galling by Cosimo's good grace in victory. Dante had smarted from the defeat too, as if the shame had been his, and he'd barely spoken to Fon in the days since. The message was clear: Fon had dishonoured the Giannelli name and undone some of the progress made to their reputation in recent weeks. He wondered if that was why they were here now, leaving the port just as everyone else clamoured into it.

Weddings here were always a community affair. Nonna Masina steamed Father Tommaso's matrimonial robes; the grocery ordered extra deliveries of Primitivo wine; the men strung fishing nets across the narrow streets along the route from the bride's house to the church; the village women always made the lace, embroidered the veil, decorated the cake . . .

They waited for the procession to disappear from sight before Dante switched on the ignition and drove through the tall stone gateposts of the Parisi agricola. All the labourers had been given a day off for the wedding, but Fon strongly suspected Pablo and Francesco would be here somewhere.

He said nothing as Dante drove along the narrow estate roads but he noted that they were heading in the opposite direction to the water tower. He felt as he had that night on the boat, heading out into international waters – oblivious to what was coming. But he had told his brother he wanted in and he had to go through with this, even if he didn't understand how it circled back here, to the Parisis.

Presently they ran out of road.

'We have to walk the rest of the way,' Dante said, cutting the engine and jumping out. He reached down for something beside his seat, slipping it into his back pocket; Fon caught the flash of a blade.

Dante began to lead the way through the grove, moving with utmost assurance over land that was not theirs. They had not gone far when, as Fon had expected, they saw the two men waiting by a wall, smoking cigarettes as they talked, their backs to the Giannellis' approach. Francesco said something that made Pablo whoop with sudden laughter.

'Hey!' Dante barked, making them jump and whirl around. They quickly ground out their cigarettes. 'Are you trying to broadcast that you're here?'

'Sorry,' Pablo apologized as Dante fixed them with a questioning look. '... Francesco was just telling me how that Antonia gave it to him against Greco's wall last night.' His toothless grin grew again. 'Greco thought it was foxes in the bins and threw a bucket of water on them!'

Both men slid back into laughter again as Dante gave a slow, cold smile. 'Well, you've only got a week left with her, so make the most of it.'

Francesco stopped laughing. 'What?' he asked, confused. 'But—'

'She's needed in town. It's time she started earning. Training period's over.'

Fon looked at his brother in alarm. What?

'In fact, you can take her out there for me,' Dante said to Francesco.

'You want her to ...?'

'Yes.'

'But ... what do I say?'

'You don't say. You tell.'

'But what if she won't?'

'Then you threaten to break her legs.'

'And if she still won't? ... I don't think she's frightened of me.'

Dante shot him a hard look. 'Then you break them, and she will be. It's simple enough ... Unless that's going to be a problem for you?'

Fon could hardly believe what he was hearing – his brother casually talking about breaking a girl's legs, a girl they had had ice cream with just the other night. Pimping her out ...!

Francesco shook his head quickly, looking ashen. He liked the girl, Fon could tell, but not enough to defy Dante's orders.

'Don't look so troubled, Francesco. I've got another one lined up for you. It's not like you're going to go without.' Dante checked his wristwatch. '. . . Come. We don't have all day. This needs to be done quickly, before we're missed.'

'OK, this way,' Pablo said, leading them into the trees. 'We had to go deeper after the Parisi girl found us.'

Fon stiffened – the Parisi girl? Did he mean Rafa or Silvana? And what had she found?

'You're sure she didn't suspect?' Dante asked.

'Not at all.' Pablo shook his head firmly. 'And it's been quiet since then.'

Fon saw that some of the tree trunks had been marked with red clay dots – enough to catch the eye, but presumably soluble in the rain or easily washed off, leaving no permanent mark. He followed the others in silence, the only sound the sharp crack of twigs snapping beneath their feet.

They had been walking for several minutes when they heard soft lowing ahead, distinctive because it was incongruous here. Pablo stopped as a herd of cattle came into view, tethered among the oaks.

'Twenty-two,' he said.

Dante seemed pleased. 'Good.'

There were a few of the estate's deep-sided carts, used for transporting the olive harvest, lying around the trees – and a carpenter's bag. Fon saw the handles of several saws protruding, and his stomach pitched.

He looked at his brother. 'You're going to slaughter them?'

'You make it sound like that wasn't always their fate,' Dante said, bemused. 'We're just doing it sooner rather than later and taking the profits ourselves.'

Fon looked across at Pablo and Francesco, aghast. How many times had they done this? It didn't look like a first event for the men gathered here.

'Don't worry about them,' Dante said. 'They've got the

hard part – butchering and carrying it all back. They have to carry it a lot further now, thanks to your little girlfriend getting in the way.'

So it had been Rafaella? Fon felt sick – sick to his stomach – at the thought of her getting caught up in something like this . . . A massacre in the woods. Blood in the dirt.

Some of the cattle had looked up and were watching them with huge, dull brown eyes. Did they feel any fear? Did they sense danger from this paltry gaggle of still, quiet men? Fon himself could feel the energy radiating from his own brother, a powerful force field that could either sweep him along or crush him. It had always been this way, since boyhood; he didn't know what it was like *not* to feel it.

Pablo pulled a knife from the bag and slowly walked around the trees towards the back of the herd. He moved casually, without haste, his free hand trailing over the rippled tree trunks, humming lightly.

He approached a beast standing right at the back, patting its flank reassuringly as he walked alongside – and in one fluid movement, so fast it made Fon freeze, he slit its throat. A scarlet arterial plume sprayed upwards. The animal made no sound as its eyes rolled back and it buckled immediately at the knees. It was dead within seconds.

Dante and Francesco were watching him as Pablo repeated the exercise again, the other animals seemingly oblivious to the silent assault, their attention on the men in front of them. Down they went, one after another, Pablo knowing exactly where to stand to avoid the spraying blood.

Fon knew he couldn't panic. He couldn't show alarm or disgust, even though his stomach was threatening to turn. Dante was right – these animals had been bred for slaughter. This was an issue of timing and ownership, that was all, he told himself.

'Whose are they?' he asked in a quiet voice.

'Lobascio's.'

Fon hesitated. '. . . Renato Lobascio?'

'Is there any other?'

Fon swallowed. 'But his house burned down the other week. He's –'

He'd been about to say the poor man had been through enough; but as he caught the look in his brother's eye, he suddenly understood.

'He's been holding out,' Dante said, watching him. 'He wants to do this the hard way.'

'Do what?' Fon's brain was working fast as the animals fell, adrenaline pumping as he tried to make sense of connections that had been hidden from him. But they were being revealed now; it was why his brother had brought him here.

'Resist. We represent the common man, Fon. The politicians are all in it for themselves, making the rich richer. They don't care about us. Look at all the industrialization in the north – they don't care about what happens down here. Papa has worked his whole life, and for what? No money, no respect. He and Mamma grow thinner and poorer year by year. The only way things are going to change is if we take control, and that means working together, as one. Us against the system. Uncle Teo showed me how it's done, and slowly I am getting everyone here to see the sense in it. They work with us, and in return we protect them and their interests.'

Fon was confused. 'Like who?'

'Well, look at Pablo and Francesco here, protecting this place.'

'But the agricola's not under threat?' Fon frowned, looking at the two rough labourers.

'. . . Not yet, but soon, perhaps.' Dante shrugged. 'Things might start going wrong –'

Might?

'– and then they'll need people they can trust on their side. Just as Lobascio is discovering that he could lose everything – his house, his livestock . . . He needs to see that if he's not with us, then he's against us.'

Fon's chest felt tight at the thought of Rafaella's father being threatened. Of Rafaella somehow getting caught up in Dante's ruthless ambition.

A sound, the snap of twigs just off in the trees, made them look up and they saw a figure creep forward and freeze. It was a young boy, no more than eleven. Fon saw him pale as he took in the scene in the clearing – a dozen dead cattle, a river of blood coagulating on the dried earth, the toolbag, the olive carts . . . *them*.

For a moment, their eyes all locked in an energetic hold – the understanding was instinctive, even to a child – and then the boy broke away, turning and fleeing back through the trees. Dante didn't stir, but Pablo and Francesco were on his tail, breaking into an immediate chase. The remaining cattle scattered, spooked now and trampling over the corpses of the slain beasts, but Fon saw that the labourers had already wound thick rope around the trees, containing them in a temporary pen. They gathered in a tight huddle while the men ran after the intruder.

Fon found himself holding his breath, willing the boy to make it away from here, praying that youth would outpace old cunning . . . Desperate shouts told him otherwise and several moments later Pablo and Francesco reappeared, dragging him over, the child frantically wrestling in their grip.

'Help! Help me!' he yelled, even though they were deep into private land with no one else around.

'It's Lobascio's boy, Mattias,' Pablo panted, struggling to hold him still.

'Obviously came looking for the herd,' Francesco added.

'Let me go!' Mattias cried.

'I thought you said no one saw you coming up here,' Dante said, displeased.

'No one did. But they're animals,' Francesco shrugged. 'They shit anywhere. There's going to be a trail of sorts, if you look for it . . . And he's come looking for it.'

'Let me go! My father's going to kill you! He'll kill you! Fucking Giannellis!' the boy yelled, wriggling again and kicking out his legs so that he propelled himself off the ground momentarily. He was skinny but strong. Pablo lost his hold long enough for him to lunge, but Francesco still had a good grip on him, and they fell heavily to the ground together.

Pablo drew the knife from his pocket and pressed its bloodied blade against the boy's neck. 'Enough,' he said menacingly, towering over the child's sprawled body.

In an instant, Mattias was still and quiet. Dante stared at him as Francesco hauled him back to his feet. Everyone was silent for a few long moments. Fon could hear the frenetic drumbeat of his own heart, blood rushing in torrents through his head as he tried to think, to find a path out from this on which everything could still be all right.

'This is a problem,' Dante murmured.

'It doesn't have to be,' Fon said quickly, looking at his brother intently. Smuggling cigarettes was all well and good; cattle raiding, arson, intimidation, even selling women . . . He didn't like it, but if this was what diversification looked like, he could . . . he could live with it. But to even think about killing a witness – a child! His brother's ambitions didn't extend to murder.

Did they?

Dante turned to look at him. 'How do you propose we move on from this?'

'The boy's got a mouth on him and a bad attitude,'

Francesco argued. 'If we let him go, he'll never stay quiet. The *carabinieri* have been sniffing around since the fire as it is.'

'My contacts there are suppressing the investigation,' Dante said calmly, still watching Fon.

'You have sway over the *carabinieri* too?' Fon asked. Bribing the harbourmaster was one thing, but the police . . .?

'Some. It's growing, but slowly. I prefer the velvet glove to the iron fist . . . So, Fon, tell me – what do you propose we do with this problem?'

Fon felt the weight of all their stares, watching, assessing him for his reaction. He took a few steps towards the boy. 'Can we trust you?' he asked the cowherd, staring into his eyes and reaching for his soul, willing him to cooperate. Did this child understand the danger he was in?

Seemingly. The boy nodded frantically.

'And you won't tell a soul what you've seen here today?'

He shook his head. 'No one.'

'You swear? Swear it on your mother's life.'

'I swear!'

Fon looked back at Dante. 'I believe him.'

Dante gave a sigh as he smiled. '. . . And that's your problem, brother.'

He glanced back at Pablo and gave a small nod. Before Fon could even react, the older man had plunged the knife between the boy's ribs. His head dropped back and his legs went from under him, but Pablo and Francesco held him up.

'*No!*' Fon screamed, running forward, but Dante caught him and held him back. Fon fought against him, trying to get past, but he would never match his brother's strength. 'He's a child! A child!'

Dante held Fon firmly as he flailed, watching the blood seep through the boy's shirt. 'No, he's a liability. He's a witness. He's an informant. He would endanger everything we're building here,' Dante said quietly, his voice against Fon's ear. 'And you need to understand that it's not just about trust. It's about respect . . . He can't get away with disrespecting us like that.'

Fon pulled back and stared at his brother with wild eyes, his chest heaving. 'You stabbed him because he *disrespected* us?' he cried. He felt like he was going to collapse. His body, his mind, couldn't support this.

'It's a shame it had to come to this, but he left us no choice. I don't like it any more than you, but this is the way of the world, Fon. Fear breeds respect – obedience, compliance. His father will fall into line now, you will see.'

A sob escaped Fon as he looked over at the boy. He was making strange sounds.

'His lungs are filling with blood,' Dante said quietly. 'He's suffering.'

'We need to get him to a doctor!' Fon begged. 'Please, Dante, *please*! We can still make this right.'

'It's too late for that now. He's beyond saving.' Dante shook his head, pity in his eyes as he reached for the knife in his own back pocket and held it out on his palm. 'But he doesn't need to suffer, Fon. Are you man enough to show him mercy?'

Fon stepped back, horrified at the suggestion. He couldn't speak. His heart was like a battering ram, trying to break his ribs.

'Put him out of his suffering, Fon.'

'No! *No!*'

'You said you wanted in.'

'But not to this! Never! . . . Dante, no! . . . Why me?' He looked over to Pablo and Francesco, both of whom returned blank stares. They would not save him from this, any more than they would save the boy.

'Because I need to know if you can.' Dante rested a hand upon his shoulder and Fon felt himself shrink several inches beneath the weight of it. His failure at El Ciolo had been graver than he had feared. A moment of fright had revealed the yellow blood coursing in his veins. Cosimo had seen it – it was why he had pitied him – and now everyone knew exactly what he was and had always been. A coward.

More than that – it was no longer enough to *want* to be in, nor was it enough to be Dante's brother or Uncle Teo's nephew. He had to prove himself once and for all. Dante's grip tightened on his shoulder as he eyeballed him intently.

'He's dying already. This is the only way you can help him,' Dante whispered. 'Give him mercy.'

Slowly Fon met his gaze, feeling himself sucked into the vortex as Dante placed the knife in his hand.

'Show me you've got what it takes, brother.'

Chapter 24

Cosimo

The wedding procession was coming back down the hill from the church, jubilant cheers ricocheting through the narrow streets as Silvana and Luchino led the throng towards Villa Maria, where the reception was being held. Cosimo wove through the tangle of men and women in their finery, past the nonnas, slow on their thick legs and stiff feet. The widows in their black lace mantillas were talking rapidly – something about the bride's dress, he couldn't quite hear. Somewhere up ahead, someone was playing a tambourine as the little children raced and played.

But ahead of them all was her.

'Rafa!' he called.

Her name landed like a bird on her shoulder and he saw how she looked back with giddy happiness, her eyes shining with joy. When she saw him calling for her, reaching for her through the crowd, her smile grew even brighter, and it made him feel like Superman that *he* might be capable of making her even more radiant.

He had felt as if time itself had stopped when she'd walked into the church wearing a dress he knew could only be his sister's, and yet looked as if it had been made for her. She made Valentina Fabiani look cheap. She made his mother look tired. Even the bride's light shone a little less brightly beside her.

He hadn't been able to take his eyes off her throughout the entire service. Every time she'd looked his way, he'd already been staring. He had tried to laugh it off – pulling faces, singing out of tune, as if they were still ten years old, but it was no laughing matter; he knew that. Finally he understood what had happened to him. The truth he'd been trying to outrun all year had caught him by the scruff of the neck and dangled him like an errant puppy. Cosimo Franchetti, second son of the Duke of Paliano and playboy-in-chief of Rome, was in love.

'Hey,' he panted, coming to walk alongside her. 'Thanks for waiting back there!'

She smiled. 'I'm in the wedding party! My sister's the bride, in case you'd forgotten? I can't hang around for you, you know,' she said archly, giving him a little side-eye as they walked.

'Don't I know it.'

'And what does that mean?' she asked, her tone playful.

'Just what I said,' he shrugged. 'You've left me behind in every way.'

'Mm, perhaps,' she smiled, seeming pleased by the thought, closing her eyes briefly as she tipped her face to the sky. It was a day that was golden, everything about it perfect, and he realized, seeing her so happy here, how very unhappy she had seemed in all the days before this. Because of him. Because he and Romola and Fon had all hurt her.

But today she was untouchable.

'Nice dress, by the way.'

'Thanks. It's your sister's.'

He grinned at her unapologetic honesty. 'Well, whatever you do, don't give it back to her.'

She grinned. 'And where would I ever wear this again? To Tito's?' She stroked a hand on the bodice, her features softening at the luxurious fabric.

'I'll take you somewhere you can wear it.'

She laughed, as if he'd cracked his best joke.

He caught her by the elbow, hating the way she dismissed the idea out of hand, as if it was inconceivable that 'they' might exist beyond the port. 'No, I will! You should come to Rome.'

'Cosi!' She laughed harder, shaking her head at the ridiculousness of it all.

'I'm serious. I could take you out there, introduce you to my friends . . .'

Her laughter died away; she was still smiling, but a sadness had come into her eyes now. He could feel her pulling away from him, as if a dangerous current was eddying at her feet. 'I hardly think I'd be of any interest to them.'

'How can you say that?' he protested. 'You're interesting to me!'

'I'm not even interesting to myself, Cosi!'

He stared at her. How could she even think such a thing?

'Rafa!' They both turned to see her mother standing at the ramp that led down to the beach, beckoning her over.

'Photographs,' she groaned. 'Catch you later.'

'Wait –' He caught her by the elbow again, wishing he could just hold onto her for the rest of the day. 'You'll save me a dance later, yes?'

She laughed again. 'Why? So you can step on my toes?'

'I'm a very good dancer. Excellent, in fact.'

'If you say so!' she said with a roll of her eyes.

He watched her go, teetering in heels and the narrow skirt, looking the very definition of Venus. 'That's a yes, then?' he called after her. 'Rafa?'

Chapter 25

Rafaella

Rafaella sat at the top table, looking out at the sea of faces staring up at them. She wondered if this was what it was like to be a schoolteacher watching over the assembled children, waiting for the bell to ring. Villa Maria's main reception room had been dressed with coloured streamers that looped across the ceiling and long tables draped in cloths. The wedding cake was displayed on a stand in the corner, and there was a dance floor and a small stage for a band with a drum kit already set up. At the far end of the room, large arched windows gave onto the beach below, but no one was lying out on the promenade – none of the *anziani* were standing on the steps or in the shallows today. Everyone was in here.

Luchino was giving his speech. He had been talking for at least forty minutes now and it seemed to her that the more he talked, the more the villagers drank. She could see Gina, Luigi and Gino all sitting together with Donatella, Antonia and Clara. Cosimo, Romola and Fede were at a table with their mother – Filippo's chair still empty, although he was expected back from Rome 'any second'. Fon and Dante were with their parents and El Greco . . .

Dante kept looking over at Gina's table, his finger tapping on the back of his chair as he watched her flirting with Luigi. Rafaella knew perfectly well what her friend was doing: she was getting revenge for Dante's on–off treatment of her. He would come in hot one day, wooing her and saying all the right things, only to disappear again for days afterwards. Gina might be mad about him but she was nobody's fool. Two could play at his game, and from the jealous look on Dante's face, it was working.

Fon, beside him, just kept drinking, his head hanging down. Everyone was drunk, but he looked wrecked. He'd been avoiding her for the past few days again – ever since the picnic at El Ciolo, when Cosimo had humiliated him – but then, she hadn't exactly sought him out either. It wasn't her job to salve wounded pride and male egos. Especially when she had asked both him and Cosimo to accept each other in her life, to no avail. The tension between the two of them was still at breaking point and she didn't know how else to ease it.

But she frowned now as she watched Fon running his hands over his face, looking as if he wanted to be anywhere but here. He wasn't talking to anyone, and he looked so wretched that she suddenly regretted not having made a point of speaking to him. Things had been so crazy all day, tending to her sister, calming her mother, enduring photographs and small talk with Father Tommaso . . . To her shame, she realized she hadn't even looked for him in church, but how could she when every time she'd raised her head, Cosimo had been staring straight at her? He had kept trying to make her laugh, almost succeeding several times, and on the walk over here he had bounded around her like a puppy wanting to play.

In truth, he was the real reason she'd let the days slip past without searching out her boyfriend. She had been enjoying having fun again, and for the past few evenings, after they'd finished their shifts at the beach caffè, she and Gina had gone over to the villa and hung out with him and Romola.

She was determined to show them they could all go back to how things had been before, and on the surface, their return to friendship had been seamless – it really had been just like the old days, the four of them telling wild stories and silly jokes, raiding the kitchen for food. Romola had got her old spark back and even decided that if she couldn't beat them, she'd join them, coming down to help out at the caffè several mornings so they could all have more time together.

But below the surface of bright smiles, it wasn't so simple with Cosimo. For all their well-intended declarations at the caffè, their truce felt as fragile as a fairy's wing – as if a lingering look could tear through it, an enquiring touch could set it alight. Their renewed friendship existed more as a concept than a concrete reality. At first she had thought it was all in her head, that she was imagining the way the air seemed to crackle between them. But then she would catch him staring at her; she felt his eyes on her back whenever she left a room, the pressure in his fingertips when they messed around in the pool. And when they came inside and lounged on the sofas, his arm was always slung across the cushions behind her shoulders, tantalizingly close. Slowly, she was beginning to wonder if, far from being something they had left in the past, the kiss had become a ghost, haunting them both.

She looked over to find him already watching her. His black eye had faded now, his atrocious sunburn turned into a deep tan, and he was distractingly handsome in his suit. Sometimes she wished she could hate him. It would be so much easier to foster contempt than to keep on suppressing the emotions he really aroused in her. It took so much energy not to look at him, to force from her mind memories that had danced for so long they had worn grooves into her very being. He'd hurt her in his efforts to show they were nothing but friends, but as she met his eyes now and she felt that familiar charge in her body, she didn't think that even Valentina Fabiani could stop what was happening between them.

In a flash, she understood it at last. Their kiss hadn't been an ending to last summer but a beginning to this one, revealing a story neither of them had been ready for.

But as he smiled from across the room, it was like watching flames race towards her over an oil slick. There was only one direction of travel, and it was unstoppable. This fire was going to consume them both.

Chapter 26

Fon

Fon felt distanced from the spectacle even as he sat in the midst of it. Everything was colourful and bright but his world had sunk into a palette of black and white and red, of ringing silence. He kept staring down at his palms, sure they would be stained for evermore. He couldn't stop shaking.

All around him, his neighbours and friends were celebrating, oblivious to his murderous morning. He felt certain the stain on his soul must be as visible as the trembling of his hands, but not a single person seemed to notice his haunted eyes or pallor. No one saw that the young man who'd walked into those trees was fundamentally different to the one who'd walked out.

He couldn't stop the tremors from coming – it felt as if his nerve endings had been set alight. He poured himself another glass of Primitivo from a jug on the table, drinking it down quickly.

'*Ciao*, Fon.'

He looked up to see Luigi standing beside him. The speeches had finally come to an end and everyone was chatting again as the band struck their first tuning notes. '*Ciao*.'

Luigi was staring into the crowd, tracking the bodies as

people mingled. Irma Parisi was laughing and talking ecstatically as the women flocked around a preening Silvana, touching her dress and cooing over her. Even Rossanna Franchetti was nodding approvingly as the bride recounted the story of the satin procured from a Lollobrigida film set in Rome.

Like Fon, Luigi seemed unsettled. He knocked back a glass in several gulps.

'You OK?' Fon asked, but he already knew the source of his friend's misery. Dante had made a beeline for Gina the moment the toasts had finished; she had been taunting him throughout the meal by flirting with Luigi, punishing him for keeping her hanging.

Now she was standing with Rafaella and Romola, her body barely contained in a jade-green dress with a hobble skirt. Dante flanked her, talking intently into her ear, his breath hot on her neck as she jutted her chin in the air. She was making him work for her, but it was already obvious how this evening was going to end.

'Why's your brother even messing with her, anyway?' Luigi muttered.

Fon shrugged. 'Because he can.' Dante could do anything and get away with it.

'He's never given her the time of day in all these years. And now he's all over her?' Luigi tutted, his lip curling with contempt.

'She never used to have a body like that.' It was a simple truth.

'So, what – I'm just supposed to wait for him to tire of her and hand her back? Who says I'll even want her?'

'No one,' Fon shrugged, his hand still shaking as he drank down more wine. 'It's your choice.'

Luigi growled beside him, turning away. 'And she was so close, too.'

'Close to what?'

'Giving it up. I put in all the spadework and now your brother's getting it!'

'I'm not sure what he's getting yet,' Fon mumbled.

'No?' Luigi asked, sounding hopeful.

Fon didn't know the details of his brother's romantic life, but they shared a bedroom, meaning he knew his comings and goings – and their evenings had been busy lately with the *bionde*. Much of Dante's business was conducted in the shadows and moonlight. It didn't leave much opportunity for dating, especially since Gina worked in her parents' shop and at the beach caffè by day.

'Well, at least it's looking good for you. Rafaella forgave you when not many would,' Luigi smirked, punching Fon's arm. 'Sly dog. Look at the two of them – they look good, you've got to say. And you've had them both.'

'Watch yourself, Luigi,' Fon snapped. He didn't want people talking about Rafaella like that. She wasn't like the others – Antonia, Romola . . . She was pure. Good. Everything the others weren't. He wasn't.

'You know what I mean, though. By summer's end, you will have done . . . She's a beauty.'

Fon watched Romola and Rafaella together. It was true they were both coming to the height of their powers: beautiful young women with hypnotic bodies, mesmerizing smiles . . . He watched Rafaella in her borrowed dress, looking so demure and graceful. She didn't have Romola's sophistication, but she still looked as though she belonged somewhere greater than this. She was shy, not taking up much space as she carefully held her glass and listened to the others talk.

Romola, though, held her glass almost like a cigarette, carelessly letting it tip as she gesticulated and held court. She knew she looked good in that spotted dress and she moved with the self-assurance of someone well used to attracting attention. After all, parties were her *milieu* – he remembered her saying that, glassy-eyed and crying, the night of the party, when he'd run into her after the fireworks and she'd put her hand down his trousers ... He shook the image from his mind, not wanting to remember.

Fon kept drinking until the shaking stopped and everything began to feel numb. His gaze kept creeping over to Antonia, watching as she laughed, her breasts too much on display in a tight dress and jiggling as she moved. Several times she caught him staring and winked at him, mistaking his sympathy for interest. The third time, she pressed the tip of her tongue provocatively between her lips, teasing him.

He looked away, feeling nothing, remembering Francesco and Pablo laughing over last night's escapade outside the harbourmaster's house; remembering Dante's plan. Did Antonia have any idea that her sexual power was about to be flipped against her?

Francesco and Pablo had arrived late, during the meal; they'd had much to do after Fon and Dante had left early, needing to be seen at the wedding. The henchmen had gone home to thoroughly bathe and change before they could come here and Dante had made a show of bringing them 'more drinks' when they appeared, as if they'd been here for hours. Fon had seen Pablo open his jacket just enough to flash the thick envelope of cash in his pocket, indicating that the cattle meat had been traded with Dante's man in Specchia. Business had continued as planned, in spite of the so-called 'interruption'.

How did his brother do it? Just carry on normally in the wake of such brutality?

The dancing was beginning now, a crowd forming, the villagers holding hands in a circle as Silvana and Luchino took to the floor to dance the tarantella. Fon stayed slumped in his chair. He had neither inclination nor ability to dance.

Dante was standing, holding hands with Gina and Donatella, but Fon saw Donatella's thumb rubbing over his brother's in an inconspicuous motion . . . A tiny but telling detail; there was an intimacy to it. Was she the one his brother planned to pass over to Francesco next, then? He watched Gina, too, on his other side. She looked happy now, laughing with Dante as he gave her all his attention. Perhaps that was his brother's secret: escape, distraction, the comfort of the flesh.

Even in Fon's compromised state, it hadn't escaped his attention that Rafaella had not sought him out during the reception. As far as he was aware, she hadn't even looked his way. As the bride's sister, she had to stay with the wedding party and support her mother, who was alternately euphoric and overwhelmed. Her father was drinking grappa with the men – including Filippo Franchetti, who had returned especially for the celebration, arriving right at the end of the speeches and causing much excitement when he unexpectedly gave a small toast to the happy couple. Irma Parisi would be boasting for months that her daughter's wedding had been graced by a cabinet minister.

Of course, the Franchettis knew how to be good guests. Fon watched Cosimo join the dancing, standing on Gina's other side and with Romola to his right – but although his feet moved in perfect time with the music, instinctively knowing when to switch direction, his gaze never lifted off Rafaella, directly across the dance floor from him. She was laughing, watching in delight as her sister was twirled and spun in the centre of the crowd . . . And yet her gaze, when it did shift, always went back to Cosimo too.

Fon watched them from a distance. He might be drunk, but he wasn't crazy. They never did or said anything to indicate there was more between them than friendship, but from here – looking on like the outsider he was – he could see that they were connected as if by a golden thread that only shone in certain lights. Their attraction seemed like a secret he alone was privy to. He could feel it inching towards them, as heavy and slow as a sloth, and he felt powerless to stop it.

Powerless to stop anything.

Images flashed through his mind again of eyes growing empty . . . red earth staining redder . . . He shook his head, dropping his face into his hands. He didn't know how to live with this.

The music kept playing as he drank one glass after another, watching the villagers each acting out their own dramas: the nonnas gesticulating wildly with Father Tommaso; Luigi trying it on with Clara now that Dante was in the corner with Gina, her hand snaked up his neck. Feminine comfort.

Fon looked around for Rafaella as he felt a sudden surge of jealousy and anger. He needed her! Didn't she see he was suffering? If she knew what he had seen today . . .!

He found her still on the dance floor, but now dancing with Cosimo – the tarantella long since finished – his eyes pinned on hers as he spun her around and her hair flew out. She was laughing, his hand splayed on her waist . . .

Fon felt the breath stolen from him, despair prickling his eyes as he watched them. She had no interest in comforting him. She had no real interest in him at all. Despite his best efforts to be the man she needed, he still wasn't the man she wanted – and now, somewhere in the course of this terrible day, he had lost her.

He knew exactly what was coming next. She and Cosimo were two stars moving through the night sky, their paths set for inevitable collision. There would be a brilliant, dazzling flash at the moment of impact and afterwards, when the meteors had finished falling, the world would have changed around them. Nothing would ever be the same.

And he couldn't stop it. He—

Someone fell back against him, the heel of a leather shoe sharp on his foot.

'I'm so sorry!' Fede Franchetti reached back towards him with an apologetic look. He had the dopey, happy expression of someone who hadn't yet tipped over his wine limit. No doubt he was well practised in when to stop, thanks to all those cocktail parties he attended in Rome.

'It's fine,' Fon muttered.

'Are you sure?' Fede frowned, hesitating as he – he alone – seemed to notice the state Fon was in.

'Yes.'

Fede crouched in front of him, looking closely now. 'I don't think you are, Fon.' There was concern in his voice and he put a hand on Fon's shoulder, prompting Fon to look at him. 'Come on, let's get you outside. Some fresh air will help.'

Slowly, blearily, Fon lifted his gaze and stared into Fede's brown eyes, seeing kindness there. Compassion. And something else, too . . . He felt a deep stirring in his spirit, like a beast turning over in the darkness – only, its shadow was golden, the lumbering body concealing a hidden brightness . . . Suddenly the world felt back to front, or upside down, or inside out. He wasn't sure which, exactly, just that it was wrong.

He recoiled from the shock of it. 'I don't need your pity!' he spat, swatting Fede's arm angrily away so that Fede toppled backwards onto the floor. Sprawled there, he regarded Fon with a new expression, one that Fon could read clearly: disappointment.

'Hey! What's going on here?' someone said crossly. Fon looked up to see Fede's plus-one – a law school friend, according to Luigi – staring down at them both. His suit was well cut, like his accent, and he had an arrogant, haughty look to him. Fon knew that he looked vastly inferior by comparison.

For a moment he wanted to square up to this stranger and tell him exactly what he was capable of – show him the blood on his hands. See how superior he looked then!

Instead he turned away, confused by the rage that had risen up in him.

'It's nothing,' Fede said, springing to his feet and patting his friend on the chest in a placatory gesture. 'Let's get another drink, yes?'

They headed for the bar, Fede lurching a little, slightly drunker than Fon had first appreciated. He watched as the friend said something to Fede, but the music was loud; Fon's eyes followed Fede's hand as he rested it on the friend's hip, leaning in to hear better.

It was a tiny detail, but telling – as quietly intimate as Donatella's circling thumb. Fon's eyes narrowed as he realized that without even trying to, he had stumbled upon another secret. He watched them get their drinks and then head for the door, going outside.

For several moments he sat there, trying to process what he'd just seen. It was almost too incredible to believe, and yet . . . His heart began to thud. He knew he had to see it with his own eyes.

He got to his feet and headed for the door too, lumbering outside. The night air was steamy and he had almost pickled himself in wine, but he wasn't the only one. As he looked around at the terrace that overlooked the beach, he could see small groups of people drinking and laughing, dancing too . . . but not Fede and his friend.

He staggered round to the side of the building where the kitchen was located, and there, by the bins, he saw a shadow moving . . .

There they were, figures in the moonlight, doing exactly what he'd suspected: hands on faces, bodies pressed together. He stood motionless as he watched, listening to their muted sounds, muffled groans barely audible over the music that drifted through the open windows.

He felt the ground tip beneath his feet as the moments passed and their urgency grew. The blood was rushing in torrents through his head. Everywhere. He felt horrified but also excited, his animal instincts quivering on high alert today, and without thinking, his hand moved to his flies. Even in this state, he was growing hard, and he held his hand there, frozen in place as he felt the dreadful proof of his own perversity.

Tears pricked at his eyes. He felt sick. Sickened by himself. Had the entire world gone mad? Had he?

He thought of the boy, bleeding to death in the trees.

He thought of Rafaella, still dancing inside. He loved her goodness, her pureness. She was the one who was supposed to save him but she was, this very moment, spinning towards a fairy tale with another hero while he stood out here as an ogre, as much a monster as his brother.

If he had lost her, then he was lost, he knew that for sure.

He turned away and threw up, trying to expel the poison in his body, his very being. He heaved and retched, wishing he could pull himself through like a jumper and be worn fresh again. Something new.

Finally, when there was nothing left to come up, he leaned against the wall, closing his eyes and feeling empty. He swayed, his body limp, one hand on the railing. He knew he should sleep. Go to bed and escape the waking nightmare that had been this day.

Just as he resolved to go, a voice carried from below on the beach.

'. . . editor wanted to break it weeks ago, but he decided it would be better used as leverage against the permits story . . .'

Fon frowned. Editor? Leverage? Story? . . . They weren't

words that were usual in conversation in the port. He looked over the railing and down onto the sand, where a couple of men were sitting on the low beach wall, smoking. They wore light suits, unlike the wedding guests. At the top of the slope which led down to the sand, Fon could see two Vespas.

'Think it'll work?' one of the men asked.

'Not sure. This isn't his first time on the hook, and he's a slippery fish . . . He always knows exactly who to call to make it go away. He's protected, isn't he.' It seemed to be a rhetorical question. The man took a deep drag of his cigarette and Fon saw the lighted tip glow more brightly in the night air. For a brief moment he caught sight of something dark against the man's chest. A camera? 'But this is different. It brings in his son.'

'And you've got actual proof of the affair?'

The first guy shrugged again. 'Yeah, although he could still just say he was there on official business.'

'But in Gallipoli? On the beach?' The other one scoffed. 'Even *he* can't build there!'

Fon frowned, feeling the hairs on his neck rise. He was drunk and physically battered, his brain was lagging several seconds behind his ears, but somehow, even befuddled and beleaguered, he knew this was . . . important.

Devastating.

Helpful?

'. . . I need to piss.'

Fon watched the first man walk off across the sand. He fell back against the wall, forgetting all about the unnatural entanglement that had played out a few minutes earlier, as he tried to put the jigsaw pieces together to make a picture – *paparazzi, photographic proof, leverage, affair* . . . His mind strained, trying to fill in the gaps of what and who.

His eyes opened as suddenly it slotted together: a truth he never could have guessed at before today. But now – in this state, in a world he had learnt was so fundamentally corrupted – he could imagine just about anything.

His breathing came heavily as he ran it through his head over and over, looking for evidence to the contrary. But the more he played it, the more the paparazzo's words solidified in form. They were like pieces on a chess board moving into formation, and he realized that *he* had been holding a piece of the story, too: a knight in his hand, a duke's daughter's drunken ramblings about 'betrayal' and 'family' as she pulled at his belt buckle, hell-bent on reprisal.

He'd had the lowdown all this time. He just hadn't known it.

But now that he did, suddenly Cosimo and Rafaella's destiny didn't seem so unstoppable.

Fon was still so drunk he couldn't walk in a straight line, but he didn't need to. He could zigzag over this board if he wanted to. All paths led to his target.

Checkmate.

Chapter 27

Cosimo

They were dancing. Her hand was in his, her breath against his neck as they moved with the music. He could feel the tiny contractions of her back muscles as they swayed, his fingers brushing over the embroidery on her dress, and it was as if they were completely alone.

He couldn't pinpoint exactly when things had shifted between them. It would be like capturing slackwater, identifying that one moment of stillness when the tides switched from one direction to another. But somehow, amid the carnival of the wedding, the realization had crept upon him as the weight of their stares began to build: she felt the same.

Just the thought of it made him mad with joy. All he wanted was to tear her from this room and take her somewhere private where he could make her promises, make her his. But her sister was the bride, her mother was hysterical, her father drunk . . . He'd had to wait, counting down the minutes until the obstructions between them began to part.

'It's hot in here,' he murmured.

'Yes.' She turned her head just a little and he felt her hair, so soft, against his cheek.

He hesitated. 'Do you want to go out for some air?'

'Yes.'

He pulled back to look at her, feeling gravity shift and gather, tipping his world towards one inevitable point. Everything was about to change. He knew it, and so did she. No one took any notice of them, the childhood friends, as they walked past.

Outside, the moon was shining on the sea, but they heard voices from the terrace and, from a single shared look, it was understood they were going back to Villa Agosto – where they could be alone in a shaded garden, where they could hide in nooks, get lost in countless rooms.

They walked, her hand in his, in silence that was somehow deafening. Chatter and laughter had always been the soundtrack to their friendship, but that wasn't what this was anymore. He could scarcely hear anything over the rush of blood in his ears, only the staccato clip of her heels on the pavement as he watched her delicate shadow walking beside his. She was beautiful even in silhouette.

It was less than a minute's walk from the reception to his grand garden gates, but it felt like it had taken them a lifetime to get here, and no sooner were they on the grass than he had clasped her head in his hands and was kissing her.

She didn't resist; her desperation matched his, small gasps escaping her as he covered her face and neck in hundreds of kisses. She smelled so good – not like the girls in Rome with their Paris perfumes, but like fresh laundry, lavender on the breeze.

They stumbled on, locked together by grasping hands and hungry mouths, the shadows slipping over them as the moon played hide-and-seek through the lemon trees. In the distance, the music from the wedding still played, laughs and shouts of revelry pitching skywards like fireworks into the darkness.

A curved stone bench pressed against his legs and he realized they were near the round pool. Close, too close still, to the street.

He pulled away, leading her into a run towards the next garden, her laughter fluttering like a dove as they headed for the jasmine wall. They kissed again, their desperation only building, not subsiding. The first time, last summer, had been different – a sudden awakening, slow realization. Shock had overtaken them both, lips pausing for eyes to absorb an unexpected truth. But a year had passed in which that memory had become legend. It had been held back for all that time but desire, like water, must flow.

He pushed her against the flowers, the scent springing up around them. Somewhere in here was a nook, but he couldn't open his eyes, couldn't move his feet. He felt her press herself against him and knew he couldn't hide what she was doing to him. There were no secrets left.

He groaned, surprised, as her hand moved to explore him, her mouth opening wider in reflex to what she found. He had to hold back somehow, he knew that, but he felt himself beginning to tremble with the effort. She was too much for him. All he wanted—

She pushed him back suddenly, and his eyes opened in alarm.

'Rafa,' he said weakly as she shimmied the tight dress up her hips.

'I want to,' she whispered.

There was no coming back. With one hand, he unbuttoned his flies, freeing himself and pinning her against the flower wall. She lifted herself onto him, her long legs gripping him tightly.

'Say you're mine,' he groaned as he eased himself into her with what little control he had left. 'For always.'

Her head fell back, her neck exposed, her arms wrapped

around him. 'Yes, yes,' she whimpered, her breathing ragged in his ear and almost ending him before he'd begun. 'I'm yours. I'm yours. For always.'

The refrigerator hummed loudly in the silence, its light glaring in the dark kitchen as he peered in at the plates of food left by Signora Cinzia: prosciutto, tomatoes, burrata, peaches, her signature *millefoglie* . . . He was ravenous but completely sated, his body basking in the afterglow of claiming the girl he loved. Twice. She was upstairs, lying on his bed, shy again now that the first waves of passion, which had consumed them like fire, were falling back to something steadier.

They had crept in like cats, furtive and stealthy as they strained for sounds of life, but they had soon been persuaded that the villa lay empty. Only the sea breezes were tiptoeing through the arches and shuttered windows. He had chased her through the rooms, unzipping her dress, slipping off her brassiere until she was wearing nothing more than that sweet smile.

He was dressed in only his boxers now and the chill wafted onto his bare chest as he reached in for a selection of *antipasti* and a bottle of prosecco. The glasses were kept in a high cupboard and they tinkled as he got them down with his good hand.

In all the passion, he had forgotten his broken thumb – or ignored it at least, his body receiving too many pleasure signals to register the dull pain; he could have lost a leg and still not stopped out there. But it was throbbing again now, and he stacked the plate of food, the bottle and glasses awkwardly as he made his way back through the kitchen.

He walked through the sitting room towards the front of the villa. The run of arches of the loggia lay beyond the main corridor and part of him had wanted to sit out there with Rafaella, looking out into the night and watching the stars reflected like diamonds in the sea. But the bigger part wanted her in his bed. He had waited too long to pass up that opportunity.

She was his wife. That much he already knew. She loved him for who he was, not what he was; with her, the world finally made sense. She was the lock and he was the key. They would only ever fit one another perfectly.

'Cosimo!'

The sudden shout caught him off guard and he stopped in his tracks. The voice was fogged with drink, too thick and slurred to identify. He stepped out onto the loggia, silhouetted in the arch at the very centre point of the building as he looked down the long drive.

'Who's there?' he asked into the darkness, peering around the stone urn.

'. . . Is she here?'

He turned to see Fon staggering up the right side of the split stone staircase. He was holding on to the balustrade with one hand, swaying as if it was pitching beneath his feet. He looked wretched – pale, with dark moons cradled below his eyes, the inside of his lips ringed with red wine.

Cosimo realized he hadn't given Fon any thought all night. Not once. He hadn't seen him in church earlier, and afterwards he'd been too hypnotized by Rafaella to notice anyone else at all. He had entirely forgotten Alfonso Giannelli's existence.

'What are you doing here?' he asked quietly. Fon had never struck him as a menacing figure – not like his brother, who seemed to bristle with animalistic caprice – but it was unlike him to be this bold, this aggressive.

'You heard me,' Fon growled. 'I said, is she here? They said they saw her with you!' His head lolled a little but his eyes came to focus on Cosimo's state of undress, the food, bottle and two wine glasses in his good hand. It told a story with no words.

In a flash, Fon knew. He caught his breath as the realization whipped through his body like a bullet, tipping him forward and back.

'Ha!' he cried, but the bark of laughter fell like a dead bird from the sky. He looked crazed with grief. 'So then I'm too late . . . It's done.' His voice faded to a whisper.

'Go home and sleep it off,' Cosimo said quietly, watching him with concern. Fon wasn't simply drunk; something bad had happened, he could tell. 'This isn't the time.'

'. . . But it *is* the time. If I have to lose something precious, then so do you. It's only fair,' Fon said, his body folding forward from the hips as he balanced precariously for several moments before lurching the rest of the way up the steps onto the loggia.

Cosimo stepped back, giving him space, and half turned to set everything down on a coffee table. He prayed that Rafaella wouldn't come down here, wrapped in a bedsheet and wondering at the noise.

'I've been looking everywhere for you,' Fon slurred. 'Did you know that?'

'I'm sorry, I didn't know that,' Cosimo said calmly.

'Of course not. You were *busy*.' Fon leaned on the word as if it was a ball he was trying to push under water. 'But this couldn't wait, you see.'

'I'm sure that's not true.'

'No, no. It's important, you know. Time is of the essence . . . Who knows when they're going to run the story? It could be tomorrow.'

Cosimo frowned at the abrupt change in direction of the conversation. 'Look—'

'Did you *see* the paparazzi outside?' Fon swung his arm back towards the sea behind him, almost spinning himself off his feet. 'They're right there, on the beach. They're still there. They're going to confront—'

'If this is about my father, he has people in his office who deal with the press,' Cosimo said evenly. 'It's not for you to concern yourself with. Or me.'

'Well, now, that's not true!' Fon argued. 'She was your girlfriend, after all. Yours!'

Cosimo frowned. 'Fon, you're not making any sense. You need to go home and sleep this off.' He walked over and manually turned the other man around, facing him back towards the stairs.

'It will be a sensation! A scandal!' Fon cried, raising his arms in the air. 'The Duke and the Starlet!'

What? Cosimo's hands dropped down as he stared at Fon swaying like a windsock, his words whistling around their heads. 'What did you say?' he whispered. The duke and the starlet?

There was simply no way—

'Yes! Your father's fucking your girlfriend!' Fon cheered, throwing the words into the air like wedding confetti. 'It's why your sister fucked me! If he goes low, she goes lower!' He laughed, the sound almost demonic in its glee.

Cosimo fell still. He felt gears that had been stuck in neutral easing into position at last as the mystery of Romola's despair on the night of the party fell into lockstep with Valentina's benign acceptance of his disinterest. He remembered his father's close attention to their guest – more than just good manners . . .

I'm trying to protect you, Romola had sobbed the next morning. What exactly had she walked in on? Echoes of his father's voice at breakfast chimed in Cosimo's mind. The way he hadn't been able to look at his own daughter. *She sees things she doesn't understand.* And then his fearsome bullishness, daring her to say the dreadful words he knew she couldn't . . . *Is there something you wish to get off your chest?*

'What will your poor mother do?' Fon asked, his face now like a Greek tragic mask as his hands pulled down on his cheeks. 'She'll be humiliated!'

Cosimo felt time slow at his words, an anchor dragging on the seabed and stalling the world's thrust. He felt the blood pool at his feet as he forgot to breathe. This drunken idiot's ravings were on the pulse. His mother would be destroyed by this. Their family would fall apart.

His father's affairs were the great unmentionable thing in his parents' marriage; he and Fede and Romola all knew why their mother was so sad, her cold anger lying behind every smile. But they had seemed to have an understanding of sorts. Be discreet. Choose wisely, from among their own. Those who had just as much to lose . . .

But Valentina broke the mould, and not just because she wasn't aristocratic.

His father was betraying *him* – his own son – as well as his wife . . .

Distantly Cosimo heard laughter, a taunting cackle that grew louder and louder in his ear. He snapped back into the moment and saw Fon, in his face, with tears in his eyes. He was laughing but crying too, like a man teetering on the very edge of insanity.

In a fury, Cosimo grabbed him by the lapels. Fon didn't try to protect himself; he dangled limply, careless of his fate. He was too out of it to understand the danger he was in, coming here, saying these things . . .

'Where's your proof?' Cosimo yelled, shaking him wildly, but Fon simply stared back at him with dull eyes. He almost looked as if he wanted to be hit. 'No? I thought as much! Baseless slurs! You just want your pathetic revenge—'

'Photos.' The word was little more than a breath. 'Gallipoli.'

Photos on the beach. He recalled his father's tan when he had come back today to the wedding; he had thought it odd, given he'd come from the city . . . Cosimo wheeled back, releasing Fon from his grip, his hands in his hair as he realized there was no stopping it now. They were undone. Ruined. His father had destroyed them all. His mother, Romola, Fede—

'Cosi?'

He heard her voice just as the rage exploded from his body and he threw himself at his old enemy. Fon staggered backwards, the breath knocked from his lungs as Cosimo tackled him and he fell against the stone urn. They both went down heavily, a violent crash sounding as stone met flesh. Cosimo felt a sharp pain in his shoulders, his thumb more than broken now; the skin on Fon's neck was badly scraped and bleeding from the rough stone, but still Fon didn't try to fight back. He looked defeated, and Cosimo dragged himself away as huge, gulping breaths of despair rolled up through his torso. He felt as if he'd swallowed a thunderstorm.

'. . . Cosi?'

He raised his head. Rafaella was standing at the far end of the loggia, wearing his shirt and a horrified look as she took in the sight of him and Fon sprawled on the ground.

'My God, what has happened?' she cried, running over. 'Are you hurt?'

'. . . I'm fine . . .' Cosimo mumbled, his voice a croak as he looked over at Fon trying in vain to pull himself up. '. . . He's just drunk.'

She looked troubled. 'What happened? I heard shouting.'

Cosimo stared at her beautiful features, her eyes wide with concern as she cupped his face. How could he tell her what his father had done? How could he reveal his family's shameful underbelly?

'He – he . . .' The words wouldn't come, but his eyes were

shining with pain and she folded him into her, pressing his head against her chest.

'Shh,' she whispered. 'I can guess.'

She assumed they had been fighting over her – which, to an extent, they had. Now wasn't the time for details. He needed to think, to accept. Cosimo felt himself surrender as she sank onto the tiles beside him, holding him more tightly. He felt relief as her actions made it clear she had chosen him. Fon was forgotten beside them.

'. . . Where's Romy?' she asked.

'What?'

'Romy. She was just coming up the drive. I saw her from the window.'

Cosimo pulled back and stared at her, hearing an echo to her words as the anchor caught on the seabed once more, slowing down the earth's drag.

His mind replayed the events of the past minute. Timings . . . tone . . .

'Cosi?' she asked again, her voice rising as she watched the expressions flicker over his face. '. . . Where's Romy?'

His sister would have seen him as she walked down the long drive. She would have seen him standing here in the loggia, arguing with Fon. She would have heard his pain and known something was wrong.

She had called his name.

In the very moment they had fought. And fallen.

He caught his breath as he looked back at the central arch, denuded now. The stone urn had toppled from its perch, gone from sight.

And that was when time stopped.

Chapter 28

Rafaella

Shock exploded like a bomb, the silence in her brain so deafening that her hands went to her ears, trying to drown it out.

No.

That was all she could think as Cosimo flew over the tiles and down the stone stairs.

No.

That was all she could think as Fon crawled up the wall and peered over it.

No.

That was all she could think as his knees buckled and he fell back with an expression she had never seen on any person in her entire life.

No.

No!

But then the stress fractures broke apart her chrysalis and the silence shattered. She heard Cosimo's screams, like meteors tearing the sky into ribbons. She saw Fon throwing up.

She staggered over to the stairs and made herself look down. Cosimo was on the ground, cradling his sister, her legs outstretched, one red shoe fallen from her foot. She could see Romola's right arm flung out, her beautifully manicured fingers gently curled. The stone urn lay beside her, not even fully smashed, the geranium flowers deracinated so that their roots were exposed like fish bones.

Cosimo rocked back and forth as he held her, his face tipped to the sky as he roared at the moon and the stars. He was like an animal, feral, non-verbal.

Somehow – half dragging, half falling – she got herself down there too. Was he sure? Was he really sure?

'Romy!' she cried, kneeling in the dirt beside her. '. . . Oh God, Romy, no!'

She sobbed, unable to comprehend the scene they found themselves in. How had their lives pivoted into this moment, when everything had been so good, so happy, so *destined*?

Cosimo looked back at her with a blank gaze and she knew that he wasn't the man of five minutes ago. In a single moment, his entire world had been destroyed. Nothing would ever be the same again. He would never be the same.

He caught his breath suddenly as he seemed to recognize her through the shock, looking frightened now, like a little boy who'd woken up into a nightmare. '. . . Rafa! . . . It was an accident!' he sobbed as she scrabbled over to him, clutching him as he clutched his sister.

'Of course it was!' Tears were streaming down her cheeks as the horror seemed to layer up like a wedding skirt: Romola's death. Cosimo's fear.

'I . . . I didn't mean to!' He juddered, pinning her with a desperate look.

'Of course you didn't! No one thinks that!' But her words were just sounds. He wasn't hearing her, his eyes wild as he looked around them frantically. He startled as he looked up and she followed his gaze to find Fon, white-faced, staring back at them. A ghost, haunting them.

'I didn't mean to,' Cosimo repeated, not seeming to recognize his old adversary.

'I know. You didn't do anything wrong,' Fon replied.

Rafaella tuned in to his voice – calm. Controlled. Almost commanding – and she felt herself latch onto his presence here. They weren't alone.

She watched as he disappeared, emerging a few moments later, coming down the steps. He was unsteady on his feet but in the glare of this crisis, he alone was holding it together.

He fell to his knees beside them and Rafaella watched him steel himself to look down at Romola. Her beautiful face was untouched but her hair was matted with blood, a crimson pool spreading in the dirt and seeping into the knees of his trousers. Death was touching him.

For a moment, Rafaella thought he was going to throw up again as his eyes scrunched shut, his body literally flinching from the shock.

'Fon?' she whispered.

He took several deep breaths and steadied himself. He looked down, as she had, and the vain hope he had cradled at a distance dissipated. Rafaella watched a tear slide silently down his cheek as the hopelessness of the situation became fully apparent.

Without a word, he reached his hand forward and shakily closed Romola's eyes.

Cosimo cried out again, completely broken, and Rafaella threw her arm around him as if trying to physically hold him together. She looked back at Fon desperately.

'What do we do?' she asked him, her voice thin with terror.

Romola was dead – but it wasn't going to end there. The police would come and there'd be an investigation. Someone would have to pay for this. An eye for an eye.

'Fon, help us!' she cried, feeling herself begin to shake as she faced the prospect of losing Cosimo too. 'You have to help us! What do we do?'

Fon looked back at her, seeing how she needed him – she

had never needed him more – but he couldn't seem to find his voice.

'Help us!' she screamed. 'Cosimo can't be arrested, Fon! It was an accident. If it was anyone's fault, it was yours! You came here and you . . . you pushed him to it! You pushed him too far!'

Fon recoiled at her words, his feet scrabbling in the dirt, and she reached for him with her free arm, clutching his hand so hard it blanched white.

'No! No! I didn't mean that!' she gasped, her voice ragged and her own eyes wild. 'I didn't mean that. I didn't. I'm sorry! I'm upset. I'm panicking . . .' He blinked back at her as her fingernails dug into his skin. She wouldn't let him leave them here. He couldn't leave them here. 'I need you to help him, Fon. You're the only one who can. Please, just help him! I'll do anything! Anything!'

She saw his expression change then, and she caught her breath – her life had constricted down to this tiny moment of existence where surviving it was the only thing that mattered. She stared at him, feeling as if she could see into his very soul.

'What is it you want from me, Fon?' she asked him, her voice lower now. Slower. She spoke intentionally, understanding she had some kind of leverage. 'Because I'll do it. Anything at all. Just tell me what you want.'

He looked into her eyes and she saw that he was every bit as broken as Cosimo. 'I only ever wanted you to be mine,' he whispered, his words slurring again.

'Then save Cosi,' she pleaded with him. 'And I will be.'

Summer 1958

Chapter 29

Rafaella

Tricase Porto, 12 August 1958

Rafaella sat on her bed, staring out at the treetops. Stray birds flew past the open doors, the cicadas at full pitch as dusk rode in on a fiery chariot. The sky was alive with defiant streaks of coral and peach, but darkness was coming, and already stitched to its far side was tomorrow.

The day when the rest of her life began.

Whispers tiptoed beneath the balcony, suppressed laughter leaking out as everyone gathered outside, the attempt at secrecy little more than a charade; they all knew she knew they were there but *la serenata* was the final ritual before she walked down the aisle, and as she looked around at her bedroom, she could scarcely believe this would be her last night ever sleeping here. Tomorrow she would cut the white ribbon pinned across the farmhouse door, symbolizing her abandonment of this, her home as a Parisi, and she would become a wife. Her childhood would be over.

She looked across at the dress hanging on the mannequin Silvana had brought over from her studio. The hem hovered less than a centimetre off the ground, the puffy, bell-shaped skirt ballooning from a narrow waist, cinched with a pleated cummerbund and topped with a tight lace bodice. Silvana had fashioned a scalloped lace cap that would be pinned to the back of Rafaella's head so that the veil bunched at the nape of her neck and splayed over her shoulders. This bride would be a model of propriety, not a fashion mannequin.

Her sister had outdone herself. Her own dress, last year, had been a sensation, albeit not without its detractors – the nonnas had taken some time to recover – but this was a step up again: zibeline silk from Paris and lacework embellished with real pearls, which the local women had worked on for months. Thrice weekly since February they had been meeting in Silvana's atelier above the cobbler's, armed with needles and thread, gathering in a large circle as they talked and worked on the tulle base.

Rafaella had tried to resist any extravagance – the pearls were too much! – but she was told this was what it was to marry into money. No expense would be spared, just as no moment would pass uncelebrated. Everyone was determined it should be a happy day, but their dogged resolve to laugh and celebrate was like a steel lining on a rainbow.

It was the villagers' first wedding since the Franchetti Tragedy (as it had come to be known in the papers) and a scar from that night ran like a seam through the port now. Rafaella could still remember the keening chaos of her sister's wedding morning, when their mother had cried and wrung her hands, despairing of God's wrath – until Romola had burst in with smiles and solutions. The calm tomorrow would feel funereal by contrast, her mother sitting doll-like in the chair and watching as Silvana fastened the silk buttons of her modest dress in near silence.

But it had to be endured. The world had continued to turn against all odds.

Outside, the first few notes rose up as the tambourine

was shaken and the accordion squeezed, and any lingering attempt at discretion was abandoned. Rafaella flattened her palms on the bedsheet as *la serenata* began, the villagers giving her betrothed a backing voice, and custom was observed. She rose after the first verse, knowing her part too, and walked towards the balcony, to her groom.

Chapter 30

Fon

She looked like an angel, standing at the entrance to the dimly lit church with her father. The late afternoon sun was still blazing, sending a heat shimmer off the cars and throwing a nimbus around her dramatic silhouette.

A murmur of appreciation swept through the congregation as the organ played and she slowly came down the aisle. Chiesa di San Nicola was a humble church, little more than a chapel, with peach-painted arches, whitewashed walls, and a fresco of the Assumption of Mary in lieu of an east window. No gilding or high Catholic crucifixes, no life-sized saints standing watch in niches. She could have been married in the cathedral in Tricase town – or anywhere she had wanted – but this was her home and Father Tommaso was her priest.

Fon felt awash with pride as his bride passed by the familiar sunburnt, windswept, weather-whipped faces of their neighbours. No one was used to beauty for beauty's sake here but toothless grins beamed, rough, calloused fingers automatically fluttering for a touch of her skirt as she passed, looking like a princess.

Father Tommaso was standing just behind him, waiting

too as she reached the end of the aisle and her father pulled back her veil, kissing her lightly on the cheek.

'I love you, Papa,' she whispered, clutching his fingers for a moment as tears stood poised in her father's eyes.

For a moment, Emilio Parisi's gaze swept over him, and Fon felt the chill in his look before he stepped away, unable to do anything else.

Fon stepped closer then, his breathing shallow as he realized the dream – the promise – was coming true. She was his at last.

'You look so beautiful.' He held out his arm chivalrously, and she took it as together they walked up the couple of steps to the altar. Father Tommaso made the sign of the cross, the altar boys standing either side of him, holding large crucifixes almost as big as themselves. The Mass server had his back turned, making final preparations for communion.

They knelt to pray as Father Tommaso began reciting the Collect. Fon was aware of Rafaella clasping her hands tightly, as if praying for fortitude – as if marrying him was a prison sentence, but they both knew it was because of him that Cosimo wasn't behind bars. He had saved his old foe in his darkest hour; he had been Atlas on bended knee, holding the world aloft as everything threatened to fall.

Two lives had been lost that day, but in the midst of all the blood and wine and reckless sex, he had saved his own. He had stared into the abyss, and from the midnight void he had understood what he needed to do.

He had taken all the risk. Now he got to take the reward.

Chapter 31

Cosimo

Cosimo watched her pray. Her eyes were squeezed shut, her lips moving in silence as she called for the power of the Spirit to come upon her. For all the good it would do. How many prayers had he sent forth in the twelve months since his sister's senseless death? Not a single one had been answered.

He watched Fon, nervous beside her, glancing at her every few moments as if expecting her to gather her skirts and sprint away from him. But Cosimo knew she wouldn't. This was the plan they had agreed on, and it was for his sake that she would keep to it.

Fon had made it all go away after all, pulling strings that were out of reach even to Cosimo's father. He had convinced the police of his account of the events that night – that he had persuaded his girlfriend to meet him at the empty villa when everyone else was at the wedding. Yes, he had hoped to seduce her. But in his incapacitated state, he had tripped on the terrace and fallen against the urn, which was already known to be loose. He was wholly unaware of Romola following at a distance behind him . . .

That version of the accident had been recounted so many times – by the villagers, by the press – that Cosimo could almost believe it was true. It gave him momentary comfort from the guilt of what he'd done, but his mind never lay in the lie for long. He had killed his own sister and his spirit would never be at rest again.

Of course, Fon's alibi had come at a cost. He had made himself the fall guy, assuming all the risk of a manslaughter charge, on two conditions: Cosimo left the port, and Rafaella – if he went free – became his bride. She had agreed to both, for them both, without hesitation; she had been trying to save him when he was incapable of helping himself in those first bleak, traumatic moments. But in the days that had followed, losing her too had come to feel like another death. The cards had all fallen in Fon's favour. To the victor, the spoils.

Cosimo knew enough of the world of politics to recognize the stink of bribery but he hadn't known, back then, that the Giannellis had far more money and reach than anyone realized. And it had only kept on growing. A year on from that night, Fon was a rich man.

Had Fon played him a cold deck? Cosimo couldn't shake the suspicion of it, and yet he knew there was no way Fon could have predicted the events of that night. He couldn't possibly have laid out in advance the plan that would give him everything he had ever wanted.

'Amen.'

Eyes opened and he heard the whistle of gasps as the villagers' gazes settled upon him standing behind the priest.

In robes.

They changed him at a fundamental level, cloaking him with an anonymity that had never been possible in his old life. They stripped him of colour, personality. Free will. His noble legacy. Cosimo Franchetti, second son of the eleventh Duke of Paliano, no longer existed. The golden playboy of Rome, scion to a great fortune, had disappeared from the public face of the earth and now only existed in a single dimension, hidden behind a high wall.

Rafaella looked straight at him, visibly shaken to find him here suddenly, the Mass server at her own wedding. The gates of Villa Agosto had remained closed this summer and she hadn't seen him since the funeral last year. He had stolen away before first light the following morning, having accepted the game was lost. His family was destroyed; Rafaella was Fon's. He had told no one of his plans, leaving only letters to be found.

Hers had consisted of two words: *Forgive me.*

Had she? Did she understand what he had realized too late – that freedom meant nothing without her beside him? That the guilt of his own hand in his sister's death couldn't, after all, be erased with a 'Case Closed' stamp on a file?

Father Tommaso raised his hands up. 'Dearly beloved . . .'

Slowly, Cosimo walked forward to perform his duties. He saw a jolt of shock ricochet through Fon as he approached; he and his brother had become formidable figures in the port in the past year, but Cosimo Franchetti could still unnerve him.

It had been nothing for Cosimo to choose this life, to walk away from his family's material riches when they were so broken and emotionally impoverished anyway. But to stand here now and watch the girl he loved marry someone else . . .

He watched in silence as the couple recited their vows before God; Father Tommaso; the village. *Him.*

Rafaella's eyes openly, defiantly locked on his as she promised to love and obey, through sickness and health, as if she was wedding herself to him and not her groom. He saw Fon see it too – her longing, her yearning for him – and he knew she loved him still . . . But it was too late for them.

Life was made up of the actions not taken as much as those that were. If he had only remembered to tell the gardener to fix the urn; if he had only been able to see past his grief as he lay in the dirt cradling his sister . . . But he hadn't, and here they were, wearing the wrong clothes and speaking their lines to the wrong people. They were lost to one another now, and he felt his last remaining hope wither and die as Fon slipped the ring over her finger, sealing all their fates.

Summer 1961

Chapter 32

Rafaella

Otranto, 28 June 1961

'*Basta!*' she called, standing by the desk as the bell rang and the children noisily sorted themselves into a line at the door. She waited for them to fall quiet, which they quickly did. They had worked out the formula with Signora Giannelli: obedience equalled release.

She nodded, smiling at the earnest faces now arranged in orderly fashion, and they burst out of the classroom, immediately erupting into chatter and squeals of laughter again.

'Nico, remember your lines for tomorrow, please!' she called sternly.

'*Si*, signora,' he replied, already halfway out the door. Term ended the day after tomorrow, and if he wanted to matriculate to the next year . . . But the children's excitement for the summer break was reaching fever pitch and it was like herding cats, getting them to do what needed to be done.

Peace settled in the room for the first time in three hours and she wiped the blackboard clear of the sums they had been practising, plumes of chalk dust billowing. The large clock ticked on the far wall as she gathered the exercise books into her bag to mark at home later. She too was looking forward to the summer break.

She walked out into the long corridor. Maddalena, who taught the other class, was just ahead of her and she turned at the sound of Rafaella's footsteps.

'It sounded like you had your hands full today,' Maddalena smiled, waiting for her to catch up.

'Oh, always.' Rafaella rolled her eyes. 'Some of the boys thought it would be funny to keep a frog in their pockets.'

'That explains the screaming,' Maddalena grinned. '. . . It is pretty funny.'

'Yes, but they must never know that,' she whispered with a laugh as they walked down the stairs and outside. The school fronted onto Piazza Castello right beside the monumental Aragonese Castle, replete with moat and battlements which encircled the historic town centre. The morning market sellers were closing up for *riposo* but there were still people everywhere.

She said goodbye to Maddalena and wove her way through the bodies, wending a well-worn path through Otranto's narrow cobbled streets. She moved like a native now but it had taken her a while to adjust to living in a big town. The historic port attracted tourists on a grand scale – unlike in Tricase, they even visited out of season – and she still struggled with the lack of trees and the blinding whiteness of the buildings. For a girl who had grown up on an olive grove in a tiny, richly coloured port, it had been a culture shock, even if she now lived only twenty-five kilometres away.

She passed tiny boutiques selling hand-painted tiles and ceramics; a deli that sold her father's olive oil; cats sleeping on narrow steps; lines of laundry strung between balconies. Eventually she came out into the piazza. The cathedral itself was a monumental but simple eleventh-century building, made of warm Lecce stone with granite pillars, its west wall dominated by a single, huge rose window. On the north side was the seminary adjoining the cathedral. It was an austere three-storey building with narrow windows along one side through which faces could occasionally be glimpsed.

Rafaella stopped on the south side of Piazza Basilica, outside a wide stone villa with a noble aspect. It had large green double carriage doors centred onto the street and, on the level above, green-slatted shutters on the windows and French doors with Juliet balconies. The villa was dwarfed by the ecclesiastical buildings on the opposite side of the square, but it was double the size of anything else in the area. It had once been the mayor's residence.

She opened the pedestrian door inset in the carriage doors and stepped into the large courtyard beyond. The tourists walking right past would have been amazed by the oasis hidden within. A majestic pomegranate tree stood at the centre with a table and chairs set below; fig trees were trained up the inner walls, their leaves splayed like hands against the stone; lemon trees stood in planters and water tinkled lightly from a fountain set into a niche. A small red tricycle was lying on its side, a leather ball wedged under the rim of a plant pot, a watering can left by the door.

The door to the house was open, as ever, and Rafaella walked straight in and up the gracious stone staircase.

'Gina?' she called, kicking off her shoes at the top step and immediately enjoying the coolness of the stone beneath her hot bare feet. It was still only June but already so hot; August was going to be unbearable if temperatures continued to rise at this rate.

'In here.'

Gina was in the kitchen, making orecchiette her mother's way. Dozens of dirty pots and pans were stacked on the counter. Little Lorenzo sat at the table with an empty plate and tomato sauce all over his chin.

'Zia Rafa!' he cried, throwing his arms up in excitement as she set down her bag and kissed his cheeks.

'What a state you are!' she laughed, reaching for his napkin and wiping him clean. 'That's better . . .' She kissed the tip of his nose. He reached for a drawing on the table in front of him. 'Is that for me?' she asked, pointing to the indistinct crayon scribbles.

'*Si!* Guess what it is!'

'Is it a . . . tricycle?' He had been given one for his second birthday and had scrawled its likeness at least a dozen times. Rafaella had five other copies of this taped to her kitchen wall at home. They were treasure to her, every last one. She loved him like he was her own.

'*Si!*'

'I love it,' she said, clutching him to her tightly for a moment and wishing she could hold onto him for longer, but he was already wriggling, his attention moving to the next thing. 'Have you finished eating? Has Mamma said you can get down?'

Gina nodded her assent and Rafaella pulled out his chair. 'Stay in the garden!' his mother called as he darted from sight. '. . . He's obsessed with that bike.'

'I know.' Rafaella walked over to the sink and washed her hands, finding yet more dirty dishes there. 'Gina, what's going on? Are you feeding the ten thousand?'

Gina shot her a weary look. 'He's got the councillors coming tonight.'

'Tonight?' This meant Fon would be going too, but there had been no mention of it this morning.

'A last-minute thing. They got word of a dignitary visiting in the area.'

Rafaella looked over at her friend as she dried her hands – her feet were swelling up and she looked drained, her hairline beaded with sweat.

'I guess I should count myself lucky he gave me an afternoon's notice,' Gina said wryly, pressing a forearm to mop her brow but only succeeding in putting flour all over her face.

'Go and get a drink and sit down, I'll finish up here. You've been doing all this plus running around after Lorenzo.' She gently barged her friend out of the way and began pulling up her hair into a messy bun, securing it with a toy drumstick left on the side.

Gina's hand went to her rounded stomach. She was due in just over two months but it had already been a long and testing pregnancy – her body had swelled dramatically, her sensational curves swamped. Even with another trimester to go, she was struggling with swollen ankles and heavy legs. The doctor said something about carrying more fluid and to take more rest, but of course she had paid him no heed. She could easily afford a housekeeper but, like Rafaella, she didn't want someone else washing her underwear or 'spying' on her in her own home. They were products of their upbringing, too rooted in doing things themselves to feel comfortable with delegation and sitting around.

'You've got flour on your face,' Rafaella said as Gina walked to the refrigerator and brought out a jug of lemonade. She poured them each a glass.

'You've got chalk dust in your hair,' Gina shrugged back, collapsing into her son's abandoned chair.

Rafaella began rolling and pinching the flour into little ears. The pastry table was overlaid with a blue enamel top that stayed cold no matter how long they worked. She liked the feeling of her hands in the flour, the steady repetition of the work. It reminded her of home and of her mother. Of a time before this, when they'd had freedom and not known it.

'So is this meeting to do with the new apartment block on Via Faccolli?' she asked Gina. Modern flats were springing up all over the town, set outside the thick fort walls; Fon kept telling her no one wanted to live in the historic centre anymore – it was impossible to bring cars down the narrow, winding streets; it was difficult to dig the drains for better sewage . . .

Gina threw her hands up in the air. 'Who knows? Who cares?'

'Do we have to be there?'

'No. Men only.'

'Well then, that's something.'

She finished up the last of the dough and set the orecchiette in a large flat-bottomed dish, covering it with a damp cloth. Their lunch was already plated up on the side – burrata, tomatoes, basil, some prosciutto and sliced peaches – and she brought it over to the kitchen table. They ate together most days, without formality, their bare feet up on the chairs and hair twisted back, skirts pulled up to bare their thighs to catch what little cooling breeze they could. In this kitchen they could go back to being the creatures of their girlhood, but on the other side of the shutters, they could only be seen as the Giannelli wives: polished, elegant and rich, representatives of their husbands' success.

She had never imagined they would come to be living here together, as sisters-in-law; when Gina had first revealed that she was pregnant, Rafaella had worried that Dante would leave her high and dry. Their relationship was tempestuous and he made no secret of the fact that he had other women, coming back reeking of perfume, lipstick on his collar . . . But then Rafaella had confided her fear to Fon and a few days later, Dante had proposed to Gina. Fon had simply shrugged when she'd asked him about it, and to this day she still didn't know exactly what he'd said to make his brother commit to her best friend. She was only grateful that he had.

It worked, their foursome living in the same town. She and Gina were a familiar sight together, taking Lorenzo to the beach or shopping in the market, and people were eager to be their friends, always putting an extra ounce of cherries in their basket or the fattest fish. It helped that Dante had quickly risen to prominence here, Fon too as his right-hand man.

Against all odds, their marriage was proving to be a quiet success. Rafaella knew her husband was proud to have her on his arm; as a successful businessman, he couldn't be let down by a woman who didn't know how to act or dress. She had to be charming but not flirtatious, beautiful but not bawdy; she had to be able to cook and make a cocktail and know how to wear her hair. In turn, he allowed her to fill her days with meaningful purpose, raising no protest when she told him she wanted to train as a teacher. Most importantly, he had kept his promise to her, the one condition *she* had insisted on when he had proposed his plan that fated August night: he wouldn't touch her in bed until she was ready. It was to his credit that he had waited for two years before she finally surrendered, when despair and too much wine got the better of her one night, Cosimo's memory growing faint, like a thumbprint on a window. She still loved him but she had lost him, and if she wanted other things – to be a mother, a proper wife; to live a full life and not exist as a shadow – then how could any of those things happen with a barren bed?

She wasn't sure what she had expected – an explosion of pent-up passion? – but it had been surprisingly perfunctory, a quiet, unsatisfying rocking that bore no resemblance to her experience with Cosimo. Fon never said anything about it afterwards but she knew she had been a disappointment to him and he hadn't 'troubled' her with his needs since; he had a mistress to deal with that side of things, she knew. Rafaella felt the shame sharply but she couldn't deny she was relieved too. Even Gina didn't know the truth of what *didn't* go on behind their bedroom door.

'Did I tell you about Antonia?' Gina asked abruptly, stabbing a tomato with her fork.

'*Antonia?*' Rafaella frowned. It had been years since they had seen her. The girl had run away from home the summer of Silvana's wedding. Rumours had swirled that she had a secret boyfriend. 'No.'

'Papa saw her in Lecce. He was meeting with a new supplier and he swore he saw her across the road in a bar with some other girls. And when I say girls, I mean . . .' Gina lifted her eyebrows in disapproval, which Rafaella understood to mean whores.

'Did he talk to her?'

'Tried to. He called over to her and she looked right at him, but by the time he got there, she had gone.'

Rafaella frowned. 'Did he tell her parents?'

'Sure. They went looking for her, but . . .' Gina shrugged. 'No sign of her.'

'It's a big place, I guess.'

'Yes.'

Rafaella looked out of the kitchen window, watching a pigeon sitting in the pomegranate tree, cleaning its wing. 'Well, at least she's still alive. That's something. After what happened to Donatella . . .'

'Don't.' Gina crossed herself. Rafaella knew her friend had always felt guilty that her dance with the devil had somehow ended fortuitously; her life was far from perfect, but she had married the father of her son and she had respectability if not peace. Donatella hadn't been so lucky. The guy who had knocked her up wasn't interested in doing the right thing by her and she'd gone to a back-street doctor to 'get the situation taken care of'; she'd died from an infection five days later. The last Rafaella had heard, the guy was married now with a kid.

They heard the slam of the pedestrian door downstairs,

footsteps on the stairs taken two at a time. Both women pulled down their skirts and took their feet off the chairs just as Dante came through, taking off his tie. Sweat patches had formed on his shirt under the arms and his hair was slicked back. He looked hot but handsome. His brooding features had somehow deepened over the past few years, like patina on wood, and he seemed to exert more power over women than ever.

But Rafaella still didn't like him. His stare always lingered on her a little too long, as if suspicious of her immunity to his charms. Or perhaps he worried about her having Gina's ear, for she too was often disdainful of him; but Gina's passion for the man always overrode her dislike of him and sometimes, when Rafaella listened to her friend's stories of their tempestuous fights and make-ups, she wished she loved or even hated her own husband enough to scream.

'Rafa,' he said, greeting her with light kisses on the cheek as usual. There was no doubt he wielded the power in all their lives and he was always quick to assert it, but with her, he held back. She was Fon's wife and that gave her a special status in his eyes, almost equal to Gina's. His brother's happiness rested with her and he wouldn't do anything to shake it.

'Why are you back so early?' Gina demanded, reluctantly getting up, a hand on her thigh.

'I came to wash and change. There won't be time la—' He frowned as he finally noticed the state of the kitchen – their empty lunch plates and current lack of industry at the table told a false narrative. 'What is this?' he asked angrily. 'I told you this meeting is important! How are you going to be ready if you're just sitting around?'

Gina groaned, waving a hand at him dismissively. 'We were just having lunch! I have to eat, don't I? Or do you want this baby to starve?'

'No fear of that!' he snapped, hitting her where it hurt. Her curves were the currency she held over him, the reason she was the woman he kept coming back to. It was why she was so agitated about this pregnancy – she couldn't afford to lose her figure.

'The pasta is made and I will make the sauce fresh!'

'When?'

'When they're all here! Seven thirty, you said!'

Rafaella sat quietly; they were forever shouting at one another and would fight savagely, sometimes literally.

'Always the last minute with you!'

Gina walked over to the fridge. 'Look – tiramisu, like you asked!' she said, holding up the dessert. 'Who is this important visitor who has you in such a fluster, anyway?'

'That is none of your concern.'

'No? He's coming to my house, eating my food, and I'm crazy to want to know his name?' Gina put her hands on her hips, her bosom wobbling with indignation, and Rafaella watched Dante's look change. She had seen it before, the sudden switch from irritation to desire. Gina saw it too, and her chin lifted a little across the kitchen.

'I'd better head back,' Rafaella said quickly, reaching for her bag as the silence grew weighty. 'Fon will be waiting for me.'

'Take Lorenzo, will you?' Dante muttered, not taking his eyes off his wife. 'He needs his nap.'

'Sure. See you later,' she said, hurrying from the room before their flames could burn her.

Chapter 33

Fon

The streetlights shone through the shuttered windows, falling on the tiled floor in thick stripes as everyone waited for their guest of honour. Bruno Collura, the council leader, had arranged the meeting, telling them the ring of a bike's bell outside would signal the dignitary's approach. The energy in the room was shifty, everyone on edge except for Dante, who was supremely relaxed; he had even forsaken a tie and was sitting in his purple velvet chair in his reception salon holding a glass of brandy, one leg splayed over his knee.

Gina had done a good job of showing the villa to its best. The gilded mirrors were polished to a shine, a majolica vase filled with Madonna lilies, Lorenzo's toys tidied away for once. Dante had insisted she stay upstairs; she had let herself go with this pregnancy and he didn't want her showing him up. Appearances mattered, and never more so than this evening. No advantage could be lost.

Fon took another sip of his drink. Unlike his brother, he couldn't shake off his nerves so easily. There was a gap between how he was commonly regarded and how he saw himself, and it was at times like this that he fell back into his old insecurities. It was true they had succeeded beyond their wildest dreams – Dante kept telling him the Giannelli family business was on the way to becoming something he would never have believed possible: an empire. Smuggling *bionde* and pimping blondes had been lucrative, of course – everyone wanted cigarettes and women – but it had only been the start. Dante had always had not just the vision for more, but the backbone too. Fon, as his first lieutenant, did what was required when it was asked of him; he just had no natural appetite for it.

He would never command respect in the same way as his brother. He didn't have courage or charisma; he didn't bristle with menace. What he did have was a quick brain and good instincts about people. A lifetime of being on the edge of things meant he could read a room with a sharp eye, and that made him an asset when it came to doing deals; he had 'smarts', and his brother not only needed that but respected it too. They had fallen into a sort of double act over the past few years, with Dante always the star and Fon forever a shadow, the quietest man in every room. While Dante performed, Fon observed. He had learnt to make a virtue of being overlooked, find the opportunity in being underestimated. It was the tactic that had won him his wife, after all.

This occasion, though – stepping back into their past – was unnerving, and he couldn't pretend otherwise.

The bike bell rang loudly outside, making everyone stand taller as the messenger boy's shadow streaked past the window. Moments later, a black *cinquecento* rolled up; it was the only car small enough to navigate these narrow, winding streets, and privacy had been stipulated for this meeting. Walking or even taking a scooter were far too risky with these crowds.

Fon listened for the slam of the pedestrian door, for leather-shod footsteps on the staircase, and he downed the rest of his brandy.

'Senatore,' Collura said, meeting the visitor at the door and inclining his head respectfully before offering his hand. He welcomed their distinguished guest with a hushed reverence.

'Signore Collura,' the cabinet minister replied in smooth tones, as stately as the pope. 'So very nice to see you again. This is a beautiful home you have here.'

'Actually, it is not mine,' Collura replied. 'But we thought the space and privacy afforded here was preferable, with so many tourists around now. I believe you know our host, Signore Giannelli?'

'Gian—? . . . *Dante?*' Filippo Franchetti said with surprise as Dante stepped forward.

Fon watched as Franchetti's supercilious smile faded. He took in Dante's sharp suit, the handsome residence and vastly elevated circumstances. Even if it wasn't entirely to his taste, no one could deny it was a long way from the *casino vecchio* in every sense.

'Senatore, it's good to see you again,' Dante said, holding out his hand. 'Thank you for coming tonight.'

Franchetti looked as if he'd been ambushed. 'Well . . . I had no idea I was being reunited with old neighbours.'

'Would you have come if you had?' Dante smiled. 'A lot can change in a few years.'

'So I see.'

'Come. Allow me to introduce you,' Dante said, presenting the councillors, the important port men who had quickly come to see the benefits of doing business with the Giannellis.

Fon waited patiently for the minister's attention to fall on him.

'And I'm sure you remember my brother, Alfonso . . .'

'Senatore,' Fon said, offering his hand and seeing how the politician's smooth smile faltered once again as their eyes locked. The other councillors had no idea of how their fates had become so inextricably linked. It had been almost four years since they had last met – blue lights flashing, screams through the moonlight . . . Filippo had returned home to a hellscape and Fon holding his hands up to it . . .

The Franchettis hadn't returned to Tricase since the accident, and on his last visit Fon had seen the garden was becoming overgrown, the gates rusting closed. Was neglect helping them forget?

Franchetti could only nod in reply. He had noticeably aged. Always lean and in shape, he was now decidedly thin, his dark hair more salted than peppered these days, and his eyes looked rheumy behind his glasses. It was hard to see in him now the ladies' man who had once bedded Valentina Fabiani. Even Dante – thinking he'd had a chance as he flirted like the devil on the speedboat – had been stunned by that revelation.

Of course, it had all come out in the newspapers in the end; even Dante had only been able to hold off the dogs for so long. A period of grace had been extended to the duke in the months after his daughter's death, but eventually the finger had been removed from the dam and the story had run for weeks: exposing the notorious bed-hopping antics of the Roman upper classes, sexual promiscuity, underage drinking . . . The fallout had been severe: Romola's reputation was compromised in death and Rossanna finally left him. Franchetti had been demoted to minister of public education, though not kicked out of politics altogether. Valentina's career took a hard knock, too. Cast as the villainess in this real-life morality tale, her new film had bombed at the box office, and then she had run off with the married director of her next one.

'It was good of you to agree to see us, signore,' Dante said, handing him a glass of brandy. Fon could see the surprise in Franchetti's eyes as it became evident it wouldn't be

Collura leading the meeting; as his brother addressed their former noble neighbour as an equal; as Franchetti began to see that this dinner was not the provincial glad-handing he had anticipated.

'Well, I was in the neighbourhood,' Franchetti murmured, trying to regain his footing.

'Yes, Lecce is beautiful, isn't it? The Grand Hotel does a very good martini,' Dante said, casually dropping the name of the hotel where Franchetti was staying forty-five minutes from here – a casual warning the politician would pick up on. 'Are you here on business?'

'. . . A private visit, actually,' Franchetti replied.

Dante nodded, knowing exactly what that meant. He had several mistresses in different towns in the region, too. He didn't like sleeping alone. None of them did.

'I must admit, I wasn't aware you had moved here,' Filippo added.

'Well, I would prefer to be in Tricase Porto still . . . Did you know we bought the Villa Blanca?'

'. . . No.'

The other wealthy summer visitors had gradually sold off their villas once the Franchettis stopped visiting the port. Death had tinged the glamour of the place, like a poison rotting the bougainvillea.

'We're doing a lot of renovation work, naturally, so this place is fine in the interim,' Dante shrugged, as if 'this place', the mayor's villa, was little more than a hovel. 'And being in a thriving trading port is helpful for many of our business operations. Not to mention my wife prefers it here.'

'Wife?'

'Gina . . . Crespi, as she was.'

'Oh – from the grocery?' Franchetti asked.

A flicker of annoyance crossed Dante's face as their humble origins were reannounced for the benefit of the other councillors, most of whom had been born middle class. 'So you remember her? She's very beautiful, it's true.'

Franchetti's mouth opened and Fon saw a realization come into his eyes, enlivening him for a moment. Was he going to say he remembered her running through his villa every summer, with his daughter? '. . . The tomatoes were always very good,' he murmured, sinking back into himself again.

Dante smouldered at the slight but, like the duke, controlled himself. 'I trust the duchess is happy in Florence?' Their divorce had, of course, made the papers too.

'. . . As she can be, thank you for asking.'

'Beautiful city.'

'You've been?' Franchetti asked with a sceptical look.

'Not recently.' Dante gave a dazzling smile. 'I really should rectify that. Gina would enjoy a trip before the baby comes.'

'Oh – you're expecting?'

'Our second,' Dante nodded.

'I see,' Franchetti murmured, looking him over again. 'I must be honest, I never took you for a family man, Dante.'

'No? Well, I suppose we come in all guises.' Dante held his gaze as a silent point was made: Filippo Franchetti was in no position to preach about family men.

It was a warning shot, both men knew, as they vied for the upper hand.

From another room, the dinner gong sounded.

'Ah, we are being called . . . Let's go through and eat.'

The men all filed through, Fon bringing up the rear and observing the responses of the councillors ahead of him as their distinguished guest settled in. Much could be gleaned from the roll of an eye, lips read.

The room was decorated with dark red silk on the walls and heavy oak chairs arranged around a long table. Gina had set out the gold tableware and candelabras, but the young women serving were local whores prepped to double up on their duties if they caught the eye of the cabinet minister. Dante called it an 'insurance policy' – booze and women always loosened the tongue – but from what Fon had seen of the man's altered state tonight, he wasn't sure Franchetti would succumb. He met Dante's eyes with a brief look, silently communicating his thoughts.

Dante nodded almost imperceptibly. It was the advantage of being brothers: they had always read each other like books.

'So tell me, do you still live in your beautiful villa in Rome, Senatore?' Dante asked as they took their seats, bosoms almost poking them in the eyes as napkins were draped over their laps. As host, Dante sat at the head of the table, Filippo to his right and Fon sitting opposite, on his left.

'No, I . . . I have no need for so many rooms these days. I'm in the process of moving to a smaller apartment on the Via Veneto at the moment, actually.'

'Still very gracious, I'm sure.'

'I like to think so.'

Fon understood understatement and knew that meant there'd be a Botticelli or two on the walls and a Bourbon bed from Francis II, the last king of Naples.

'It must be difficult, though, scaling down from – as you say – so many rooms to just one or two. What are you doing with all your furniture?'

'Why? Do you wish to buy it?'

It was a sharp response – too sharp – and as Dante looked back at him, offended, Franchetti gathered himself. 'Forgive me. That joke was in poor taste. I . . . I'm tired.'

'Of course.'

'In truth, Rossanna's taken much of it to Florence.' Franchetti shrugged. 'I don't need all those mirrors and chairs.'

'Mm,' Dante nodded, agreeing. 'Although you're much more of an antiquarian, aren't you? A noted man of letters.

Surely you didn't give up your books and papers? Dividing up your collection must have been—'

'No, no, she had no interest in any of that,' he said dismissively. 'I kept all that. It was really quite simple in the end.'

Fon watched him closely, seeing how Franchetti smoothed the napkin on his lap as he spoke. It was a self-soothing gesture – the end of his family life hadn't been as simple as he liked to imply.

'Well, I'm glad to hear it,' Dante smiled, an attentive host even as sharks swam below the surface of the water. 'And Fede? How is he? Did I hear he's working with the state attorney's office now?'

Franchetti straightened up proudly. 'Yes. He's doing very well there. I believe he'll go far.'

'Well, of course – he's a Franchetti.'

The compliment was double-edged, but Dante delivered it with a smile. Fon had never told him – or anyone – what he had seen Fede doing outside Villa Maria the night Romola died, even though that sort of information would be invaluable leverage against such an influential family. Fede's kindness and the way he had extended the hand of friendship when everyone else had turned their backs meant something. Even the night of the accident, when Fon had been in despair and lashed out at him, Fede had been restrained and compassionate. Four years on, Fon could close his eyes and easily conjure the image of the two men behind the bins and how it had taken his breath away. It was scorched into his mind, a tattoo from a terrible night, and though he squashed it down, the image lurked in his shadow self.

Now Fon sat very still, bracing instead for a mention of the other Franchetti son's name: *How* is Cosimo? *Where* is he? *What* is he? . . . His name never came up in conversation. It was as if he had dropped off the face of the earth rather than simply entered the Church. Certainly Rafaella never uttered his name, and Fon could never quite decide if that was a good sign or a bad one.

But Cosimo was of no interest to Dante, who pressed on with his agenda.

'Fede must be busy with these protests in South Tyrol,' he continued as the food was served. Just days earlier, thirty-seven pylons had been blown up by protesters seeking autonomy for the German-speaking region.

'Yes, a messy business,' Franchetti murmured.

Dante's elbows were splayed across the arms of his chair as they moved, finally, from the personal to the political. He looked relaxed, a man in his element. 'Think they'll get what they want?'

'Of course not. Fanfani knows how to send out a strong message that violence never wins.'

'I agree,' Dante nodded, glancing at the serving girl as she set down his plate of orecchiette. 'It's preferable to negotiate. In my experience, there's always a deal to be done. But of course, you know that better than anyone. You're one of the most experienced government ministers in cabinet.' He gave a small laugh. 'You know where all the skeletons are buried!'

A rumble of sycophantic laughter erupted from the other councillors, all flattered to be in the company of a Roman power player. But Fon simply watched as Franchetti's eyebrow hitched up – in response to the joke? Or because he was resistant to Dante conversing with him as an equal? Resentment glittered in his eyes even as his mouth smiled. Did he still remember that day on the boat, the Giannelli brothers working for him in the sun, grafting for coin and kudos?

'It's true I have been doing this for a long time now. Which is why, I take it, you asked me here tonight. You have something specific you want to put to me?'

It was Collura's moment, and he leaned forward as Dante sat back to give him the floor. 'Indeed, Senatore – we wanted to talk to you about the development that was refused outside Scorrano.'

Fon watched their visitor frown, deliberately oblique. 'I don't recall that . . .'

'Eight thousand new apartments. A high school and civic centre. A multimillion-lira contract.'

Franchetti allowed a long pause, as if sifting through applications in his head. 'Ah yes, that. The land there was deemed unsuitable.' The proclamation was pronounced with finality and Collura's gaze skittered over the table towards Dante.

Dante watched, as still as a rock lizard, as Franchetti began to eat. 'The land there is the same as everywhere else.' He gave a half-smile. 'And with respect, Senatore, concrete doesn't care. We're not looking to grow mangoes.'

Franchetti smiled too, amused by the image. 'Still, we can't risk another cathedral in the desert.'

Dante's finger tapped on the table. 'That money has to be disbursed, however. The whole point of the Southern Development Fund is to regenerate—'

'The winds of change are blowing, Giannelli,' Franchetti said, cutting him off with a condescending tone as he put down his cutlery and reached for his wine. 'Franceschini wants to put together a commission advising against these poorly planned developments where no consideration is given to the aesthetics or the quality. Half of them are unfinished! Pressure is growing to block new building.'

'All the more reason to get those permits awarded now, then,' Collura said.

Franchetti shook his head. 'He's advising we build less but better. He wants his recommendations to be put into policy, and I for one am behind him. Most of what's going up is a blight on the landscape.'

Fon watched him pontificate, the nobleman falling back

into seasoned superiority, as if his delicate aristocratic sensibilities were now offended by the inelegance of the developments from which he had personally profited. Fon leaned forward slightly in his chair, knowing it was time for him to put a finger on the scale and recalibrate the weighting of power.

'That never seemed to concern you when you were minister of infrastructure, Senatore. How many permits did you issue when you were in charge there?'

Franchetti looked at him in surprise. Fon could see that the duke still regarded him as the teenager who had passed round cold drinks on the boat and set the bindings on the water-skis – while the duke flagrantly seduced his son's girlfriend in front of them. 'I never counted—'

'Twelve thousand, seven hundred and eighty-three.'

'You couldn't possibly know that.'

Fon shrugged. 'We know many people who know many things.'

There was a small silence as the duke carefully set his glass back down and resumed eating. He was deliberately slow, dictating the pace of the conversation if not the topic. 'Well, clearly some mistakes were made along the way, I don't deny that,' he said eventually. 'In our haste to regenerate after the war, we took some decisions that wouldn't be taken now. But there's a new recognition that heritage and culture are important to the economy and must be protected, especially if we want to grow the tourism sector.'

'Tourism is nothing to the economy versus development,' Dante said.

'Maybe not yet, but it's growing – and fast. Look at Pompeii. Look at the impact of Hollywood coming to Rome. Italy is becoming a world-class destination.'

'But to prioritize history and tourism over the lives of real working people? Our men need jobs. We have an army of them, just waiting for the order to break ground on this project.'

'As I recall, your own mayor advised against it.'

'Yes, but he's reconsidered,' Dante said with a lazy smile.

'Reconsidered?'

'You know how local politicians are – only ever concerned with keeping their jobs. He didn't want to ruffle any feathers before the elections last month.' Dante pinned the duke with a stare in which messages – threats – were communicated without words. 'But now he's had time to think on it, he sees the benefits, and he agrees the refusal needs to be reversed.'

Franchetti shrugged, blowing off the insinuation. 'I'm sorry. There's nothing I can do.'

'This is an important contract for the area,' Dante said, still pushing. He never stopped. Not until he got what he wanted. 'It will bring us regeneration, like the rest of the country . . . My men—'

'*Your* men? Are you an elected politician too, then, Mr Giannelli?' Franchetti said sharply.

Dante blinked. 'I'm a man of the people.'

Franchetti met Dante's eyes, a small laugh falling from his lips. He knew exactly what that meant, but Fon could see he intended to put them in their place. Even now, in the midst of all this splendour and power, he was still out of their reach. 'This is all beyond my jurisdiction. I'm merely the minister of public education now,' he said disingenuously. 'Furthermore, my ministry covers the Department of Fine Arts and Antiquity, meaning I'm heavily involved with the International Council of Museums. Whatever I may have approved in the past, my remit now is to *protect* heritage. I can't be seen to be involved with this.'

'No one's asking you to be seen,' Dante smiled, still throwing out lifelines. 'On the contrary—'

'I'm sorry. You're overestimating my powers,' Franchetti said bluntly. 'I wish I could help.'

He made to stand up but Fon leaned forward again, recognizing his moment. 'You could. You are very much more influential than you want us to believe. You could make Franceschini reconsider with just one phone call, but you won't because you don't want to do business with *us*. To you, we are merely fishermen's sons.'

'That's ridiculous.'

'It is ridiculous,' Fon nodded. 'Because we are very much more than that now. We are well connected, Senatore, and we know that in your capacity as minister of infrastructure, you took bribes.'

Franchetti rolled his eyes. 'How many times have the press run with that innuendo? And yet nothing's ever come of it.'

'It will this time. If our source talks.'

There was a pause, and Fon could see the other man trying to read whether he was bluffing.

'You don't have that kind of power,' Franchetti sneered dismissively.

'No? They held off on publishing the affair because we told them to.' Fon shrugged, his tone steady as he revealed the Giannellis' hand in events.

'*You?*' Franchetti whispered, incredulous at what he was learning.

'The court of public sympathy was on your side. Everyone pitied you. It wasn't the right time to show the world what you'd done to your son, your wife.'

'Until suddenly it was!' Franchetti snapped. His world had crumbled for a second time when his scandals had hit the front pages. 'You want me to believe you held them off, then gave them the go-ahead?' he scoffed.

'Nothing lasts for ever,' Fon replied coolly, seeing the rage in the other man's eyes. He knew Franchetti blamed him for

Romola's death, and rightly so. Even though Fon had been cleared of any criminal culpability, he'd put his hands up to toppling the urn that killed her. And now Fon was saying they had extended mercy to Franchetti, then let it lapse . . .? He was demonstrating the range of the Giannellis' reach. He'd hate them too if he was sitting in the other man's chair.

'. . . I urge you to reconsider and make that call. After all, what do you have left now besides your career?'

There was a long silence. Fon saw the duke's jaw clench with contained anger. It wasn't the fact that he'd been cornered that was so enraging to him; it was that he'd been cornered by *them*.

And he wouldn't stand for it.

'You've played this all wrong, Giannelli,' he hissed. 'Blackmail won't work on me. I'm not issuing that permit.' He looked between the two brothers, unwilling to cede an inch, even if it was self-destructive. 'You think I care about my position?' He made a sharp, derisive sound. 'Just try me and see! There's no opponent more dangerous than a man with nothing left to lose.' He got up from the table, setting down his napkin and buttoning up his suit jacket as he cast his eyes over them all with contempt. '. . . Gentlemen.'

The councillors looked away, but Dante watched as he left the room before swinging his gaze back to Fon with a smile.

They both knew perfectly well it was another bluff.

There was always more to lose.

Chapter 34

Cosimo

'In there.'

'Thank you,' Cosimo nodded as the novice master walked away again, leather-soled sandals slapping against the stone floor. He pushed open the door and walked into the small room. It was supposed to be for receiving visitors but seemed designed to be deliberately uninviting, with only a small wooden table and hard chairs to hasten guests' departure.

'. . . Father?'

Filippo Franchetti turned. 'So you *are* here,' he said coldly, though relief seemed to shiver through his eyes.

'Yes, I—'

'When were you going to tell me? Or was that the point – that I wasn't supposed to know?'

'Of course not. I didn't know myself until a few days ago.'

'I went to Lecce especially to see you, Cosimo! Imagine my shock when they said you had gone!'

'Father, I intended to write.'

'Really? When?'

'When I had some time. It's been busy here.' He sighed, realizing he hadn't even shut the door yet and they were already into their first argument. '. . . It's good to see you,' he said, closing the door.

His father hesitated, seeming to catch himself too. '. . . And you.' They met in the middle of the small room, hugging briefly, and Cosimo felt himself flinch at the physical contact. He couldn't remember the last time he had been touched.

He pulled back. 'Is everything OK?'

'Yes, I just wanted to bring you this. The last of your things.' His father lightly touched the top of a small shoebox under his arm.

'What's in there?'

'I'm not sure exactly. Your mother went through and sorted everything; she said you'd want them.' Filippo shrugged and held it out.

'Oh.' Cosimo hesitated.

'Is there a problem?'

'. . . It's just we're not allowed possessions here.'

His father frowned. 'It's just some keepsakes!'

'Even so.'

'Well then, is there not somewhere safe this can be stored until . . .'

'Until what?'

'You leave here!'

'I won't be leaving here, Father.' He watched as Filippo's mouth flattened in a grim line. The finality of Cosimo's decision was something his father still failed to grasp. He relented a little. '. . . But yes, thank you. I can make sure this is kept safely for me.'

He took it, looking down at the shoebox: pale blue with white writing, sized for children's shoes. A part of him desperately wanted to know what was inside, these mementoes, artefacts from his old life – letters? Games? Knowing his mother, it could be his baby teeth. He could almost feel the contents vibrating with suppressed energy and he pressed the lid more firmly closed; he knew he wouldn't dare to even lift it.

'You're pale,' Filippo said, regarding him closely, his eyes grazing over his seminarian's habit: a long black cassock with green sash, the black, peaked, square biretta hat he was holding in his other hand. His mouth puckered with disapproval. 'Do you ever go outside?'

'Not enough, it's true. Most of my time is spent in the library.'

'Doing what?'

'Studying scripture. We're transcribing some tenth-century documents about Saint Francis.'

Filippo rolled his eyes. 'Is that what the world really needs?'

'I find it interesting. Not to mention quite meditative.'

'And to think we could never get you to open a book as a boy . . . You need to go outside and get more sun.'

'You're right. I'll take some more turns around the quad after lunch.'

Filippo turned away, unused to this agreeable demeanour; their relationship had always been fractious in the past. Cosimo had always been his mother's son. Now they couldn't even fight like they used to.

Cosimo watched him pace, sensing a disquiet in his father's spirit. He knew he hadn't known peace since the night of the accident, but this seemed fresh, like newly turned soil. 'How is Mamma?'

Filippo's eyes flashed towards him. 'You'd know better than me. Has she visited you recently?'

Cosimo shook his head. His mother had moved to Florence with his three youngest siblings, busying herself with the little ones as if trying to forget all about the older children who no longer needed her. Fede was working in Rome, rapidly ascending the legal ladder; Cosimo had deliberately absented himself, of course. But it was Romola's loss that had left a void at the very centre, obliterating their family like an exploding star. '. . . Not here. I'll write to her tomorrow and let her know I've been relocated. I only arrived a few days ago.'

'What's here that they needed you so badly?'

'There have been some departures among the novices and Father Polacco needs help with the pastoral ministries.'

'Was that Father Polacco who saw me in just now?'

'No, Father Caputo.'

'Hm. You have no shortage of fathers, it seems.' He turned away, his gaze upon the slitted window set high in the wall. 'So, what sort of *pastoral ministries* are you undertaking?' A hint of disdain frilled the words. They had very different ideas about public service.

'There's been an outbreak of polio—'

'*Polio?*' Filippo whipped round.

'We're trying to help with that as well as encourage uptake of the vaccine.'

'And they have to send you – my son?'

'I'm not *your son* here.' The words came out faster, sharper than Cosimo had intended, and his father froze. They were an echo of the cry that had fallen from Cosimo – 'You're not my father!' – in the days after the story had broken in the papers, as his mother sobbed, humiliation coming in hot after tragedy.

Cosimo turned away from the memories. 'I like it here,' he said placidly, reaching for mildness. Most of the time he could suppress the violent emotions that he knew still festered in the darkest corners of his soul, but seeing his father was always unsettling, like pulling the plug off a volcano. He couldn't recover from his father's betrayal, nor the tragedy to which it had led, and like his mother before him, he had retreated into civility. Manners threw up a barrier only a soft heart could pierce, and there were none of those here. 'I've only been out on ministry a few times, but the port is beautiful and the people are good.'

His father gave a small snort.

'They seem grateful for the work we're doing,' Cosimo continued, seeing how his father raked a hand through his hair. He was visibly agitated, unable to settle. '. . . Papa, what is it? Has something happened?'

Filippo hesitated, his eyes meeting Cosimo's. Regret lived there, but nothing could be done about it now. What was done was done. They never had been able to reach one another.

'No,' he said, shaking a hand dismissively. 'I just had a business meeting that rankled, that's all.'

'Here? In Otranto?'

'I'm a politician, Cosi. Politics is everywhere. I could go to any town in Italy and people would want something from me.'

'And what did they want?'

'Just the usual shakedown. Upstarts thinking they're the new world order and that everyone's for sale.'

The bells had begun ringing for evening Mass, the streets outside growing quiet now. Through the narrow channel of the window, the golden light of the piazza fell into the austere room. Cosimo knew the cathedral would be dramatically spotlit at this hour. There was a spectacular view of it, of the entire piazza, from a window that was hidden from the streets by the parapet wall. It was on the very top floor of the seminary and led out onto the roof; it was strictly out of bounds, but Brother Savelli, a friend of his from Lecce, had shown it to him on his first night here. Cosimo had made a secret pilgrimage on many nights since, sitting up there with the roosting pigeons when he was unable to sleep.

They heard hurried footsteps in the corridor outside, the

seminarians making their way through to the cathedral next door. 'Papa, I have to go, I'm sorry – we have Mass.'

'Oh.'

'Why don't you come? Father Polacco is—'

But Filippo shook his head. He had lost his faith along with everything else when Romola died. 'I have a journey back to Lecce in one of those *ridiculous* cars . . .' He tutted. 'I only wanted to bring you your things and check for myself you were really here.'

Cosimo frowned. 'I'm fine. I'm perfectly safe.'

Filippo nodded, but he wore a haunted look, as if losing children was a contagious state. He crossed the room and stood at the door for a moment. 'Write to your mother,' he said, before slipping out like a ghost.

Cosimo ran through the vaulted, covered stone walkway connecting the seminary to the cathedral. On one side was a courtyard, on the other a garden with fruit trees. Everyone else was seated and the organ already playing as he took his place in one of the narrow, inward-facing choir pews.

'Where were you?' Alessio Savelli whispered. He too had been at Lecce seminary until last year, when he had been seconded here. They weren't supposed to foster close friendships in the novitiate – everyone was supposed to be equal, no one more or less important than anyone else – but privately, Cosimo had been relieved to see Savelli's face when he had walked into the refectory.

Like Cosimo, Savelli came from a noble family, but as the fourth and youngest son, the money for an inheritance had run out and he had been sent into the Church largely against his will. He was due to take his deaconship next year but he struck Cosimo as temperamentally unsuited to the role; left to his own devices, he'd said once, he would have become a racing-car driver in the Mille Miglia.

Their rooms were together on the third level, where the senior novices resided. There too the windows were narrow, like castle arrow slits, but being on the top floor at the top of a hill, they could glimpse staggering views out to sea. They were supposed to resist, especially during prayer time, but if Cosimo kept his eyes averted, it wasn't for 'modesty of the eye' but because he hadn't seen the sea since leaving Tricase Porto. It was too bound up with his memories of summers and everything that had happened there.

'My father paid a visit.'

'Oh.' Savelli glanced across. Over the years together in Lecce, Cosimo had revealed his own story to him; he could have read most of it in the papers anyway, but Cosimo had gone further, confiding the pact with Fon and how its consequences for him and Rafaella had led him to retreat to the seminary. Between grief, guilt and heartbreak, the wider world had nothing left to offer him. '. . . Are you OK?'

'Sure,' he murmured. In truth, he felt unsettled that even here – hidden behind metre-thick stone walls and committing himself to a reclusive existence – his old life could still reassert itself without notice.

Cosimo let his eyes wander as Father Polacco began the service, intoning prayers in a sombre voice. He had never been a devout Catholic before Romola's death, but he had learnt to find a sort of peace in the rituals of divine observance: rising with the sun, eating at set times. He had never been an enthusiastic student but studying scripture for hours upon end left him with no time to think his own thoughts, and he was grateful for that. In the weeks after the accident, when his entire world had lost shape, it was the Church that had given him structure.

He looked around at the cathedral in which they sat. Even its form was reassuring, its solidity a comfort. The building was essentially a simple monolith, a vast stone structure with triple-height ceilings, a central nave and two aisles either side divided by Romanesque arches over marble columns. It was ancient and impermeable, still standing after centuries of wars and occupations.

As in the seminary, the only windows were narrow and set very high up so that the sanctuary itself was dark, inset in a large niche. At a first glance, simplicity abounded here – the walls were white, the glass windows clear – and yet, look up and the cathedral was dramatically adorned by gilded frescoed ceilings; look down and an exquisite eleventh-century mosaic floor depicting the Tree of Life ran the entire length of the nave. People had walked over it for nine hundred years; they had been baptized, married and carried in their caskets upon it. If it could endure, so could he, surely?

He looked down to the sanctuary where Father Polacco was taking Mass, assisted by Father Caputo, both of them performing their sacred duties with reverential gravity. No one in the congregation would ever have guessed they had had a fierce disagreement that very afternoon over the amount of butter Father Polacco put on his boiled potatoes.

It was difficult to see the faces of the congregation from where he sat. At best, Cosimo could glimpse some people sitting at the very front of the right side of the aisle. He recognized the owner of the taverna on Via Rondachi with his wife, and Signore Russo, who ran the bookshop. He saw the man with the fruit stall on Piazzetta de Ferraris and the woman who wove baskets sitting on a ledge at the top of the steps beside Chiesa di San Pietro. It was early days; names still eluded him, but he was pleased that traces of familiarity were beginning to creep in. They were crumbs of comfort in a new place.

Afterwards, the novices all filed out, walking slowly and erect over the historic floor, the eyes of the congregation upon them as they headed for the side door that led back into the seminary. He felt the weight of expectation in their gaze. They saw not the young men but their ecclesiastical robes. They were already seen as symbols of the Church, instruments of God's power on earth. But the moment the door closed behind them, the younger seminarians broke into sprints along the walkway, black cassocks swinging as they held onto their birettas.

'Did you see that girl in the third row?' whispered Brother Barbieri, gesturing with his hands to suggest large breasts. Another boy shoved him, laughing.

Cosimo looked away, trying to pretend he hadn't heard. He had sequestered himself in the closest thing he could find to a living tomb specifically to suppress the passions that had once throbbed through his veins. It had been his desire for Rafaella and his enmity with Fon that had led to his sister's death. He couldn't pretend otherwise, and he had to find a way to live with it.

But the truth was, behind the heavy church doors and beneath the robes, he wasn't an emblem, any more than the rest of them. They were young, fallible men, and though his body was here, there were no walls he could find to hide him from his own mind.

Memories of Rafaella refused to die – and the road ahead was still long.

Chapter 35

Rafaella

This part of the port was like a warren, the streets so narrow that Rafaella's hands could brush the walls on each side as she walked. In the two years she had lived in Otranto, she had never been down here before – she'd never had occasion to come this far – and now she realized how very limited her experience of this town really was. Without even noticing it, she had become a rich man's wife and her world view had changed along with her address. Every day she walked from her pretty villa to the school, or the market, or down to the water's edge to choose the best fresh fish . . . but that was only half the picture. The poverty here was far greater than the privations she had known in Tricase Porto. There, their very smallness had insulated them: everyone looked after each other, sharing their catches and harvests when someone was down on their luck.

It was different in a big town. Scale dialled up the misery. Patched and stained bedsheets flapped like flags on the washing lines above her head; stray cats slunk at every corner, bristling with fleas. Women sat on crumbling steps with children on their laps, dull-eyed in the heat as they pressed themselves against the walls, seeking comfort in narrow, ever-shifting shadows. Men stood around in their vests and trousers tied with string, playing cards, smoking cigarettes and worse things besides.

A cobbler had set up a rickety table outside his shop and was listlessly hammering tacks into the sole of a shoe. 'Conte?' she asked him.

He looked at her for a moment – taking in her strawberry linen dress, her gold cuff – and pointed to a house three doors down, as if too tired to talk.

The door was open, of course. No one had need of locks here. They all knew each other and there was nothing to steal.

'Signora Conte?' she called into a shadowy room. It was small but a square of light shone from the back window, alleviating some of the gloom. She peered around the door.

A woman was lying on a mattress, five children sitting on it around her. None of them was Nico, but one child – not more than three years old – was sitting on the woman's legs. The whites of their eyes shone in the darkness as they blinked back at her like owls.

'Signora Conte?' she repeated, but her voice automatically contracted to a whisper as she came and stood by the patient, becoming aware of a rancid stench.

Oh God.

The woman was staring at the low ceiling, her gaze fixed, and Rafaella caught her breath as she waited, aware of the children watching her . . . Their mother was—

The woman blinked, the unexpectedness of it making Rafaella jump. The woman's face was glistening with a sheen that was at odds with the thick dustiness of the room, her breathing shallow and strangled. Beside the mattress was a small tin pail quarter-filled with vomit, and Rafaella felt her own stomach turn.

'I'll get help!' she said to the inert children, turning and running from the room, gulping for fresh air as she staggered back out into the street. '. . . Please, help me!' she called out. 'There's a woman sick in there! She needs a doctor!'

Faces slowly turned but no one came running. It wasn't the shock to them that it was to her.

'*Si*,' they nodded, turning away again.

'Is there a doctor?' she asked a woman who was cracking open some almonds into a bowl held together with staples.

'No doctor,' the woman said with a slow shake of her head.

'Her husband, then? Where is he?'

'Gone. Looking for work in Brindisi.'

Brindisi was over an hour away. 'Where in Brindisi?'

The woman shrugged.

'But the children . . .' Rafaella panted, looking back at the contaminated dwelling. Without help, they would all fall ill, if they weren't already. 'I'll . . . I'll find someone. I'll come back.'

The woman's eyes moved slowly up and down her, like the cobbler, taking in the tailored linen sundress and her fashionable sunglasses too. 'Mm.'

Rafaella gave a cry of despair that this woman didn't believe her, running back down the street and around the corner. She would get her own doctor; he lived on the other side of the port, where the large villas of the old sea merchants were located, but she ran as fast as she could anyway.

The cobbles were shiny from ancient wear, from the unremitting sun, and her sandals had no grip. She felt her feet slip and threw her hands out on the ground as she fell forward, banging her knee hard. 'Ow!' she cried, on all fours. '*Bastardo!*'

Someone heard her curse and looked out from the open doorway opposite. A young priest.

'Signorina,' he said, rushing out to assist her as he saw

her grip her knee. He gave her his hand to help her up and caught sight of her wedding ring. '*Scuzi*, signora. Are you OK?'

'*Si, si*,' she said quickly. 'But I need help, please! I need a doctor urgently!'

'You are ill?'

More people came to the door now.

'Someone needs a doctor?' asked a man with a stethoscope around his neck.

Rafaella cried out with relief. 'Oh, thank heavens! There's a woman in the next street. She's very ill and she's got five small children with her . . .' He looked back at the room he was standing in, as if he had the same scenario in there too. 'Please, please come with me!' she begged. 'I think she's dying!'

At her words, the young priest and the doctor swapped looks. 'I'll get Father Caputo,' the priest said, beginning to run up the street.

The doctor ducked back into the building and emerged a few seconds later carrying his bag. 'Show me,' he said.

Rafaella ran back down the street, leading him to the house, past the amazed looks of the almond woman and the cobbler. '. . . In there,' she said, pointing to the dark doorway.

The doctor rushed in and Rafaella followed, picking up the two smallest children from the bed; they were like bags of bones. They protested weakly, like mewling kittens.

'Shh,' she shushed them gently. 'Come with me while the doctor helps your mamma . . . Come, come.' Slowly she herded them out towards the sunshine, where she could get a better look at them. Their condition was startling. They were emaciated and filthy, with sunken eyes and skin filmed with sweat. They all blinked, recoiling from the bright sunlight as if it burned them.

She tried to find shade on some steps, but the sun was high in the sky at this hour and what little there was offered no relief from the heat. A cockroach scuttled across the cobbles and over her sandalled feet as she began checking the children for signs of temperature, rashes . . .

'There!'

She looked up and saw two priests rounding the corner. The younger one, who she saw now from his cassock was a seminarian, had brought, presumably, an ordained priest. He hastened inside with a stern look. He and the doctor were a tag team: one tasked with saving lives, the other with saving souls.

'Thank heavens, I thought we'd lost you! We've been down all the wrong streets,' the younger priest panted as he came over, his cheeks flushed. She wondered how he could bear the heat in his heavy robes. 'How is she?'

'I don't know. The doctor's still in there but I thought I should bring the children out here.'

'You were right to do that . . . What can you tell us about her?'

'Nothing beyond her name – Conte. I've never met her before. She's the mother of one of my pupils.'

'Pupils?'

'I'm a teacher. I came by to get some schoolwork from him so he can graduate the year. I didn't expect to walk into . . . a scene like that.'

'No.' The young priest's gaze flickered over her, as the almond woman's and cobbler's had, and she realized just how out of place she looked here; in her head, she would always be an olive farmer's daughter, but on the street all people saw was a rich man's wife. 'It's a terrible thing what's happening. The doctor has been doing his best to contain this polio outbreak.'

'Polio?'

'Yes. We've been going around trying to convince the residents to take up the vaccine but it's difficult to win their trust. They're naturally cautious of having a virus injected into them.' He looked down at the children. '. . . How do they seem?'

'Well, these two have a fever,' she said, pressing her hand to their small clammy foreheads again. 'And I think this little one is holding her head strangely.'

He nodded, looking at them more closely. 'Fever and muscle stiffness can all be symptoms. It can take a few weeks for symptoms to appear and if their mother is very badly afflicted, then they'll have been exposed.' His concerned expression matched her own.

'Oh God,' she murmured, before catching herself. 'Oh, I'm sorry, Father.'

He smiled. 'I'm not ordained yet. I'll become a transitional deacon next year. I'm Brother Savelli, by the way.'

'Signora Giannelli,' she said back, trying to gather herself, but the enormity of the past quarter-hour was beginning to catch up with her. 'This is all . . . it's all so terrible. I had no idea there was a polio outbreak in the town.'

He nodded placidly but she knew what he was thinking: of course she didn't! 'It has been very bad,' was all he said. 'We're doing what we can to assist the sick, but the hospital is overwhelmed and the children's home is overflowing. We're having to send them as far away as Lecce now.'

She looked back at him in dismay. Lecce?

'Signora Giannelli?'

She heard the note of surprise in the voice as she saw Nico coming up the street. He was carrying a hunk of bread and two pears she suspected had been harvested from a fruit tree in one of the grand gardens. His body slumped at the sight of her holding his siblings with the young priest, as if she represented an endgame.

'Nico!' she gasped, relieved to see him at last. 'Are you all right? I came looking for you and—'

'Is it Mamma?' His eyes were wide with fear. '... Is she dead?'

'N-no, but, Nico, your mamma is very sick.'

He nodded, his eyes wide. He knew that, clearly. It was evident from the size of the others that he was the eldest child – and without his father here, the man of the house too. 'I went to get her food.' He held out the pears and bread like a gift.

Her heart ached for him. 'That was very good of you, Nico. She will be so proud of you.'

'I'll give it to her.' He went to move past her, but she stopped him.

'Nico,' she said gently. 'Let's wait here while the doctor is in with your mamma.'

'Is he making her better?'

She swallowed, knowing she couldn't give false hope. 'He's trying to.'

'Can I see her?'

'Let's just wait here for a few minutes, shall we?' she said, patting the kerb beside her.

Brother Savelli crouched down in front of the boy. 'Nico, can you tell us – how long has she been unwell?'

'A while.'

'OK.' Savelli nodded but he looked concerned.

'She had a stomach ache and then she got hot. She started making funny sounds in the night.' He looked anxiously from the priest to Rafaella. 'Is she going to die?'

'The doctor's doing everything he can to make her well again,' she said.

'She can't die!' Nico said to her desperately, as if she had the power to stop it.

'I promise he'll do everything in his power to help her and

whatever treatment she needs, we'll make sure she gets it.' That was a promise she *could* make. She looked back at Brother Savelli. 'Should we take the children to the hospital and get them checked over?'

'No!' Nico cried. 'I'm not leaving Mamma!'

The other children squirmed too, agitated by his distress.

'OK, OK,' she said quickly as the little girl in her arms began to cry. 'Shh-shh, we'll wait to see what the doctor says first.'

They sat down again, but who knew how long they might be out here.

'So . . . you're a teacher?' Savelli asked after a few moments.

'Yes.'

'Do you enjoy it?'

'Oh, I do. I couldn't bear to just sit around all day being . . .'

'Ornamental?'

'Something like that,' she smiled, seeing a look in his eye, as if he recognized the plight of pretty women. 'Besides, I believe in the value of a good education to help people lift themselves out of poverty.'

'It's a shame more people in your position don't think like you.'

'Well, I haven't been in this "position" for very long,' she said quickly.

'You married well?'

'. . . I suppose that's one way of looking at it,' she nodded. 'How about you? Do you enjoy being in the Church?' Was that the right term? Was one supposed to 'enjoy' a life of abstinence and penance?

She thought of Cosimo. How could she not? He had hidden himself away too, trying to reject his old life – her – like a jacket that could be shrugged off. Had it worked? Did he ever think of her anymore? It had been three years . . . She had tried so hard to move on with her life, to accept their changed circumstances and to let his memory go, but it lingered like a watermark, always there.

'It's not without its struggles,' he conceded frankly. 'But that's like anything worthwhile, I suppose. I'm told that once I'm ordained, the fun will really start . . . I'll have miracles at my fingertips then.'

She looked back at him blankly, her thoughts still snagged on Cosimo.

'That's a joke,' he said hurriedly, blushing furiously as he saw her slightly frozen expression.

'Oh!' she smiled. She wasn't used to joking novice priests – and he didn't look used to being one, either. His gaze lingered on her a little too long to be wholly pious and she sensed something in his manner that was resistant to his fate.

'Signora Giannelli,' Nico piped up beside her, interrupting them. 'Did you come to get my lines?'

'Oh . . . no, Nico . . .' She shook her head, cupping his cheek with her hand as she saw his wide eyes. How much had he had to contend with, while she had been asking for lines? '. . . I came to tell you we won't need them after all. You're going to be just fine for next year.'

The doctor came out, wearing the same stern expression the priest had been wearing on his way in, and she understood immediately what it meant. The priest was the one working hard now.

He shook his head. 'Too far gone . . . Her breathing muscles are paralysed,' he murmured, scarcely moving his lips, but Nico was standing to attention anyway, his body rigid. 'The children must come to say their goodbyes. Father Caputo is administering the last rites.'

'No!' Nico cried, dropping the food and sprinting into the house before she could catch hold of him. 'Mamma! Mamma!'

The other children followed after him, a pitiful line of

wounded animals trailing back into their cave, as heads turned on the street. Comprehension of the situation rippled like a wave over the cobbles. Death was recognized all too well in these parts and steadily people began to walk up, gathering outside the tiny dwelling in silence.

She followed Savelli back into the deathly space, still carrying the two smallest children. Father Caputo was almost entirely shrouded in the darkness in his black cassock, his voice low as he administered the sacrament. He had none of Father Tommaso's gentle, enveloping nature but was brisk and officious, as if the dispatching of Signora Conte's soul was something to tick off before Vespers.

The children cried and wailed as they felt heaven being called downwards to kiss their heads and take their mother away from them. Rafaella did what she could to comfort them, but they were ill too, their bodies already fighting the disease. She knew they needed medical care quickly.

Nico stood stiffly like a soldier, sobbing bitter tears as he swayed on his feet, watching Father Caputo gently close his mother's eyes for the last time. Their father was somewhere in a city ninety kilometres from here – no one knew where exactly, nor when he would return.

She looked around the wretched home. There was almost nothing in it save a table, one chair, the bed and a wooden washing tub. It was clear they couldn't stay here. Which prompted the question – where, then?

'What on earth . . .?' Gina stood in the doorway, taking in the sight of Rafaella feeding three filthy children at the kitchen table.

'*Allora*!' Rafaella smiled brightly; too brightly. 'You got my message, then?'

Gina stared back with a confused look. '*Si*,' she said warily. 'Dante said you needed me to come over as soon as I got back.'

'And he's got Lorenzo?'

'Sure,' she nodded, coming in and standing behind a chair, as close as her belly would allow. 'What's going on?' She smiled at Nico, who was pushing pasta around his plate. He had said scarcely a word since they had left his home to come here.

'Gina, this is Nico Conte, one of the best pupils in my class,' Rafaella said proudly – and still far too brightly. 'And these are his little sisters, Vittoria and Caterina. They're twins. Aren't they beautiful?'

'Beautiful,' Gina cooed, but there was concern in her eyes; she had an instinct for crisis, and this was very clearly a crisis.

'Nico, I'm just going to run a bath for you all. Will you be a big boy and help the girls to eat up?'

He nodded, watching cautiously as Rafaella caught Gina by the elbow and led her through into the hall. Her villa wasn't as grand as her friend's but it still had a genteel air with noble proportions and was a palazzo in comparison to what she'd visited earlier.

'Rafa, *what* is going on?' Gina whispered. 'Where did you find these kids?'

'Their mother died this morning. From polio.'

'Polio?' Gina gasped, retreating immediately, her hand pressed protectively over her swollen stomach. 'But that's so contagious! How could you let me come here—?'

'Don't worry, they're fine. I've been at the hospital all afternoon getting them checked. Turns out they were given the vaccine a few weeks ago and it's worked, thank God. Mainly they're malnourished and sick from living in squalid conditions – there's another two brothers and a sister who've been admitted with pneumonia. Gina, they're all under ten.' Her eyes shone with pain. 'The mother had been ill for a few weeks and lost the ability to walk and take care of them. The neighbours didn't realize the full extent of it. Nico was covering for her, pretending everything was OK.' She pressed her hands over her mouth.

Gina took a breath, ever the logic to Rafaella's emotion – the very reason why Rafaella had called her over. 'Where's the father?'

'In Brindisi, looking for work. No one knows where he is or when he's coming back.'

'Or *if* he's coming back,' Gina said worriedly. 'He wouldn't be the first man to taste freedom again and turn his back on all that . . .'

'I know; that's what I'm worried about.'

'How did you even end up getting involved?'

'Nico's in my class. He was going to fail the year unless he handed in an assignment. His attendance had been patchy in the last few weeks and he didn't come in for the final two days of term – now I know why,' she sighed. 'I went round, intending to sit down and do it with him. Instead I found the mother literally taking her last breaths and all these sick children lying on her.'

'My God, that's awful.'

'It really was. I found a doctor working nearby with some priests who've been trying to help the sick. They were the ones who had convinced the mother to give her children the vaccine.'

'So then why didn't she have it, too?'

'The doctor said she didn't want it. The number of adult cases is so low – less than five per cent – she thought only the children were at risk.'

Gina winced. 'Have they got any other family here?'

'We don't know yet. Brother Savelli is going to ask around.'

'Brother Savelli?'

'The seminarian who was working with the priest today. He helped me take the children to the hospital.'

'Oh.' Gina frowned, thinking it all through. 'So if they don't have family here, and the father doesn't come back . . .?'

'Well, that's a lot of ifs. We've got to hope for the best.'

'But *if* . . .?' Gina pressed.

Rafaella inhaled sharply. 'Then they'll end up in the orphanage. In Lecce.'

'Oh, Rafa,' Gina whispered, putting her hands over her face. 'This is *not* what I thought you wanted to talk about.'

'Tell me about it,' Rafaella muttered. She glanced at Gina. 'Wait – why? What did you think I wanted to talk about?'

'Well, when Dante said you needed to see me, I assumed it was because of . . . you know, the Franchetti thing.'

Rafaella felt the walls of the villa bow inwards. '. . . What Franchetti thing?'

Gina looked surprised. 'Fon hasn't told you?'

'Fon's not here,' she said, struggling to keep her voice level. 'What's happened to Cosimo?' She braced herself for whatever was coming, but her heart had gone into an immediate gallop.

'It's not Cosimo,' Gina said, putting a hand on her arm, seeing how her cheeks had paled. 'It's Fede.'

'*Fede?*' Rafaella frowned. She saw his name in the newspapers occasionally. He was a big legal hotshot in Rome now; some people were even talking about him as a future state attorney general. 'Is he OK?'

'We don't know. Apparently he was attacked outside his office today—'

'What?!'

'People witnessed it. He was bundled into a car and driven away . . .' Gina blinked back at her with big brown eyes. 'Raf, they think he's been kidnapped.'

Chapter 36

Fon

It was late when Fon left his brother's house, pulling the green pedestrian door closed behind him till it clicked. His own home was only three minutes' walk away but he slid off his jacket and slung it over one shoulder as he walked. It was still suffocatingly hot and the day had been long. His body ached, but a cold shower would put everything right.

Fon turned the corner and walked past the bakery that sold Rafa's favourite *pasticciotti*; he knew the lights would be on again in a few hours, the ovens heating up . . . A dog trotted past him, its nose in the air curiously, as if he had a stray sausage in his pocket. A small run of scooters had been badly parked alongside a graffitied wall and he was briefly transported back to his younger self and the years when he had run with Luigi and Gino, getting up to the same antics. He still saw them, of course, when he went back to Tricase Porto, but so much had changed in the past few years, it was as if they were all entirely different people.

From this direction, he approached his villa by the garden first. Unlike his brother's extravagant courtyard, with its fountain and trees and riotous flowers in pots, this was much smaller; but it was private and still large for the port. He'd had some olive trees planted for Rafaella when they moved in but they had struggled to take here, the narrow street and high walls thwarting the sunlight. They weren't dead, but nor were they thriving, and they hadn't produced any harvest at all as yet.

The irony wasn't lost on him.

He stopped at his front door. It was narrow and unassuming. People walked past every day, unaware of the identity of the man living here, and he preferred it like that. Dante was drawn to money and luxury – swagger – but Fon was more interested in quiet power.

'Rafa?' he called down the hallway.

He peered into the kitchen. It was clean and tidy, all the dishes cleared away – unlike his brother's house, which more often looked as if an earthquake had hit it. He glanced in at the sitting room, too: the cushions were plumped, the flowers set in fresh water. The new television gleamed in the corner like a trophy, but he wasn't convinced Rafa had ever switched it on.

He climbed the stairs. Was she already asleep? It was after midnight . . .

He passed the guest bedroom, which no one had ever stayed in, and immediately stepped back again, his brain taking a moment to process what his eyes had shown him: his beautiful wife, asleep on the covers, surrounded by three very clean and scrubbed children wearing pyjamas so new they still held the fold creases.

He stared down at them, trying to make sense of the scene. The two girls looked to be no more than four, although the boy was nearer to ten, eleven maybe. For a brief moment he had a flashback to that morning, all those years ago, among the oaks and the cattle. A slaughter of the innocents . . . The usual wave of nausea rose up through his throat, but he was familiar with it now and could swallow it down.

He placed a hand on Rafaella's foot and her eyes flew open. He saw her relief on recognizing that it was 'only him' and felt a rush of pleasure that the sight of him consoled her.

'What's going on?' he whispered.

She pressed a finger to her lips, checking on the sleeping children before inching off the bed. He watched as she drew the sheet over their shoulders, pressing a hand to their foreheads and cheeks as if checking their temperatures. She was a natural mother, as he had always known she would be.

They walked through into their bedroom next door and he listened as she explained the events of her day.

'Brother Savelli is going to let me know more tomorrow,' she said. 'The Church keeps up-to-date records of its parishioners, so with any luck they'll have an aunt or uncle or grandparent here who can look after them.'

'Yes.'

She looked at him, pinning him with her gold-flecked eyes, knowing he had never been able to refuse her when she held him in their gaze. 'But until then, until we know more, I'd like to keep them here.'

He swallowed. 'Rafa, it's best to let the authorities take care of this. The Church is well equipped to deal with this sort of situation, not to mention there are procedures to follow. We can't just take in a stranger's children.'

'Their mother's just died, Fon, and their brothers and sister are still in the hospital. They're completely alone. We can't abandon them in their hour of need . . . Please.'

He looked into her eyes. She had so much love to give; just not to him. Or at least, not in the way she had given to Cosimo. No matter how much Fon gave her or how long he waited, it was never enough. And he feared it never would be.

'. . . Fine.'

'Thank you,' she said as he moved away, beginning to

untuck his shirt. He could feel her watching him. '. . . Did you hear about Fede Franchetti?'

He glanced over. 'Yes, I was just with Dante. He's making some calls.'

'Do you have any idea who would do such a thing?'

He sighed. 'Fede works for the state attorney, Rafa. I'm sure there are many people who've got a grudge against him: people he's convicted, their families . . .'

'Has a ransom demand been issued?'

'Not as far as I'm aware.'

'So then, do you think they'll . . .?' Her voice rose with fear.

'I'm sure there will be one tomorrow,' he said quickly. 'There's usually a lag between kidnap and ransom demand. Whoever's got him has probably been too busy covering their tracks today. Once they're sure he's somewhere secure, they'll make contact with the family.'

'I just can't believe this could happen to them! As if that family hasn't been through enough . . .'

'It's callous,' he agreed.

Rafaella was pacing now, biting her nails.

'You mustn't take it to heart,' he said softly, wishing he could take her in his arms and that she would find comfort there. 'Everything will be fine. The Franchettis are rich. They'll pay the ransom and it'll all be over within a few days. That's usually how these things work.' The papers were full of such stories lately, particularly in Palermo and Naples.

'Sometimes they drag on, though,' she fretted. 'Don't you remember that mayor who disappeared for nine months, and he was so weak by the time they released him, he died a week later?'

Fon sighed again, pushing off his shoes with his opposite foot and sinking onto the bed. He had been on the road for several days and was weary. 'Like I said, the Franchettis have money – not to mention Filippo must have people working on it behind the scenes. He's a government minister. They'll know how to bring an end to it quickly.'

'Who is Dante talking to?'

He glanced up at her as he pulled off his socks. 'What?'

'You said he was making some calls.'

'Oh. His supplier in Rome is asking around for him.'

She turned away, agitated. 'As if a cigarette importer can shed any light on the kidnapping of a lawyer!' Her tone was unintentionally withering, drawing a sharp look from him.

'You'd be surprised. Lawyers smoke a lot of cigarettes.' He shrugged. 'He has his sources . . .'

She wheeled back to him. 'What if you went up there?'

'*Me?* What good would that do?'

'You're clever, Fon. You can read people and you pick up on things most people miss. If you were to speak with Fede's colleagues or . . . or even go to the Franchettis' place of residence.'

He frowned. 'Why would I do that?'

'Because you're from Tricase. Old bonds matter at a time like this. They know you.'

'They know me as the man who accidentally killed their daughter!' He paused, seeing how she recoiled, still, at any mention of Romola. 'You really think they'd want to see me, of all people, at a time like this?' He shook his head. 'There's nothing they would tell me they won't have told the police.'

'But you know better than anyone what the police are like – they make all the right noises but they're always in someone's pocket, being paid off.' She pinned a suspicious look on him. She had never explicitly asked him how the police had been dissuaded from pressing charges for Romola's death but he suspected that, as the years went by, she had come to understand there had been offstage manoeuvrings of some sort; that his agreement to 'save' Cosimo had been pledged with his foot already on the scales.

He looked away again.

'Please, Fon,' she implored him. 'We owe it to Romola's memory. We can't just sit by and do nothing! We have to do everything we can to help her family.'

He rubbed his face in his hands. 'But it would take most of a day travelling each way, and I've got meetings booked. I'm supposed to be in Taranto and Bari and . . .'

She came and sat beside him, somehow dogged and gentle at the same time. 'Can't you reschedule them? You're the boss, after all. I would go to Rome myself, but now, with those children needing looking after . . .'

His head lifted at the prospect of her going to the capital and reinstating herself with the Franchettis. '. . . Fine,' he nodded. 'I'll go. But don't get your hopes up.'

She had been his wife for three years now, and Cosimo was practically living as a monk somewhere – but the Franchettis still cast long shadows. He couldn't take any chances.

Breakfast was quiet, even with five of them in the room. The children stared at Fon from across the table as if *he* was the intruder. Their eyes were too large in their heads, their cheeks sunken. It was the look of lack, poverty's hard mark upon the body, and he felt his sympathy stirred for these helpless creatures. He himself hadn't been so very far off that mark when he'd been their age.

But look at him now, with his noble house and beautiful wife. Happy endings could come from harsh beginnings. He was living proof.

He watched as Rafaella made the coffee, barefoot on the tiled floor, her apron tied tightly around her small waist. She was still so slim, her body practically unchanged from when they'd been teenagers in Tricase, and he was grateful she wasn't like Gina, her abundant flesh always jiggling and her clothes struggling to contain her.

Rafaella had prepared a meal for him to eat on the road and packed his bag carefully. Always so dutiful and attentive; he couldn't fault her.

'I'll let you know if I hear anything,' he said as he was leaving, planting a kiss on her cheek and eliciting disapproving stares from the silently watching children. Even scrubbed, well rested and fed, they had a feral look to them, like the foxes that peeked out from under bushes along the roads at night, amber eyes catching in the headlights as he sped past.

'Ask for Father Caputo when you go back to the church today.'

She looked thoughtful. 'I think it was Father Caputo who was there yesterday.'

'Good. He'll help you.'

'You know him, then?'

He smiled as he left her. 'I'm a good Catholic, am I not?'

His Fiat 100 Berlina was parked in the usual spot; he kept it on a street in the new quarter where the modern apartments had gone up and where he had installed Gabriella, his mistress. For a moment he considered dropping off his bag and telling her to expect him tonight, but experience cautioned otherwise; the element of surprise applied to mistresses as well as adversaries.

Fon got in and drove out of town. Dante drove a glossy Lancia Flaminia, but he preferred something that was fast enough for the open road but incognito too. He turned off the highway after two junctions and headed inland, then pulled off again after a couple of miles. The land here was agricultural, huge fields sprouting grains, a few almond groves too. He hung a right onto an unmarked dirt track. He could see plumes of dust billowing up behind him in the rear-view mirror; donkeys nodded in a field, unconcerned, as he sped past.

The land rose here in a gentle slope and ahead he could see a farmhouse. It was long since abandoned, the roof partially caved in. Someone had told him the old farmer had hanged himself from one of the beams; someone else said he'd simply left for work in the north. Certainly no one was here now. Francesco had scoped the place for two weeks before they'd moved in; he had stepped into the breach and become the brothers' top man on 'security measures' ever since Pablo's unexpected death from a short illness a couple of years earlier.

He drove over the hump of the hill, finally coming to a stop outside the farmhouse. A small round stone *trullo* sat opposite the yard. It had no windows, and the walls were half a metre thick. He reached for the *panzarotti* Rafaella had prepared and the bottle of water and got out, walking over the stony path.

He looked around him; somewhere, behind a wall or in a tree, Francesco was watching. But if Fon couldn't see him, no one else would.

He opened the door and let the fetid air fall out of the confined space before he stepped inside. The figure on the chair looked up; his hands were tied before him, the chain tethered to a bull ring in the wall. He stood, as if anticipating an attack, but a grain sack was over his head and he moved jerkily, trying to discern the direction of movement, noise. Threat.

'Who's there?' Fede's voice was bowed with stress.

'Relax. I've just brought you some food,' Fon said, though his animal instincts were on high alert at being so close to his quarry. If Fede was a true enemy, it would be easier to go through with the charade, but this man had only ever shown him kindness, friendship, respect . . . Memories of Fede flashed through his mind: sitting on his scooter and inviting him back to the villa for a drink; swimming up to the boat when the others, on the rocks, had ignored him. Sprawled on the dance floor with a disappointed look as Fon rejected his help—

'What do you want?' Fede asked angrily. '*Money?*' He spat the word out as if it was dirty. Pathetic.

'A ransom demand has been made, stipulating our requirements. As long as you cooperate, there's no reason for this to end badly.'

Fede tutted as if this was all a poor joke. Something beneath him. '. . . You'll never get away with it.'

'It's in your best interests that we do,' Fon said coldly. 'Sit down.'

'Why?'

'Because I'm going to hand you your food.'

'Why?'

Fon frowned at the question. 'Well, unless you want to starve . . .'

There was a pause before Fede sat begrudgingly, and Fon carefully set the parcel of food on his lap. He watched as Fede's hands clasped it, examining it warily as if it might be a bomb or a blade instead. Reassured, his fingers fumbled with the paper, but as he went to pull off the hood, Fon stopped him.

'Wait until you hear the door click. Then you can take it off.'

'So I have to eat in the dark too?'

'Yes.'

'Why?'

Fon gave a small laugh. '*Why?* I would have thought that was obvious.'

There was another pause. 'Forgive me. It's my first time being kidnapped.' Sarcasm trimmed the words. 'I assume it's because you don't want me to see your face?'

'Exactly. There's no walking away from this otherwise,' Fon said in a warning tone as he turned away. 'Wait until the door clicks. Then take the hood off.'

'Fine,' Fede murmured. 'Thanks for the advice, Fon.'

Fon stopped in his tracks, so stunned he felt like he'd been shot. He turned back and stared at his captive: hooded, bound. Defiant.

'What? You thought I wouldn't recognize your voice?'

Fon had been counting on it. It hadn't crossed his mind that he would have been anything but completely unmemorable to this person with whom he had shared, at a distance, almost twenty summers.

But Fede was a clever man, not just a charming one. Suddenly the reason for the inane questions made sense; he'd been getting him to talk – trying to see if he could recognize an accent, gain trust, elicit a clue. Instead, he'd hit the jackpot.

Fon watched Fede reach up and slowly pull the hood off his head. They looked at one another. Over the years they had both filled out, become men, but Fon would still have recognized him anywhere, and his heart beat in triple time as he came face to face again with the man who had lingered in his memory beyond all others. He felt a rush of emotion – of power – at the thought that he knew Fede's secret; he knew what he was, and Fede had no idea.

Fede was blinking rapidly, dazzled by the light after so long in the dark, his left eye purple and swollen. He had unwisely fought back the previous day as Fon and Francesco had bundled him into the car.

Fon watched as Fede looked around the tiny hut, trying to get his bearings. There was nothing here to help him; this place had been chosen for its lack of identifying landmarks. It was miles from the nearest road or occupied house. The last thing Fede had seen as they jumped him had been his office street in Rome; he could have no idea where he was now. The car journey back here yesterday had taken almost seven hours.

Slowly he returned his gaze to Fon as the desperate reality of his situation stared back at him, unblinking. No one would find him here.

His anger grew.

'What the hell do you think you're playing at, holding me here?' Fede demanded, his voice a low growl. He began to pull and rattle the chain, a little at first, then wildly, scraping the chair's legs on the dirt floor. His characteristic poise vanished as he became like a rabid dog suddenly, frenzied and dangerous, as if enraged that he had been kidnapped by *him* – Fon Giannelli, Dante's kid brother! – of all people. Was he indignant that he hadn't been taken by someone more fearsome? A professional? Was the ultimate indignity in this situation not his capture, but his captor?

Fon watched dispassionately, refusing to show his shaken nerve. The eldest Franchetti had a surprisingly strong fighting spirit beneath those polished manners.

'Get this chain off me immediately!'

Fon bristled at the imperious tone. Fede had always been the most equable of the Franchettis, less arrogant or conceited than Romola or Cosimo – but it appeared he quickly reverted to type when the chips were down. A shame. 'That won't be possible until our demands are met. But there's no need for you to go hungry, and there's a bucket in the corner for ablutions too. You might want to use it while the door is open and you have some light?'

'. . . A *bucket* . . .?' Fede stared back at him in disbelief.

'Yes. I'm afraid it's hard to come by en-suite facilities in most kidnap-and-ransom places.'

The sarcasm triggered another stunned pause. '. . . You won't get away with this!' Fede cried. 'When my father hears what you've done . . .'

The echoes sounded again and Fon looked away, steadying himself.

'It's because of your father that this is happening,' he said calmly. 'But yes, we hope that once he understands the new arrangement, he'll work quickly to assure your release.'

Fede was dumbstruck as he stared at Fon. His expression reminded Fon of the look on Filippo's face as he sat at Dante's dining table and tried to pull rank, completely miscalculating the real source of power in the room – or even the real reason for the dinner. He had thought it was about building permits, or showing how far they'd come . . . Greed and ego.

Fon walked out of the *trullo*, leaving the door wide open.

'Where . . . where are you going?' Fede cried in a panic, startled by his sudden disappearance.

Fon came back and stood in the doorway again.

'I'm giving you some privacy to use the facilities,' he said magnanimously, lighting a cigarette with a careless shrug. 'Fede, we're not savages.'

Chapter 37

Cosimo

The sliding panel to his left drew back, revealing a silhouetted profile through the mesh. Cosimo stared ahead at the wooden door.

'Bless me, Father, for I have sinned,' Brother Barbieri said in a sombre tone, but Cosimo could hear the curve of a smile in his voice. 'It has been one week and four days since my last confession. Father, I have something important I wish to confess.'

'Go on,' Cosimo murmured.

'I met a woman a few days ago – a married woman – and I have had bad thoughts, Father.'

Cosimo rolled his eyes. He had thought Barbieri might at least start small, say with feelings of jealousy, or kicking a cat. They all knew the parishioners generally rotated their sins from a longer list. It didn't do to bring too many, but they needed to have enough to appear contrite; three was generally agreed to be a good number.

'Have you acted on them?'

'Not with her, Father, no. But privately, I . . . I have struggled to remain chaste.'

'Is that all—?'

'No! No! No!'

Cosimo jumped as a disembodied voice to his right side suddenly started up.

'Come out at once!'

Cosimo let himself out of the confession booth just as Barbieri was getting up from his kneeling position on the ledge outside. Alessio Savelli met his gaze as the three of them waited for the priest to come round from the far side too and join them. The cathedral was quiet but not empty, and they had come downstairs to the older confession booth in the crypt.

Father Polacco appeared, looking weary. 'Brother Franchetti, that was the opportunity to ask what he meant by "struggled". Did he remain chaste or not? This is fundamental to what, Brother Savelli?'

Savelli straightened up. 'Matter and form, Father.'

'Precisely. Matter and form. For serious sins, the details must be given – the matter – and it is your job to elicit them – the form – for the sin to be validly confessed and the sacrament of penance given.'

'Yes, Father,' Cosimo nodded. He knew perfectly well about matter and form, but he also knew Barbieri was trying to taunt him, having failed to force him to listen to the details of his latest temptation over dinner last night and again at breakfast this morning.

The priest gave Barbieri a worried glance. 'Was that a true sin to which you were confessing, Brother Barbieri?'

'Of course not, Father. It was just made up for this practice session.'

Cosimo kept his face impassive, but he could feel Savelli twitching anxiously beside him.

'I'm glad to hear it,' Father Polacco said with relief. 'Brother Franchetti, you must stop skirting around the issues the penitent is confessing. You need to look into yourself. To err is human. If we are to help, we must engage, not rush through as if we are ticking off a to-do list.' He looked at Savelli, who was watching with a concerned expression. 'And don't look so alarmed, Brother Savelli. Taking confession is like being pecked by ducks . . . annoying, but perfectly harmless.'

To everyone's relief, the cathedral bells began to peal.

The priest sighed. '*Allora*, that's enough for today. We'll try again tomorrow. But Franchetti, think on what I'm telling you, please. We keep going round in circles with this issue.'

'Yes, Father.'

'Hm. Now go to lunch, all of you.'

'Thank you, Father,' they said in unison, taking the ancient stone steps two at a time and heading for the door that led back to the seminary.

They walked out into the quad, a light breeze scurrying at their long hems, and Cosimo was suddenly reminded of standing on a balcony in shorts and bare feet, looking out to sea . . . It was a snapshot from another life, so unimportant at the time, and yet the memory of it took his breath away. He tried to bring himself back to the present moment: walking past orange trees, behind high walls.

'You'll go to hell for lying to him,' Savelli said with a wry look.

'Not if I add lying to my list of sins at my next actual confession,' Barbieri grinned. 'Besides, I need to take any opportunity I can to confess. He'd have a fit of apoplexy if he knew what she's really been doing to me—'

Cosimo looked at him sharply.

'In my *dreams*!' Barbieri laughed. 'Relax.'

'How you made it this far I'll never know.'

'I always say, observing chastity is about resisting desire, not denying it exists,' he grinned. 'But if you'd seen her, you'd be questioning your life choices too, believe me.'

'Aside from the fact you're a novice priest, she's a married woman—'

'Oh, but they're the best – everyone says it. We're forbidden fruit and so are they.'

It was true. Women being attracted to men of the cloth wasn't an uncommon phenomenon. Some liked the 'challenge' of trying to get a priest to break his vows; others fell for the emotional intensity that could bloom instead when the physical realm was denied. Cosimo certainly sometimes felt stares lingering upon him in the cathedral, and he was careful never to lift his head and make eye contact.

Not that he could ever be tempted.

'Barbieri!' Some of the other brothers were sitting on the grass under the orange trees, beckoning him over.

'See you later,' he winked at them, peeling away and crossing the quad to join them.

Cosimo watched him go, feeling his irritation stirred. Barbieri's flippancy felt like a middle finger to Cosimo's more earnest ambitions. He was light-hearted and unserious, erring on the side of irreverence, as if all this was part of a slightly ridiculous experiment which would soon end; whereas Cosimo was here because the wider world had failed him. There was nothing left for him but this. But Cosimo also knew the reason he disliked Barbieri so much was because he reminded him of himself – his old self – and he was jealous that Barbieri could still somehow exist as a red-blooded, three-dimensional man in this place.

'Are you and Caputo going back out with the doctor this afternoon?' he asked Savelli.

'No. We've got a meeting with the teacher again today to discuss the next steps for the children she took in yesterday. We've gone through the records now and there's no other family here; the father's gone missing. She's adamant they can't go into the orphanage but it doesn't look like there'll be any choice about it now.'

'Six children, you said?'

'Yes. Although three are in hospital with pneumonia currently, but they should recover well. It won't be long before they're released.'

'There's not many people who would take on six children.'

'Exactly! She's not just got the face of an angel, she's got the heart of one too. She's so sweet and gentle and . . .' He stopped, as if becoming aware of Cosimo's curious look. Had he really said 'face of an angel'? He cleared his throat. 'Plus, she looks like she can afford it.'

'I thought you said she was a teacher?'

'Teacher with a rich husband.'

'Does she have children of her own?'

'Not that she's mentioned,' Savelli shrugged.

They opened the door into the seminary and headed down a long corridor, lined with portraits of the popes, towards the refectory.

Savelli glanced at him. 'Actually, I wanted to ask if you would go to the next meeting for me?'

'Instead of you, you mean?'

'Yes.'

'But why?'

They turned into the dining hall. Three hundred seminarians, some as young as fourteen, all wearing their black house cassocks and green sashes, were eating at long tables and talking in low voices. Silence wasn't stipulated here, but nor did anyone assert themselves in any way.

Savelli looked uncomfortable. He was never self-doubting and rarely prone to introspection but he seemed apprehensive now. 'I just think this case needs someone who can handle it properly. You're better at this sort of thing than me.'

'Well, that's not true,' Cosimo said as they sat down opposite one another. One of the first-year novices was already approaching with their meals. They waited for him to set down the plates. '. . . Thank you.'

They began to eat – fava beans and chicory.

Cosimo watched Savelli. 'Is it because of the teacher? You're attracted to her?'

Savelli wouldn't meet his eyes as he ate. 'No, I'm not,' he protested. 'I'm just not . . . neutral to her. And I don't think it's helpful to put myself in the way of temptation.'

Cosimo knew his friend struggled with the requirement for chastity in particular. It was difficult to adapt to the demands of the Church when it hadn't been his personal choice to come here. Cosimo had come through the gates at a sprint, seeking refuge as he tried to escape his sense of guilt and loss, but it had never been the same for Alessio, who would have chosen many other lives before this one: if not a racing-car driver, then a soldier in the Noble Guard or an Olympic skier. Alessio had once told him, during one of their late-night talks, that being asked to live without desire felt like being robbed of his soul.

'Listen, just because we're in here, wearing these –' Cosimo indicated their cassocks – 'doesn't mean we're invulnerable to the baser, messier elements of being a man. God knows I never want to say Barbieri is right, but he wasn't wrong just now. It's not about denying desire but resisting it.' He knew none of them were alone in their struggles in that regard. Sometimes when he couldn't sleep he heard sounds in the night, muffled groans from beneath blankets.

Cosimo kept his voice low. 'At the end of the day, we still feel, and that's a good thing, because we're alive and we're men – not statues. Not saints. We're not immune to those feelings because we're in here. We just have to find a way of living with them.'

'So you're saying I should face her down?'

'You make her sound terrifying,' Cosimo grinned.

'That kind of beauty is,' Savelli replied wryly. 'Men go to war over faces like hers. Seriously, I couldn't stop staring, Cosi; she made me want to be free of here. I scarcely slept last night.' Savelli shook his head, giving a weary sigh. 'I've got my exams coming up in a few months. The last thing I need is a dark night of the soul.'

'OK, how about this as a compromise? I'll go with you later. At least then I can see her for myself, and I can tell you whether or not you're going mad.'

Savelli chuckled as he reached for his water glass. 'Well, there really are no guarantees on *that*.'

They crossed the piazza ninety minutes later, taking all of thirty seconds to reach their destination. Savelli stopped outside a pair of green carriage doors inset in the facade of a smart villa.

'Really?' Cosimo smiled, glancing back at the seminary on the other side. 'I knew the port was small, but . . . *really?*'

'This isn't her place. She just thought it would be helpful to meet us here instead; she thinks our days are busier than hers. Little does she know she's saving us from catechisms,' Savelli said drily.

'Ah.'

Cosimo followed him through a pedestrian door into a verdant courtyard. The shade from a mature pomegranate tree offered welcome respite from the blistering sun, and the sound of water tinkling in the fountain stirred distant memories of a party and fireworks . . . a wall of jasmine flowers . . .

He shook his head as Savelli led the way up stone steps. 'Caputo said to keep her talking till he gets here,' Savelli was saying. 'He has to press the flesh with the bishop first.'

'Sure.'

They stepped into in a small, square reception hall with a kitchen leading off in front and other rooms off a salon to their left. It was gaudy to Cosimo's eye, with gilded Empire chairs and ceilings poorly painted with cherubim, but the bones of the place were good: historic terracotta-tiled floors, high ceilings, stone arches.

They could hear voices coming from a room on the far side of the salon.

'Signora Giannelli?' Savelli called through. 'It's Brother Savelli.'

Cosimo whipped round to face him, feeling as if the world had just tipped to a slant. '*What* did you say her name was?' he hissed – just as the lady of the house emerged.

Cosimo watched her approach, feeling dismay and relief in equal measure. She was heavily pregnant – as she had been the last time he'd seen her, at Rafaella's wedding. Sure enough, a little boy followed behind her, pedalling madly on a red tricycle, curious to see the visitors.

Gina, by contrast, didn't seem to recognize him, at least not immediately; the uniform had a way of obfuscating them. But as he removed his biretta she stopped in her tracks, looking as if she'd seen a ghost.

'*Cosi?*'

The little boy looked up at the two seminarians with reverential awe. He had his mother's dark brown doe eyes, but even at his fledgling age, Cosimo could clearly see Dante's impressive bone structure beginning to emerge.

Gina had married Dante Giannelli? Or rather ... Dante had actually married her? Cosimo had been sure he would leave her stranded.

'You know each other?' Savelli asked in surprise.

It was several seconds before Cosimo's brain processed the question. He couldn't believe what his eyes were showing him: a ghost from the past, his sister's memory stirring from the tomb in which he had buried her. He couldn't see Gina and not think of Romola. Nor of—

'From . . . we're friends from childhood,' Cosimo mumbled.

'Really?' Savelli looked mildly concerned now as he witnessed their ongoing mutual shock.

'Gina,' Cosimo managed. 'What are you doing in Otranto?'

'We moved here two years ago,' she replied. Her voice didn't sound how he remembered it. There was none of her suspended laughter, as if giggles were being held in; no hint of teasing or ribaldry. But he saw how, automatically, her hand rested on her son's head, tousling his hair and reassuring him, her other hand on the hump of her stomach. She was a mother now. Her life had changed just as much as his own. Beyond all recognition.

'. . . Well, Signora Giannelli, I'm Brother Savelli,' Alessio said slowly, trying to draw their attention away from the ghosts of the past and remind them of the purpose of the visit. 'It's good of you to allow us to meet here . . .'

Gina looked back at Cosimo again, paling before his eyes. 'Actually – no.'

Savelli continued as if he hadn't heard. 'I'm afraid Father Caputo has been a little delayed, but he will join us shortly—'

'This isn't a good idea,' Gina broke in.

'I'm sorry?' Savelli blinked.

'Yes – I must ask you to go,' she said more firmly, finding her voice and some of her old spirit again.

'But the meeting,' Savelli protested. 'The children . . . Your sister—'

'I know, but . . . I've just heard from her. One of the children is . . . running a fever. She can't make it. She asked if she could reschedule.'

'Oh.' Savelli looked bewildered.

'I must ask you to go,' Gina repeated.

Cosimo recognized that his old friend was lying. She knew

the truth – that he, not Fon, was the one who had toppled the urn that terrible night. If Rafaella hadn't told her, Dante would have done. She must hate him for it.

He felt the old guilt and remorse beginning to push up inside him like weeds. He could only cut them back; nothing would ever kill them off. 'Of course,' he said, replacing the biretta, subsuming himself into an emblem again. No longer Cosi, but Brother Franchetti. 'We understand. It was good seeing you again, Gina.'

'But Father Caputo—' Savelli tried again.

'Alessio, *now*,' Cosimo said, catching him by the sleeve and all but dragging him back out and down the stairs. He turned into the courtyard and walked straight into someone coming around the corner. His arms shot out instinctively to catch them—

Rafaella stared back at him, delicate and fragile and more beautiful than ever.

Suddenly he understood the true reason for Gina's distress, her urgent need to get him out of here. Too late, he realized what should have been apparent from the very moment Savelli had called out to 'Signora Giannelli'. His old friends were sisters through marriage, wedded to the two brothers he had grown to hate ... *Of course* Fon would have followed Dante here. He was incapable of independent thought, a sheep to his brother's wolf.

But dangerous, all the same.

'Rafa,' he breathed as she broke away from him with a gasp. She had a young child in her arms, two others by her legs. Her chest heaved with shock, her eyes wide as she tried – like him, like Gina – to understand how he could be here.

'Cosi?' She took a step back from him, the children moving with her again like ducklings, but it was too late; he had felt her warmth, her silky softness sweeping against his arms, and his soul was unfurling like a spring bud. For four long years he had removed himself from the natural world, stepping out of the sunlight where even the shadows danced, away from the breeze that skittered and skipped, sheltered from the rain that soaked and renewed; locking himself instead into a suspended, arid atmosphere of sharp edges and precise angles, where nothing was soft, nothing was fallible.

'What are you doing here?' she whispered as her eyes ran over him, taking in the uniform with its intended blankness that stripped him of all identity. He saw her recognize that nothing remained, in physical form, of the boy she had loved. Her lover. It was impossible to imagine now that he'd once sat on a beach, cocky and defiant, getting sunburnt and risking heatstroke, demanding to be forgiven. Now his pleas for forgiveness were whispered in confession booths, or while kneeling in prayer at the end of his bed.

She shook her head, her eyes feverish as a heat came to her cheeks, their past crashing over her in one devastating wave. Memories of that night – the joy and the despair – played over her face as she tried to comprehend this violent assault on the senses. He felt it all too.

What they had lost, they had lost for ever. They were both bound to vows in which they had forsaken one another. And if it was difficult living with her ghost, seeing her again in the flesh was a torture he couldn't endure.

Nor she.

'I can't do this,' she whispered, turning and rushing back out through the gate with the children in her wake, her silhouette immediately bleached out in the midday sunshine as if the daylight had swallowed her whole. He ran after her to the gate, but the little group had already rounded a corner and gone.

His heart was pounding, his veins flooded with hot blood as he felt himself colour up, his hands still tingling from the touch of her. He wasn't sure whether to cry or laugh, punch the sky or start dancing. She had run from him, yes; but he knew now that she was here, and suddenly he understood that he would see her again. Because if this proved anything, it was that all roads led to her – even the ones he had taken to forget her.

Chapter 38

Rafaella

'Did you know?' Rafaella's voice was sharp, defensive, as she paced around her kitchen, pressing her bare feet to the terracotta tiles as if trying to ground herself. The children were scattered throughout the house, playing. Nico had worked out how to turn on the television set.

'Raf, do you really think I'd have let you walk into that if I had known?' Gina had walked through her front door mere minutes after her, Lorenzo on her hip and worry in her eyes.

'. . . No.' She ran her hand through her hair, her other hand on the small of her back. Her body felt as if a flock of starlings was trapped in her ribcage, trying to get out, beating, fluttering, agitating . . . The past had thrown an iron hook into her flesh and kept dragging her back to that moment again, when she had found herself in Cosimo's arms . . . Like in her memories. Her dreams.

'I swear, the first I knew of it was when he walked in with the other priest, a minute before you arrived. I was trying to get rid of him precisely so that what happened *wouldn't* happen!' Gina threw her hands out.

Rafaella felt guilty for her accusing tone. 'It's not your fault.'

'Well, if it's any consolation, I don't think he knew we were here either. He looked how I felt!'

'Right.' She nodded, still pacing.

'. . . So, how do you feel?'

'How do I feel?' Rafaella laughed, sounding crazed. 'Like another man's wife! That's how I feel. Another man's wife.'

'He looked different, I thought.'

'Well, yes. He's a *priest* now!'

'Trainee priest.'

Rafaella looked over at her. Why did she want to cling to that word – *trainee* – as if it held out any hope? 'How did you think he looked different?'

Gina thought for a moment. '. . . Like he'd been . . . halved, if that makes sense?'

'You mean thinner?'

'A bit of that. But I meant more like he's cleaved away parts of himself. Taken away the flesh and left just bone. He seemed sort of *bloodless*, you know? At least when I saw him, anyway.'

'Yes,' Rafaella breathed; but she had seen a look flare in his eyes, like a firework exploding, as he found himself holding her. It had faded again with every step back she'd taken.

'Don't look so worried,' Gina soothed.

'But I am worried! He's here! He's across the piazza from you!'

'Yes, but it's not as if you're at risk of just running into him. It's not Tricase. That seminary's like a prison.'

'For him to be *here*, though. At this seminary, here. Why not Lecce or Taranto? What were the chances?' Her voice was rising through the octaves, disbelief mutating into panic. She couldn't do this – live a few streets away, knowing he was behind those stone walls. She would never know a moment's peace. She would look for his face now in every crowd. It had been hard enough to subsume him in her thoughts when she'd thought there was no hope of ever setting eyes on him again.

'Listen to me. He's probably lived here all this time, side by side with us, and we never knew it,' Gina shrugged. 'And if you hadn't become involved with these kids, we still wouldn't know it.'

Was that true? Had Cosimo been living here all along, her neighbour for the past two years? Had there been thousands of 'almost' moments when he'd walked past the narrow seminary windows mere seconds after she'd slipped through Gina's green carriage doors? Sat at the far end of the cathedral from her at the same Sunday Mass? They had always slept under the same moon, but now they were breathing the very same air.

'But that's another reason why you should get this kids business all wrapped up sooner rather than later.' Gina's voice pulled her attention back to the present. 'You can't be having meetings with Father Caputo, not knowing whether Cosi's going to be there too.'

'You're right.' Rafaella nodded blankly, trying to imagine it. She desperately wanted it. She desperately didn't. The life she'd built here – ordered and calm, peaceful, *bloodless* – had been dashed apart at a stroke. With a single look, everything was chaos.

'How are they getting on with finding the father?'

'Uh . . .' Rafaella struggled to get her thoughts in order. 'Father Caputo's in contact with the bishop at Brindisi,' she murmured. 'All the priests in the district have been asked to take special notice of new members of their congregation. They think there's a good chance they might find him at confession. For a man to abandon his family is one thing, but to not ask forgiveness for it . . .'

'Yes. Men are reckless with their hearts but not their souls,' Gina nodded. 'Well, until they find him, you're going to need help. You can't just take on six children overnight, especially when Fon's on the road so much.'

'Maybe,' Rafaella murmured, stopping in front of the garden doorway and looking out at the withered olive trees. There was no breeze today, the heat clinging and oppressive.

'Not maybe. Definitely,' Gina said bossily.

Rafaella turned back to her. 'I think I'm doing pretty well with them at the moment.' Bathing them last night, reading bedtime stories and watching them sleep had filled a void in her soul she hadn't even known was there. The children needed love, and she needed to give it. Only now did she see how stunted she had become, emotionally, in these past few years, closing herself down and withering into something mannered, poised and all but dead inside. But mothering those children and seeing Cosi again had changed that, rousing her from her torpor. How could she go back?

'Yes, because this is only half of them!' Gina said, speaking plainly. 'Not to mention they're in a state of shock at having lost both their parents, *and* they've been ill . . . Wait till they start to settle in and become bolder. You're going to be run off your feet.'

'You forget that is my day job. Looking after a roomful of kids is what I'm paid to do.'

'But you can't give these ones back at the end of the day! I'm telling you, you're going to need help.'

'Perhaps,' Rafaella said again, drifting back into her thoughts.

'*Luckily for you,*' Gina said, raising her voice and getting her attention again. '. . . I happen to know just the person to help you.'

Rafaella waited expectantly. She should have known this was leading somewhere. 'You do?'

'Mamma called me the other day. Remember Sonia Lobascio? From the wash-house?'

'Yes.'

'Well, her daughter just got married, and she's moved to Otranto with her husband. Flavia Cassano's her name. And she's looking for a job.'

'Oh. Is her husband working for Dante, then?'

'No. He's a carpenter, from here, but Mamma thought we might be able to help Flavia. I was thinking of taking her on as a housekeeper – Dante's losing patience with all the mess, but I'd like to see him bend down and pick up toys with this strapped to his front!' She cradled her huge bump with a marbled look of annoyance and affection.

'You should definitely take her on,' Rafaella said calmly. Gina could argue with Dante even when he wasn't physically there.

Gina sighed. 'No, your need is greater than mine right now. I can last a few more weeks. You can have her help you out with the kids.'

'But I might not have them for very long.'

'But you might,' Gina argued. 'And how is Fon going to take coming home every night to a madhouse?'

'. . . He wasn't thrilled last night,' she conceded. It had been disconcerting how unmoved he had seemed by the children's plight. She had always thought – hoped – that having children would bring life to their marriage. Now she wasn't so sure. He seemed so happy with just her.

'You see? Take Flavia,' Gina said as if that was that, pulling a chair out and sinking into it with a groan of relief. 'So when is he back?'

'In a few days.'

'What's he going to do up there?'

'Look for leads,' Rafaella shrugged.

'Will he go to see the family?'

'He said he'll try to see Filippo, although he doesn't think he'll have much luck. But the others don't live there anymore, remember? Rossanna's moved to Florence with the little ones . . .'

'Not so little now,' Gina mused. 'The older boy must be, what, fifteen? Sixteen?'

'Really?' Rafaella looked at her, startled by the realization. Romola's death had seemed to stop the clocks, all of them frozen in time.

'Well, it's been four years . . .' Gina's voice trailed away. They rarely talked about Romola. It was too painful, for one thing, and too interlinked with Cosimo for another. She and Rafaella had both pinned their flags to the Giannellis. They had to accept how things had turned out and move on.

They lapsed into silence for a few moments, watching through the garden doors as a sparrow landed on the outside table and pecked for fallen seeds.

Gina frowned, seeming to think of something.

'What?' Rafaella asked, watching her.

'. . . Do you think Cosimo knows? About Fede, I mean?'

'Well, of course. He's his brother. The family would have been in touch with the seminary and alerted them to what's happened.'

'Yes, you're right,' Gina nodded. 'It must be really hard for him, though, being stuck in there and not able to do anything about it.'

'He can hardly do any more about it out here. Fon's wasted trip has shown that.' Rafaella shook her head and rubbed her hands over her face. 'Oh God, when he finds out Cosi's here . . .'

'Why should he find out?'

Rafaella frowned. 'Because we're all living within a quarter-mile of one another.'

'Yes, and Cosi's all but locked up in there. It's not as if we're just going to bump into him. You shouldn't tell him. You know how paranoid Fon's always been about him.'

'But that was before we were married. I'm his wife now.'

'Precisely,' Gina nodded. 'So keep things simple, Raf. We've all rebuilt our lives in Otranto; we like it here. We can all coexist in the same town together, so long as we don't poke the bear.'

It was the last week in July and the tourist season was in full swing, but they had no difficulty getting a table at Osteria Origano, Dante's preferred restaurant. It was tucked away from the Via Seminario along a warren of roads, little more than alleys, that led to an elevated, walled garden. Only the more discerning visitors frequented here, and it was well out of the price range of all but the most successful port citizens. That was precisely why the Giannelli brothers liked to use it for business meetings.

Rafaella sat at the table, decorous in a new dress Fon had brought back from his trip to Rome. It was a deep magenta colour, not a shade she had ever imagined for herself, but it seemed to complement her tanned skin and bring out the caramel highlights in her light brown hair; she had been aware of one or two people looking at her and Fon as they'd walked the short distance here. More than once they had been told they made a striking couple. It was just a shame that strike had never led to a spark.

Gina and Dante had arrived first, of course, and chosen seats by the wall, looking down onto the street; Dante didn't like 'the element of surprise', according to Fon. They were dining with the council leader, Bruno Collura, and his wife, Letizia, and the men had dominated the conversation all evening with discussions about budget deficits, the upcoming Ferragosto celebrations next month, and a rogue mayor who was attracting press attention 'for all the wrong reasons'. They still had dessert to come, but Rafaella was bored and Gina was restless.

'Ah! Father Caputo!' Dante said, raising a hand in greeting as a robed figure passed by below, in the direction of the seminary.

The priest, momentarily surprised, made his way up the steps and over to where they sat as Rafaella cast about for Cosimo or even Brother Savelli. Gina pinned her with a stern look as she pulled her attention back to the table.

'Signori. Signoras,' the priest said politely, though she knew he wasn't given to handing out smiles unnecessarily.

'Father – it is late for you to be out, is it not?' Dante asked him with a slight frown.

'I'm on my way back from ministering to some of the sick who were too unwell to make Mass,' the father explained with a humble nod. Rafaella noted that his demeanour with the men was more supplicatory than she had seen in the community the other day.

'This outbreak has been troubling,' Dante nodded, wearing an expression of concern that Rafaella knew he didn't feel.

'I believe the vaccine uptake is improving now?' Collura said.

'I believe so,' Caputo agreed. He looked at Fon. 'Of course, signore, your wife has shown tremendous Christian charity fostering the Conte children to keep them all together. As you know, the orphanage is overrun.'

'My wife is an angel. I don't deserve her,' Fon said, patting her hand on the table.

Father Caputo nodded, almost in agreement. 'Well, if you will excuse me . . . I must get back to the seminary,' he said, retreating. 'Enjoy your meal.'

'Thank you, Father,' Dante said with a satisfied look, aware of the other diners glancing over curiously at their special attention from the distinguished priest.

Across the table, Gina winced, rubbing her stomach as she shifted her position. She still had weeks to go, but Rafaella was concerned she might deliver early. This pregnancy had been difficult all the way through, with Gina becoming crankier the larger she grew.

'Are you in pain, Signora Giannelli?' Collura asked solicitously.

'No, they're just twinges,' Gina said stoically, even though Rafaella knew she'd had difficulty walking for the past few days. 'They come and go.'

'Your husband makes big babies, I fear,' Letizia laughed.

Gina looked at her sharply. 'Or possibly *I* am petite?'

It was true that Dante was almost a foot taller than her, so both comments were true, but a light had seemed to glint off Letizia's words that caught both Gina's and Rafaella's attention. Neither of them were fools; they knew their husbands kept mistresses, but the men were discreet about it, respectfully so. If it was conceivable that Dante would seduce a business associate's wife, it was inconceivable that he would bring her to their dinner table.

And yet . . . he was a man with appetites. And his wife was very, very pregnant.

Rafaella looked between Dante and Letizia with sudden comprehension, feeling a stab of anger on her friend's behalf.

Collura cleared his throat and reached for his drink, looking uncomfortable, as if he too knew the secret. 'And perhaps you too, soon . . .?' he asked Fon.

'I'm sorry?'

'Will make big babies,' Collura laughed with a shrug.

Rafaella felt herself freeze as Fon's hand squeezed hers a little tighter on the table. 'Well, that is very much our wish, yes.'

'I'm certainly looking forward to becoming an uncle,' Dante said, regarding them both with quiet scrutiny. 'I want our children to grow up not just as cousins, but as close as siblings. Like me and Fon, yes, of course; but you girls were friends too before you were sisters. You understand it.'

'We do. And I agree it would be lovely,' Rafaella smiled benignly, but she felt his probing scrutiny. Could he see the lie at the heart of their marriage?

'So then you need to get on with it!' Dante laughed, flicking his wrist as if sending them off to try right now.

'. . . Fear not on that score,' Fon said coolly, the lie slipping from him smoothly.

'You need to try harder, then, brother,' Dante proclaimed. 'What's stopping you? You've got a beautiful wife who's ready! Give her a baby!'

Heads turned at the boorish remark and Fon shifted, embarrassed; unlike Dante, who lived for attention, he was never comfortable in the spotlight. 'We're leaving it to God's grace. He will bless us when the time is right.'

'And in the meantime, they've got a house *full* of children,' Gina butted in defensively, changing the subject.

'Yes! Did I hear correctly on that?' Collura asked, taking the bait. 'Fon came home to find six orphans in the bed?'

'Well, it wasn't exactly like that,' Rafaella demurred. 'But yes, the six of them are staying with us now.'

'Six?' Letizia sighed, shaking her head disapprovingly and drumming her long nails on the tablecloth. 'Ai-ai.'

'The walls are bulging,' Dante said, lighting a cigarette and drawing on it hard. 'You will have to buy a bigger house, brother. It's not like you can't afford to.'

Fon's eyes flashed towards him. 'We're perfectly happy where we are. Rafa loves the garden, don't you?'

She nodded, smiling.

'Besides, everything's settled down since the nanny started,' Fon added. 'Hasn't it?'

'She's very good,' Rafaella agreed. 'I can't imagine how I would have got away tonight without her.'

It was true that Flavia had come in and made an immediate impact. Gina had been right: a second set of hands was vital when there were six mouths to feed, six faces to clean and six beds to make.

'Still, to take on a stranger's children,' Letizia frowned.

'It seemed like the right thing to do,' Rafaella said quietly. 'They had just lost their mother, and if you saw the conditions they'd been living in . . . I couldn't let them be separated after all that.'

Collura sighed, shaking his head with admiration. 'Fon, your wife is not just beautiful, she's a saint too,' he grinned. 'You're a lucky man!'

'I know. I knew it from the first time I laid eyes on her,' Fon said loyally, still squeezing Rafaella's hand. He was unaware of Dante watching them, but Rafaella saw the look of jealousy in his eyes.

And something else too.

Chapter 39

Fon

Fon cut his ignition, listening to the engine idle down as his eyes tracked the landscape for something – anything – that shouldn't be there: a distantly parked truck, the glint of sunlight reflecting off binoculars, branches chopped from a tree to give a better sightline, a still-warm cigarette butt in the red dust . . . In his experience, it paid to be paranoid.

He stepped out, the door closing heavily behind him as he stared at the tiny round stone hut ahead, the *trullo* stuffed with hidden treasure: millions' worth, in human form.

He walked over and put his key in the padlock, hearing the locking bar clunk and turn, the shackle unclipping. He saw the dust motes spin in the air as daylight fell in with heavy indolence. It took him a moment to find Fede on the ground, his back pressed against the wall. He had curled into a foetal position, perhaps to sleep, and his head lolled heavily as he slowly pushed himself up, his palms spread on the ground.

Fon watched him adjust to the brightness and wondered if his captive listened out for the sound of his car with anticipation or dread. After all, the abduction notwithstanding, Fon had made sure Fede was treated with kindness and civility during his spell here. He had insisted Francesco treated him with as much respect as possible in the circumstances. He was brought good food and fresh water every day, and the mess bucket was cleaned and replaced without comment. He was afforded his dignity.

'*Polpette di melanzane*,' he said, holding out the package wrapped in baking parchment.

Fede's eyes flickered towards him in surprise at the upgrade on his usual *bocadillo*.

Fon shrugged. 'We don't want you losing weight. We don't know how long this is going to go on for.'

There was a pause before Fede reached for the package. He held it in his palms tenderly, as if it was a newborn. '. . . My father has not paid?'

'Not yet, no.' Fon paused. 'I'm sorry.'

'*You're* sorry?'

'Of course. I wish it hadn't come to this. This isn't how I like to do business.'

'Business.'

A small scoff echoed the word and Fon felt himself bristle, retracting like a hermit crab back under his shell.

Fede watched him. 'And how *do* you like to do business?'

'With mutual respect. Negotiation. I have a talent for contract work and homing in on detail.'

Fede smirked. 'We could do with you in the state attorney's office, then.' His eyes flashed. 'You're wasted here; nothing more than a paid thug. Is this what you imagined your life would be? Kidnapping and ransom? Bribery? Extortion? Racketeering?'

'I never dared to dream that high,' Fon hit back. 'I never imagined I would get to marry my wife or live in my villa; I never thought I would be able to do more with my life than fish for mackerel and drop lobster pots. But perhaps such lack of imagination is impossible for you to consider. You, the son of a duke, to whom anything and everything is available.'

'So I'm being punished for being born rich?'

'It's not personal, Fede. It's not about you at all. You are simply leverage. All this is nothing but a waiting game.'

'And if I fall ill?'

'I won't let that happen. It's in our interests to ensure you remain a viable transfer commodity. You are no good to us dead.'

Fede smiled, resting his head back on the wall, the sunlight falling on his throat. It had been several days now since his capture and his beard was coming in thickly; it made him look older. 'You're lucky, then, that you took me and not my brother. He would die just to spite you.'

'I believe you. He would do anything to spite me.'

'Can you blame him?'

Their eyes met as they trespassed into another area of shared history. Cosimo hadn't been the only brother to lose Romola.

Fede looked away first, the silence between them filled by the song of a distant blackbird, and Fon glimpsed the pain behind his eyes. Like him, Fede was a master of repression, hiding his true feelings beneath smooth manners and a ruthless intellect. Fon felt a rush of pity for him, knowing he was living a lie. Was he lonely too? Did he sit in filled rooms as a stranger among friends, showing his family a face that had no reflection?

'. . . For what it's worth, I want you to know how sorry I am about what happened to Romola.'

Fede winced. 'You're very apologetic today. Why the bleeding-heart confessions?'

Fon shrugged. 'There's no one else to hear them.'

'You mean you can't be *seen* to be a decent human?'

The comment was like a whiplash and Fon inhaled sharply. 'We all hide in plain sight, Fede. Even you.'

Fede's eyes narrowed at the pointed comment but Fon

turned away and stepped back into the light, refusing to reveal what he knew just yet. He was a keeper of secrets and that gave him power here, even if Fede was unaware of it.

'I'll give you some privacy,' he said – it had become their code phrase – as he lit a cigarette and paced slowly outside. There was no rush to leave.

Fede had finished by the time he came back in, and he emptied the contents of the bucket into the hole Francesco had dug on his initial stakeout. He had brought another bucket and soap on his second visit, specifically for Fede to wash in, and he filled that too from the standing tap outside the farmhouse, watching as Fede washed his face and hands. Fon had meant what he said when he'd told Fede he wasn't a savage. He knew his captive would never see him as a social equal, and any long-held hope of becoming friends was unthinkable now; he accepted that. But it mattered to him that he rose in Fede's estimation at least as a businessman.

'So . . . married life,' Fede said, unwrapping his meal as Fon leaned against the doorway. 'Does it suit you?'

Fon shrugged. 'Three years now and we've never been happier.' He watched Fede's eyes travel over him curiously, sceptically – as if it was inconceivable to him that Fon might have found a woman prepared to pledge her life to his.

'And where does your lovely wife think you are right now?'

'Today? In Taranto.'

'*Are* we in Taranto?' Fede asked quickly, glancing at him.

Fon gave a wry smile. It was easy to forget that his captive had no idea at all where he was. For all he knew, Fon could have taken him over the border into France, Switzerland, Austria . . . 'I'm afraid not.'

'Ah . . .' Fede's fingers were slow and clumsy unwrapping the paper. He was stiff from lying immobile for so long. 'What does she think you do?'

'Import cigarettes.'

Fede laughed at that, truly amused, the sound sudden and unexpected so that Fon almost jumped.

'It is technically true. It's just, it's only one of the things I do.'

'A cover story.'

'If you like.'

Fede nodded as he took a bite of the *polpette*, a small groan escaping him as the flavours burst on his tongue. Deprivation of light, comfort, touch . . . any positive sensation at all was enough almost to break a man. Fon had discovered this over the years when needing to extract information. Once someone was in a state of privation, the carrot was usually far more effective than the whip. It played better to Fon's nature, whereas Dante *loved* the whip.

'Good?' he asked, taking pleasure in this small mercy as Fede nodded appreciatively, too overcome to speak. Fon took no joy in these baser aspects of his job, and Fede was a cultured companion, after all. 'Then I shall bring some more tomorrow. Unless there's something else you'd prefer?'

Fede pinned him with a look. 'You're taking requests now?'

'No, I—'

'Am I your prisoner or your king?'

Fon swallowed, immediately regretting his hospitality and rueing his need to impress this man who was by turns a bear cub, then a viper. He had been supplicatory, not commanding, and had relinquished his authority by trying to chase Fede's respect.

'I must go,' he said abruptly, turning and reaching for the door.

'No, wait!' Fede cried, just as it was slammed shut and darkness fell upon him again like a velvet cloak. 'Alfonso, I'm sorry! I didn't mean—'

Fon clicked the lock shut and strode back to the car, blood rushing in his head. He'd been such a fool to think there was a place here for compassion. For decency.

Even here, with the keys in his hand to freedom and riches, he was nobody.

He stood at the window of the apartment, looking out towards the sea. The restaurants and bars were filled up along the promenade, the castle walls dramatically lit, tourists weaving in and out of the boutiques that stayed open late in the hopes of selling a decorative tile or handwoven basket after dinner.

Behind him the television was playing a game show, canned laughter setting his nerves on edge. Gabriella was through in the kitchen, fixing him a drink. She had been surprised when he'd turned up here unexpectedly again, agitated.

Fede's disdain had wounded him more deeply than he cared to admit and Fon was already resolved not to go back tomorrow, to teach him a lesson and show him who wielded the power between them now. Alone in the dark, with no food or water, Fede would soon feel the minutes begin to stretch like hours, realizing too late that he had deprived himself of the only person in the world who could keep him alive. Fon might even leave him for two days. Could he survive that long without water? He remembered the second bucket – it had been freshly filled for washing, but the soap . . .

He turned away from the window. He would decide tomorrow, he told himself; see how he felt after a good night's sleep. He might feel more merciful on a full stomach.

'Here.' Gabriella crossed the room and gave him his martini.

He took a deep drink and closed his eyes with fleeting pleasure as it slipped down, but he was still angry and discomfited at Fede's scorn; he couldn't throw it off. It was as if a piece of his soul had been turned over and now sat at an odd angle to the rest of him, jarring with every movement. Why did Fede's opinion matter so much to him? Why did he care what that man thought, when he was the one with all the power?

He looked back out of the window, trying to recover his equilibrium before he went home. His wife was seven minutes from here in their beautiful home, caring for six orphans with Flavia.

Flavia. He didn't like having a stranger in his house. Her eyes followed him, watchful. Lustful? Money and power attracted women, but the wrong sort. He wanted her gone. They needed her while the Church was still looking for the children's father, but if that went on much longer without success, Fon would send one of his own men up there to find him and haul him back here to face his responsibilities.

'Will you stay tonight?' Gabriella asked him, grazing a nail against his chest. She had had them filed into sharp talons and he knew they were supposed to excite him, but she could rarely satisfy him in the way he liked. Most of the time she earned her money simply by living here; it was far more important to him that he was seen to keep a mistress than it was to enjoy having one.

Rafaella was expecting him home – he had told her he wouldn't be late. She would be feeding a stranger's children their dinner, running their baths, brushing their hair . . .

Gabriella pressed the nail harder against his skin, looking up at him through slitted eyes, before she slowly sank to her knees and reached for his flies.

'Yes, I'll stay,' he murmured, dropping his head back and closing his eyes. Images – always the same image – stepped out of the shadows and filled his mind as she began to work on him. This was what he needed. It was the only release that would bring him peace.

Collura had been right to call Rafaella a saint. She was the Madonna.

But when he was like this, there were things only Gabriella could do for him – and tonight he needed the whore.

Chapter 40

Cosimo

'I thought I might find you here.'

Cosimo looked up as Savelli came to sit beside him, setting his biretta on the bed. There would be serious consequences if he was found in Cosimo's room during prayer time, but he was taking the risk anyway. Cosimo had been thrown into crisis.

Cosimo saw his cheeks were flushed from the walk back here, the rosy bloom of fresh air settling upon his body like a taunt, and he felt the flicker of rage again in his stomach. He felt it every time now when Savelli came back from his pastoral visits with Father Caputo, because he himself had never felt so confined. He longed for these walls to fall and the wind to rush in. He kept tipping his head back, trying to breathe. Why couldn't he breathe?

'Did you see her?'

Savelli nodded. 'She's doing well. It's been hard for her, juggling them all, but she has a woman helping her now, so things are easier. She said she even managed to get out to the market this morning to buy some fruit.'

Peaches, Cosimo guessed. They were her favourite.

'And she's planning a trip to Lido la Castellana for them later, for an evening swim and picnic.'

Cosimo stared at him as if he was being deliberately provocative. Peaches, swimming, a picnic? All these things embodied the world of softness that he was denied. Colour, taste, sensation . . .

Memories of a long-ago day bubbled up: diving from the rocks at El Ciolo, the girls lying on their towels and laughing as he and Fede took turns rating their dives. It had been the first day that summer when things had gone back to normal between them all. Looking back, he realized it had been perfect. The Giannellis had turned up on their speedboat, intruding, but even that hadn't spoilt the day. Cosimo had vanquished Fon, and he'd felt like a king.

But hindsight had shown him he'd only won the battle, not the war. Now the wild hope he had nurtured following his reunion with Rafaella at Gina's was fading fast. One day had run into another, into another, and no word had come from her . . .

'Was her husband there?'

'Yes. That was the point of today's meeting – he wanted to see Father Caputo himself. He's going to send someone to Brindisi to help with the search. He's lost patience with the situation. Clearly he isn't as charitable as his wife.'

His wife. Even the words made Cosimo flinch. The thought of Fon lying with her in their bed at night . . .

Savelli gripped his shoulder, seeing the storm flicker over his face. 'I'm worried about you, Cosi. It's been days now and your spirits are getting worse. You've got to try to move past this.' Savelli, to his credit, had made no further mention of his own feelings towards Rafaella. He knew Cosimo's story; he knew exactly who she was to him.

'How can I, knowing she's outside these very walls?'

'She doesn't want to see you,' Savelli said, as gently as he could.

'She told you that? You actually asked her?'

'Yes. I said everything you asked me to say, but she said no good could come of it. She's married now.'

Cosimo shook his head in disbelief. 'But she doesn't love him!' he cried. A sudden, sickening thought hit him – unless . . . unless she had grown to love him? 'Did she tell you she does?'

'She didn't say.'

'Well, what did she say?' he cried.

'She asked how you were.'

'And you said . . .?'

'That you were fine. I didn't think it would help for her to know you're suffering like this.'

Wouldn't it?

Cosimo got up and paced across the narrow room; it was more like a cell, the bed like a bench, the window set so high the only light was a thin slit that fell across the door. And everywhere immovable, ancient stone.

He pressed his hand to the wall, feeling its coldness against his palm, the stippled texture reminding him it was worn and marked but enduring. As he must endure now. This was his penance, after all – the closest he could come to a life for a life. This was his storm to weather, the test he must not fail.

Ever since that night when the world had literally crumbled around him, he had walled himself away from any feeling: the colours were too bright, the sensations too deep, excoriating him inside and out. He couldn't survive it. The guilt of what he'd done was too immense, and later, when he'd realized that saving his freedom meant relinquishing Rafaella – even though it had been her bargain, her pact – he had found safety only in absolute stillness, in total silence. It hurt too much to feel. He had willed himself to turn to stone until, slowly, all those flashing, blinding, swirling emotions of anger, envy, lust and regret had sunk to the bottom of a muddy pit, out of sight and range. He had reassured himself that as long as he moved with care, without provocation, there was no reason for them ever to rise up again.

It was this very denial of the senses that had helped him survive, but now everything felt airless and suffocating. He had buried himself alive but his spirit was fighting back; it still wanted to breathe. It refused to die.

He could no longer find refuge in this stone mausoleum, because *she* was here in Otranto and she was everywhere. She scaled his walls and came to him in his dreams. He saw her face in every crowd. She was behind his every confession of despair, anger, ingratitude ... of impure thoughts. The feelings rushed at him in a flailing, screaming constant assault on the senses and he couldn't stop them. Seeing her had been like a drowning man's last gasp, a final clutch at life. She was a rose in the desert: fresh and fragrant, delicate, but also strong. Because she had thorns as well, and she was intent on keeping him back.

He told himself it was just a walk. There was no sin in wanting to feel the sun on his face, to warm his bones away from the cold, cold stone.

Savelli had advised this. Urged it, even. Fresh air and sunlight ...

People nodded at him as he walked by, through the streets of the new quarter where modern apartment blocks seemed to spring up almost every week. Cars were parked nose to tail along the roads, bunches of scooters left askew outside garages and back doors. He heard music playing from the bars. Most tourists stuck to the historic centre, and it was the locals who congregated here; he heard their sullen shouts at one another from doorways or across balconies, as they stood smoking cigarettes.

Some of the prostitutes were out already and he sped up as he walked past. His cassock didn't inspire reverence in them but mischief, as if he was a challenge to be overcome – they made a point of swaying their hips and squeezing their cleavages for him, especially when they got a closer look at his face.

'For shame!' they cried after him angrily, as if he was denying womankind.

He crossed the street, feeling the wind pick up and his pulse quicken as he drew closer to the water. It glistened in small winking blue pockets at the ends of streets.

He walked until he left the blocks of the new neighbourhood behind and the land spread out into a patchwork of fields, groves and copses. The beach lay beyond a stand of eucalyptus and fir trees and he crossed the open grassland, aware he was conspicuous here in his long seminarian's habit.

The white sandy bay was broad, curving around to low-lying rocky points at each end. Even at this time, as the sun was descending rapidly, there were still plenty of people lying out on towels, others on sunbeds with orange umbrellas. The water was pale like celadon, lacking the dazzling intensity that had characterized Tricase Porto in such unapologetic terms; but it was clean and no doubt warm in the shallows. He recognized the tribal activity here: the *anziani* floating as they talked; the *ragazzi* jumping off the rocks. Mothers on the sand, building sandcastles and . . .

He found her. Rafaella was sitting on a blanket, towelling off a little girl, the droplets flying off her like she was a dog in full shake. They were laughing about something and the sound of her voice carried to him, light and percussive.

Everything in his body slackened. His muscles, his soul . . . Running into her the other day had been a karmic shock for which he wasn't prepared, but to come here, knowing he would find her . . . Because it wasn't just a walk. It was a temptation he had been unable to resist. She was refusing to see him and this might be his only chance to rest his eyes upon her, to nourish his soul with a closing look that could last the ages.

He stopped behind a eucalyptus, only half hidden, but telling himself there was no reason for anyone to be peering into the trees here. He watched her and it felt as if time itself was unwinding, the spring on a watch spooling the hands backwards to the easy days of their Tricase summers.

She was his best friend. Rafaella Parisi, the girl he had known and loved his entire life. He had beaten her at running races; she had beaten him at chess. She had taught him how to dive deeper; he had taught her Roman swear words and slang. They had been separated for too many months in every year, and yet everything momentous that happened to him was only truly celebrated once he had shared it with her. He remembered his jealousy as they'd moved into adolescence and Romola's door had been shut on him while the girls gossiped about boys; how he would stand at the door straining to hear who *she* would mention. And how, when she grew tall and lanky, he teased her and said she looked like a boy, because he knew she wanted to be petite like Gina and he was terrified that his attraction to her would be revealed.

He moved closer, unable to stop himself as he watched her recreate the idyllic scenes of their own childhood. She was so good with children, a natural. He couldn't understand why she wasn't yet a mother. Savelli had told him she was a teacher now and it pleased him because she'd always been too clever, too enquiring, to settle for serving drinks and cooking dinners.

There was a little boy, around ten or so, organizing the bigger kids into a circle as they threw a ball around. A young woman was helping Rafaella with the younger ones, drying them off from their swim and trying to poke skinny arms through sleeves. There were a lot of failed attempts, the clothes sticking to their damp skin, ill-coordinated limbs at the wrong angles as their giggles drifted over the sand to where he stood hidden.

He felt himself sinking into the halcyon scene, his body remembering these soft, comforted feelings, and had to forcibly draw himself back. Because it was also a mirage. To a stranger's eye, the two women could have been sisters, sitting on the beach together with their children; but the nanny was paid and the children . . . borrowed.

This, this right here, he reminded himself, was the fallibility of the feeling world. Things were never as they seemed. Lies and deception were everywhere. Death might lie around every corner—

'Go and get it, Rosa!' he heard one of the children cry, and he looked up to see the older boy pointing in his direction. The ball was rolling his way, at speed.

Rafaella looked over too, squinting as she watched the young girl run onto the grass, arms outstretched to catch it though it was far ahead of her. Cosimo hid himself behind the trunk, but although it offered some cover . . .

'Not too far, Rosa!' she called.

Cosimo held his breath as the ball rolled past his feet and came to a stop just beyond him. He couldn't kick it back without being spotted, but if the child saw him here, hiding behind the tree, she might scream and then . . . She stopped running suddenly and he froze. Was he visible around the slim trunk? Was his cassock caught in the breeze?

'Brother!' the little girl cried excitedly.

He stiffened, realizing he'd been caught; that despite his best efforts to remain hidden, he had been found out anyway. Was it a sign? God's will that they were supposed to meet? Just like they had met the other day? They needed to talk. There was so much to say.

He began to step out—

'Rosa!' said a familiar voice as Alessio Savelli moved across

Cosimo's field of vision, stopping just in front of him and holding out the ball. 'Is this yours?'

'*Si!*' she cried, taking it happily and unceremoniously, running back towards her brothers and sisters on the beach.

Cosimo felt himself sag as the moment passed as quickly as it had come. His subterfuge was still safe. God's will remained unknown.

He looked up and met Savelli's eyes. '... How did you know?'

Savelli fixed him with a knowing look, but he shrugged. 'I just thought I might find you here.'

Chapter 41

Rafaella

The morning light had an apricot tint to it, throwing a pale blush onto the stone buildings of the piazza. The air was fresh, cooler than it had been in weeks, and Rafaella, moving through the market throng, detected rain on the wind. It would be welcome – summer had been blistering this year, and the hot days always led to humid, sticky nights in which sleep was only ever light and fleeting.

She was used to sleeping undisturbed, but now she slept alone most nights too. Fon had been on the road more than usual lately and she'd had the luxury of a double bed to herself, stretched out on smooth sheets as she watched the ceiling fan spin round and round, almost hypnotizing her.

Her dreams were troubled, but that was nothing new; it was simply the intensity of them that frightened her now. She would awaken with a gasp, almost certain she could still feel Cosimo's hands upon her, or hear his breath in the room, or see his shadow pass outside the door. Several times she had even got up and stood in the corridor, drenched in sweat and moonlight as she searched for phantoms.

But she wasn't imagining this.

He was following her again, keeping his distance as she

moved from stall to stall, talking with the market sellers. It was almost becoming a routine. The market was set up every other day and she was becoming accustomed to the weight of his gaze on her back as she filled her basket. As if it was an arrangement they had tacitly agreed.

Did he know that she knew he was here?

He would make no spy, that was for sure. She had been shocked when she'd caught sight of him hiding in the trees at the beach the other week, unable to fathom how he'd known ... But as Brother Savelli returned the ball and joined them on the sand, she'd realized they had a messenger (unwitting or not). So she had tested him. At their next meeting she had deliberately shared her plans again, by way of conversation, only to hear an echo to her footsteps a few hours later.

Cosimo had her in his sights. He had found her again and he wouldn't give her up.

She told herself she could ignore him and still take comfort in his gaze. His company might no longer be an option, but to have him as her shadow ... She welcomed the respite of shade, however faint. She had stood in the glare of the sun for too long, her every movement, every emotion it seemed, scrutinized by Fon and his brother as if they were waiting for something from her, though she knew not what.

But she knew this wasn't innocent. She luxuriated in Cosimo's scrutiny, yearning for the weight of his stare upon her profile, her legs, her arms. She started doing her hair, showing more skin: a higher hem, a ruffled sleeve. It was a power she had never known before. To be watched, missed, untouchable.

But she wanted him to touch her again – it was all she could think of. He invaded her dreams, dominated her waking thoughts. She found excuses for more meetings with Brother Savelli even though they both knew – though it went unspoken – that he was their intermediary, passing over news and plans . . .

Right now, Flavia was at home, cooking breakfast and dressing the children, allowing her the time to buy only the very best grapes, cucumbers, beans . . . It began to spit with rain as she spoke with the sellers, chatting about Ferragosto and the influx of visitors, wanting to draw out every moment of this slow-motion chase. Because she didn't want it to end. She didn't want to go back to that house and that empty life with Fon. All she wanted was to be in his presence, wrapped up in his gaze . . .

The rain started falling more steadily, fat drops splashing onto hard cobbles, and the market sellers pulled tarpaulins over their stalls as she walked and wandered, walked and wandered. She wanted to stay out here for ever – the hot rain washing the dust from her skin, slicking her hair and soaking her clothes – but eventually she ran out of road, reaching the far end of the market. There was nowhere to go but back.

But she didn't do that. She couldn't.

How long were they going to play this game? Already it wasn't enough. Why was she giving up the man who wanted her for a man who didn't?

She stood motionless as a rumble of thunder sounded far off in the distance, the sky growing ominously dark as she stared past the stalls, her basket full, her heart racing. She felt as if she was standing at the very edge of the world, overlooking a precipice into the great beyond – and she wanted to jump. To double-dare destiny and stare it down, because it was all her fault, this. She had condemned them to it. In the shock of the aftermath of the accident, she was the one who had placed their fate in Fon's hands – she had been trying to save Cosimo from what felt like certain imprisonment, but all she'd done was lock him up behind different bars.

Was he behind her now, watching her pause?

People were beginning to run for cover, disappearing into the shops as the rain came harder. Heavier.

She turned her head a half-turn, able to feel him at her back. They were tethered still, tied together by an invisible thread.

She stepped into a narrow alley, turning left and right into other streets without intention, losing direction, listening only to the footsteps echoing hers.

She walked faster, trying to match the rhythm of her pulse, but as she hurried her pace, she heard the percussive rhythm of his feet matching her beat.

She broke into a sudden run, breaking cover now. He would know she knew he was behind her. The chase was out in the open.

She was lost but it didn't matter. The back streets had become a maze with no destination and no way out, but she didn't want to escape. Or win.

She turned another corner and saw a cavity between the wall of a house and a steep set of stairs – just enough to park a couple of scooters – and she ducked into it, her heart clattering. She pushed her hair back from her face, her skin wet, her clothes soaked, waiting.

She heard him coming up the street, giving chase; he was only twenty metres behind her – fast and determined not to lose her. Not again. She caught sight of his profile as he ran past, saw the jolt travel through his body like an electric shock as he glimpsed her in his peripheral vision, hiding in the nook, trembling in the rain. He turned back in the next breath and suddenly – just like that – he was standing before her, saying nothing and everything at once in the silence.

When she had seen him at Gina's, the sight of him – so altered, so unlike himself in his robes – had made her snap shut like an animal trap; the shock had been too great to absorb in the moment. But now here were the eyes that had held hers as she said her vows, here was the mouth that caressed her in her dreams. Here was the soul that belonged with hers. She felt his gaze fall over her like a rainbow, shelter from any storm, and she saw all his longing, all his pain. Four years had passed since that night when they had claimed and then lost one another, but if their lives had changed beyond recognition, their feelings hadn't. He loved her still. She could see it in his heaving breaths, even though his feet were now quite still; the way his body stood taut, almost trembling from the tension of holding himself back. Rain was pouring down his face as if the sky itself was crying for them.

'Cosi,' she whispered. Her hand fluttered towards him – tentative, frightened – and that was all it took to rip past the ties that had separated them. He swooped down and kissed her in a seamless movement, his hands clasped upon her cheeks, holding her to him now as for ever.

It was done.

Nothing would keep them apart any longer. Not life, not death. And not, for a single day more, Fon Giannelli.

His body pressed her back against the wall, as it had the first time in that ancient olive tree. His breath was hot and ragged as his urgency was matched by her own. He didn't care who saw them and neither did she. It had been an unnatural act, their separation. *This* was right. This was love.

She felt the pressure of his fingertips through her clothes, and she pushed into it. She didn't care if he bruised her. Let her body wear the marks of their passion! She felt no guilt and Fon would never see it anyway. All the things she wanted to be – a full woman, free to love, a mother – she could never be with him.

She gasped for air, her hands in his dark, wet hair, her fingers twining tightly, binding her to him. 'I love you, Cosi, I love you,' she whispered.

He moaned in response, the sound coming from a place deep inside him as he buried his face in the crook of her neck. 'You're really still mine?' he asked, pulling back, his eyes burning like pools of fire.

'Always. I've always been yours. All this time.'

She saw her words land, healing him somehow as he kissed her again, over and over.

Her hands ran over him, marvelling at the body that had claimed her so completely four summers ago and never relinquished its grip. 'What do we do?' she whispered as his mouth covered her face, his hands on her breasts. He couldn't get enough of her. He had to hold her, touch her, taste her. 'Tell me what we do.'

In the face of crisis, it was his turn to choose. They had both made vows. Could they choose one another before everyone, before God . . .?

He looked back at her, clasping her face in his hands. 'We leave,' he panted, the rain running in rivulets down his cheeks.

She nodded, tears of happiness slinking from the corners of her eyes. It was all she had wanted to hear. 'Yes.'

He stared, drinking her in. She was his sustenance and he hers. '. . . Will he let you go? Or will he fight?'

'He'll let me go,' she said urgently, but she saw – as his breathing slowed and he began to regain control of himself – a cautious reserve come into his eyes, as if he knew better than that. Their past was scarred by his battles with Fon. 'He will,' she insisted. 'It's not what you think between us. He doesn't want me, Cosi. He wants . . .' She struggled for the right words, trying to articulate the thoughts herself. 'He wants the idea of me, I think.'

'The idea?'

'We're not intimate together.'

He sank against her at the words, burying his face in her neck again and holding her close like something precious.

'You don't know how it's tormented me, Rafa . . . giving you up to him,' he said, his voice choked with emotion. 'Thinking of you with him.'

She clasped his face in her hands this time, making him look at her. 'I was always yours.'

'But I don't understand. He was relentless about you. Obsessed. How could he have you and not . . . have you?'

'I don't know,' she whispered. 'But I was grateful for it. I never pressed him for fear of him changing his mind.'

Cosimo frowned. 'But will he give you a divorce?'

Rafaella hesitated. 'No.' Fon's reputation came before everything. 'But I don't care, Cosi.'

'You know what that would mean . . .' He looked back at her worriedly, stroking her cheek. Being together would come at a high price.

'It means both of us leaving, turning our backs on our vows.' She swallowed. She didn't care about living in sin. They could move far away, where no one knew them. No one else would ever have to know. They knew what was between them was pure. 'I can do it. Can you?'

He nodded. 'But we'll need to be careful about how – and when. Leaving the Church is . . . bureaucratic. There are procedures to follow.'

'Fine,' she said, not caring what they had to do as her eyes roamed over him hungrily. She couldn't believe they were here, together. Their bodies touching. Their souls joined. He kissed her again, making her moan, and he had to pull himself back after a few moments, pressing his forehead against hers as he struggled for composure. Clarity. They still needed a plan. 'We'll need to think about how you break it to Fon.'

'I'd rather do it sooner than later. I've never been a convincing liar and he's good at reading people, but especially me. He'll know something's up. Better to do it quickly. No lies. He hates liars.'

He watched her. 'What will you say?'

'The truth. That we can't go on in a loveless marriage. It's not fair to either one of us. I want a family. I want to be a mother. To be your wife.'

'You can't say that bit. He'll never allow it.'

'But Cosi, you don't know how it's been between us. Truly, I think part of him will be relieved it's over. I think he only married me to appease Dante.'

'*Dante?* Why does he care?'

Good question. She swallowed as she remembered Dante's look at dinner the other week. He'd had so many women over the years but he'd never once come near her; he had earmarked her for his brother and it had given her a protection of sorts, put her off limits. But lately, she had sensed a new intensity in his scrutiny of her. She felt his eyes following her every time they were in a room together and as Fon's distance from her grew, Dante's shrank. He was getting closer by single degrees. She could feel it.

'Does he know I'm here? In Otranto?'

She shook her head. 'I haven't told him.'

'Probably better to keep it that way until we work this out,' he murmured. 'It'll only complicate things with him. If he so much as hears my name in relation to you . . .'

Her brow furrowed as something occurred to her. 'Do you think he'd go to the police? If we renege on the agreement, might he tell them what really happened that night?'

Cosimo fell still. He was silent for several moments. 'It was an accident. *I* know that,' he said slowly. 'I've . . . made my peace with it, as much as I ever will. I've prayed for forgiveness and tried to become a better man. And the police felt there was no case when they thought he was the one who had tripped, so I don't see why that would change if they learnt it was me.'

'But he has contacts with them,' she whispered. 'I didn't

know it then, but . . . he's connected. And so much more powerful now than he was back then.'

Cosimo nodded. 'Well, I'd still rather take the chance of ending up behind bars than continue living without you behind those walls.'

She took his hands and kissed them. 'I love you,' she said with bright eyes.

'And I love you. I won't let you go again, for anything.'

'You promise?'

'Let me think of a plan.' He kissed her forehead as he cradled her to his chest and the rain continued to fall. 'But I promise, Raf – one way or another, we're getting out of here. Together.'

Flavia was stripping the beds when she returned.

'Oh, signora!' she exclaimed. 'You are soaking!'

'I'm . . . I'm fine . . .' Rafaella said, laughing at herself as her clothes dripped on the floor. 'It came on so suddenly. I couldn't get back in time.' Too late, she realized she had left the basket of food in the nook in the side street.

'You have caught a chill, I fear,' Flavia said, regarding her with concern. 'You have a fever?'

'Me? No,' Rafaella said, pressing a hand to her neck, but she went to the mirror and caught sight of her reflection. Her eyes were shining, her cheeks flushed. Her hands automatically flew to her face as if she scarcely recognized herself. Joy was written all over her face. She would never hide this from Fon. He would see at once she had come alive again – and he would know why. It was an instinct he had.

'You should have a hot bath and get into some dry clothes quickly, signora,' Flavia cautioned.

'You're right. I shall,' Rafaella nodded, moving to go but stopping again. 'The children have been OK?'

'Of course!'

'I feel bad I was gone so long.'

'Spoken like a true mother,' Flavia smiled as she beat the dust out of a pillow.

'Oh, I don't know about that,' Rafaella demurred.

'I do. You're a natural, signora. They are so lucky someone as kind as you found them and took them in.'

'Anyone would have done the same.'

Flavia shook her head. '*Non*, signora . . . Only you.'

'Well, I'm lucky to have you helping me.' Rafaella smiled, embarrassed by the compliments. 'You make it look so easy. You come from a big family?'

'Not really. We were four children, but then my little brother died, so . . .'

'Oh Flavia, I'm sorry,' Rafaella said sympathetically. 'How old was he?'

'Eleven.' Flavia had fallen still. 'I miss him.'

'Of course you do. I lost someone very close to me a few years ago. She was a sister to me in all but blood and there's not a day goes by when I don't think about her.'

'It's very hard,' Flavia murmured, turning away now, her head bowed.

Rafaella watched her for a moment. She felt ashamed that she'd been so busy looking after the children, this was the first time she had bothered to learn more about the young woman working beside her.

She went into the bathroom and opened the taps, watching the water rush into the tub as she slowly unbuttoned her blouse, sinking back into the memories of this morning's encounter. Cosimo danced through her head, the heat from his touch still vivid on her skin. She took off her wet shirt and brassiere and looked down at herself, wishing he had left his mark after all. She wanted to be branded by him. Made his own.

She ran her fingers over her body, closing her eyes as she

remembered his hands on her breasts, his face in the crook of her neck—

A sound in the hallway made her start and she looked up to find Dante standing in the doorway. A slow smile had spread over his face at the sight of her, half naked, touching herself. He was perfectly unabashed to be found watching.

'What are you doing here?' she gasped, covering herself with her blouse. How long had he been standing there, enjoying her nakedness? 'Who let you in?'

She could hear Flavia in the bedroom, still moving the beds.

'I have a key, Rafa. You know that.'

She stared at him. She had never known that. She knew his influence extended into almost every aspect of her life, but to have a key to her own home . . .? Fon had kept it from her.

'What do you want, Dante?' she asked, but her voice was thin, betraying her fear. The mannered artifice that always existed between them in Gina and Fon's company was missing in their absence and he regarded her now, seeing how she hid from him, her dislike of him evident. She didn't think he liked her either, but a man could detest a woman and desire her at the same time, and she could see the debate flash through his eyes. Flavia was here, but that wouldn't stop him.

His gaze raked along her bare stomach, arms, her smooth clavicle, the nub of her shoulders, and it felt like his hands were running over her skin. Her body had awoken under Cosimo's touch not an hour before. Could he see it?

'I want to talk to you,' he said after a moment, pulling back, the tone shifting again. 'Cover yourself and come down to the kitchen.'

He disappeared and Rafaella stared into the void he left behind, her heart like a jackhammer.

Turning off the taps, she ran back to her bedroom and took off her sodden skirt, which was clinging to her thighs.

She changed into a plain dress, the plainest she could find, coming downstairs just a few minutes later. He had already found the coffee and was setting the Bialetti pot on the stove. He was so perfectly at home in her house, she had to wonder whether he let himself in while she was out. She wouldn't put it past him to go looking for things. What, though? What was it he wanted from her?

He turned as she entered the room, taking in the sight of her lissom body now hidden beneath frumpy cotton, and gave a gloating smirk at her overt modesty.

'So you were caught in the rain?' he asked, conversational now.

'Yes,' she said, smoothing back her wet hair and beginning to loosely plait it. 'I was at the market.'

She remembered again the lost basket, evidence of her trip there. If Flavia was to ask, or him . . . Regret at her wild recklessness was beginning to creep up on her. Had she lost her mind? If someone should have seen them . . . Cosimo was in his seminarian's uniform! She was a Giannelli wife! And yet it had been unstoppable, worth any risk.

Flavia walked in, carrying the sheets. She stopped abruptly at the sight of Dante there, seeming to pale.

'Signore Giannelli,' she murmured, dropping her gaze to the floor.

Dante nodded, seeming to enjoy her deference. 'Flavia.' His voice was so low the word came out as more of a growl.

Flavia hurried through, setting the sheets in the washing basket before rushing from the room again. Dante's eyes followed her until she was out of sight. Had something happened between them, Rafaella wondered.

'Pretty girl,' he murmured, watching as she made her way up the stairs.

Rafaella said nothing, wondering if he had forgotten he was married to her best friend – or just didn't care.

He stuffed his hands in his trouser pockets as she walked past him to check the coffee. '... You know, most women wouldn't be happy about having such an attractive woman around their husband.'

Rafaella made a noncommittal sound as she lifted the lid and peered in. There seemed little point in reminding him Flavia was also married, nor that Fon wasn't like him, chasing down every skirt on the street. 'Maybe I'm not most women, then.'

'Tell me something I don't know.'

Rafaella let the comment pass.

'How are you finding her?' he asked, watching as she moved around the kitchen, restless and unable to settle. She just wanted him gone.

'She's great,' she said mildly. 'I couldn't do without her. I think I could cope with four children, but the extra two is just ...' She held her hands up in surrender, trying to look relaxed, to regain her dignity. Whatever her private feelings about him, she reminded herself it was better to have Dante as a friend than an enemy. 'I'm so grateful Gina offered her to us. I know she must need the extra help too.'

'Well, she'll have her soon enough now the father's been found.'

Rafaella looked back at him. 'What?'

'Fon didn't tell you?'

'No.' She frowned. 'I mean, I know he was fed up waiting so he sent one of his team to look instead – but he hadn't told me they'd found him.'

Dante rolled his eyes. 'Well then, pretend you don't know! He probably wanted to tell you himself and I've just ruined his big surprise.'

She stared at him. He said it as if it was a relief the father had been found and the children would be taken away from here, but she thought of the single-room house and its lack of sanitation and comfort, the one bed where their mother had died . . . How could they possibly go back to that? They had just started settling in here, finding a routine and eating well; she'd been reading to them in bed at night and making sure they got enough sleep.

She rubbed her face in her hands dejectedly. 'This is a disaster.'

Dante scowled. 'Why? You should be pleased! The family will be reunited. You did a good thing, taking them in like this, but clearly it was never a long-term solution.'

She knew he was right. She couldn't just *take* someone's six children because it had felt good having somewhere to put her love at last. But the thought of giving them up, of sending them back out there . . . 'But the father,' she pressed. 'How's he going to support them all? Did he get a job in Brindisi? Is he going to move them up there?'

Dante held his hands up at the rapid-fire questions. 'Slow down . . . I don't know and I don't care.' He shrugged. 'That's his business, not ours.'

Her mind was racing with disaster scenarios. She and he had both lived among poverty throughout their childhoods; they knew the toll it took on people. Or had he forgotten? Surely Dante could remember how it felt to go to bed with an empty stomach?

She couldn't let it go so easily. 'And what will he do now his wife is dead? Who will look after the children?'

'He'll find a job and he'll remarry.'

'But it's not that easy . . . Can't you give him a job?'

She knew she was pushing her luck, and as he looked back at her she felt the weight in his gaze, as if there was something to be negotiated. 'Perhaps,' he said finally. 'I'll think about it.'

'Because those children deserve—'

'It isn't your concern any longer, Rafa!' he said sharply,

losing patience. 'They're not your kids. And more to the point, they're not Fon's.' An edge to the words caught her attention and she pulled back, taking the pot off the heat and pouring them each a cup.

Dante watched her as she took a sip. 'Every man needs his own bloodline.'

'I know that,' she said quietly.

'So then, perhaps you should be concentrating more on having your own children than rescuing other people's.'

'I want to have children of my own. I do. I just can't bear to think of these ones suffer—'

He interrupted her again. 'Have you talked to any doctors?'

'What?'

'You and Fon. It should have happened by now. I'm not the only one to have noticed it. Mamma too is fretting. She thinks there must be something wrong.'

'There's nothing wrong!' She felt offended that her intimate health was being discussed so freely by others.

'You bleed every month?'

'*What?*' She couldn't believe he was asking her these questions.

'Just answer me.'

'Y-yes, of course.'

'And the act? How often do you do it?'

Her mouth opened in disbelief. Was this really happening? '. . . Enough.'

'How often is that? Every day? Three times a week? Twice a month? What?'

'Dante, I'm not telling you that! It's private!' Her cheeks flamed with shame that they were having this conversation.

'He's my brother, and you, as his wife, have one responsibility – to give him children. So I'll ask you again, how many times do you do it?'

'. . . It depends! There isn't a schedule!' Oh God – could

he hear her lies? 'Besides, he's been on the road so much lately . . . I've scarcely seen him these past few weeks.'

Dante frowned; it was his turn to look surprised. 'You mean he's not coming back here at night?'

'No, he's been travelling.'

He didn't reply, but she saw the slight narrowing of his eyes and could see he was holding something back. She could guess what: Fon was, in fact, coming back to Otranto each evening – but he was staying with his mistress.

She turned away, not wanting him to see that it suited her this way; that she would be happy if Fon never shared her bed again.

She heard Dante replace his cup on the table. 'You know, there was a reason why I wanted to talk to you today, Rafa.'

Another one? 'Oh?'

'How has Fon seemed to you lately?'

She frowned. 'Fine.'

'Fine? He hasn't seemed distracted? Low?'

'*Low?*' She met Dante's eyes as he stared back at her, always regarding her so closely. 'No. Why? What's going on?'

He clicked his tongue against the roof of his mouth. 'I'm worried about him. He's not been himself recently. I wondered if you had noticed it too.'

She shook her head. 'But then, he's been away so much . . . Do you think he could be staying away deliberately?'

'I'm sure not,' he replied offhandedly.

Rafaella lapsed into thought, trying to think of reasons why Fon would avoid coming back here. '. . . He hasn't been thrilled about having the children here, but I didn't think it was anything more than an irritation to him.'

'And you didn't think to relieve your husband's irritation by getting rid of them?'

'They're *children*,' she protested. 'They had nowhere else to go.'

'They could have gone to the orphanage. Children go there every day.' Dante regarded her as if she had disappointed him. 'You know, there's nothing Fon wouldn't do for you, Rafa. My brother loves you very much.'

'I do know that,' she swallowed.

'The question is – do you love my brother?' She felt them moving into choppy waters again. She remembered the edge to his words the night of the dinner with Bruno Collura and his wife, the insinuation that she was failing in some way . . .

'He's my husband, isn't he?'

'We both know they're not one and the same thing.'

'. . . I love him, Dante.'

'Are you *in love* with him?'

She didn't reply immediately. Cosimo's kisses were still upon her lips; her blood was still racing from his touch. Her every waking moment for the past three years had been a lie, and now she was being pressed on semantics? 'I don't know what you want me to say to that.'

'It's an easy enough question. You're supposed to say you are.'

She threw her hands in the air, frustrated. 'Well, I'm sorry, but being "in love" isn't something that can be conjured at will,' she replied, the words bursting from her in a rush. 'I married him. As I agreed to do. You can't force my feelings as well as my actions.'

'. . . Is that what we've done?' A dangerous tone glinted in the question. 'I don't recall making you do anything against your will. As I remember it, you were the one who made the offer to Fon.'

Rafaella looked away, her heart thudding in her chest. She was shocked she had said the words aloud. It was the first time she had ever alluded to the shadowy manoeuvrings of the brothers in the months following Romola's death. She had acted in good faith cutting that deal – Cosimo's freedom for her hand – unaware she was just one such transaction as they steadily ramped up their pressure tactics in the port and stepped into power.

They had been clever about it. Nothing was ever too conspicuous, just a litany of small acts of attrition designed to wear down resistance: intermittently cutting off the water supply to the port, damaging some trees in the groves, reducing the oil yield of the villagers' olive harvests . . . It was the very pettiness of the grievances that meant nothing could ever be said. But the wider knowledge of what was happening had hovered unarticulated in the port, fear and suspicion growing among the villagers as confirmation was transmitted with dark looks. Rafaella's father had tried his best to keep her out of the Giannellis' clutches when she had announced her engagement to Fon, but for reasons she could not disclose, she had refused to change her mind.

The brothers' reach had grown quickly. Everyone saw the explosion in their wealth but no one could account for it, and its unexplained presence only furthered the whispered rumours of ill-gotten gains and corruption. In the space of a few years, people were saying they had politicians in their pockets, the police chief and council leaders too, not just in Tricase but in the Salento region overall . . .

For all this time, Rafaella had kept her suspicions and misgivings to herself. But no longer.

'I'm a good wife to him, Dante,' she said quietly. 'I do what is asked of me and, in all truth, it is no great hardship; Fon has only ever been sweet and gentle to me.' That much was true. 'But asking me to be in love with him? . . . Some things are simply not possible.'

She saw an ugly look come into Dante's eyes at her small

act of resistance as he took several steps towards her, standing so close she could smell the coffee on his breath.

'Well, let me tell you what is going to be possible, Rafaella,' he murmured, looking down at her, and she felt a frisson of terror that the thing she feared most from him – a horror she had never dared to acknowledge to herself – was finally in the room with them. 'You're going to give my brother what he wants – what he *needs* – to have: children. A son.' His gaze ran over her and she saw a shiver of lust in his eyes, like the flicking of a lizard's tongue. 'Get him to put a boy in you.'

She caught her breath, knowing what was coming next.

'Or I will.'

Chapter 42

Fon

Fon looked down at the footprints in the dust, his eyes tracking the big, booted treads marking the earth, prowling a perimeter and keeping their prisoner captive. Francesco had done his job well. He always did. He wasn't an intelligent man, but he was loyal and obedient – Dante had been right to keep him close as he rose in wealth and position.

He hesitated, taking a breath and steadying himself before he put the key in the lock and turned it. Sunlight fell into the dark space with its usual indolence and he watched as the inmate retracted from the sudden assault. Fede moved slowly, gingerly, pressing his body from the ground, and when he lifted his head his eyes seemed to bulge in his face. The difference in him was marked. He had lost weight and looked filthy; his hair had lost its smartly clipped Roman shape, and his beard was thick. He no longer looked like a duke's son but like any of the *campieri* around here.

He blinked several times and Fon saw him flinch as he realized it was he who had come this time, not Francesco. Had Francesco been rough with him these past weeks? He looked for signs of assault – wounds, bruises, inert limbs lying at awkward angles; the henchman had developed a love for pain – but Fede seemed in decent shape. Just weak.

'You came back.' Fede's voice was hoarse, as if the darkness was robbing him of substance.

'. . . Francesco's on a job,' Fon said roughly, moving in and setting down the food. Gabriella had prepared some arancini and he crouched down, opening the parcels carefully. He handed them to Fede, the food lying within like jewels in paper crowns.

Fede said nothing, watching him closely as if bracing for a kick. The traces of their last meeting hung in the air, like whispers that had been unable to escape this room too. *Am I your prisoner or your king?* Fon still felt the humiliation of the encounter; it sat on his skin like a tattoo, branding him as the weaker man. Inferior. The yellow-bellied coward Fon knew he really was – and that Fede had known he was, too, ever since that day on the rocks.

'. . . I didn't think I'd see you again.'

'As I said, Francesco's needed elsewhere today.'

'So? You could have let me starve,' Fede shrugged.

'As I've also told you before, we need you alive.'

'So then I have *some* leverage.'

The comment was pointed and Fon regarded him more closely, seeing how the delicious food remained untouched. Had he been deliberately refusing his meals – was that why he'd grown thin? If so, Francesco hadn't reported it. But Fede was an intelligent man and Fon knew he'd be looking for any advantage he could find.

'If you mean by going on hunger strike, then no, you don't. We would still continue as planned, but on receipt of the ransom we would simply hand back your body for burial.' Fon stared at him, his eyes as cold and hard as his words. He would not leave here today on the back foot. '. . . But that would be regrettable, Fede. Death does not have to be the outcome of this.'

'As if you care whether I live or die!' Fede scoffed, tipping his head back against the wall. He sighed, the sound ancient and deep. 'You really think I believe you're going to let me walk out of here?' He looked back at Fon through slitted eyes. '. . . I know how this ends . . . I know you. I've seen your faces. And you know that if I get a shot at freedom I'll go straight to the police . . .' His voice trailed off as he saw Fon's slight smirk. 'Ah . . . But you've got your people there too, of course,' he sighed, too exhausted to even sound defeated.

There was another silence.

'Eat,' Fon commanded.

Defiance flashed in Fede's eyes as he refused to move. He had nothing left to lose and denial was the only control he had left.

Fon walked over to the wooden chair and sat in it. Fede seemed to prefer the floor. 'You know, it takes a surprisingly long time to die from starvation,' he said, his elbows on his knees as he looked down at his captive.

'Not if I stopped drinking.'

'True – you could be dead within days,' Fon conceded. 'And we would have to bring up our timings accordingly.'

'Timings? Like a schedule?' Fede gave a laugh that almost reached his eyes. 'So you've done this before?'

Fon gave him a puzzled look. 'Of course, many times. Why would you think you're the first – or even the only one? You're not *special*, Fede.'

Fede's eyes flashed at the insult, and Fon felt himself grow in stature.

'Although usually the ransom has been paid by now, so I suppose you are unique in that respect. Your father really doesn't seem that bothered by your fate.' They were cruel taunts, he knew, and he watched the pain flash behind Fede's eyes. 'I'll be honest – we've been surprised. We thought he valued you more than this.'

Fede looked away, sinking further back against the wall, his arms limp in his lap. 'Then you really don't know my family at all,' he murmured.

Fon looked at him in surprise. He had been expecting more comeback, more fight than this. He had been gearing himself up for this confrontation for days; it was all he had been able to think about, but this wasn't the man Fon had left here eighteen days ago. Something in Fede was breaking: his hope in his father, his spirit. '. . . Eat.' He picked up an arancini ball from the paper by his feet and held it out.

Fede stared back dully at him.

Fon leaned in closer, holding it up to his face. 'I said, eat,' he snarled. He knew the insubordination was intended as another humiliation, and he wouldn't lose this time. He would not walk out of here until it was written in stone which one of them was king.

Still Fede didn't stir. He just blinked. His hands were chained together in front of him, but at this proximity, Fon knew Fede could hit upwards with his bunched fists and get the chain around his head and neck . . . Fede was the bigger man, it was true, but he was diminished after weeks spent motionless and alone in the dark.

Fon took the risk as he suddenly launched himself forward off the chair, falling to his knees and, in a swift movement, pushing Fede's head against the wall. He gripped his jaw hard, forcing it open, and with his other hand put the curve of the arancini ball to his mouth and held it there – but Fede wouldn't bite down.

'*Eat!*'

Fede eyeballed him, the whites of his eyes like a skittish horse, as they remained locked, immobile, on the ground.

Fon could feel the muscles in his hand shake as emotions flooded him: anger. Rage. Contempt. He would not leave here as the loser.

Fede groaned as the flavours seeped onto his tongue, glaring at Fon as his own body worked against him, crying out for the meal. Fon knew it must be a worse torture to the starving man to endure this than to abstain from it altogether. For several seconds they remained locked in suspension . . . until Fon saw a tear slowly slide from the outer corner of Fede's eye. His jaw relaxed and he bit down.

'Good,' Fon said quietly, sinking back onto his heels and watching as the prisoner slowly chewed, head hanging down in shame.

It was a victory. Fon had won this battle convincingly, but he felt somehow spent after the confrontation. He'd wanted to break Fede, to enforce his power, but now that he had . . . He had never hated Fede. The Franchettis, yes. His arrogant father, his spoilt sister and Cosimo, of course, the lifelong thorn in his side. But Fede had always been different, a better man than the rest of them. If only it could have been Cosimo chained up here, not his brother.

'For what it's worth, I want you to get out of this alive, Fede.' His voice was low, barely more than a whisper, even though there was no one else around for miles.

'Why? Why do you care so much?'

'Because I know you.'

'We were never friends, Fon.' It was intended to hurt but Fon felt bulletproof now. He had anticipated exactly this slight.

'No,' Fon agreed. 'But I still know you far better than you think . . .' The urge to reveal Fede's secret sat on the tip of his tongue. He couldn't help it; he wanted him to know he knew.

He watched Fede eat, knowing he should remain silent. That to show compassion was weak, every word eroding his hard-won advantage. And yet . . . 'You never noticed me, growing up . . . No one did. But I always saw you. I watched you all. I wanted to be just like you.'

Fede's eyes disinterestedly flicked in his direction. Now that he had started to eat, he seemingly couldn't stop, his fingers cramming the food into his mouth with increasing urgency.

Fon gave a small smile as he sank back into the memories, crossing his legs at the ankles, elbows looped on his knees. '. . . I looked forward to your return every summer. I admired you more than you could possibly know . . . Your family's return to the port was always the highlight of the year, for everyone – even Dante, though he'd never admit it.' He watched Fede reach for the other paper parcels, dragging them over the ground towards him. Defeated. Compliant. 'I don't want to see you die here.'

But there was no reply. Fede wasn't interested in *making friends* with him. He just wanted to survive him.

Fon got up and went outside, clearing out the mess bucket and refilling the washing one with fresh water. He smoked two cigarettes, pacing in the sun and trying to enjoy the quickening in his body of the small victory in the hut. It was an inconsequential triumph, not worthy of this rush, and yet he felt he had reclaimed that part of himself which had been lost last time. He had shown he had the power. He had absolute control over this man who had been above him in every way for his entire life, up until today. He could hold him here or release him whenever he wanted; starve or feed him according to his will; keep him alive or kill him on a whim – and he realized he wasn't just Fede's king now. He was his god.

He felt a strange sensation running through his body. It was unfamiliar and unsettling. He thought it might be happiness, but he wasn't sure.

Fon walked over to the abandoned farmhouse across the

way, puffing on his cigarette, staring idly through the broken windows, reading the old graffiti ... He looked back at the *trullo*. Fede had finished eating at last and was lying on his back on the ground, his bound hands above his head, his arms outstretched and the chain pulled taut from the bolt in the wall as he positioned as much of his body as possible in the sun. Like a dog.

The dog and the god. Words reversed. Worlds reversed.

He watched how Fede's muscles relaxed, his face slack as he breathed fresh air and sunlight for a few precious moments ... It was a simple pleasure. Perhaps the simplest. Fon smoked another cigarette and walked another lap around the house. There was no rush, and these were the small mercies he could grant.

'I brought something for you today,' he said when he finally returned, almost an hour later.

Fede's head turned on the ground to look at him. He looked better already, his cheeks gaining some colour, his eyes enlivened from the meal. 'What is it?'

'You'll need to stand up.'

Fede hesitated but did as he was told, a look of alarm spreading over him as Fon pulled the razor from his pocket. He drew himself back into the shadows. 'You said—'

'Relax,' Fon said, holding up a hand to calm him. 'You need a shave.'

An astonished silence followed.

'Don't look so stunned. I told you the first day, we're not savages. I'll do what I can to help you through this – bring you good food, let you wash, lie in the sun ...'

He saw that look come into Fede's eyes, the same slightly mocking, haughty expression he'd worn when he had asked Fon last time, *Am I your prisoner or your king?* But kings, he told himself, could be gracious. Magnanimous in victory.

'I thought it might make you feel better, more like yourself. But if you're not interested . . .'

He went to put the razor away again.

'Wait,' Fede stopped him. A note of desperation sounded in the word. He had been almost entirely deprived of human contact these past few weeks. The lure of comfort, any small kindness, was impossible to resist. '. . . I am.'

Fon nodded. 'OK, then.' He took over the washing bucket and set it down before him. 'Soap yourself.'

Fede obeyed, getting on his knees and splashing his face so that the dirt came off in streaks, his eyes looking brighter. He wet the soap, rubbing it into an extravagant lather over his beard.

Fon watched, seeing how Fede's eyes kept falling to the blade in his hand. He tightened his grip on it, his mind working fast. What if the desperation and despondency – the weakness – was all an act? Was Fede deliberately luring him in, preying on his compassion and kindness and decency? Might he lunge for the razor?

'OK,' Fede said, when he was seemingly satisfied the hair was soft. He held his hand out for the razor.

Fon shook his head. Did Fede really think he was so stupid as to hand him a weapon? Another tension developed between them as each man held back, wary and suspicious of the other.

'. . . Tilt your head back,' Fon commanded.

Fede didn't stir, and Fon could read the conflict in his eyes. What kind of fool exposed his own throat to the man who was keeping him in chains? But also, what other choice did he have? He was already incapacitated.

Slowly, he lifted his chin, his eyes trained upon Fon's every move like a sniper. Fon adjusted his grip on the blade, feeling his heart rate accelerate as he approached. Fede was the bigger man, even half starved. Even with a blade in Fon's hand, this was a dangerous moment for them both.

He raised his hands up, pulling the skin taut, aware of Fede's eyes tracking him closely. He pressed the blade flat against his neck, alert for the smallest twitch of a muscle, before gradually tipping the angle and bringing it down through the beard.

The sound of the bristles shearing was all Fon could hear in the silence of the tiny stone hut. They were both breathing heavily, on guard against one another as if fear was something they could smell, trust flapping like a bat about their heads and unwilling to land.

The first stroke completed, he dipped the blade in the water to clean it and reached up again. Fede still instinctively pulled away from him but as Fon repeated the action again and again, their animal instincts began to settle fractionally.

'You know, I saw you outside Villa Maria with your friend at Silvana's wedding,' Fon said quietly. 'I know what you are.'

He saw Fede's Adam's apple bob in his throat as his prisoner took the revelation on board. 'If you know that . . . why haven't you used it?'

'Used it?'

'Surely it would be easier to blackmail me than kidnap me?'

Fon smiled at the lawyer's logic. It was the same question he had asked himself. One word to Dante about Fede's proclivities and this would all have been done very differently. Blackmail was a lot cleaner, quicker and safer for them all than this; the last thing Filippo Franchetti could afford was another lurid family scandal making the headlines. And yet Fon had remained silent, for reasons he was still trying to understand. Was it mercy to the one Franchetti who had ever treated him as worthy? Was the favour repaid? Or was it because, try as he might, he couldn't quite detach himself from the scene between Fede and his friend the night Romola died? The men's shadows had fallen upon him, dragging him into their underworld with them, and it exercised a hold over him like nothing else in his life.

'Yes, that's true, but then it would follow you everywhere. It would define you, Dante would make sure of it . . . At least this way, you can walk away unblemished in body and reputation. You're only a pawn in these negotiations; there's no need for your life to be ruined over it. Within a few weeks, you'll have put it behind you as a sore inconvenience, nothing more.'

Fede's eyes tracked him as he moved. 'Can I ask you something?' he murmured as Fon dipped the razor into the bucket again.

Fon nodded, but as he pressed the blade to the skin again, he felt Fede temper the instinct to speak. He looked back at him, the movement paused as he waited.

'. . . Why do you let Dante push you around?'

Fede had barely moved his lips, the question little more than a whisper. And yet it reverberated around them like a screaming devil, all Fon's fears thrown up like a bag of butterflies.

'He's dominated you your entire life . . .'

'Stop,' Fon said in a low voice.

'You're better than him—'

'Don't talk about my brother,' Fon warned, calmly pressing the blade closer on Fede's skin in a clear threat. But his prisoner didn't flinch and Fon wondered – was this what Fede wanted? Was *this* his plan – to provoke him into an angry slash, bloody and brutal but quick? It would be over within seconds.

'You're a good man, Fon. I know you are. But he's not.'

Fon felt his breathing become ragged as Fede refused to look away, to back down. He was defiant – fearless and provocative – and they both knew such disrespect could not be borne. Dante would never have allowed it . . .

'He's rotten to the core and you know it.'

'Stop!' But images were flashing through Fon's mind of another knife-edge pressed to another throat . . . of desperate pleading, shallow breath, the rolling whites of eyes. His hand began to shake as the memories of the murdered boy crashed upon him, but to his shock and dismay, Fede covered his hand with his own.

Fon caught his breath at the unexpected tenderness, the razor still pressing ominously against his prisoner's neck. Fede stared into his eyes, and it was like a flashlight shining into the heart of him, exposing everything he'd kept hidden – had had to keep hidden – all these years.

Fede was looking at him, really looking at him, as if peering into his very soul, and he realized that Fede knew. He had always known. His secret was Fon's too.

They were the same. Both monsters. Both liars.

Both alone.

He recognized his brother's silhouette even in the dark, leaning against a car as he parked up.

'What are you doing here?' Fon frowned as he got out.

'More to the point, what are *you* doing here?' Dante replied, watching as Fon walked over to him.

Wasn't it obvious? 'I'm going to stay with Gabriella tonight.' He shrugged as carelessly as he could. There was no possibility of going home. He felt made of glass, transparent and thin, as if his skin had been peeled away and everything he truly was could now be seen by the whole world. He had always taken such care to hang back, to set himself at angles and deny a clear view into the heart of him, but now he felt lit from within, exposing his fatal flaw.

Hiding his true nature from Rafaella was hard at the best

of times but he feared that if he walked through the door tonight, she would instinctively know. He knew she suspected something was wrong – he didn't desire her the way he ought to; he could too readily accept that she loved another man. He needed her not for sex but safety. Their marriage was his badge of respectability. With her in his house, in his bed, he could be seen as normal – because there was one person, more than any other, from whom he had to hide himself.

Dante pulled on his cigarette, regarding him through slitted eyes. It was the look he gave to business associates about whom he hadn't yet made up his mind. 'Is that so?'

'. . . Is it a problem?' Gabriella lived in the same block as Dante's own side piece, Renata, though he had been more absorbed with Bruno Collura's wife lately. His appetites were legendary and seemingly insatiable.

'I spoke with Rafa today. I went over to find you, but she says you've barely been home in weeks.'

'Oh.' Fon shrugged. 'I guess I have been here more than usual lately . . .'

'Why?'

'Why do you think? I keep Gabi for a reason and it's not conversation.' He went for dismissive disdain, but Dante wasn't buying it.

'You've been distracted lately. Off the mark. Forgetful. Not to mention no one can keep tabs on where you are.'

Fon threw his arms out. 'Well, I'm not hiding.'

'Your wife thinks differently.'

'Dante, what's the issue?' Fon sighed. 'As far as Rafa's concerned, I'm on the road – and what she doesn't know won't hurt her.'

Dante's eyes dragged over him and Fon felt a wave of fear that his brother could see what Fede had seen; as if Fede's attention had left marks on his skin like lipstick kisses. 'You need to get rid of her.'

'Who? Raf—?'

'Gabriella. She's distracting you from your marriage. Get rid of her!'

Fon blinked, seeing his brother was deadly serious. '. . . OK,' he said quietly. 'If that's what you want, I'll get rid of her. It doesn't matter either way to me.'

'Good. And then go home and start paying some goddamn attention to your wife.'

Fon stared at him, feeling a trickle of fear creep through his bones. 'Dante, where's this coming from?'

'If you don't want people to start talking about you, you'll do as I say. You've been married three years with nothing to show for it. I want her knocked up within the month, you hear?'

Fon nodded. He knew the Giannelli reputation came before everything. They needed heirs. His brother's impatience with the issue had been building for months – but why had it suddenly cracked now?

He took his cigarettes from his jacket pocket and lit one too, drawing hard for a moment before exhaling a plume of smoke. It always made him look more confident than he felt.

'Why did you come to see me earlier, anyway?' he asked, trying to change the subject altogether.

'Francesco is back from Rome.'

Fon coughed on the smoke. '. . . Already? I thought he wasn't due back for another few days.'

'Yeah, well, if you'd been around you would have known he came back early. Our contact came good on the warrant for Franchetti's office . . . It's clean.'

Fon frowned. 'And the apartments too? They're sure?'

'The diary's not in his new or his old place. He went back twice, once when Franchetti was sleeping. Checked his suits.'

'So do you think the wife has it after all?'

Dante shook his head. 'He wouldn't entrust it to her. She loathes him now. She'd happily throw him to the wolves if she could, and that diary would do it for her.' He looked thoughtful. 'No, Franchetti told us he kept all his books and papers in the divorce. He's no fool. That diary's his insurance policy. If it's not on him – and we know now it's not – then he's put it somewhere safe.'

'Fede's apartment is probably worth another look.'

'Francesco was thorough. It's not there.' Dante pushed himself up to standing from the car bonnet. 'It's time to up the ante. We've had his son for weeks now and he's not handed it over – he thinks we won't do anything. He thinks he knows us, that we're just Carlo Giannelli's sons. We can't play in the big league.'

Fon stared at his brother, a chill spreading through his heart. 'So what are you thinking?'

'We show him otherwise. If he won't play ball, we'll have to force his hand.'

Fon knew what that meant. 'We said we weren't going to do that. Straightforward kidnap and ransom, you said. Nothing more. No bloodshed.'

'He's calling our bluff, Fon. Are you going to let that stand? He's happy to let his son rot because he doesn't think we mean business?'

Fon could only stare at him.

'We've been patient long enough. I'm a reasonable man, but I will not be disrespected. I'm going to send Francesco over tomorrow to pay Fede a visit—'

'No!' The word burst from him before he could stop it.

Dante looked at him in surprise. '*No?*'

'. . . I mean, let me do it.'

'You?' Dante scoffed. 'As I recall, you're a lot less handy with a knife than him. You couldn't even stick it to someone half dead.'

It was the accusation Fon had never been allowed to shake off. Even now, all these years later. 'He was a kid!'

'Yeah,' Dante muttered. 'And he was suffering. You let him suffer rather than put him out of his misery.'

Could murder ever be mercy? Fon swallowed, staring down at the ground. 'Dante, look, I've never pretended to be capable like that. I know what I can and can't do – and what I can do is read people and work them over. I talked to Fede today when I took him his food. I think I can get him to talk to me. He still thinks we're holding him for money. If I tell him it's the diary we want . . . that we'll let him walk if he gives it up . . .'

'It's a lot quicker to send Francesco in and let him do what he does best with a scalpel and a box-cutter.'

'I agree – but let's keep that as back-up,' Fon said quickly. 'Nothing's off the table, but we don't want to play our hand too early. Fede's a lawyer. He's a rational man with a logical mind. I think I can persuade him without things escalating.'

'What do you care about escalation?' Dante scowled, looking at him closely. '. . . He doesn't know you're *you*, right?'

'Of course not!'

'You've kept the hood on him? At all times?'

'Obviously.'

'But if you've been *talking* with him—'

'He never knew me well enough to identify me by my voice alone. I don't think he'd even remember my name! He was always your friend, not mine.'

His brother looked unconvinced.

'We need to keep our heads on this,' Fon said, keeping his voice steady. He couldn't afford a misstep here. 'Maiming a Franchetti – much less killing one – is hazardous. They're too high profile and we can't risk that kind of scrutiny. If I can get him to give us the whereabouts of the diary without spilling any blood, then so much the better for us all.'

He could see Dante was considering it and he felt the desperation surge in him, like sap rising.

'Please. Just let me try tomorrow. If I can't make any headway, you can send in Francesco with his toolkit.'

Dante nodded. '. . . Fine. You can have one run at him. One. But make sure you put the frighteners on him so he sees it's in his own best interests to talk.'

'I will. I'll do that. I'll get through to him.'

'Call me tomorrow when it's done.' Dante flicked his cigarette to the kerb and turned towards the building, his jacket slung over one shoulder as he headed for Renata's apartment. 'And in the meantime, go home and fuck your wife.'

Chapter 43

Rafaella

A cat with amber eyes slunk over the wall, on the prowl for its dinner as it surveyed the scant garden, peering disinterestedly past the withered olive trees and scattered toys. A small paddling pool was half filled with water, reflecting the moon, a plastic duck gliding in serene silence.

Upstairs in the umber-coloured villa, a cotton lace curtain was fluttering at the open window. The sound of children's chatter had long since died down and the only noise now was shuttered gasps pinching the night sky.

Rafaella watched their shadow dance on the wall as Cosimo moved above her, his face burrowed in the crook of her neck, her legs wrapped around him like a bow. Somewhere on the floor lay their clothes, shed alongside their past as they both reached for the future and brought it into the present. Into now.

Waiting hadn't been an option. Just this day had been endless, and tomorrow felt like it would never come. She'd had a taste of him again and she needed more. She wasn't sorry for it. She was a traveller in the desert, parched and needing to drink if she was to survive; one drop wasn't enough to sustain her.

It had been her last day with the children but he was all

she could think about as she played with them in the garden, lost in her thoughts as she fed, bathed them and read their bedtime stories. Flavia had noticed her distractedness, giving Rafaella a funny look when she'd asked the nanny to stay a few minutes longer after putting them to bed so she could pop out to thank Brother Savelli for all his help.

Tomorrow morning, Signor Conte would be taking the children back again, and this house would fall quiet once more. Like her, they were being returned to the person to whom they belonged.

Savelli had been a good friend, passing on the coded message she had slipped to him earlier as the priests walked past each other in the busy corridor. Cosimo had let himself in just before midnight, coming through the garden gate, which she had left unlocked. They had come straight up here to her private sanctuary, saying scarcely a word, instead letting their bodies talk through hands, mouths and intertwined limbs. Fon was away again, and they had all night to reclaim one another and soothe their scarred souls.

She felt his urgency gathering now, his body tensing as he panted hard, his mouth pressed to her ear. She clutched him tighter, holding him as he cried out, and she knew his ecstasy was marbled with sorrow. Reclaiming her meant, at some level, relinquishing Romola. Giving Rafaella up had been the price of his freedom, but submitting to life in the Church had been his own form of penance for his part in his sister's passing. He had lived these four years in the shadow of death. Now he was choosing life.

She ran her hands through his hair, looking up at him as he gazed at her. He was more handsome than ever; grief had etched its lines into him and scrubbed the arrogance from his eyes. Gone was the blank architectural beauty of youth and, in its place, something more flawed, but richer and deeper, like the burnished spot on a lucky bronze statue.

'I love you, Raf.'

'I love you,' she smiled, revelling in the weight of him and his powerful physicality. Her heart was roosting in its rightful place again. They had returned to the point from which they had been diverted that night when Fon had turned up at Villa Agosto while she had been waiting for Cosimo in bed.

He rolled onto his back with a contented sigh. It had been years since he'd lain in a double bed and his legs stretched out on the smooth sheets. He groaned happily.

Rafaella turned her head and watched him as he closed his eyes to enjoy the downbeat of cool air on his bare stomach. A film of sweat glistened on his skin and she could see sleep was hovering over him like a whispering angel.

The wall shadows had fallen still at last and her eyes closed too, her lean body limp in the twisted sheets. Somewhere outside she heard a cat yowl, a lover's shout, the slam of a door, as the moon continued her stately ascent.

Cosimo's fingers were softly stroking her bare thighs, growing slower, scarcely moving at all . . .

Her eyes flew open as an echo reverberated through her mind . . . The slam of the door.

Her door.

She sat up with a gasp, staring into the darkness and straining for the sound of footsteps in the hall.

'What is it?' Cosimo murmured, sitting up too and propping himself on an elbow. 'Is one of the children—?'

'Fon,' she whispered, looking at him with wide eyes.

There was a pause.

'But you said he was away.'

'He is! He . . . he said he was . . .' she stammered, feeling the blood pounding through her head. But she heard it still, a sound from downstairs – a thud, staggered footsteps, curses, as if someone had tripped over a shoe or a toy.

Rafaella jumped from the bed, grabbing his cassock and

shoes. 'Get dressed! You have to get out of here,' she hissed, balling them against his chest as he too got up and stood disorientated in the room.

'But how? Where?'

She jerked her head towards the Juliet balcony. 'I'll go downstairs and make him a drink. Something to buy time.'

Cosimo threw the cassock over his naked body, transformed in an instant from Adonis to a meek man of God. 'But when will I see you again?' he asked, pushing his feet into his shoes as they heard more crashes from downstairs.

'What is he *doing*?' she hissed in disbelief. Of all the nights for Fon to come back. She had scarcely seen him these past few weeks.

'Rafa!' Cosimo brought her attention back to him again. 'Meet me tomorrow. In the confession box, just before noon?'

She nodded disconsolately as he reached down and kissed her again. 'I wanted us to have all night together,' she protested, pressing her hands over his as he clasped her cheeks.

'We're going to have *all* our nights together,' he said with a wink, a flash of the cocksure boy she'd once known surfacing for a moment. 'We'll make our plan tomorrow, I promise. There's no turning back now.'

She watched as he turned for the French doors, stepping up onto the stone balustrade before reaching for the cast-iron drainpipe and carefully making his way down.

Rafaella looked around the room and saw the story it told. She hurriedly picked her clothes off the floor and laid them neatly over the bedroom chair, smoothed out the bedsheet, plumped the pillows and punched a fist into her own. She glanced outside in time to see Cosimo running from tree to tree across the lawn towards the back gate. She didn't know where Fon was in the house or what he was doing, but if he were to look out . . .

She grabbed her robe from the back of the door and ran silently down the hall, desperately trying to compose herself. Could she pull this off? Or would he look at her and be able to tell straight away that another man had just made love to her in their bed?

'Fon?' she asked, walking into the kitchen and forcing a yawn, rubbing her eyes as if he'd woken her. 'What's going on? You said—'

Her husband turned to look at her, so drunk he could scarcely stand. He was holding a bottle of brandy in one hand and swaying on his feet.

'Are you OK?' she asked, concerned. He looked wrecked. He wasn't usually a drinker, not like Dante.

He gazed at her with glassy eyes and she wondered how many duplicates of her he was seeing. Her mind went back to the night of her sister's wedding again – that wonderful, terrible night in which worlds had collided and exploded; she remembered seeing him across the room, utterly alone at the dinner table as everyone talked and laughed and danced around him.

He looked just as alone again now. Just as wretched.

'Hey,' she said quietly, walking over and taking the bottle from his hand. Carefully, she set it down on the counter. 'Fon, has something happened?'

His head was hanging, and it seemed an effort for him to meet her eyes. 'I don't want . . .' The words trailed off.

'Don't want what?'

He swayed again. '. . . To be this.'

'To be drunk?'

'To be . . . me.' The words came out as a mumble.

She put a hand on his shoulder. Something bad had happened, but what? 'Come. Let's get you to bed. You'll feel better in the morning.'

He allowed her to drape his arm over her shoulder as she slowly led him along the hall and up the stairs.

'It's too late now,' he mumbled as they walked past the children's bedrooms, and she felt her own hypocrisy that she had stood in judgement of their father when under this roof lay infidelity, inebriation and lies.

'It is late,' she whispered, feeling sickened by what she had done, and was still prepared to do, to be with Cosimo.

She closed the bedroom door behind them, her eyes scanning the room again for any glaring aberration in the domestic scene. She looked over at the wall where their shadows had danced, their silhouetted selves come to life with torrid intensity. Now there was nothing to see but a hairline crack in the plaster. This room would keep her secret.

Fon dropped his jacket to the floor and kicked off his shoes, losing his balance as he tried to step out of them. He fell against her and she almost buckled under the weight of him.

'Whoa. Are you OK?' she asked again, trying to set him straight; but he didn't seem to hear, his eyeline directed downwards. 'Fon? Can you stand?'

He raised his hand slowly and traced the edge of her robe with his finger. She had become dishevelled trying to get him up here, the belt coming loose, and she startled as he pulled it open suddenly, exposing her breasts.

'Fon!' She recoiled, releasing him and moving to close it again, but he caught her by the wrist and held her hand in place. She looked back at him, alarmed by the gesture. This wasn't like him. He never put a finger on her. 'Fon! *Basta!* Let me go.'

She tried to wrest her arm from his grip but he was too strong and, as he looked back at her, she was taken aback by what she saw on his face: anger. No, more than that – rage. Despair.

Oh God, did he know? Had he seen Cosimo after all?

'Fon,' she said, a quaver in her voice as she saw his breathing grow heavier, his grip tightening on her wrist, hurting her now.

'I have to . . . I have to do it.'

She stared at him. 'What? No!'

His eyes travelled over her, taking in the sight of her tender curves, a Giannelli violating her privacy for the second time today—

Dante. These were *his* instructions.

'Fon, no!' she cried as he tore at the robe, yanking it off her so that she stood nude before him. Instinctively she slapped him hard, skin striking skin. He looked stunned, but only momentarily; it seemed to wake him up, and he hit her back in the very next instant. The force of the blow threw her back on the bed and she tried to scramble away, but as she turned, she saw his shadow on the wall bearing down upon her, warriors in the moonlight.

Chapter 44

Cosimo

Cosimo waited in the confession box, the wooden seat creaking under his weight as he shifted position, getting comfortable before the window slide drew back. This was the safest place for them to meet in private, but even so, the cathedral wasn't empty – it never was. Father Polacco was at the far end of the nave, talking to the organist; Savelli lurked nearby as a lookout. Only ordained priests could take confession, and if Cosimo was to be found in here . . . But it wasn't his fate that mattered, only Rafaella's. It was for her sake they had to take these precautions while they worked out their next steps. He hadn't seen Fon in years, but he still didn't believe the man would give up his wife just like that.

He had slept fitfully after getting back to the seminary, hating the thought of his old adversary lying beside her in sheets that were still warm from his own body. He couldn't stand it. They had to get away from here as soon as possible.

Where was she? She was late, and his ears strained for sounds outside the confession box: Savelli's hushed greeting. Whispered words of warning. His nerves were growing with every minute that ticked past midday, but at last he heard light footsteps approaching over the mosaic stone floor and a moment later, the panel slid back. Her delicate shadow fell into the confession box.

'Cosi?'

Cosimo smiled at the sound of her gentle voice.

'*Amore mio*, you came.' He felt like a teenager again, the life force rising in him like a spring shoot, eagerly seeking the light.

'Of course.'

He heard the breath of relief in her voice too, and he pressed his hand to the mesh screen. She pressed hers back and he felt tiny diamonds of her skin through the grille, precious softness.

For several moments neither of them spoke. It was enough just to be with her. Yesterday's passion had engulfed them in a wave of desperate kisses, urgent promises; now it felt almost reverential to sit together in silence.

It was another moment before he realized she was weeping.

'. . . Rafa?' he frowned, a spike of fear spearing his stomach. 'What is it? What's wrong?' he whispered. 'Is it the children?'

Her breath skipped in small judders. 'They . . . they went back to their father this morning.'

'Yes.' Savelli had told him everything when he'd returned from the meeting: how she'd wept handing them over, giving them their new clothes and toys, food from the kitchen and all the money she had in her purse, urging Nico to contact her if they ever needed help.

He tried to find the words that would bring her comfort. 'I know it's hard. You could have given them a better life, but . . . he is their father, even if he's poor. They're a family at the end of the day. They belong together.'

'I know,' she whispered, sniffing lightly.

'But they were lucky to have had you for as long as they

did. You helped them, Rafa, when they needed it most – when they had no one else in the world. They'll never forget that.'

'I hope not,' she whispered, pressing a handkerchief to her eyes.

'It's time to think about you now. Us . . . I think I've got a plan.'

'. . . Y-you do?' She juddered, still upset.

'We'll leave tomorrow. During Ferragosto.' The high summer festival, celebrating the Assumption of the Virgin Mary, always drew in huge crowds to the cathedral towns. There would be a parade through Otranto, the streets thronging with bodies; it would give them a clean getaway, no delays. They needed to put distance between themselves and the Giannellis as quickly as possible. 'We'll go after Mass. The crowds will be so crazy, no one will even notice we've gone for hours. We'll need money, of course – for a taxi to the station and then train tickets – but I've got that covered. I've still got whatever I came in with. I'll just need to get down to the cellar tonight to get it back.' He drew breath, waiting for her response – something, anything. He'd been plotting their getaway almost all night. It was the best plan by far for getting away from here.

'. . . Raf?'

A small silence drew out. 'I can't wait that long,' she whispered.

'Till tomorrow?'

'I'm sorry.'

He frowned. 'But . . . but why? We've gone this long – what's one more night?'

She didn't reply, and a seed of fear began to bloom inside him. 'Rafa, what's happened?'

'I just have to go. Today. I can't wait. I'm sorry. It's not safe.'

'*Safe?*' His stomach plummeted to the floor. Had they been

seen yesterday – had word got back to her husband? Had their moment of abandon hurled devastating consequences upon her? Or was it even worse than that – Fon had seen him in the garden? He had smelled Cosimo on her skin and just known? He closed his eyes, feeling sick. 'What did he do? Tell me, Rafa. Does Fon know?'

'Not about you.' He could hear in her shallow breaths, the strain flexing her voice, that she was frightened.

'Then what? Did something happen when he got back last night?' He saw her hand fly up to her mouth, suppressing sobs as her head bent forward. His mind was racing. 'Did he hurt you?'

'He tried to,' she said in a small voice.

'Tried to? What does that mean? What did he do?' Urgency made his voice hard, but he had to know.

'He tried to force himself—'

Cosimo threw his head back and scrunched his eyes shut as his mind filled with words, thoughts, images . . . He felt like he couldn't breathe as anger, his old friend, pumped through his veins, as fresh and ready as ever.

'But I managed to get away. He was so drunk, and . . . I locked myself in the bathroom and stayed in there all night. I didn't come out till he'd gone.'

Cosimo could hardly speak. How could he have left her there with him?

'He did this because you told him you were leaving him?'

'No. He still doesn't know about you.'

'I'm going to kill him,' he murmured, his voice breaking.

'No. Please,' she pleaded. 'That won't help . . . I just need to get away from here. I can't go back there, not to an empty house. The children have left, and Flavia's gone to Gina's already. He'll try it again, I know he will.'

Cosimo rubbed his face in his hands, his rage so great he felt the booth could scarcely contain him. He needed to get out of here – this cathedral; this port. But he also knew their departure wasn't going to be as easy as walking through doors. They needed time to make arrangements: find somewhere to stay, get some money together. But he couldn't, he wouldn't, let her be alone with her husband again.

'OK, look . . . Can you give me a few hours?'

'What for?'

'I'll make a call. My brother will be able to help.'

'. . . *What?*'

'Fede. He'll be able to help us. He's in Rome, but he'll work something out. He's resourceful.'

There was a shocked silence.

'Oh my God,' she whispered. 'You don't know?'

He frowned. '. . . Know what?'

'I can't believe they didn't tell you.' She sounded stunned.

'Tell me what? Rafa? What are you talking about?'

She hesitated, as if trying to find the words. '. . . Fede was snatched off the street outside his office in Rome last month.'

Cosimo felt the anchor drag, catching on rocks as the world jolted again and slowed once more.

'He hasn't been seen since. It's believed there's been a ransom demand, but no one really knows for sure – well, not outside your family circle. Fon's been trying to find out more but he's not had any luck. It seems to have been kept out of the papers . . . I can't believe no one told you!'

But Cosimo could. This had his father's fingerprints all over it. Suppressing stories, behind-closed-doors negotiations . . . He would be dealing with this 'his way'. No need to make a fuss. Reputation was everything, and the Franchettis' was already in freefall. A kidnapped son was the very last thing his father needed as he tried to claw his way back from disgrace.

Did his mother even know? She had lost a daughter; now a son too?

'Cosi?' Rafaella whispered. 'Are you OK?'

No, he wasn't. This was a world of stone where no hearts beat, and his brother needed him. But he had to be practical; for Fede's sake, he had to act with logic, not rage. Until they had money, they were stranded. Rome was a day away from here.

'It has to be tomorrow, Rafa – I can't get the money until everyone's asleep tonight,' he whispered, seeing her shadow turn towards his voice. 'I know you're scared of going back to the house, but isn't there somewhere you can go tonight? To Gina's?'

She hesitated. '. . . Maybe.'

He heard the doubt in her voice. 'Rafa? You know Gina would never let Fon get near you if she knew.'

There was another hesitation. 'You're right. Don't worry about me,' she said. 'I'll be fine. Where should we meet?'

'Down by the traffic lights on Via Faccolli.' They couldn't chance being seen together in the old town, but they could get a taxi to the station from there. 'After Mass, it will be easy to disappear in the parade.'

'OK.'

'We can do this. Go to Gina's. It's just one more night.'

'One more night.' Her hand went up to the grille again, blocking the light, and he pressed his fingers as hard as he could against it, touching her in fragments as if she was pieced together from mosaic tiles.

He wanted more, all of her, as he'd had last night . . . but a moment later she was gone, the confession box door swinging open behind her. Sunshine filled the place where she had been, a violent radiance assailing him so that he could see the sun shafts spearing the air before him. He basked in her afterglow for several moments, giving her time to leave before he exited the booth too.

Savelli came and stood by him. 'Well?' he asked in a low voice.

'We're leaving here tomorrow after the service.'

Savelli nodded. He seemed unsettled by the speed at which this was all happening, but for Cosimo it was all too slow. He had to be patient.

Life would begin again tomorrow.

Chapter 45

Rafaella

'What's this?' Dante stood in the doorway, pulling off his tie, staring in at the sight of Rafaella and Gina sitting on the bed.

'Rafa's staying here tonight,' Gina said, cradling her bump and resting against the pillows beside her. 'The children were sent back to their father today and Fon's working late, so she didn't want to be at home on her own.'

Dante's gaze narrowed at the cover story. Rafaella suspected he had just come straight from being with Fon and that he knew perfectly well where his brother was tonight – and it wasn't working late. He knew exactly why she was here, while his brother went back to an empty house.

Was she supposed to think it a coincidence that on the very same day Dante had threatened her, Fon had come home blind drunk and tried to take what he'd always been happy to do without before? She'd heard him sobbing in the bedroom as she lay curled up on the bathroom floor. It wasn't desire that had driven him. It was his brother. *Why?* Why did it matter to Dante so much that they have a child?

Dante gave a small snort, as if women baffled him, and continued on to his bedroom.

Gina looked over at Rafaella. The fear in her eyes was only

visible close up. She was well practised in handling her husband and wasn't afraid to argue with him – they had a code of sorts in their relationship – but lying to him was something she never did.

But she had had to choose on this occasion, and she had chosen Rafaella. She had seen the marks on her friend's body and listened as Rafaella had recounted last night's events – how Cosimo had stolen in under cover of darkness and made love to her, how Fon had returned home unexpectedly, with one thing on his mind. Only a stray kick between his legs had disabled him long enough for her to get away and lock herself in the bathroom.

Gina, without hesitation, had helped her pack the suitcase that was now hidden under Rafaella's own bed. 'I think he bought it,' she murmured.

Rafaella nodded. Her friend didn't know the full truth about Dante's threats against her but, in the end, it had been the lesser of two evils, choosing to spend the night here: she was safer in a full house with him than an empty one with Fon. Dante wouldn't leave Gina's bed to come to hers and risk her screaming the place down. He was a dangerous man, but not a stupid one.

She looked at her oldest friend, wishing it could all be different, but they both knew there was no way either brother would let Rafaella walk into the sunset with Cosimo. She had been naive to think Fon would let her go after all. Escape was their only chance of happiness.

'I'm going to miss you,' she whispered, clutching Gina's hand.

'You have no idea,' Gina replied, squeezing her back. She was mere weeks from her due date and losing her best friend. Ever since Romola's death, they had grown even closer, marrying the brothers and moving here to live, their houses just a street away from one another. But the men they loved – really loved – were sworn enemies, and this was the fork in their road, finally.

Rafaella didn't worry for Gina's safety. As the mother of Dante's children, she was uniquely protected.

'Papa!'

They looked up as Lorenzo dashed down the hallway, past the door towards his father.

'My boy!'

Rafaella could imagine the scene occurring in the other room: Dante swinging the little boy in the air, a proud father and not a monster. The sound of their laughter travelled down the hall.

'You need to be careful tomorrow,' Gina murmured, taking advantage of the distraction. 'You know that, don't you? He's got people everywhere.'

'People?'

'People who report back to him.'

Rafaella frowned. 'Why? He's a businessman. Why would he need to have people reporting my movements to him?'

She saw Gina regarding her, as if trying to evaluate her. 'He's successful because he's ruthless, Rafa. We all know he's got fingers in many pies, but surely you suspect some of those pies must . . . taste funny? No one gets rich this quickly without cutting corners.' She squeezed Rafaella's arm. 'And if he finds out you're deserting his brother . . . *humiliating* him . . .'

Rafaella fell still. Like Icarus, Dante had always flown close to the sun. He had been handsome, cocky and ambitious in his youth and he had somehow played that combination to devastating advantage. There had always been an element of menace to him, but outright danger . . .? Until yesterday, she would have said not, but then he had stood in her own house and threatened her.

A floorboard creaked outside the room, making them both

startle and look up. Flavia rounded the door a moment later, carrying Lorenzo's clothes from the bathroom.

'... *Ciao*,' she said nervously, seeing how they were both frozen and staring at her. 'I shall put Lorenzo to bed, yes?'

'*Si*, thank you,' Gina murmured, her eyes sliding over to Rafaella's as the young woman sidled out of the room. '... Think she heard?'

Rafaella shrugged, but a thought had come to her. What if Flavia herself was one of Dante's spies? Did that explain Dante's sudden agitation about their barren marriage – could the young woman have been reporting to him about Fon's prolonged absences from the house and, by extension, her bed?

She shook the idea from her mind. Flavia had been nothing but a friend to her in the past few weeks, helping out with the children. Paranoia was making her crazy – she couldn't live a life second-guessing everyone's motives and actions.

She told herself that by this time tomorrow, she would be gone. For the first time in her life she would be truly free to live on her own terms with the man she loved. But if, as Gina said, the walls really did have ears and strangers' eyes would be watching her, then just walking out of her own front door was beginning to feel like an impossible dream.

Chapter 46

Fon

The sun beat on their stomachs, warming the skin, as they lay side by side on the ground. Fon could feel his own pulse against the red earth, a distant drumbeat in the silence. He turned his head to look at Fede. The stubble was already coming back, growing in quickly, and Fon raised a hand to brush against his cheek.

Fede smiled; he might still be in chains but Fon had done what he could to minimize his discomfort, bringing cushions with him in the car and a blanket too, for the nights could be cold. Fede's eyes closed as he enjoyed the attention. '. . . You want to shave me again.'

'Yes,' Fon smiled as he got up and walked over to the old farmhouse to fill the washing bucket. He felt oddly happy, somehow at peace as they lazed together here, doing nothing at all. He looked idly through the broken window as the water ran; the supply was weak, coming in fits and starts. A blackbird had got into the building and was flying around inside. It landed on a windowsill opposite, knocking the ash from a cigarette butt to the ground before taking flight again, skittish in its captivity.

He walked back to Fede and set the bucket down. 'Sit in the chair.'

Fede obeyed, his eyes never leaving Fon's face as he dipped the soap into the bucket and began lathering him. Fon couldn't get used to the attention; no one had ever watched him before, never looked for him. He'd seen the way Rafaella's eyes had always searched for Cosimo in a crowd, how Cosimo almost drank her in; he had never thought he would be wanted like that.

He only knew the opposite. Scenes from last night ran through his mind again – Rafaella's desperate pleas as she leapt away from his touch, her cry as he got a hand to her clothes, the viciousness to her kick as she finally got him off her and locked herself away.

He had been glad she'd escaped him, crazy though it was to admit; he was proud of her for fighting against what he himself had been too scared to deny his brother. It had broken him, not just seeing her terror and revulsion, but the toll it had placed upon him too, forcing him to take something he didn't want, to hurt someone he didn't want to. It had taken him back to that morning in the oaks, when murder had come in the guise of mercy.

He had left here yesterday so happy. He had spent his entire life avoiding the truth of what he was until Fede had unmasked him. Fon didn't want to have to pretend with him – he was the only person who saw him truly – but how could he be open with him now? The scythe was swinging over Fede's head, and Fon had only one chance to save him.

'What is it?' Fede asked, seeing the tension in his jaw. 'Tell me what you're thinking.'

Fon's hands fell from his face, soap suds on his fingers. 'There's something we need to discuss.'

'. . . Sounds serious.' Fede's eyes still roamed over him, but the heat in them was beginning to cool as he braced for what was coming. For all his confidence with Fon on the intimate plane, he was still shackled in chains.

'I want to get you out of here, Fede.'

He gave a relieved laugh. 'That would definitely be my preference too.'

'But I can't do it without your help. The ransom was never for money.'

He watched as a quizzical look came into Fede's eyes. 'Then what?'

'The diary. The one your father keeps . . . Dante is fixated upon it. He won't let it go.'

There was a long pause as Fede pulled back. He looked away, towards the distant trees on the rising hill. 'Well, then, that is bad news.'

'What do you mean?'

'If it was money you wanted, you'd have it by now. But that diary . . .? It's priceless. His entire career is built on those secrets.'

'We know. It's why *you're* here. The only thing more valuable than money . . .'

'Is family?' Fede finished for him. He gave a cold laugh. 'Not for the Franchettis! Not my father, anyway.'

Fon frowned. 'But you're his son.'

'So?'

'So he's already lost a daughter! He's not going to lose you too!'

Fede gave him a pitying look. 'He lost her *because* he had betrayed Cosi. You really think he'd pull back from doing the same to me? . . . That diary is his last remaining source of power, Fon. It's all he's got left.'

'OK, OK. So, then, he won't willingly hand it over . . . But you must know where it is.'

'No,' Fede shook his head. 'We hadn't spoken in nine months before this happened. He's moved house since. I have no idea where he's put it.'

'But there must be somewhere safe. We didn't think he would let it out of his sight, but we've gone through his office now, and his apartment, and yours—'

Fede looked shocked. 'You've ransacked my apartment?'

Fon threw his hands out. '. . . Fede, look where we are! Breaking into your place and looking around is hardly a surprise, is it? . . . We expected a quick capitulation, not a drawn-out saga, but none of this has gone to plan.' He stared at Fede, feeling sick. It was clear he still had no idea of the gravity of his situation, and Fon didn't want to have to spell it out to him.

'I need you to think,' he went on, in the calmest voice he could manage. 'If I don't give Dante the diary or its whereabouts, he's going to send someone else here to get the information out of you . . .' He looked at Fede. Did he understand what that meant? What Fon was trying to tell him? 'He wanted to send him here today, and I managed to stall him for a few more days. I said I'd speak to you.' He could see Fede was about to make a wisecrack, but he shook his head. '. . . This is serious. Dante is dangerous.'

'I can't tell him something I don't know.' Fede shrugged, and Fon could tell he thought this was a bluff. Or exaggeration.

'You need to listen to me. If Dante doesn't get an answer, then he'll . . . take something from you instead, to show your father he's serious and scare him into complying.' He willed Fede to understand what he was telling him. 'You're going to be the one to suffer and I can't . . . I can't stop him!'

Fede pinned him with a level stare. 'You could just take these things off me.' He rattled the chain.

Fon gave a shocked laugh. 'You don't think I would if I could? Francesco has the keys, Fede!'

'Then ask him for them!' Fede cried. 'You're Fon Giannelli. He works for you!'

'No, he works for Dante. And if he told Dante I was after the keys to the chain that's holding you here . . . I have no power in this.'

Fede blinked. 'So, then, we're each as helpless as the other. No key and no diary.'

'No! No!' Fon rubbed his face in his hands. 'It's not the same. A diary isn't like a key . . . It's no small thing to hide. You must know where he would put it.'

'Maybe it's not just Dante who wants it so badly. Maybe it's you, too,' Fede said, watching him. 'Maybe all this . . .' His eyes roamed over Fon, standing by the shaving bucket. '. . . Is your way of getting me to talk?'

'That's really what you think?' There was a moment of tension before Fede looked away.

'This – whatever this is between us – it wasn't planned, Fede. I didn't know I . . .' He trailed into silence; he couldn't even say the words. 'But if Dante knew, I think he'd kill us both.'

Fede looked back at him, watching as Fon sank to his heels, his head in his hands. They were quiet for several moments.

'I know it's hard for you to trust me when we're . . . here, like this . . . but I'm trying to *help* you. I want you to get out of this. I want you to be OK.' Fon gave him an imploring look. 'I would like for us to somehow continue . . . away from here . . .' He threw his hands out. 'I like you, Fede.'

Fede blinked. 'I like you too,' he said quietly. 'I don't know what to tell you, Fon. If I could point you somewhere, I would, but since the divorce, everything's everywhere. Every-*one's* everywhere! Mamma and the little ones are in Florence. Cosi's in Otranto—'

Fon sat straighter. 'Wait – what?'

'He's in the seminary down there now. I got a letter from

him the day you grabbed me . . . He was moved over from Lecce a few weeks ago . . .' He took a better look at Fon's expression. 'Why? Is that important?'

Fon didn't stir, only his mind moving fast. Fede had no sense of where he himself was right now. He had been snatched from Rome and bundled into a car with a hood on his head; he had no idea Otranto was just three miles from here.

He sat back on his heels again, hardly able to take it in. Cosimo Franchetti was living in the very same port as them? . . . The seminary was right opposite Dante's home.

Too late, far too late, he remembered Franchetti's offhand comment the night he'd come for dinner. He had said he was here on *a private visit*. They had assumed he was meeting a woman, but what if it had been his son? A son walled away in a fortress. There would be nowhere safer than . . .

'The seminary,' he breathed.

Fede caught on fast. 'You think he gave it to Cosi?'

'It's the only thing that makes sense.'

'But Cosi hates him. He wouldn't do anything to help our father.'

'He may not *know* he's helping him.'

Fede looked up as Fon jumped to his feet. '. . . Where are you going?'

'To tell Dante. This is it, Fede! This is how we get you out of here.'

'But how will you get in? It's a seminary! They can hardly get out, much less anyone else get in!'

Fon glanced over with a smile. 'We have someone who's already in . . . Not Cosimo, don't worry. We'll keep your brother out of it.'

He saw the disbelief on Fede's face as he began to understand their reach: police, local government, Church . . . He looked equal parts shocked and impressed.

Fon turned to leave but stopped and came back again,

crouching before him. He picked up the black hood and held it in his hands. 'I have to put this back on you.'

'No . . .' Fede said warily.

'I have to. Listen to me, Fede, this is important . . . When I come back tomorrow, I may not be alone. In fact, you have to assume that I won't be. Dante never leaves anything to chance. Once we get the diary, he's going to want to see for himself that you don't know it's us who've got you here – which means you have to be wearing this. If he thinks you've seen my face, we're both dead.'

'But . . .' Fede sounded defeated, recognizing the logic.

'It's vital you don't say our names, you don't say anything about Tricase . . . Don't even lift your head. He will *only* let you walk away from here if he believes you're oblivious to our identity. Do you understand?'

Fede stared back at him, blinking rapidly.

Fon put a hand to his cheek, tracing it with his thumb. 'Tell me you understand, Fede.'

'I . . . I understand.'

'Good.' Fon reached for the black hood, placing it tenderly over Fede's head again.

'I can't breathe,' Fede whispered, panicking.

'You can – you can do this. You're safe now. This is it. You're almost out of here.'

Fede fell still.

'It's just for tonight, I swear. I'll get back here as soon as I can in the morning.'

He walked over to the door and hesitated there, hating that he was locking Fede in the dark and the silence again. But it was for the last time.

The rest of their lives could start tomorrow.

Chapter 47

Cosimo

The shadows were hard-edged in the moonlight, his steps silent on the flagstones as he crept barefoot past the dormitory doors and down the stairs. Usually there was some level of activity throughout the night – the sweep of cassocks, murmured voices – but tonight there was a density to the quietude. Everyone was in their beds and getting what rest they could. Tomorrow would be a long day.

Today had been long enough. Cosimo had spent the rest of his afternoon in the library, searching the newspapers for mentions of his brother's fate. To no avail. Was Fede dead or alive? He still had no idea. There were a few accounts of eyewitness reports the day after he had been snatched, but then nothing. Cosimo knew better than anyone that press suppression of a story was one of his father's tactics. A call had been made, a promise made or a deal done, pointing the reporters to another story, another politician. It didn't always work. Romola's accident had been everywhere, throwing their family into the spotlight. Death was incontestable, after all, but kidnappings could be disproved: ransom demands kept private; no body, no crime . . .

He tried consoling himself that there was perhaps comfort

to be had in not knowing his brother's fate. It was the irrefutability of Romola's death which had almost crushed him. To live in denial was also to live with hope, surely? Perhaps not; but the lie would have to sustain him until tomorrow. He could do nothing while he was still in here.

He made his way down the turning staircase to the cellar, treading cautiously as it grew ever darker. Savelli had warned him the darkness was pervasive in the basement, but he couldn't risk flicking a switch and drawing attention to his middle-of-the-night mission. There was no plausible reason for him to be down here; he would need to be in and out within moments.

Savelli had told him what he recalled of the layout: the rector's wine collection was stored in the vaults by the stairs, and further along were the seminarians' personal effects, which were stowed on admission. Some boys arrived with trunks full of possessions, seemingly unaware they would be stripped of almost everything in their daily lives here, but Cosimo had turned up in just the clothes on his back and never had cause to go down there.

The windowless space was stale and stuffy, a strong aroma of incense ingrained in its walls. He got to the bottom of the steps, expecting blacker blackness, but to his surprise found he could see quite well. The space was dimly lit up ahead. He stopped on the step and peered around the corner. Was someone else down here? He strained, listening for sounds of movement, but all was quiet. The light was faint from here, at the far end of the long space, but hulking silhouetted shapes were clearly discernible along either side of the passage: boxes stacked, tall candelabras standing like winter trees, parts of an old organ. He could make out some rails of threadbare ceremonial robes. The extensive wine cellar was dusty, not so much as a gleam of light on the shoulders of the bottles, thick cobwebs binding them together like lace.

Cosimo moved past them and was halfway along when a small scraping sound came to his ear, barely audible. A mouse?

But then he heard the soft clearing of a throat up ahead – distinctly human – and he froze.

Someone else was down here after all.

The rector, perhaps? It was the middle of the night – it had been three o'clock when he'd left his bed. Who else had cause to be down here in the dead of night?

He heard a shuffle, as if something was being pushed, and then footsteps on the stone floor. They were coming . . .

Cosimo darted into the shadows, squeezing between some wooden boxes and dislodging clouds of dust. He felt it tickle his nose as it danced in plumes and he clamped his hand to his face, his eyes trained on the opposite wall as the light began to shift upon it. Moving . . .

He braced for it to grow brighter, coming closer. He couldn't squeeze back any further and there was no room to crouch down . . . He would be illuminated as they passed . . .

But a few moments went by and he realized the light was growing fainter, not stronger. They were moving in the opposite direction. He heard the sound of a large key in a lock and ducked back out just in time to see a door opening at the far end of the cellar and a hooded, robed figure disappearing through it.

Savelli had told him the space extended under the seminary garden, reaching into the cathedral crypt by way of an interconnecting door that was kept locked. The cathedral's doors were always open, but the seminary's were not. He listened to the sound of the footsteps retreating beyond the door, now closed but left unlocked – whoever had gone out would be coming back. He didn't have long.

Without the dim light, darkness spread through the space like a black mist, but he ran anyway. His heart was pounding and he kept knocking into things as he moved blindly, his eyes trying to adapt. There were dozens of trunks on the ground, but along the walls he saw the shelving with wooden boxes Savelli had described to him. Small white labels blinked weakly and he grabbed one, holding it up to his face and peering closely. *Cordeschi.*

He moved along a little further. *Endrizzi . . . Esposito.*
Alphabetized?
Farinelli . . . Ferrari . . . Finocchario . . .
Franchetti.

He removed the lid and reached inside. The box was almost empty but for the loafers, trousers and shirt he had worn on the day he walked through the Lecce seminary doors . . . His fingers felt the cool, familiar smoothness of his leather wallet too. It was the only thing that mattered – his ticket out of here. He couldn't remember how much money he'd brought in with him, but it would be enough to get him and Rafaella a taxi and onto the train. They could work out what to do next once they knew they were safe.

He grabbed the contents and replaced the lid, pushing the box back into position; it scraped, as if a nail was peeking through its base and catching the wooden shelf. He glanced over at the closed – but unlocked – door, checking it was safe to break cover.

All was silent and still.

He hurried back the way he'd come, moving swiftly through the passage, his relief and confidence growing as he got to the staircase and the pale lunar light falling across the floor at the top of the steps began to lead his way again; he took the steps two at a time, his growing exultation powering him through the passageways and back up to the higher floors.

He could only have been gone from his room for five or six minutes at most, but it felt as if the entire world had changed around him. The walls had fallen in at last. He could breathe! He was no longer trapped here with no way out! Tomorrow was already saddling up on the dawn. His coming freedom was a blush on the wind.

'Did you get it?'

Savelli was waiting for him on the roof. They were both on altar service tomorrow, but sleep wouldn't come for either of them tonight. They were too buoyed up, adrenaline pumping for the stealth mission that was going to get one of them out of here, at least.

Cosimo winked, holding up the wallet like a nugget of gold as he crept into the narrow space between the tiles and the parapet. He joined Alessio in lying back against the roof tiles, his body stretched long, the wallet pressed against his palm as he breathed deeply, relaxing into the brief coolness of the night. The nightmare was finally coming to an end.

'Someone was down there,' he whispered after a moment.

Savelli's head turned on the tiles. 'Who?' he frowned.

'I couldn't see. They went out through the cathedral door.'

'Did they see you?'

Cosimo shook his head.

'Strange.'

They listened to the whistling silence, eyes trained on the peeping stars overhead. Below, Piazza Basilica lay shrouded in darkness; the dramatic cathedral lights were switched off now. Tomorrow the streets would blaze with coloured lights and banners, the port ready for the carnival—

A small creak came from below. It was no more than a yawning hinge, but the noise was distinctive in the suspended silence of night and Cosimo leaned forward, looking over the parapet wall. The pedestrian door set within the green carriage doors of Gina's villa was slowly opening.

Rafaella had said she would stay there tonight. Was she

there now? Sleeping in a bed behind those green shutters? Or was she awake too, waiting for the minutes to tick past until they could be together at last? Was this her now, coming out . . . ?

He tensed as Dante Giannelli appeared in the frame instead. Cosimo recognized him immediately, although it had been years since they'd last met. The profound difference in him was striking . . . Just wearing a suit, for one thing, distinguished him from the seaside lothario bombing across the water beyond the port, shirtless, on his speedboat. But there was something new in his manner, too, that Cosimo recognized from his old life in Rome: the self-satisfaction that came with power and influence. The air of superiority.

Cosimo frowned as he watched, hidden in the shadows. It looked as if Dante was waiting for someone.

A dark figure caught his eye, emerging from the shadow of the cathedral and setting out across the square. 'Look,' Cosimo whispered. 'That's him. The one I saw in the cellar just now.'

'Who is it?' Savelli whispered back, crouching down next to him.

'Can't see,' Cosimo murmured.

They watched as the hooded figure went straight to Dante and they began talking in low voices. The priest reached into the deep pocket of his house cassock and pulled something out; Cosimo couldn't see what exactly, not from this distance, not in the darkness, but as Dante held his hand out, it fell from the priest's grasp. A small red leather prayer book, tooled with gilt, hit the ground.

The priest bent to retrieve it, and Cosimo caught a glimpse of his profile in the light coming from the courtyard behind Dante.

What . . . ?

Savelli shot him a stunned look.

They watched as Giannelli took the book and the two men said a few more words before their business was concluded. Dante stepped back inside his gate and the priest hastened back into the lee of the cathedral, where the door was always open, where he could slip silently into the bowels of the seminary with total discretion. The entire meeting had passed in a matter of minutes, almost silent, almost unseen. It had been inconspicuous, yes, but innocuous . . .?

Cosimo and Savelli stared at one another, unsettled.

Why exactly was Father Caputo having a secret assignation with Dante Giannelli in the dead of night?

The silence was profound. But for a few scattered coughs, someone blowing their nose, a baby mewling somewhere at the back, Cosimo could almost hear the collective pleas for help as the congregation prayed.

His own lips didn't move. His eyes didn't close. He was staring at the patch of stone floor before him, willing himself to sit through this charade. He no longer believed in anything but his own survival instinct, his love for Rafaella, and hers for him.

Savelli, beside him, pressed his fingertips lightly on Cosimo's knee, holding it down as he cast him a sideways look. Cosimo shrugged his eyebrows back in reply. He hadn't realized his leg was jiggling, agitation leaking from him in a multitude of ways.

'Amen,' Father Polacco intoned solemnly.

'Amen.'

'Come on,' Savelli whispered, and they rose from their appointed seats at the end of the choir. Alessio was on wine duty, Cosimo handing out the wafers, and they walked to the altar, bringing them over to the bishop on golden dishes as the congregation began to stream down the aisle in orderly lines to receive communion.

Cosimo moved automatically, staring out at the sea of faces, looking only for hers.

Where was she?

'The body of Christ...' Father Polacco intoned.

'Amen...'

Where was she? He felt racked with apprehension that something would go wrong, that there would be a stick in the wheel to trip them up. Had she been safe at Gina's last night, or had Fon come looking for her? Had Dante given her up to him?

Everyone moved in rhythm, as if in a coordinated dance: the bishop offering the sacrament and blessing his flock with the sign of the cross, reverent eyes looking up at him, mouths opening expectantly...

He saw her coming down the line at last! Her face was downturned as if trying to hide from scrutiny, but he would always find her in any crowd. She was so slender, so chimerical, it was as if the light shone right through her, golden flecks glinting in her hair and – as she looked up, straight at him – her eyes. He thought he would go crazy just from looking at her, the flagrant yearning in her eyes matching his own.

With that single look, she told him what he needed to know. They were still on track.

He held his breath as he waited for the line to move, as she knelt before Father Polacco.

'The body of Christ...'

She tipped her head back slightly as she drank from the goblet Savelli offered, her hair falling back from her face and exposing a faint bruise on her cheek. Cosimo's eyes narrowed, the sight of it like a sword swipe to his own skin. 'Amen,' she said softly.

'Amen,' echoed a male voice, and Cosimo realized that of course Fon was right beside her – also kneeling, receiving the sacrament, as if he wasn't a sinner who had laid hands on his wife!

He felt his anger surge as he waited for Fon to look at him, willing him to make eye contact. He wanted to see that look of fear come into Fon's eyes, as it had on his wedding day. It would be the release trigger Cosimo needed to act . . . but for the first time that he could ever remember, Fon appeared not even to notice him. He looked straight through Cosimo with an almost haunted expression as he received the eucharist.

Cosimo watched in disbelief as his old enemy passed right by without even seeing him. What . . .?

Dante and Gina were coming up behind them. Gina was struggling to kneel, her balance thrown off by the late stage of her pregnancy; Dante chivalrously helped her down, aware that he had an audience.

Up close, the differences Cosimo had registered in him last night were even more apparent. Wealth could be worn. Paraded. It was conveyed through glowing skin, white teeth and shiny hair; a good watch, a hand-stitched tie, a heavy gold ring . . . Dante Giannelli made sure everyone could tell he was a power player now. He wore it like cologne.

Father Polacco made the sign of the cross as Savelli offered him the goblet of wine – but Dante looked straight at Cosimo. It was the first time the two men had directly laid eyes upon one another in three years but Dante was regarding him without any apparent surprise, almost as if he had been awaiting this very moment. As if he had known he would see him here.

Had Gina told him?

Cosimo saw a crowing glory in his eyes. See how completely the tables had turned? Now it was the fisherman's son living in splendour while the duke's son embraced poverty and abstinence.

'The body of Christ . . .' Father Polacco said.

'Amen to that,' Dante said, right in front of him now and

biting down on the wafer Cosimo gave him with a wolfish snap.

Cosimo felt an echo reverberate in his body as Dante moved off. Gina caught his eye momentarily and he saw in her familiar face deep concern, a silent plea, before Dante reached for her hand and led her away.

He watched the married couples go, Fon and Rafaella just ahead – together but very much apart – as they made their way back to their seats. The difference in all four of them was startling, but something in Dante's look in particular had disturbed him. It was more than gloating. It reminded him of that day on the rocks when Cosimo had humiliated Fon with his daring and won – he'd thought – a bigger battle than just diving from a cliff. He had felt victory. Supreme victory.

That same look on Dante's face now told him something else was going on, something more than he could see.

'. . . The body of Christ . . .'

'Amen . . .'

Amen to that.

Another memory surfaced from that day on the rocks. Still Fon locking antlers with him, but there had been more going on than the two of them vying for supremacy, trying to win Rafaella's admiration. He remembered Dante's flashy entrance on the speedboat, back where it had all begun for the Giannellis: water-skiing trips, of all things. He remembered Gina's excitement as Dante aggressively wooed her in front of them all. And he remembered Romola's barbed comments as she struggled to regain her pride, her sense of self, after losing her footing with Fon . . .

He owns the entire cabinet.

He caught his breath as his sister's desperate boast sounded in his head, as clear as if she were whispering it to him now . . . And Dante's cool response? *Amen to that.*

She had revealed untold treasure to two brothers who had

been nothing at the time but now sat here like kings; two brothers whose meteoric rise simply would not have been possible without ruthless ambition.

But were they ruthless enough to snatch a man at gunpoint off the street? Ambitious enough to turn a man of the cloth for lavish reward?

Cosimo slowly turned, the movement causing Savelli to glance at him curiously, and looked back towards the choir. Father Caputo was sitting in his usual place, dressed in his ceremonial robes, a model of piety now. But last night ... the house cassock, the red leather, the pages edged with gilt ... Not a prayer book, but something else so familiar that Cosimo had become blind to the very sight of it.

His father's diary.

His father's surprise visit.

The last of your things ... somewhere safe this can be stored ... ? Too late, he realized the shoebox hadn't been in with his possessions last night.

'The body of Christ ...'

'Amen ...'

He stood motionless as the sacrament was given. Miracles really were at work all around him, because suddenly he knew who had Fede. And he knew why.

But he also knew they had achieved what they wanted, and that meant one of two things. His brother was either a free man ...

Or a dead one.

Chapter 48

Rafaella

They stood pressed against the wall as the crowds surged past with the procession, everyone cheering so loudly that Rafaella could have screamed at the top of her lungs and no one would even have turned. They were just two in a sea of faces, and she knew it was the perfect moment to disappear. Even if she was being watched, she had a good chance of losing herself in the mob . . .

She turned to Gina, who was holding Lorenzo on her hip.

'No, not yet . . . a little longer,' Gina whispered, eyes wide as she held back her tears. She had promised not to cry. Tears would be an instant giveaway to anyone watching them, a sign that something was wrong.

'It has to be now, while the crowds are biggest . . .' Rafaella squeezed her hand in apology. They both knew another five minutes – five months – wouldn't be enough. There was never going to be a right time for them to say goodbye.

'I'll be in touch once I'm settled, I promise.' She hardly dared to move her lips or show her sorrow as she talked. Paranoia had her in its grip and her eyes scanned the crowd again, looking for anyone paying attention to them.

'Dante will intercept letters,' Gina murmured.

'. . . I'll get a message to Maddalena at school; she'll pass it on to you,' Rafaella said, squeezing her hand reassuringly again. They had agreed not to hug, nothing at all to indicate a parting. They had already said their goodbyes in private. They would see one another again, they had promised, but Rafaella wasn't so sure. She might not know the depths of their husbands' reach but she did know the breadth of Dante's rage and ambition. When exactly would it be safe for them to meet again?

She took a deep breath and saw, from the way Gina stiffened, that she knew this was the moment. Their hands gripped tightly in a final hidden embrace.

'*Ciao*, Gina, I'll catch you in a bit,' she said loudly, for the benefit of eavesdroppers.

'*Certe!* I'll be right here.'

She took a step to the side, allowing Gina's fingers to slip from her grasp as she took another one. Immediately she felt the power of the crowd pull her along, a riptide dragging her from the safety of shore. She glanced back, forcing a bright smile at her friend and godson as she allowed herself a last look, but within moments their faces grew indistinct, just two among the many. Tiles in the mosaic.

She was adrift.

By a stroke of good luck, she and Gina had been separated from Fon and Dante almost immediately on stepping out of the cathedral; they would be glad-handing all the local dignitaries, but they would be back any moment too. They might already be looking for their wives in the crowd. Every minute mattered and she couldn't hesitate . . .

She let herself be pulled along with the crowd before peeling away and slipping into her empty house. The door was unlocked as always, and her ears strained for sounds of movement before she ran up the stairs. Her packed suitcase was under the bed where she'd left it, untouched. She didn't know what Fon had thought of her staying over at Gina's last night – no doubt Dante had informed him of her presence in their guest room – but he hadn't even looked at her as they'd met on the cathedral steps this morning. Shame? Or guilt?

It didn't matter. The damage was irreversible. No matter the vacuum at the heart of their marriage, they had always been friends; they had protected one another in their various ways over the years, but something fundamental had shifted between them now and it couldn't be moved back again. Undeniable truths could no longer be ignored. She loved Cosimo and always would. And he . . .? There was something at the heart of him that was stunted, oblique.

Forty seconds later, she was slipping through the garden gate – it led onto a quiet back street where her chances of going unnoticed were improved. The procession was travelling through the main streets of the old town and down towards the water's edge. Gina, if she ran into either of the brothers, was going to tell them Rafaella had gone there ahead. Instead she would be travelling in the opposite direction, heading west towards the new neighbourhood, where Cosimo awaited her. They would take a taxi to Maglie and from there a train, when they could disappear completely. Neither Fon nor Dante Giannelli would ever see them again.

She could hear the band playing from the main street and took comfort in hearing it grow ever fainter as she hurried through the narrow alleys. The modern neighbourhood was only a few minutes' walk away. She could already see the apartment blocks through some of the straighter streets . . .

She ran as fast as she could with her bag, stepping out a few minutes later into the glare of the sunlight on the wide, straight street. Here was safety. Here was freedom.

And there he was.

Cosimo was waiting for her, just as she'd always dreamed.

He was sitting on a scooter, staring down one of the side streets that divided the modern white apartment blocks. He had no bags but was wearing a shirt and trousers she recognized from the old days. There was nothing to mark him out as a seminarian, a fugitive from the Church. He was hers again.

'Cosi!' she gasped.

He turned as she ran over and flung her arms around him. 'We did it!' she whispered, hardly able to believe it had all passed without a hitch. She had been so sure Fon or Dante would be able to tell there was something afoot at Mass this morning, as if the plan was a scent they could detect. A blood trail they could follow.

She had scarcely dared look at him in the cathedral but she kissed him now, sinking into their new beginning. Only . . . his body was tense and stiff.

He pulled away, glancing back down the street anxiously, and she realized they weren't yet safe. 'Let's get out of here,' she murmured.

Cosimo hesitated as she fastened her bag to the straps on the back of the scooter. 'We . . . we can't, Raf.'

'. . . What?' Tears immediately sprang to her eyes. Their happy ending was right here – they were standing in it!

'Fon and Dante are down there,' he said, his eyes still trained on the side street, his fingers tapping anxiously on the handlebars. She followed his sightline and saw her husband and his brother – the very people she'd been hiding from – talking to someone else beside some parked cars. Even at a distance, she recognized the lop-shouldered silhouette: Francesco.

'I have to follow them.'

'But why? Just forget them! It's behind us.' She remembered the bruise on her cheek and his look of horror as his eyes had landed upon it in the cathedral. 'None of it's important now.'

He didn't take his eyes off the street. 'You don't understand . . . They've got Fede. He and Dante.'

She stared at him as if *he* had just hit her. 'What? . . . No! They wouldn't . . .'

Wouldn't they? Wasn't she, this very moment, stealing away from her own home and her entire life because she had been threatened by one brother, assaulted by the other? Hadn't Gina told her their spies would be watching her every move? Threats, assaults, spies . . . was kidnapping really such a reach?

She watched Cosimo watching the men, and knew he believed it of them.

'Oh God . . .' she whispered, watching them too. 'What are you going to do?'

'I don't know. I need to see where they've got him first.' He glanced at her distractedly, scarcely able to lift his attention off them for a moment. 'Just wait here for me.'

'No!' she cried, immediately climbing onto the back of the bike and gripping him with her arms. 'You're not going without me.'

'Rafa, no! It could be dangerous. You don't know what they're capable of.'

'They wouldn't hurt me. Or him,' she replied staunchly. 'Fede and Dante were friends when they were kids.'

'That's precisely the problem. Fede knows everything about them. He can identify them. They're not going to let him go.'

She closed her eyes against the words. Murder too? She knew she was an innocent compared to Gina's savvy and cynical world view, but was this the full truth her friend had been trying to show her? Her marriage had been a lunar landscape, never showing the dark side of the moon. '. . . How do you even know all this?'

'Because they got what they wanted last night. I saw the ransom handover happen. I didn't see it for what it was at the time, but now I do. Fede has served his purpose for them, so either they . . .' He stumbled on the words. 'Either they dealt with him last night, or they're going to do it now.' His voice was rigid with tension.

'*Now?*' It didn't feel real. Fon was going straight from church to kill a man?

His head turned back slightly towards her. 'Was Fon at home last night?' he asked over his shoulder.

'I don't know. I was at Gina's.'

'Right.' He swallowed hard. 'Well, they would have needed Fede alive for leverage, and they only got the diary late last night, and they've been at Mass all morning, so . . . I'm praying that means they've not had a chance to do it yet.' He glanced back towards the historic centre, in the direction of the parade. '. . . And who would notice if they disappeared for a few hours in the middle of a carnival?'

It was the same logic by which they'd hoped to vanish themselves. The hunted had become the hunters, seeking out the very people they'd been running from.

Cosimo's fingers tapped solidly on the handlebars as he kept watch over their movements. He looked as if he hadn't slept, pale and baggy-eyed, like he'd endured the worst night of his life. But that couldn't be true. Nothing could ever be worse than the night Romola had died.

'. . . You said they got a diary?' she asked.

'My father's. He kept records of the misdeeds of most of the cabinet. It was bad enough when it was in his care; at least all he wanted was position. But in Dante's hands . . . the guy's a mobster, Rafa. It would give him unchecked power.' He flinched suddenly. '. . . They're moving.'

She looked down the street to see the brothers getting into a car, Francesco crossing the road further down and getting into one too. He pulled out first, the Giannellis following in Dante's glossy Lancia Flaminia.

'Where did you get this scooter?' she asked as Cosimo stirred into action.

'I'm borrowing it,' he said, fiddling with the wires.

'But how do you even know . . .?'

The scooter started into life. 'My misspent youth in Rome wasn't entirely useless,' he said, kicking off the stand. He turned his head to speak to her over his shoulder. 'Hold me tightly,' he said softly. 'To be safe.'

Chapter 49

Fon

He was quiet as they drove out of the port, leaving the celebrations behind them. After a broken night spent waiting for the news to come that they had the diary, and then sitting through a cathedral Mass that seemed never-ending, he was relieved to be turning his back on the chaos of Ferragosto and heading for the farmhouse.

Retrieving the diary had been easy for Father Caputo once he'd been given his orders. It turned out Franchetti *had* visited the seminary the night of the dinner, and Cosimo, straight afterwards, had handed over a small box to be stored with his personal belongings in the vaults. After those long weeks of detaining Fede, the ransom was in their hands within a matter of hours. Their hidden treasure, their holy grail, had been on a shelf metres away from Dante's own front door the entire time.

But Fon's nerves were still up. Even though the ransom demand had been met by the hostage himself, he knew Fede wouldn't be safe until he was out of range of a bullet. He knew better than to underestimate his brother; Dante was nervous of the personal history they shared with their captive, and he would need to reassure himself that their anonymity had been preserved before a single step to freedom was granted. Fede just had to hold his nerve and feign ignorance, but Fon felt as if there was a gun to his head too.

Francesco was in the car ahead of them, ready to drive Fede back up to Rome and dump him there in the place from which he'd been taken. Fon didn't want to think about Fede being so far away – would Fede leave him behind without a backward glance? Would he hate him as soon as he was a free man? But he couldn't object without raising Dante's suspicions.

They turned off the highway after a few miles and onto the local road before splitting onto the dirt track. They passed barren fields and crumbling stone walls, a few crows soaring overhead in the pulsing sky, Dante dodging potholes with a careless air until the farmhouse came into view and, with it, the *trullo*.

Francesco was already parked and crossing the yard, unlocking the padlock to the stone hut. Dante cut the ignition and they got out too.

'You! Up!' Francesco said, disappearing inside the *trullo*.

The roughness of his tone turned Fon's stomach. Fede's voice was subdued from within.

Moments later, Francesco reappeared, half dragging Fede beside him. He had been released from the wall chain but his hands were still bound with ties. Crucially, the hood was still over his head, and Fon felt a wave of relief that the masquerade was holding up.

Nobody spoke. Fon felt the drubbing of his heart against his ribs as they all awaited Dante's judgement.

'. . . He looks well enough,' Dante said to him in a low voice, taking in Fede's bowed figure. 'Not too thin.'

'No,' Fon agreed. 'We've tried to keep him in good health. The shorter the recovery time, the quicker he'll return to normal life and put this behind him.'

'Very considerate,' Dante said, giving him a sideways look.

'Just pragmatic. We always said this was a risky job with their profile.' Fon's mouth barely moved as he spoke, his eyes slitted against the bright sunlight. 'It's as well for us Franchetti suppressed most of the press speculation. We've got what we wanted; it's in everyone's interests to let this fade away.' He drew his cigarettes from his jacket pocket and lit one, restlessly turning in a circle as he pulled hard on the first drag.

'And you'd be able to do that, brother? Let this just . . . fade away?' Dante asked, just as Fon's gaze fell on the farmhouse.

The front door was ajar . . . Only fractionally, as if the latch had slipped. But it had never been open on any of his trips out here before. It had been locked, and . . .

He remembered the blackbird in the farmhouse yesterday. It could only have got in if the door had been opened.

Had someone been here yesterday? Someone else besides him?

He willed himself to remain still, calm, as he turned back to find Dante watching him.

In a heartbeat, he saw that his brother knew – he knew everything. The cigarette fell from Fon's fingers as shrill fear pierced his heart.

Francesco.

Francesco had come out here yesterday, on Dante's orders.

Fon's mind raced. What had betrayed him? His plea for the chance to interrogate Fede first? His eagerness to get a result without violence? Or – as he had long feared – had Dante always known? Had his long-held suspicion about his little brother finally been confirmed when Fon had shaved his prisoner with tender care, thinking they were alone?

He felt the pieces that had made up the jigsaw of his life slot into alignment at last, the full picture revealed: Dante's hawk-eyed scrutiny, pushing him into marriage with a girl who loved a man she could never have. His brother's insistence on getting her pregnant and stopping the gossips from talking. Protecting their name. Protecting him.

Slowly, Fon looked back over at Fede with despair, knowing he was a dead man standing. There was no changing this course. Dante wasn't here to confirm that their identity was safe. Francesco wasn't here to drive Fede back to Rome. Diary or no diary, Fede simply couldn't be allowed to live now he was the single biggest threat to the Giannellis' reputation. Fon himself had killed him, simply by being who he was.

A tear rolled down his face at what he was about to lose. He knew it was yet another sign of the weakness his brother despised, and he looked back at him expecting to see contempt, disgust. But it was worse than that. He saw pity.

Dante clutched him suddenly, hugging him so hard Fon could scarcely breathe. Only because they were brothers, he knew, was he still alive too.

'... Let me say goodbye at least,' Fon pleaded under his breath, his brother's arm like a vice around his head.

Dante released him. Merciful.

Slowly, Fon walked over to where Fede stood, a clever man playing the dumb hostage as asked, oblivious to his fate. His boots felt made of lead, his blood like tar in his veins as he crossed the courtyard and slowly pulled off the hood. Fede blinked back at him and Fon saw in his eyes confusion at this sudden break from the plan, then dawning understanding as he tracked Fon's tears . . .

'No,' he whispered.

Fon's eyes flickered towards Francesco, standing beside them. 'I'm so sorry,' he gasped, feeling as if his heart was exploding. 'It's all my fault.'

Fede paled. 'But the diary . . . You said . . .'

Fon couldn't reply. He'd lived through much horror, but he'd never known pain like this.

Fede looked over to where Dante was standing by the car, impassive and imperious. 'Dante! Come on!' he cried desperately. 'We're friends! . . . You can't do this! You don't need to do this! . . . I'll never say—'

A sudden whine came to their ears, drawing closer fast, and they turned to see a faint red cloud of dust billowing above the hill.

Company.

'What the hell . . .?' Francesco muttered, flicking open the switchblade in his free hand which, until now, had gone unnoticed. He grabbed Fede again by the arm just as a blue Piaggio appeared over the crest, skidding to a dramatic stop as the two riders were confronted with the scene of four men standing here in the courtyard. Fede – hands tied, a knife pointed at him – made a particularly arresting sight.

Dante, still standing by the car, began to laugh, shaking his head as if he was amused. 'Well, well, well,' he called, staring at the intruders.

Fon felt the electric shock of seeing Rafaella's hair caught by the wind, her pale, horrified face peering over Cosimo's shoulder. What was she doing here?

What was *he* . . .?

'Cosi!' Fede cried, instinctively moving forward as his brother jumped off the scooter. Francesco reflexively lunged at him with the knife, but he wasn't fast enough—

'Fede!' Cosi yelled.

Fon felt the blade slip between his ribs as he threw himself in front of the only happiness he'd ever known. He gasped. The pain was sharp but clean.

Cleansing.

An exquisite catharsis, as if his sins were finally being purged in the face of sacrifice.

He heard screams – Dante's, Rafa's, Fede's – but they almost immediately faded into ringing silence as his knees buckled and he fell. Fede fell with him, cradling him in bent arms, his bound hands awkwardly angled as he held Fon's head in the dirt.

He was saying something, but Fon couldn't hear what; he could only look into Fede's eyes as the world began narrowing down to the black pinpoints of his pupils. Fede had been the only person to ever truly see him, and as he saw his sorrow swelling in heavy tears, Fon felt what he'd been searching for his entire life.

It was only his for a moment.

But it was enough.

Chapter 50

Cosimo

There was no anchor this time. The world had gone out of control, time running amok like spinning hands on a cartoon clock. Dante covered the courtyard in seconds, falling to his knees and gathering his brother from the dirt, pulling him from Fede's anguished embrace.

Cosimo looked on, frozen by what he was seeing. Death was always brazen, but love . . . love could hide its face. It could hide behind stone walls and smiles of friendship; it could go undetected, its radiance uncatchable and elusive – but once revealed, it glowed like a pearl in the moonlight. And Cosimo saw it now; he understood at last the missing piece to his elusive brother as tears rolled down Fede's cheeks and Dante railed at the heavens. Rafaella stood beside him, trembling too as the lies fell away and the carcass of her marriage was revealed. The world as they knew it had come to another end.

It felt as if the sky was splitting open, raining fire, flooding rivers of blood. Cosimo could feel Dante's roars vibrating under his feet. The beast had been let out at last, as everyone had always somehow known it would be . . . but it was as his curses began to quieten and subside that Cosimo's fear began to rise. The sky seemed to contract in an atmospheric spasm above their heads as Dante carefully laid his brother's body back on the ground.

'Dante,' Francesco said, his voice ragged and thin with terror as he felt it too. 'It was an accident. There was nothing I could do—' He staggered backwards as, slowly, Dante reached for something in his sock and rose to stand.

'. . . You killed my brother,' Dante snarled, and Cosimo saw the quick flick of his wrist. A switchblade protruded from his fist like a solitary finger.

'Dante . . .' Fede said appeasingly, holding his hands up too. He was still on the ground, looking up, and Cosimo realized to his horror that it was Fede to whom Dante was talking, not Francesco.

'It's because of you he's dead,' Dante said in a low voice.

Fede shook his head, feet scrabbling as he tried to get up. 'No—'

'Yes! You destroyed him!'

'Dante, wait!' Rafaella began running towards them.

'Rafa, no!' Cosimo yelled, chasing after her too, but his eyes were on his brother, pleading for his life.

'I cared about him!' Fede cried, holding his bound hands out defensively. Somehow he had got to his feet but he was weakened by weeks of captivity, with no way to fight back. There was no chance he could outrun Dante like this. And Dante knew it. 'Don't do this!'

'Please, no!' Rafaella screamed, as Dante's arm swung like a comet, the flash of its blade the star's tail. She was just metres away from them—

She never saw the bullet.

Chapter 51

Rafaella

Dante slumped to the ground, his body falling beside Fon's and their blood pooling together in one single sea. He hadn't even had time to look surprised, his death mask freeze-framing the dark menace that had characterized his life. He had lived in anger and died in fury.

Rafaella stared down at him in shock, swaying unsteadily on her feet but frozen, as if rooted in position. She had stopped in her tracks when the bullet grazed her, its whistle screaming past her ear en route to its target. She felt hands on her arms, holding her up, as Cosimo caught up with her.

'Rafa? Are you OK?' he asked desperately, checking her for a wound as she looked back at him blankly. She couldn't comprehend what had happened. In a matter of moments, two lives had been lost. She had woken this morning expecting to become a fugitive. Instead she was a widow – Gina too. 'Did it hit you?'

She couldn't answer him. She couldn't feel her body at all. She was in shock. None of this was real . . .

'Fede,' she whispered, catching sight of Cosimo's brother staggering erratically, his face pulled into a mask of grief, tears rolling down his cheeks. He was thin, far thinner than the last time she'd seen him years earlier, his hair shaggy, though he was clean-shaven.

Cosimo turned too and saw his brother looking close to collapse. 'Fede,' he cried, looking around and finding the switchblade that had fallen from Dante's hand as the bullet hit. He grabbed it and ran to him, cutting the ties around Fede's wrists and freeing him at last.

The brothers embraced, Fede crying out as withered muscles in his chest and arms were released, burning now from the sudden movement. He buried his face in Cosimo's shoulder as they sank together to the ground.

'It's OK, it's over,' Cosimo told him as Fede sobbed. 'It's over now.'

Rafaella looked down at Dante's beautiful, arrogant corpse by her feet. Blood was spilling from a neat bullet hole in his head and the memory replayed unbidden in her mind, still echoing through her body: the crack of the gunshot, that blistering whistle as it tore through the air . . .

She gasped, realizing that in the midst of the chaos, as bodies fell and staggered and ran, the bullet had come from a gun none of them had fired. She whipped round to look back towards the car . . . to the farmhouse . . . its door open . . .

She caught her breath as she saw who was standing there. '*You* . . . ?'

Flavia looked back at her. The gun was still in her hand, still smoking, but she dropped it into the dirt as she staggered forward, her eyes on the bodies. 'Is it done?' she asked, her voice strangled. 'Are they dead?'

Rafaella stared; she couldn't stop staring. 'What have you done . . . ?' she asked as the nanny came and stood beside her, shaking.

'What I swore to do.' Flavia met her eyes. 'Vengeance – for my brother.'

Cosimo frowned. 'Your brother . . . ?'

'Mattias Lobascio,' Rafaella said for her, seeing how Flavia softened at the sound of his name. She remembered Flavia telling her that her younger brother had died, but it was only now she remembered the young boy's death had been all the talk back home. He had been murdered around the time of Silvana's wedding, his body left on the hillside to be found the next day; the corpse had been arranged almost kindly despite the gaping wound in his chest. The case had never been solved and Rafaella, to her shame, had been too overtaken by the tragedies in her own life to dwell on it. But it had been closer to her than she'd ever realized.

She looked down at Fon and Dante, bleeding into the dirt. '. . . They killed him?' she whispered.

Flavia nodded, her mouth set in a grim line as she met the dead men's empty eyes.

Rafaella recoiled, squeezing her eyes shut. She felt sick – sickened that she had ever had a good word to say about her husband, shown him kindness, felt compassion.

'You're certain?' Cosimo asked, seeing Rafaella's shame.

'Deathbed confession. Pablo Carrieri admitted it,' Flavia said in a quiet voice, still watching Rafaella. 'He wanted to purge his conscience but Father Tommaso couldn't get to him in time, so he told his wife instead. He told her what they'd done on the morning of your sister's wedding.'

Rafaella whimpered, distressed. She had been so happy that day – celebrating with her family, dressing up with Romola, making love to Cosimo . . . but death had been all around her, within touching distance.

'Who were "they", exactly?' Cosimo asked.

'Pablo. Francesco. Dante and Alfonso,' Flavia replied. 'Pablo stabbed him, but Mattias wasn't killed outright. Dante tried to get Fon to finish him off, but he couldn't do it . . . Not that that makes him innocent,' she said quickly.

'No,' Rafaella murmured.

'Pablo's wife came and told us what she knew,' Flavia went on, her voice dull, as if she'd been steam-rollered flat. 'It was no surprise, but it gave us the certainty we needed. By then the Giannellis were behind everything in Salento. They had risen fast by being ruthless.' She swallowed, closing her eyes, the sun on her face as she thought back. '... My family knew getting close to them wouldn't be easy. By then they had moved here, and their network of informers made them almost untouchable.' Her eyes opened again. 'But my mother said no one ever pays attention to the woman looking after the children and washing the bedsheets ...' She smiled coldly, unapologetically. 'And so Big Man Dante Giannelli was killed by a woman. I lived in his and his brother's houses, right under their noses, just waiting for the perfect moment to strike.'

Flavia looked over at Fede, who was listening too, ashen-faced. He looked as if he was in shock; Rafaella wasn't sure how much of this he was taking in.

'My husband and I followed him here and saw you with Fon the other day,' she went on. 'It was clear you were important to him, even more important than you were valuable. His marriage was falling apart. His wife was leaving him.'

Rafaella remembered that moment yesterday in Gina's bedroom, when they'd heard the floorboard creak outside and Flavia had appeared a moment later. Their instincts had been right; she had been eavesdropping.

'... I knew that coming back here and waiting was my best chance of getting him and his brother together, without lots of witnesses.'

'So you would have killed Fon too? If Francesco hadn't done it for you?' Fede asked in a strangled voice. 'He was going to die today, no matter what?' Tears shone in his eyes. He looked broken.

Flavia hesitated. '... No.'

'*No?*'

'I hated him for having been there. He was no innocent. But he wasn't a monster either. It was only because of him that we got Mattias's body back. Dante had wanted Mattias chopped up ... with the cows ... to get rid of all the evidence ...' Flavia's voice wavered on the words. Everyone flinched.

'... Pablo told his wife, Fon said no. He said it was the only time he ever saw Fon stand up to his brother. He was adamant Matti's body should be left so that we could have a burial.'

'And that meant you could swear the vendetta?' Cosimo ventured.

Flavia nodded.

'I don't understand,' Rafaella said, looking between them.

'Vengeance can only be sworn in the presence of the body,' Flavia murmured. 'If they'd done it Dante's way, there would have been no body, no proof – and I wouldn't be standing here now.' She jerked her chin in the air defiantly. 'So take me to the police if that's what you want. I've done what I set out to do, and I am proud of it.'

Rafaella looked between Cosimo and Fede. Flavia had killed a killer, and it seemed to her that a bullet between the eyes had been a mercifully quick death for a man who had slain a child. He had deserved worse.

She raised her eyes to the horizon, her gaze fastening on a lop-shouldered figure tearing over the hill and growing ever more distant. Francesco was getting away.

'He won't get far,' Cosimo said, following her line of sight. 'The police will catch up with him.'

'And when they do?' she asked. 'What do we tell them? ... Because as far as I'm concerned, Flavia's done nothing wrong here. In fact, as far as I'm concerned, Flavia was never even here today.' She stepped closer to Flavia, interlocking her arm through the nanny's.

Cosimo watched, getting the drift of her argument. 'We did all see Francesco kill Fon in cold blood,' he agreed.

They looked over at Fede, the lawyer among them. '. . . When Dante came at him, he pulled out the gun and defended himself. It was kill or be killed,' Fede murmured. 'We were all witnesses.'

They shared looks, understanding the implications of their agreement. Francesco would be convicted of a crime he hadn't committed – but they all knew he would never be convicted of many he had. And who could pity men who were butchers? Justice didn't always follow the letter of the law. Just as love was more than vows.

Cosimo held his arms out and Rafaella walked into them, closing her eyes as he kissed her hair.

Finally it was over.

Finally, it was beginning.

Epilogue

Rafaella

Tricase Porto, 28 April 1963

The church bells sounded, pealing into a peerless sky above a vivid cyan sea. Distant boats moved on the horizon but the Tricase fishing boats were still in port; harried wives up and down the Via Borgo Pescatori were telling their husbands the hauls could wait another day as they fastened their neckties and brushed the lint from their Sunday best suits.

Villa Aymone's yellow shutters had been pushed back against the walls and Rafaella stood on the balcony, letting the sun warm her face. She was wearing the new dress her sister had made for her – white silk printed with poppies – and her hair in a low bun, with a fresh flower that Cosimo had picked and brought up with breakfast.

Below, Fede was wandering in the garden with a watering can, drenching the flower beds before the shadows moved to the other side of the wall and sunlight became the enemy. Gardening had become his passion after his release from the *trullo*; ever since Fon's death he'd had a yearning for abundant life, as if the colour and scent and teeming activity of a garden were an antidote to his weeks of sense-starved privations.

He had inherited Villa Agosto after their father's sudden death last year. Pills and a note had been found beside the body, but that had never made it into the papers, which reported Filippo's death as a heart attack. Now Fede came down from Rome most weekends to work on the garden – and on theirs, after Cosimo, with his share of the inheritance, had bought Villa Aymone.

She looked over the treetops towards Villa Blanca. It sat slightly forward of them here, fronting onto the coast road, but she could see on the near side that the doors onto its grand balcony were open outside the master bedroom. Gina would have been up for hours already; her nights were finally getting better now that Angelica was almost two and Lorenzo had recruited her as a playmate.

It hadn't been easy for Gina, coming back here. There had been real anger among the villagers towards Dante as the extent of his depravity came to light. No one would ever forgive him for the murder of Mattias Lobascio, and his parents had been forced to slip away in the dead of night. But Gina never once defended him or tried to talk people round. She let them have their anger – it was justified, she said, nothing if not a pragmatist. She had loved Dante once and he would always be the father of her children, but she was glad that he was dead. Rafaella knew she would never forget the look on her friend's face when she'd shared what they had learnt at the abandoned farmhouse.

Gina had returned to the port – and her family – almost immediately, taking up residence in the newly renovated Villa Blanca. Her baby's birth was imminent, and it was no time to be alone. At first everyone shunned her, too; she had profited from his crimes, they said. She must have known! But her refusal to defend the indefensible soon showed them that she was still the girl they had always known – and when her mother was seen hurrying to the villa and the news spread that her waters had broken, the village women had gone over anyway with clean towels and salts, delivering her baby with laughter and tears.

Rafaella saw the *anziani* coming slowly along the street now, talking all the while, walking sticks tapping the cobbles as they made their way towards the church, where Father Tommaso awaited them. She turned back towards the bedroom.

'We should go,' she said, smiling as Cosimo – so handsome in his shirt and tie – looked up from the bed. 'Mamma wants us to greet everyone as they arrive.'

'*Certe*,' he murmured, but making no move. This was their sanctuary. Neither one of them liked leaving it.

She sank onto the mattress beside him, her hand cupping around the tiny silken head of their daughter in his arms. 'She's so beautiful,' she whispered.

'Like her mamma.' Cosimo's eyes held hers and she leaned in to kiss him, their lips lingering. '. . . No,' she smiled, knowing that look. 'We have a baptism to get to.'

'Fine,' he conceded with a grin, knowing they would be picking it up later. Their hunger for one another was still rabid, fifteen months after their wedding. 'You take her while I put on my jacket.'

Carefully he laid the baby in her arms and Rafaella kissed her pretty face over and over, and then over again. She cooed and smiled down at her, admiring too the christening gown the nonnas had spent months working on in Silvana's atelier. Their lace was always beautiful and meticulously made, but even by their standards, this was extra fine and extra soft. It had to be special, they had said. This baby was a gift to them all, a salve to Tricase Porto's greatest hurt.

Rafaella cradled her child tenderly as she got up. 'Come,

then, little one,' she whispered, stroking her cheek with a crooked little finger. 'It's time to be blessed, Romola Rossanna Franchetti.'

She looked up just in time to see a sad look flicker over Cosimo's face, like a shadow running over the ground. 'Are you OK?'

'Of course,' he said quickly, looking away and fiddling with his cufflinks.

'. . . You just wish she was here,' she said for him.

He shrugged, deflating at the simple truth. 'She would have loved all this.'

'Of course she would. She loved any opportunity to celebrate! She'd be bossing us on the flowers, or she'd be making me change my dress, or my hair. The *only* thing she would approve is our choice of name.'

He smiled, but his eyes were still haunted. How many prayers had he offered up in the seminary, asking for forgiveness? Begging for a sign he was absolved? Rafaella didn't think he would ever find peace with his part in Romola's death.

'I miss her so much.'

She walked over and rested her head against his chest, the baby lying tranquil in her arms. 'Me too.' She knew he felt Romola's presence here, that coming back to the port had been a way for him to feel closer to her.

'We mustn't be late,' he said, kissing her hair. 'I don't want to get in trouble with your mother.'

'My mother loves you more than she loves me,' Rafaella laughed, following him downstairs.

'Fede, time to go!' Cosimo called, knocking on the window at his brother. '. . . Fede!'

Rafaella could see her brother-in-law refilling the watering can at the tap. He couldn't hear anything over the rush of water.

'I'll get him,' Cosimo murmured.

He went outside, taking the steps two at a time and running over the grass, tapping his brother on the shoulder. They talked for a moment, Fede checking his watch and looking surprised by what it showed him. He always lost track of time in the garden.

Rafaella watched them from the window as she rocked the baby, kissing her downy head. The brothers had grown close in the past year and a half, bonded by everything they had lost but also, increasingly, by what they had gained. Coming back to the port had been a homecoming for them all.

Fede bent down to wash the soil off his hands, the spray from the tap catching the sunlight and casting out tiny rainbows. He was saying something to Cosimo when a small barn swallow flew down suddenly from the lemon tree, settling on the handle of the watering can, right beside them.

It was the first swallow Rafaella had seen this year; they must be nesting nearby, but they were rarely so tame.

She saw Cosimo look at it too, no longer listening to his brother but watching as the bird ruffled its feathers in the periphery of the soft spray, preening in the morning light. It basked for a moment before taking off again and settling, incredibly, on Cosimo's shoulder.

He completely froze, Fede too. They all knew barn swallows were shy and cautious creatures but this bird was unafraid on its tailored perch as it began to twitter and cheep excitedly. From Rafaella's vantage point, it looked almost as if the bird was chattering to them, and she saw the brothers exchange stunned looks.

The swallow flew off Cosimo's shoulder onto Fede's – making him, too, freeze – and then back again to Cosimo's, hopping lightly as it chirruped in the morning sun.

Rafaella pressed closer to the glass, hardly able to believe what she was seeing. Cosimo was saying something to Fede now, and Rafaella felt her skin tingle at the look dawning on Fede's face as he watched the tiny bird play.

She saw a change come over Cosimo too, starting in his eyes, then his mouth, his muscles softening and expanding with each passing moment, as if he was somehow being released from the trusses that had bound him so tightly for the past six years. She saw his chest heave, the tears gathering in his eyes, as at last the bird took off from his shoulder, and through the glass she heard his delighted shouts as it began swooping around him and Fede in joyous ellipses.

Both brothers were crying and laughing, hugging one another as the barn swallow began darting around them and cutting through the air. Rafaella was crying, too, as she watched from the window, somehow understanding. She wanted the moment to crystallize and keep them all contained within it for ever. But gradually, inevitably, the swallow began slowly gliding up, up on the thermals and they could only watch, entranced, as she danced through the peerless sky, a portent of another summer and all the happy days still to come.

Acknowledgements

I have written almost thirty books now, but it never gets any easier. If anything, it's getting harder and I really rely on my various support teams to help me get these books over the line, so this is my chance to give sincere thanks.

To my editor, Sally Williamson – well, that was a baptism of fire! You received a skinny first draft which had the will to live but no pulse and somehow you fed it up into this hefty beast! Thank you for being so rigorous and thoughtful and really pushing me to keep building and refining both characters and plot. This was one of my difficult books when I didn't know what it was about till the last lines, but you glimpsed the arc early on and I'm so grateful for your belief that I would somehow get there in the end.

Thank you, too, to Kim Young for championing me and spearheading this exciting new chapter for my books. I could not be more excited, nor invigorated, by your vision, and I cannot wait to continue to create, develop and build with you.

To the team – some of whom I have not yet met, so forgive me for any omissions at this point, but I do include you all in this – Eloise Austin, Lucy Upton, Sarah Ridley, Tom Chicken, Oliver Martin, Cara Conquest, Vivien Thompson and the *absolute legend* that is Alison Barrow: just wow. Mind blown. I'll do anything you say.

Special thanks as always to Camilla Rockwood, who knows my writing incredibly well at this point and somehow manages to perform incisive copy edits without making me cry.

Amanda Preston, my agent – we've discussed this. You're stuck with me and that's all there is to it. I can't do this without you, and I give thanks every day for that lunch in Charlotte Street when we turned up wearing matching Zara tops!

Finally, to my family – no matter how many worlds I create, I would always choose this one with you.

About the Author

Karen Swan is the *Sunday Times* and international bestselling author of twenty-nine books, which have sold over five million copies around the world. A prolific author, she writes two novels a year and her books are known for their evocative locations. Karen sees travel as vital research, and likes to set deep, complicated love stories within twisting plots. A former fashion editor, she lives in Sussex, England, with her family and three dogs.